The Monk's Habit
The Disinherited Prince - Book Two

THE MONK'S HABIT

THE DISINHERITED PRINCE
BOOK TWO

GUY ANTIBES

SALT LAKE CITY, UT

THE MONK'S HABIT

This is a work of fiction. There are no real locations used in the book, the people, settings and specific places are a product of the author's imagination. Any resemblances to actual persons, locations, or places are purely coincidental.

Published by CasiePress LLC in Salt Lake City, UT, October, 2016.
www.casiepress.com

Cover & Book Design: Kenneth Cassell

ISBN-13: 978-1539483632
ISBN-10:   1539483630

AUTHOR'S NOTE

This is the second book in the Disinherited Prince series. In order to survive, I have Pol taking a more active part in his life. There are still mentors to be found, but Pol develops a different relationship with them. The story contains plenty of action, but Pol is confronted with challenges that he would never confront at Borstall Castle. I liked writing this book and seeing it develop. I hope you enjoy reading it.

I'd like to again thank Judy for her editing and Ken in the interior and exterior design of the book.

— Guy Antibes

MAPS OF THE DUKEDOMS OF EASTRIL
AND THE BACCUSOL EMPIRE
IN THE WORLD OF PHAIROON

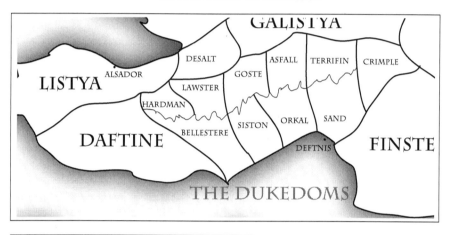

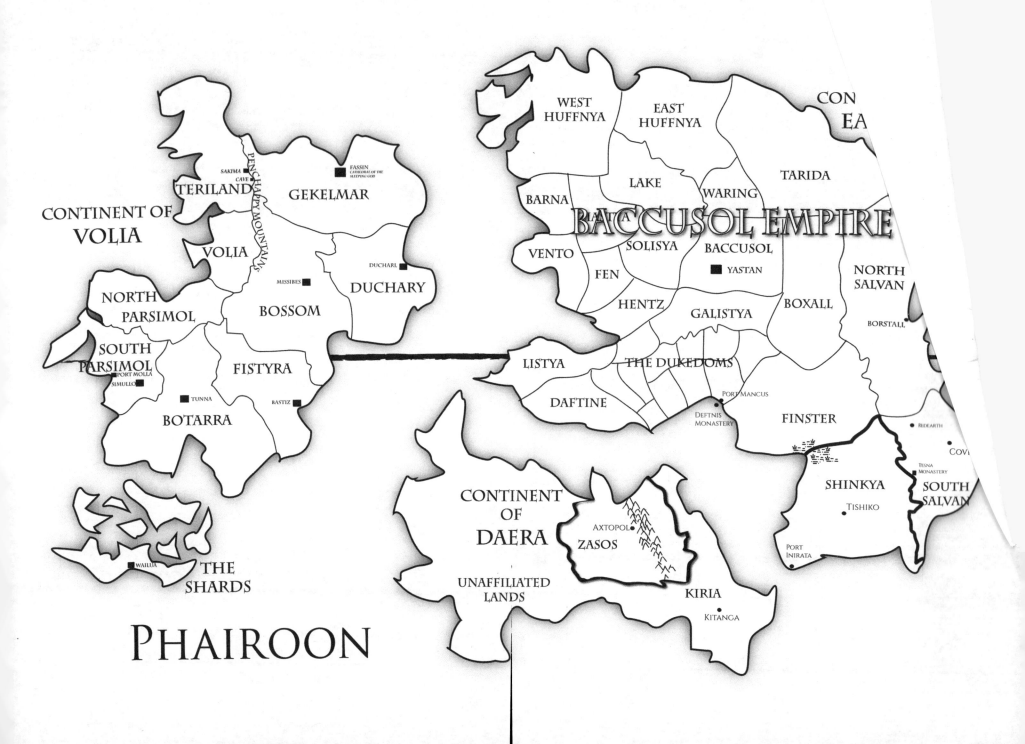

CONTINENT OF
VOLIA

TERILAND

GEKELMAR

SAKIMA
CAVE

FASSIN
CATHEDRAL OF THE
SLEEPING GOD

VOLIA

DUCHARL

MISSIBES

DUCHARY

NORTH
PARSIMOL

BOSSOM

SOUTH
PARSIMOL

FISTYRA

PORT MOLLA

SIMULLO

TUNNA

BASTIZ

BOTARRA

THE
SHARDS

WAILUA

PHAIROON

WEST
HUFFNYA

EAST
HUFFNYA

CON
EA

BARNA

LAKE

TARIDA

WARING

BACCUSOL EMPIRE

VENTO

SOLISYA

BACCUSOL

FEN

YASTAN

NORTH
SALVAN

HENTZ

GALISTYA

BOXALL

BORSTALL

LISTYA

THE DUKEDOMS

DAFTINE

PORT MANCUS

DEFTNIS
MONASTERY

FINSTER

REDEARTH

COV

CONTINENT
OF
DAERA

AXTOPOL

TESNA
MONASTERY

ZASOS

SHINKYA

SOUTH
SALVAN

TISHIKO

UNAFFILIATED
LANDS

KIRIA

PORT
INIRATA

KITANGA

The Monk's Habit

Chapter One

~

A COOL WIND WHIPPED THE CLOAKS of the four riders looking out over the estuary towards the large island that held their final destination, Deftnis Monastery.

"There it is," Valiso Gasibli said. His dark curly hair flitted this way and that in the wind. "It's a bit of a boat trip, but I'm sure you are all up to it." He turned his mount and kicked the sides of the horse to urge it back towards the coastal track that led down to the coastal town of Mancus, which served as the mainland port for those heading to Deftnis.

Pol Cissert, a refugee from Borstall Castle where his mother had been the Queen and he a prince, looked at the whitecaps on the angry sea and blinked his eyes. For all his time as a prince of North Salvan, the nearly fifteen-year-old had never ridden in a sailboat on the ocean. His gaze lingered on the little craft coming in from the island and worried about all the bobbing. He didn't look forward to the final leg of his escape.

"Worried about a little boat ride?" Paki said. His fifteen-year-old companion rubbed his hands in anticipation before taking off after Valiso, or Val, as the boys called him.

Actually Pol thought that 'terrified' better described his current emotional state. His large horse quickly caught up to Val, Darrol Netherfield, his sworn man, and Paki. Pol thought he would feel the relief of reaching the refuge of the monastery, if it weren't for that boat ride.

"What's the matter with you?" Val said. He followed Pol's eyes out to the ocean. "Does the little trip out to the monastery worry you? Think about your horse who will have to follow you in that big barge sitting at the dock."

A barge with ungainly sails bobbed in the water at the end of a stone dock. Pol instinctively reached down and patted his mount's neck. He had yet to name his horse, once the property of his stepbrother, Prince Landon. It had served him well in the two weeks they had been on the road. Their flight from Borstall Castle, where Pol's mother had been poisoned, and he had been disinherited, had been slowed by the necessity of traveling cross-country rather than using North Salvan's roads.

At least Pol's fragile constitution had held up during their ride. He wasn't so sure what would happen on that boat, but the monastery was the only sanctuary available to Pol. Val thought the healers at Deftnis might be able to cure Pol's heart and lung problems. As it was, Pol was convinced he would die before he reached the age of twenty, if he made it alive across all that water to the island.

They stopped at a stable yard serving the monastery and removed their bags. Pol regretted leaving his horse in the care of someone else, but then his horse, along with Darrol's and Paki's, would make the crossing later when the sea had calmed. Val told them that he intended to stop just long enough to see him settled at Deftnis, and then he would be heading due north to the Imperial capital of Yastan.

"I'm hungry," Paki said, earning a scowl from Darrol.

The former Borstall palace guard clapped Paki on the side of his head. "Not until we are across. You might lose whatever you shove in that bottomless maw of yours, otherwise. I know. I've made the crossing in conditions as bad as this and fed the fishies."

Val smirked, the shape of his usual smile, and called them over. "I can put you under during the crossing."

Paki shook his head. "I'm brave enough."

Pol thought his friend looked a little uncertain of his claim. Pol had no desire to make a fool of himself for the sake of bravado. "I'll take you up on that. Maybe another time I will take a chance." He worried more about his heart beating out of his chest with anxiety and losing his breath, if the ride made him nauseous, than about losing whatever he had in his stomach.

The boat they had seen from the cliff had put in alongside the dock and let passengers off. Three men wore the gray robes of monks, but Pol could see the men wore swords and had boots with spurs hiding beneath the folds of thick cloth. One of the monks had to be assisted off the boat, and then threw off the helping hands once they reached the solid footing of the dock. The monk continued to walk a bit unsteadily right past them. The men nodded to Val, maybe recognizing him, since Val had trained for years at the monastery.

Pol looked at Paki, who swallowed a bit, but took a deep breath and gave his bags to one of the sailors.

Once Pol was seated, Val joined him. "Are you ready?" Val said.

Pol nodded.

A bump awakened Pol. The boat bobbed against a thick wooden pier. "Are we here?"

Darrol put Pol's bag on his lap. "This is yours, but I'll carry it up to the dock. Val will do the same with Paki's. You might want to help your friend up the ladder."

Pol looked over at Paki, whose pale face held a sorrowful expression.

"I'm a fool. I'm a fool. I'm a fool," Paki said as he struggled up the ladder.

Pol followed him and helped his friend walk around on the pier for a few steps.

"Did you feed the fishies?" Pol teased.

Paki nodded, and Darrol laughed. Pol looked back at the angry stretch of water, knowing he had made the better decision.

Val didn't seem to pay any attention to them and stalked off the pier into the town that made up the little port on the Isle of Deftnis. "Don't bother about gawking. You'll be down here often enough," he said. "I want to get to Yastan as soon as I can, so let's not waste time."

It was a struggle to keep up with his former bodyguard, but they all followed Val like ducklings waddling after their mother. Darrol had spent some time in the monastery, but even he still examined the buildings as they trod through the village to an inn. A carriage that looked more like a covered cart stood in front.

"We'll take that the rest of the way," Darrol said, as he put his bags in the back of the wagon. Pol did the same, and soon his teeth shook and rattled as the cart made its way up the rough cobblestones that led to the Monastery sitting at the top of a hill.

As they approached the monastery wall dressed in black stone, Pol thought the place looked sinister and unfriendly. "It looks foreboding," he said.

Darrol pulled on his lower lip and looked at their destination. "It's not a particularly happy place, but I have mostly positive memories."

Pol shuddered at the term 'mostly positive'. He expected to be worked hard with a monastery filled with men as severe as Val. "What are you going to do now that you are back?" Pol asked Darrol.

"I may teach arms to the young things," Darrol said, "or learn a bit more about Seeking." He looked at Val. "Or both." His face broke into a smile.

"Pol can help you with that," Val said. "He'll do well in the Seeker category."

The way Val spoke put an end to the banter. They rode on in silence, and their conveyance finally clattered underneath the portcullis of the monastery gate. It looked more like a castle than a spiritual refuge. Pol remembered that monasteries these days were mostly secular orders in the Baccusol Empire.

"Stay here," Val said as he left his bag with them in the large courtyard and walked up the steps into a newer-looking building on the castle grounds. Pol just absorbed the feel of his new home. He would probably die on the monastery grounds, he thought, unless the healer-monks cured him.

A short time later, Val emerged, along with three older monks. They all shuffled down the stairs in their gray robes. Again, Pol thought it odd that they wore swords and boots, but these didn't have spurs. They eyed the trio.

"Darrol, we know. You are always welcome amongst us," the

oldest-looking of the monks said. "Pakkingail Horstel?"

Paki halfheartedly raised his hand.

"You are accepted by virtue of this letter of recommendation from Malden Gastoria, Court Magician to North Salvan." The monk waved a document in his hand and then turned to Pol. "You are the newly-disinherited prince, so Valiso says."

"I am, sire. Please refer to me as Pol Cissert. I am no longer a Fairfield and I still fear for my safety."

"I don't care what we call you, Pol Cissert. Show me some of your power. Malden writes that you are somewhat of a prodigy."

Pol drew within himself and detected the pattern of the seven of them standing in the courtyard. "If you will excuse me," he said. He pointed to one of the monks and raised him six inches into the air, then moved him backward and forward before lowering him down onto the cobbled courtyard. "Will that work?"

The monk who had been moved smiled, once he shook off the shock of being transported. "You are what Val described."

Pol smiled and then collapsed to the ground. His heart beat too fast, and his breathing began to get out of control. "I can do more, but if I do, I will faint."

The monk helped Pol to his feet. "Val said you get overcome with fatigue. We will see what we can do about that. I'm sure you have stories to tell."

The old monk nodded. "That will have to wait. A quick meal for Val—"

Val held up his hand. "The sea is a bit rough today. If you don't mind, I'd like to enjoy my dinner only once, going down. I think I will be heading back on the next trip, after all."

"Well, we will let you leave before the boat returns to the Mancus shore. Say goodbye to your friends." The three monks returned to the building.

Pol looked at Val and really didn't want him to leave. "You really aren't staying?"

Val shook his head. "The Emperor must know the true story of what went on in Castle Borstall, even if he likely won't do anything about it. Your father plays a shrewd game, and the Emperor won't forget your mother's murder. He won't forget you, either. It's hard to get an audience with Hazett, but if you need anything in Yastan, you can contact Farthia's father, Ranno, for assistance."

Val looked around at the buildings in front of him. "I learned most of my craft within these walls." Val put his hands on the boys' shoulders. "Neither of you will lack for training. Work hard. I'm sure we will run into one another in the course of time." He threw his bag back on the covered cart and climbed up on the front seat. The driver turned in the courtyard and drove Val out of sight. The man never turned to wave, which disappointed Pol.

The sparsely-furnished dormitory wasn't what Pol had been used to, but it met his expectations. Darrol merited his own personal cell, as they called individual rooms in the Monastery, but it looked like the boys would be sharing their living space with fourteen others, so Pol and Paki found two empty beds next to one another.

"Appreciate the solitude. A number of those identified during the Emperor's processional are due to start arriving in a week or two, along with our normal raft of new inductees. The dormitory will fill up. As far as I know, you two are the youngest pair of acolytes to be taken in at Deftnis in my lifetime, at least," Gorm, a younger monk, said. "Tomorrow both of you will be given a battery of tests to determine how you can serve Deftnis. There are a number of specialties, but you will be required to learn a bit of everything."

"What kind of specialties?" Paki said. Pol noticed the excitement build up in his friend.

"Archery, Swordsmanship, General Weapons, Seeking, Scouting, Healing, Strategy & Tactics, as well as a few others that we won't talk about today. This dormitory is for those with magical abilities. Magic has a training regimen all its own."

Pol thought. "Where does knife throwing come in?"

"Valiso taught you how to use knives?" Gorm couldn't hide the surprise in his voice.

The question brought a nod from Pol. "I needed to defend myself from assassins."

"I'll note that. It fits in a few of our categories, but I think you will be a special case." Gorm frowned, and Pol didn't know why. Was it his frail constitution?

They both ate in the half-empty commissary. No one introduced themselves to the two boys, and Paki's presence became a comfort. Pol finally felt that he was safe.

They returned to the dormitory just after dark to find a few of the beds now occupied. Pol collapsed onto his. He had no idea what Paki dreamt of, but Pol kept waking up after having dreams about his struggles during the summer. He had had to fight for his life time after time, and his survival had come at a cost. Pol had more battle scars than any fourteen-going-on-fifteen-year-old should have. He pulled back the right sleeve of his nightshirt and ran his finger along the latest one. An arrow had skittered along his forearm and carved a line. He could feel the newly-healed wound in the dark.

How many more scars would he collect at Deftnis?

~ ~ ~

Chapter Two

P OL WOKE TO THE PEAL OF BELLS. They sounded like they rang just above his bed, but then he wondered if magic enhanced the sound. He sat up and saw others struggling out of their beds, pulling on robes. Paki and he hadn't been given any robes to wear, so Pol pulled out the cleanest clothes that he had.

Paki still snored, but Gorm whacked him with a long, thin rod and then proceeded to do the same to the other few who hadn't responded to the bells.

"What?" Paki said rubbing his leg. Pol could see a red welt rising on his friend's skin. "He didn't have to do that."

"Get used to it," one of the older acolytes said. "You'll learn quickly that oversleeping isn't tolerated." He nodded to the both of them. "Get to the commissary, or you won't have breakfast either. Eat well since you are being tested today."

Pol knew well enough that eating always helped with his magic and let Paki follow behind him as they joined the loose line of men and youth heading to the commissary building. He looked at the brightening sky and figured that he'd have to get used to rising at dawn from now on.

Breakfast was better than he thought. He pictured monks eating gruel and water, but their plates were filled with bread, bacon, eggs, and baked apples in a sweet cinnamon sauce. Pitchers of fruit juice littered the tables, along with little pots of pepper and salt. It didn't match breakfasts in the royal family's dining room at Borstall, but he'd had worse in the castle's kitchens.

Paki certainly had no problem with the food. He didn't say a word while he wolfed down his breakfast. He might be slow rising from his bed, but he made up for it.

Gorm approached their table. "Time for testing. Follow me." The monk turned and didn't look back to see if Paki or Pol trailed behind.

Pol used his location magic to keep from being turned around as they walked up and down, and then took turns that would have left Pol lost otherwise. Gorm had purposely led them in circles. Paki's face showed confusion, but Pol knew where they were about to enter the new building from a newer corridor that led from the older keep. At least that's what Pol thought to describe the main building.

Gorm turned around. "Do either of you know where we are?"

Paki twisted his face in thought. "Deftnis Monastery?"

Gorm gave Paki a hard stare. He turned to Pol. "How about you?"

"We are about to enter the building where the Abbot has his office." He stated it as a fact because it fit his location sense and the pattern that he still was developing for the monastery layout.

The monk's eyebrows rose on his face. "A lucky guess?"

Pol shook his head. "Something Malden Gastoria taught me," he said. "Do you want me to tell you how many people are in the room on the other side of this door?"

Gorm squinted at Pol. "How many?"

"Six." Pol tried to keep a smile off his face. "Oops. Five. One has just left by a different door."

The monk threw open the door and counted the three monks and two acolytes. "Did someone just leave?"

"Anosto did, just a moment ago," one of the monks said.

Gorm pursed his lips and shook his head. "Follow me." He continued through the room.

The wood paneling on the walls looked much newer, and the flooring wasn't worn at all. They walked past alcoves with statues of monks, and Gorm stood in front of a set of double doors. A little plate at the side said 'Testing'. They had reached their destination. Pol looked up and down the corridor at the chairs lining both sides.

At least they wouldn't have to wait. Pol wanted to be done with this, and he wiped his suddenly wet palms on his pants as Gorm knocked. He heard someone say 'Enter' from the other side. He used his location sense to note that five men were in a row. That meant they sat behind a long table.

He walked in and recognized two of the three monks, the man who he assumed was the Abbott and the monk that he had levitated. The room had no windows, but the ceilings were high.

Gorm grabbed two chairs from the wall and put them about three paces from the front of the table.

A monk Pol had never seen looked down at a piece of paper. His hands were ink-stained. "Pakkingail Horstel?" Paki stood when the monk called his name. "Approach the table."

Paki wiped his hands on his vest, showing that he had the same anxiety as Pol. "Yes, sir." He gave the monks a little bow.

"What magic do you know?"

Paki shrugged. "I don't know much. I recognized some writing on a drawing of dots and nudged a penny a little on a board."

"How much of the penny moved across a line?"

He shrugged again. "Maybe half of it, maybe more. I didn't pay a lot of attention. I was surprised I could do it at all." He looked at his questioner. "Sir,"

"Show me," the monk said and put a coin on a grid.

Paki narrowed his eyes in concentration and must have moved the penny, but Pol was too far away to see.

"Good. We generally don't take anyone into our order below the age of sixteen, but you were recommended as a companion for Poldon Fairfield. Welcome to Deftnis," the Abbot said. "Quarter of a penny-width," the Abbot said to Pol.

Pol felt his face burn with embarrassment. Had he looked too eager to see his friend's result?

"You may sit in the hall, Horstel," the monk with the ink-stained hands said while he scribbled on a paper. "Pol Cissert. You may stand where your friend did."

Pol looked behind him as Paki gave Pol a thumbs-up and closed the door behind him.

"You represent a conundrum. Do you know what that word means?"

Pol nodded. "I have a good vocabulary, sir. It means I am a hard-to-solve problem."

"Good. Tell us what spells you know," the Abbot said.

After thinking for a few moments, Pol let them know what he had done. He didn't call them all spells, but he thought the men might want to know the times he had 'tweaked' the pattern.

"Third Level, or even more if he had stamina," one of the monks said.

"What is a third level?" Pol said. He had heard Malden say something about third level something or other.

"Multidimensional levitation is a key element. Levels are determined by a basket of capabilities, if you will. Not all magicians have equal abilities in the same spells. They may be better than their peers at one spell, but worse with others," the monk he had moved said. "What spells do you have trouble with?"

"I can do location spells without losing strength and I can anticipate moves with sips of magic in a sparring match. If I move large objects, I can faint. You saw that in the courtyard yesterday. I didn't faint, but if I had done anything else or moved you for longer, I would have."

"Malden Gastoria mentioned that you have discovered spells on your own?" The last monk to ask him a question just did again.

"I think I made myself invisible. I have no way to verify it," Pol said shrugging. "It's a matter of thinking of a pattern and then tweaking it. That's the term Malden used."

"It is the acceptable term among magicians," the monk said. "More spells?"

"I figured out how to enhance hearing. I was eavesdropping on my mother." Pol took a deep breath and pressed his lips together to avoid getting emotional about his late mother. "I remembered learning about sounds bouncing in a room, and then expanded the pattern to my ears."

"It worked?"

Pol nodded. "Yes, sir. I can't say I heard things perfectly, but well enough."

"Well enough," the Abbott snorted. "Tell me about patterns and magic."

"On a basic level, magic is about detecting patterns and the corresponding ability to tweak the patterns. That means to use your powers to change the pattern. Val taught me—"

"Val?" one of the monks said.

"Valiso Gasibli. He called me Pol and I called him Val. He taught me to use patterns in non-magical ways. We solved some mysteries together."

"As Seekers?" the Abbot said.

"Like Seekers," Pol said, nodding. "He was my bodyguard, and we spent a lot of time together in the summer months."

"How long have you been studying magic?" one of the monks asked.

"Since late spring," Pol said.

Pol didn't know why, but the monks looked impressed.

The Abbot nodded. "It's all here." He pointed again to Malden's letter. "You may go. Welcome to Deftnis. I am sure you will find your experience here illuminating. We are aware of your physical limitations, and once things have settled down, you'll be under the treatment of our Healers."

Pol bowed to them. "Thank you for accepting me." He turned and left to find Paki looking out one of the windows lining the corridor.

"Gorm said we should return to our rooms and unpack our things."

The two of them found their beds and pulled their packs out and emptied them into the wardrobes that stood on the right side of each bed. Keys had been inserted in the locks while they were gone. On the chain that held the key was an amulet depicting a braided circle behind a symbol of fire surrounding a sword. Pol noticed the device elsewhere around Deftnis.

He began to fold his soiled clothes and put it into the wardrobe. Gorm walked by. "Only clean things go in there. You'll find a place to wash your clothes and a clothesline through the corridor." Gorm pointed towards the back door that they hadn't yet used.

Everything that Pol possessed was dirty, but he would have to wait to wash the clothes that he had on tomorrow. Paki groaned, but Pol just shook his head.

He rarely had to personally wash anything until his days-long trip north to the Taridan border weeks past. It seemed like the time he spent in North Salvan was a long time ago rather than just weeks. Pol wouldn't mind getting used to fending for himself now that he was out of danger; in fact, as Pol Cissert, he had to learn how to be independent.

He had no desire to return to Borstall Castle and constantly avoid his murderous siblings—no longer siblings, since he now knew they weren't related by blood. The revelation from his mother, that King Colvin wasn't his real father, shocked him, but now that she had died, he had accepted the fact that he was truly an orphan. Pol didn't feel sorry for himself. He had to learn what he could and accept as much time as he had left to fulfill his life.

If the gods wanted him to avenge the death of his mother, the opportunity would come. If it didn't, Pol might feel disappointed, but he was grateful for the very fact that he could feel the disappointment.

The pair of them returned from washing and hanging their clothes to complete their unpacking. Two robes had been placed on both of their beds. Paki's had a white rope belt, and Pol's was orange.

I'll be wearing clothes under that," Paki said. "It's wool, and it's scratchy."

Pol rubbed the material. He agreed with Paki's decision. Pol had never worn anything so uncomfortable, but then he currently lived in a strange place compared to Borstall Castle.

He plunged his hand to the bottom of his pack and felt the bag of books that Malden had given him. He noticed a ledge above the back of his bed that could be used as a bookshelf and looked around the room and saw that the other magic acolytes had books on their ledges. He heaved the bag onto his bed and pulled out the sack. He hadn't touched it after Val had repacked his things for their trip.

Pol gently shook the contents onto his bed. He found a book on magic spells and another book on patterns, but as he thumbed through them, it looked like he knew most of what was written. His notebook on religions had been included, but Pol didn't know why Malden would have included that unless Mistress Farthia had made him do it. Another book talked about herbs.

What intrigued him was a large pouch. He vaguely remembered Malden putting it in the sack during the burning of his mother's funeral pyre. He opened the pouch and poured the contents onto his bed.

Paki whistled. "Your mother's jewelry, I'll bet."

Pol examined the items piece by piece. "I never saw her wear some of these, and others have stories that Mother used to tell me over and over. I think all of these came from Listya." He ran his hands over the worn items, knowing that his mother had done the same.

Pol treasured the amulet that his mother had given him when she told him of his heritage and his real father, Cissert. He didn't know if he could believe that he had shared ancestors from an alien race that gave his mother and him silvery hair, and his father and him a bad heart. He fingered the amulet underneath his shirt and wondered at the value of the gold, silver, and jewels that lay before him. He quickly bundled it back up and tossed it in the back corner of his wardrobe.

"Pretend you never saw this, okay?" Pol said to Paki. "I don't want anyone to know about these."

"Those are worth a lot, Pol. It would tempt anyone, except me, of course."

"Of course," Pol said. "Look at these books. He tossed the herb book, which looked pretty new, to Paki. "Do you know these?"

Paki thumbed through the illustrated pages. "Lots of pictures. This is an expensive book." He spent a bit more time looking at it. "I know a few of them, and there are a bunch I've never seen before," Paki said.

"If you want to learn healing, I guess this is part of it."

"I want to be a scout." Paki said, putting the book on Pol's bookshelf.

"I want to be a Seeker," Pol said. "Less muscle, more brain."

"Suit yourself."

Pol smiled. "I will, if they let me."

Pol and Paki wandered around the monastery after their testing. Gorm had told them there would be nothing more today, but the boys would be evaluated for specialties tomorrow. They passed by the stables, but their horses had not yet arrived on the barge, since the seas were still too rough. They helped the stable master groom horses. Paki asked about gardens, but there were no ornamental gardens in the monastery, and the healers liked to tend to their herbs without outside help.

They washed the clothes they hadn't done the day before, and when dinnertime finally came, the boys drifted over to the commissary. A few more acolytes seemed to be present. Gorm had told them that classes wouldn't start until after the harvest break that took place during the last month of summer and the first two weeks of fall.

Pol had never thought about harvests before, but it made sense to him. Families might be willing to give up their sons to the monastery, but harvest time needed as many helpers as possible, and the monastery understood that. He wondered about those who lived far away from Deftnis, but perhaps a lot of acolytes and monks might just take the time to get away from Deftnis Isle for a bit.

The food was as good as the previous evening. Pol remembered reading about religious orders where the members endured severe diets as part of their worship. He didn't have to worry about such a thing in a monastery that was pledged to arms and magic. Both disciplines required strong bodies. Pol would endure as long as he could until his own body gave out.

Even though they didn't have any reason to, the boys got up at dawn and rushed over to the commissary. A monk they hadn't met before gathered the boys and showed them to the armory. They hadn't made it around to the back of the castle on the previous day. The armory and other buildings sat in the back. Pol noticed that an open gate led outside the castle down to practice grounds.

They waited for some time before an old monk called them over.

"Pakkingail and Pol?"

"He's Paki, and I'm Pol," Pol said to the man.

"You can call me Edgebare. or Sir."

"Yes, Sir Edgebare," Paki said, giving the man a bow.

The monk laughed. "Paki, right?" He pointed at Paki. "What arms specialty are you interested in?"

"I want to be a scout," Paki said.

"Swords and Archery," Edgebare said. "Archery is not my area, but you should also learn Seeking and Survival."

"Seeking!" Paki said, grinning.

Edgebare grunted. "You won't be so happy after you've been in training for a few months. What about you, Pol?"

"I'm most suited to Seeking. My physical condition isn't very good."

"Hmmm," Edgebare made the sound as he rubbed his chin. "Any experience with swords?"

"He nearly won the North Salvan tournament when the Emperor visited."

"Is that right?"

Pol nodded. "For fifteen-year-olds. I can use a little magic to help boost my strength."

"A pattern-master, already?" Edgebare said.

Paki furrowed his brow. "What's that?"

"Not all magicians can perform anticipation magic. It requires a fast mind and disciplined thinking." The monk squinted at Pol's belt. "A Third, eh? You anticipated to make short work of your opponents until your magic gave out?"

Pol shook his head. "Not my magic, my strength. If I overdo things, my heart begins to pound, and I can barely breathe."

"We can try to fix that. It's a shame Searl isn't still with us."

"Searl?" Paki said.

"A Master Healer. Probably the best to ever walk these grounds. He'd have you fixed soon enough. Hopefully our current crop of healers can help. If you are a pattern master, you will eventually find yourself under my tutelage for swords. You won't have a choice. Any other weapons skills?"

"I can throw knives."

"Do you use magic to guide them?"

Pol had to think. "I don't think so. I practiced really hard. I had, uh, challenges before I came, and I actually used the knives."

"Against a real person?"

Pol nodded.

"He's killed with his knives before," Paki said. "I was with him."

"Perhaps a story for another time. You did this in self-defense?"

"I did. Valiso Gasibli taught me. He served as my bodyguard."

"Ah. That explains it. He probably flashed all of those fancy knives he owns."

Paki nodded. "We both had to learn how to handle them."

"Knives are good for Seekers, but we don't have a Knife Master in the Monastery right now. We have a few monks who might be adequate to teach you enough skills to be dangerous, but not at Valiso's level." Edgebare looked at both boys. "Knives are not an especially popular specialty. We don't encourage the training of assassins at Deftnis."

Pol had wondered about that. "But don't Seekers need to learn knives?"

"A Seeker might be in a position where wearing a sword or other weapon might not be advisable, so you need to be prepared with a defense."

Pol asked the question that had always bothered him. "Is Val an assassin?"

Edgebare pursed his lips. "He has been called on to kill in the Emperor's service. He's not an assassin for hire, but are his hands clean?" The monk shook his head. "Valiso has his own code. I consider him an honorable man called upon to do dishonorable things."

That answer would have to do, thought Pol. "So swords, knives, and what else?"

"For an undersized youth? I think what you've identified is enough for now. You will learn about all weapons while you are here, but when you get older and bigger. Neither of you want to become battle healers?"

Both boys shook their heads.

"Paki needs to learn basic magic, and I think I've been classified Third Level," Pol said.

"Third Level, and at fourteen, fifteen? You could ditch the weapons and become a magician."

"I have strength problems when I cast spells," Pol said. He didn't want to be a magician like Malden Gastoria, as much as Pol liked him as a mentor at Borstall Castle. Pol didn't like the way Malden was always called away to talk to King Colvin, his stepfather.

"Then do your best. I think Seeking might be a good start for a bright boy. Come back tomorrow, and I'll have a few monks here to evaluate your present skills. Don't worry about having to decide today or even in a year. Most acolytes are with us for years and often change their specialties. That's why you'll be exposed to a lot of different aspects of healing, war, and magic at first." Edgebare looked up at the sun. "Time to visit Jonness, who is both a Survival and Seeker Master, although his assistants are still out on Harvest Break. Go on, now. I'll spread the word. You might even get some instruction in before the hordes return," Edgebare said.

After getting directions to find Jonness, the boys crossed the keep to a large room, but not as large as the armory. Jonness was a tall, spare man. His head was shaved. He looked exactly like Pol imagined what a monk at a religious order looked like.

After introductions and a conversation with each boy that was similar to Edgebare's, Jonness took them through small gate into a wood that grew right to the castle wall. Pol had to smile. This was a larger version of the little wood where Paki's father had taught them how to hide and walk in the forest.

"So you've learned a bit?" Jonness said. "I want you both to hide. No tree climbing permitted. I'll find you."

Pol had done this drill a number of times with Siggon, Paki, and even Val. He nodded and took off. Once the trees hid him from Jonness, Pol stood and soaked in the pattern of the woods. He noticed a person located to both his right and his left. That brought a smile to Pol's face. So Jonness had observers. He watched his footsteps to make sure he didn't leave any tracks. He moved towards the observer on the left and made sure to keep trees between both of the observers' lines of sight.

Pol's senses saw that Paki had moved towards the opposite side, and that would be fine with Pol. Finally, he found the spot he sought, a dense area of the trees. He found a suitable place and stopped.

He sat with his legs drawn up, and with his back to observers.

GUY ANTIBES | Page 19

Jonness went after Paki first. He noticed that the tall monk moved quickly. Jonness consulted with the observer on Pol's right and found Paki.

The three of them walked to the observer on the left and stood for a bit. Pol could imagine them conferring on Pol's whereabouts. Pol just sat where he was, seeing the four of them wandering about the woods until Jonness spotted Pol.

"How did you do it?"

Pol smiled. "I cheated. I used a locator spell. I found your two observers and kept out of their sight. I found this cluster of trees and waited. I tried to imagine myself invisible to magic."

"No tracks," Paki said. "I told you he was good at this."

"Indeed. It's obvious I can't locate as well as you," Jonness said. "You wish to be a Seeker?"

Pol shrugged. He fought off being giddy at defeating a Deftnis master. "It is something that I think I can do."

"Pakkingail did a credible job, but as you said, you cheated. I wouldn't call it cheating, since our graduates use whatever they can to succeed. We encourage such creativity, if that's what you call it. Well done."

Pol finally broke into a grin.

"Yeah, well done," Paki said putting his arm on Pol's shoulder.

~ ~ ~

Chapter Three

~

TEN DAYS LATER, ACOLYTES FILLED THE DORMITORY. None of them wore an orange belt like Pol. Evidently there were no new Third Level acolytes. Perhaps now that magic classes were to begin, Pol could learn what the levels actually meant.

Gorm instructed Pol to follow two acolytes who joined them as Gorm escorted Pol to the first magic class right after breakfast. Both of them were in their early twenties, and Pol felt like a little puppy following his masters as they walked through the keep towards the administration building. They looked alike with dark hair, tall and thin. One had blue eyes and the other brown.

The plaque that had said 'Testing' had been replaced with one that had the single word 'Magic'. Pol let the two men proceed before him as they entered the large room. It looked as it had before, but now Pol noticed that the wooden paneling had been removed, revealing stark stone walls. Magic lights still lit the room, and the table and chairs still remained, with more chairs lined up against the walls.

One monk sat behind the table, and three chairs had been drawn up on the other side.

"Pol is new, so I will do the introductions," the monk said. "I am Vactor." Pol nodded to the monk. Vactor had been the one he had moved in the courtyard when he first came to Deftnis. "Sakwill is on your right, and Coram is on your left." Vactor turned to the older

GUY ANTIBES | Page 21

acolytes. Sakwill had the blue eyes and Coram had the brown. "Pol Cissert—"

Vactor's eyebrows turned up, but then he nodded. "I amend myself. The Emperor's Processional discovered Pol. He has raw talent, but was under the informal tutelage of one of our former monks. He has mastered patterning to the point he has created his own tweaks."

The two men, still standing, looked at Pol with new eyes.

"A prodigy, eh? Don't see those often, do you, Vactor?" Sakwill said. "We'll take care of you." Sakwill's smile didn't reach his eyes.

Pol had been 'taken care of' by his brothers, and he didn't want a repeat. He felt his temper rise. "And I'll take care of you, in my own way," he said with a little too much heat.

"You may sit," Vactor said. "We don't permit animosity in our little group. Is that clear?" The monk looked at Sakwill.

"Yes, sir."

Pol scrunched down in his seat a bit. "Yes, sir."

Vactor stood. "Pol, I want you to move me like you did in the courtyard."

"Can I sit?" Pol did not want to faint or collapse in front of his two classmates.

"Of course."

He lifted Vactor up and moved him to the left and to the right and diagonally from where he started. Pol had to grip the edges of the chair to keep from swaying.

"How about you, Sakwill?" Vactor said. Pol could hear the challenge in the monk's voice.

Sakwill moved Vactor to the right and the left. Pol could hear Vactor's boots sliding on the floor, so he didn't lift him up.

He looked over and saw sweat beading on Sakwill's face. At least he didn't faint, Pol thought. He felt a little angry, or was he jealous? He wished that Paki sat next to him. Pol felt isolated and lonely for the first time since he had arrived at Deftnis.

"I hope you don't mind, Pol," Vactor said. "We had a detailed report from Pol's teacher. One problem with learning magic so young is that Pol can't tweak on a sustained basis. He loses energy quickly. As you can see, he is powerful, but only in spurts. It will be useless to put him in a lower class, since he can already do or find out on his own what he needs at the lower levels, so he will practice along with you." Vactor said.

Sakwill grunted, and then Coram did as well. Pol felt badly about having his weakness so blatantly discussed, but what alternative did he have? The pair would see him collapse when he overdid it soon enough. At least he had an excuse, although Pol didn't put his weakness down to being almost fifteen. He knew it was because of his ill health.

"This year, we will be looking more deeply into patterns."

"It's always patterns," Coram complained.

Pol thought the man's voice sounded a little whiny.

"You'll be able to put patterns into your swordsmanship soon enough," Vactor said.

Pol raised his hand up to shoulder level. "You mean anticipation magic?"

Vactor nodded. "Pol has used it before." Vactor turned his gaze toward Pol. "Will you help me teach it to these two? They are both wanting to become pattern-masters."

Pol really hadn't heard of that category before coming to Deftnis. Pol realized how little he understood his capabilities, of what he knew and what he didn't. He couldn't refuse Vactor's offer to demonstrate in front of his fellow students.

"I'd be happy to."

Sakwill snorted. "Taught by a snot-nosed kid?"

Vactor stood. "I'll have none of that. Arrogance, or rather the lack of arrogance, is what we are known for. I'm not asking you to bend a knee to Pol, but once you have left Deftnis, you need to seek out knowledge wherever you can, and anticipation magic is known only to a limited number of magicians, and fewer can put it into practice. I'll bring practice swords tomorrow. It's not something you can do without a lot of practice."

Pol looked at Sakwill, who didn't look very friendly.

The monk went over the magic program. It looked like variations on what Pol already knew, but with only the three of them with one teacher, Pol hoped Vactor would teach him more efficient magic like Val and Malden had done with locating.

They were dismissed, and Pol decided to seek out Darrol to learn more about magician-swordsmen. Darrol didn't claim to be one, so Pol wanted to know why. Perhaps he could better understand Sakwill's personal pattern if Darrol helped him.

The monastery had changed with the monks and acolytes returning from Harvest Break. It seemed that all the empty spaces had filled up, and that would make it harder to find Darrol.

Pol returned to the armory where he had previously interviewed with Edgebare.

"I am looking for Darrol Netherfield. Do you know him?" Pol asked an older monk.

"He's just finished evaluating new swords in the practice room." The monk pointed towards a pair of double doors. One was partially open, leaking young acolytes. They wore tan leather belts. Pol looked down at the orange cord. Belts and cords. He shook his head. He'd have to figure all of that out.

Pol wished that he were taller. It would ease looking past the young men coming out of the practice room. Finally the stream became a trickle, and Pol slipped inside. Darrol stood at a table putting away various kinds of swords.

"Coming to spar?" Darrol said. "How are you doing? We haven't seen each other since arriving at Deftnis."

"I'm doing okay. No one has threatened to take my life... yet." Pol smiled at Darrol. "Are you adjusting to the monastic life?"

Darrol laughed. "Not really monastic. Many monks and acolytes have families living at Deftnis Port or at Mancus on the mainland. I can go to the pub whenever I'm not teaching." He shrugged. "To tell you the truth, it's a fine life, but a bit boring. I came to make sure you are treated fairly. Had a talk with Edgebare. He was impressed after I backed up everything you told him. The man thought you were lying." Darrol nodded. "I set him straight."

"I liked him. He reminded me of an older Kelso Beastwell."

Darrol shook his head. "I hope Kelso hasn't been sacked from his Captaincy by your father."

"It is my intent never to know," Pol said. "That is all behind me."

Darrol grimaced. "The past is never behind you. One just has to put the past into the proper perspective. You learned a lot of valuable lessons that probably aren't apparent right now, but they will be as you get older."

Pol felt he had had enough 'life lessons,' but he recognized Darrol's advice. Perhaps he was too young to think much of anything but the past year.

"I wanted to ask you about anticipation magic and pattern-masters. Are you one?"

Darrol scrunched up his eyebrows. "Me? Not at all. Having a little magic and being a Deftnis magician—anything requires third or fourth level magic." His eyes went to Pol's belt. "They rated you third level, eh? Malden would be proud. I'll bet you made them think hard about how to classify you. Val thought if you had more endurance, they would have to rate you a Level Four. That is monk-level competence."

"And a Third Level isn't?"

Darrol shook his head. "Not by itself, it isn't. The leather belts are monks who fight with little or no magic. That's me. Black is a Master. I wear the green. It's the lowest for a monk, and I never thought I'd get higher, so I left. It's different with you around. I'll get to see you grow."

"Why don't you get married and have boys of your own?" Pol said. He realized that he had probed too far with the look on Darrol's face.

"Not something I want to talk about, at least not now," Darrol said. "So there are white, yellow, orange, red, purple, blue, gray, and black that correspond to each magic level. For fighters, it's tan, brown, green, red, purple, and black. Less colors to confuse us that use more muscle and less magic." Darrol laughed.

"What about pattern-masters?"

"Level Four is probably the minimum rating for true competence, although a Third Level can learn it. Anticipation magic, what you just talked about, has to be mastered, and it generally takes a Level Four."

"So I'm between a Three and a Four."

Darrol nodded. "At fifteen," he rubbed Pol's hair since he knew Pol's birthday would be in the next few weeks, "there has never been a Level Three, to my recollection."

Now Pol understood Sakwill and Coram's resentment. Pol knew

anticipation magic well. His life had depended on it fighting in the tourney King Colvin had arranged for Emperor Hazett's visit.

"Got time for a little sparring? I've got a couple of practice swords that are waiting to be broken in."

Pol grinned. "A bit for as long as I last. We've never really sparred before."

"No, we haven't, although I've certainly seen you in action."

This was an opportunity to think about and practice anticipation magic before he had to show Sakwill and Coram. He'd make the most of it.

~ ~ ~

Chapter Four

POL TRIED TO TEACH ANTICIPATION MAGIC to the two others in his class, but they didn't seem to be picking it up, or they chose not to respond to Pol's effort to teach.

"We will let the sword masters teach you," Vactor said after their second session with swords. "I have another task for you three." Vactor pointed to three square metal tubes about a foot long and an inch wide. "I want you to twist the bar in the middle."

His two partners had no trouble putting a single twist, but that particular effort made Pol faint, trying to tweak a twist into a square metal bar.

Pol woke up a few minutes later. Someone had removed his robe and rolled it up to make a pillow on the hard stone floor.

He struggled to get up, but his heart beat fiercely in his chest.

"I think it's past time you visited our healers," Vactor said, kneeling next to Pol. He looked up at Sakwill and Coram sitting in their seats. "This is the difference between you two and Pol. He's got one good tweak in him."

"Did I twist the bar?" Pol asked. He wondered if his fainting had been for nothing.

"Good enough," Sakwill said, picking the bar up from the top of the table that Pol couldn't see.

Pol nodded and closed his eyes, willing his heart to slow and his breathing to even out.

A healer in a lighter gray robe entered the room, carrying a rolled up stretcher. "Fainted?"

Vactor nodded. "It happens to him after an ambitious tweak. He successfully performed the spell and then…" The monk shrugged his shoulders.

Pol didn't want to be carried anywhere, but he didn't have the strength to walk and had to put up with the embarrassment of riding the stretcher to the infirmary. They put him in a ward. No private rooms at Deftnis, he thought.

Three healers, all youngish to Pol's mind, leaned over to examine Pol.

"Heart murmur," one said, laying his hand on Pol's chest. "It's a big one."

More probing and unintelligible sounds from the healers resulted in another commenting on Pol's spleen.

The youngest healer took Pol's wrist. "We can help with your symptoms, but we can't offer a cure. There was a monk who had the ability to heal the way you need healing, but he left the monastery five years ago."

"Searl?" one of the monks asked.

The younger one nodded. "He could change the pattern of organs. We haven't had a monk since then that came close in that ability."

"Does that mean I'll die before I'm twenty?" Pol said.

"No. It means you'll struggle with your heart and your lungs, but not as badly with our treatments. I don't recommend that you go very far from a healer. Stay at Deftnis, and you can live as long as the three of us."

Pol didn't quite know how to take that. They recommended that he stay in bed until dinnertime, and then he could resume his normal activities.

The bed was more comfortable than the thinly-padded cot in his dormitory, so Pol lay back and thought about what the healers had said. He could live longer if healers were close. Pol wondered what would happen to him if healers weren't close. Would he be any worse off than he was now?

He wondered about Searl, the monk. That would be a question

for another time. He closed his eyes and let sleep take him.

A hearty dinner helped Pol regain his strength. The healers wanted to see Pol once a week, and he had to admit that he felt better than he ever had.

Pol didn't want to push his strength in the evening to test his condition, so he waited for morning and the first class for Seekers in the morning. Pol knew Paki among the attendees until Darrol slid up next to him.

"They're going to let me attend some of the classes," Darrol said, grinning. "I enjoyed my time too much on our little jaunt in the woods, except for the Lirro's death, of course. So we get to learn together."

Paki looked excited. "I thought they'd split us up."

Darrol shook his head. "Only one master this year for both Seeking and Scouting, Jonness, but he's a good one. He may do some splitting later on, since he has two monks to help him."

The master had tested them when they first arrived in Deftnis, and Pol thought that he had impressed him well enough.

Jonness stood in front of the participants and had them sit on the floor of the practice room. "We will work together for the first part of this term. I do survival and stealth. There are a number of you who will want to stick with me as we transition into scout training. We start with an introduction to Seeking, as it is less stealthiness and more discerning patterns.

"Why is everything seemingly disorganized?" Pol asked Darrol.

"Initially, its a winnowing process. You'd be surprised how many times an acolyte, or even a monk like me, will change their minds about their specialty. That's why the Abbot is open to the notion to let everyone try what they want. The classes will change, you wait and see."

Pol wrapped his arms around his knees and smiled. Now he felt like he could wait for a while. Perhaps he wouldn't die young. He'd have to think beyond his teenage years, and that made him a little uncomfortable. There was a part of him that had become too complacent about his short life horizon.

Pol settled into his classes. Magic for the Third Levels was moved to late afternoons for an hour and a half. Pol had to work in the kitchens during lunch. He spent all morning long with Jonness and the afternoon with different monks.

He didn't know that acolytes had to learn the same things that Mistress Farthia had taught him. He talked to the monks about repeating what he had learned. Most of them told him to wait at least a year before going to the more advanced classes.

With more time on his hands, Pol decided to practice knife throwing on his own. He found a smaller practice room that was usually empty and moved a few broken-down targets inside. He liked the time alone, so he could just contemplate all kinds of things.

One morning just outside the walls of the monastery, while practicing fire-making without magic out of whatever was at hand, something Pol had learned from Siggon Horstel in North Salvan, Jonness stopped Pol.

"This is Kell Digbee," Jonness said.

Pol looked up. He saw a well-built blondish boy, probably eighteen or older, looking down on him with his fists on his hips. "This is an acolyte?" Kell sneered at Pol.

"He's the one that's going to catch you up to the rest of us."

Pol sighed. He hadn't succeeded in trying to teach Sakwill and Coram the basics of anticipation magic, and now he would have another chance to fail at teaching. At least this time Kell was closer to his age. Pol stood.

"I'm Pol Cissert," he said, "I learned this last year, so it shouldn't be too difficult for you."

Kell snorted. "Who let you in here? You must be all of thirteen years old."

'Fifteen, just," Pol said. "But Master Jonness will vouch for my competence." Under previous circumstances, Pol's heart would be racing, and his breathing would be all he concentrated on, but with the healers' help, he felt his heart beating a bit faster, but that was it.

Jonness sighed. "Just listen to him."

Pol told Kell to bend down, but the boy still stood with his hands on his hips.

"You won't learn unless you watch."

"I am watching," Kell said.

The defiance in Kell's voice irked Pol. "Suit yourself," Pol said as he went ahead describing the set-up and explaining what one had to do. After he started the fire, he stood and said, "Now, you can do it." He destroyed the twisted bark that he had used to wind around the turning post.

Kell grimaced and tried to reassemble Pol's apparatus, but the bark couldn't be used again.

"Master Jonness won't want you to use my set-up again," Pol said, "We're supposed to use materials that you scavenge among the trees."

The youth kicked Pol's stuff aside, but bent back down to look at what Pol had made. Kell ignored Pol as he stomped off deeper into the wood and stripped ropy bark from a tree and cut two reasonably straight sticks from a recently fallen tree. He could see the anger in Kell's posture as Pol sought out possible patterns that might have caused the youth's ill temper.

Pol stooped down and picked up a thicker branch and grabbed some dry moss from the fallen tree and put them behind his back, as he followed Kell back to the rest of the fire-makers.

Kell stood over the remains of Pol's fire making and growled. Pol tossed the moss and the branch on the ground. "The moss is used to help start the fire, and you'll carve a base and a holder from the branch," Pol said.

"But I didn't find them myself."

Pol looked up at Kell's truculent face. "I just let you know what you missed. Can you remember what I just said?" Pol could nearly see the dark cloud over Kell's head. He wondered if Kell ever smiled.

Kell just nodded, and then got down on one knee and looked at the others at work and at Pol's things. He cut the thick branch in two and carved a notch into one section and used his knife to cut a tiny bowl in the other part to accept the top of the spindle. Then he tried to wind the bark around the ends of the stick, but it kept falling off.

"Twist the bark to make it thinner, and cut a notch at each end the bow."

"Bow?" Kell asked.

Finally a question, thought Pol. "Yes, that's what the stick with the twisted bark is. If you can't find the right bark, you can make a cord out of reeds, or even tall grass. A shoelace will work even better, if you have one."

"Hmpf."

What did that mean? Maybe Kell just accepted Pol's words.

At least Kell wasn't stupid. He finally got the idea of what to do, and his bow began to twirl and hum like the rest of the fire-makers. Pol looked over and saw the tiny coals that Kell needed, but Kell had no idea what to do.

"Slide the smoking bits into the moss and gently blow to get the fire going. That's how you get it started."

"Oh." Kell looked around. He would find no help by looking around, since he was now the only one making a fire. He slipped the coals into the moss and blew gently until the moss began to smoke. "Then I put shavings on?"

Pol nodded. He couldn't give Kell a smile of encouragement, but he nodded. "Have you always used tinder boxes?"

"I've generally used servants, but yeah," Kell said. He kept blowing on the moss and shaved off some of the edges of one of the sticks to give the fire more fuel and finally made a respectable tiny blaze.

"Good work, Kell," Jonness said. "That's enough. Pol taught you well. Now do it entirely on your own."

"Why should I do it again? Isn't once enough?"

Pol started at Kell's outburst. He wasn't respectful enough to Jonness. "The rest of us have done this twice, today," Pol said. He got an angry look in return.

"Do I need to help him?" Pol said, looking at Jonness.

"No, but let me know that he's been successful."

Pol didn't like having to report Kell's results, but he just nodded. Kell began to remind Pol of a smarter Landon, surly with a dislike of Pol. He hung around as the others went back to the Seeker practice room, leaving Pol to observe. Luckily, Kell only needed a tip or two and picked up making a fire quickly enough.

"Good," Pol said, getting up. "We can go back to class now."

Kell stomped out his tiny blaze, while Pol grabbed the bucket left to quench all the fires. He was going to give the bucket to Kell, but the youth had already headed towards the building, leaving Pol standing by himself.

Pol ground his teeth and poured water over Kell's and his fire-making efforts. He took the bucket back to the room and slipped in the back. Kell sat up front, closer to Jonness.

"One other thing, the Abbot asked me to announce that we have a thief in our midst. Keep your valuables locked up. Hopefully, if we are all careful, the thief won't have an opportunity to steal. If not, maybe a few of you will have an opportunity to use Seeker skills to find the culprit," Jonness said, joking. He then reviewed the fire-making technique, and talked about alternate materials for the bowstring and tinder. "If you can't find string, you can move the spindle by rubbing it between your palms." Jonness demonstrated how to make the spindle turn.

Siggon had taught Paki and him the same things. Pol looked over the group and wondered how many had learned any survival skills before coming to Deftnis. Kell obviously came from a privileged household. Pol wondered how many of the other boys came from humble circumstances. Darrol and Paki certainly did. He couldn't imagine Malden growing up poor.

The acolytes filed out, but Pol stayed behind.

"Want to catch the thief?" Jonness asked, smiling.

Pol shook his head. "I don't know enough."

Jonness crinkled his eyes. "I think you know more than you think. So you have another question?"

"I do. How many acolytes come from wealthy families and how many come from poorer circumstances?"

"Thinking about your new friend Kell?"

"He's hardly a friend."

Jonness chuckled. "Our magic acolytes can come from anywhere in Imperial society. What recommends them is their magic. That's true with most monasteries that I know of, except for Tesna, who generally accept only the noble-born. For training in arms, an acolyte needs a recommendation. Most of those on the lower rungs aren't exposed to Deftnis graduates, so our fighters tend to come from better families."

"Kell said he had servants light his fires."

Jonness nodded. "Undoubtedly true, but I let the Abbot worry about that. I'm only concerned about my students. I know all about your circumstances, since you and your friend Paki came with Valiso Gasibli and Darrol Netherfield. You are the surprising one. I had expected Pakkingail to be the woodsman, but it's really you. I only wish I had the time to work individually with you, Pol. That kind of training comes later, so be patient and help me with the others."

"I will, sir." Pol said. He bowed to Jonness and left the practice room. Gorm had just told him he had a new class to attend on political geography. From the title, he thought Mistress Farthia had already worked with him in Borstall on such things. That would be another class where Pol might be ahead of acolytes much older than him. Pol thought that he would be more challenged at Deftnis, but disappointment filled him as he dragged himself to a building he'd never been in before.

He entered a classroom. Tables and chairs for ten students were set on each of two raised tiers overlooking a large table. Pol took a chair in the back on the side. Someone had hung a huge map of Eastril on the wall opposite the seats. Pol groaned when he spotted Kell talking to an older acolyte across the room from him. Kell met his eyes and turned away with a disagreeable expression on his face.

A balding monk about thirty years old with dark olive skin walked down the steps to the floor. He looked like a bird of prey, with a ruff of dark, curly hair and large brown eyes behind a sharp beak of a nose. That said, the man looked very intelligent to Pol.

"You are all at various stages of the Seeker track at Deftnis and have been invited to attend this class. I come to the monastery every two years to bring the world to Deftnis for a few months. At other times, I work for the Emperor in Yastan, the capital. I am to be addressed as Master Akonai. My full name is Akonai Pulau Haleaku. If you are curious, I originally grew up in The Shards."

Pol had never come across anyone who came from the large island group that sat to the south of the Volian continent. His name certainly sounded exotic.

Akonai walked around the room, checking off the attendees,

starting on the other side of the room. He finally stopped at Pol and looked down at his roll. "Pol Cissert?" he said quietly.

"That's me," Pol said.

That brought a smile to Akonai's face. "We have mutual friends, I think." Akonai lowered his voice. "Ranno Wissingbel sends you his regards, as does his superior. I work in Ranno's ministry."

Ranno's superior was Hazett III, the Emperor of the Baccusol Empire, and Pol could feel a blush running up his neck. Pol met the Emperor personally when he visited North Salvan in the summer. "Is Mistress Farthia in Yastan?"

Akonai grinned. "She is, along with Malden Gastoria, an esteemed graduate of Deftnis."

The master turned and walked back to the center of the room. "We will be talking about each of the countries in the Empire," he pointed to his back without turning, "and about the power structures governing all of them. The information that we will discuss is highly confidential, but it has a short life as circumstances quickly change." Akonai's gaze lingered on Pol.

Pol had lost what little power he had in North Salvan, but the subject matter excited him. Farthia, his tutor for the past few years, had only taught him geography and the briefest of what happened in each country, except those bordering North Salvan. To know the political situation, new or not, in all of the Empire would be exciting. No matter what transpired, Pol could learn new patterns that swirled in the countries of the Baccusol Empire.

The rest of the two-hour class consisted of a review of the different kingdoms and of The Dukedoms, a band of smaller countries. Deftnis was part of the Sand dukedom. Pol had been through all this before and had finished memorizing all the political entities and their capitals last year. Akonai still put in a little bit of inside information or intimations of information while he talked, and that kept Pol interested.

Pol heard the hourly bell outside.

"I must leave you. I have some advanced courses for monks only. Same time tomorrow." Akonai rushed up the steps to the door and left them. They had no books to read, so Pol would bring paper and ink tomorrow to make notes.

Kell bumped into him on the way out. "What did the monk tell you?" he said. "You always get special treatment. One would think you were royalty." Kell sneered.

"I know some people who he knows in Yastan, and he relayed their greetings, that is all."

Kell just grunted, pushed Pol aside, and moved on ahead. He couldn't have been more like Landon that time, except Landon wouldn't have talked to him as long.

The next day Darrol joined him in Master Akonai's class and sat beside him.

"Do you know all the countries of the Empire?" Pol asked.

"I know most of them. Don't quiz me on all the Dukedoms, though."

"There they are," Pol pointed to the huge map, still hanging in front of them.

Master Akonai walked into the room. He walked up to Darrol. "Netherfield. I haven't seen you in years. Are you behaving this time?"

Darrol reddened a bit. "I am. I want to learn a bit about Seeking this time around. I can't be teaching swordsmanship all my time here."

Akonai looked at Pol. "Take good care of this rogue, will you?"

"He's here to take care of me," Pol said with a smile.

"Not in this class." The monk strolled back to the center. "I hope you brought some paper and ink. It is permissible to take notes. If you don't, you might not be able to pass the test you will all take at the end. Understood?"

Pol heard some grumbling, but he stayed quiet and sharpened the quill of his pen. It looked like he was the only one to come prepared to take notes. Perhaps the others were far enough from their schooling not to realize they might need to record Akonai's lectures.

"We are going to move from west to east on the map behind us. I will lay out a map of the country that we talk about on this table," Akonai pointed to the table in the center of the room, "where we will discuss the merging of geography and politics."

They spent the next two hours talking about the relationship between West Huffnya and East Huffnya. Pol knew quite a bit about East Huffnya since the Emperor's Processional went through that country, and Mistress Farthia discussed each visited country when she had returned from her visit to Yastan. However, Akonai delved more deeply into the political conflicts internally and how that affected the external relationship between the two countries.

Two hours sped by for Pol, but he had to nudge Darrol awake. He looked down and Darrol had written all of two sentences compared to nearly three pages of notes that Pol took.

Akonai rubbed Darrol's thick brown hair. "Wake up, warrior," he said gently, with humor in his voice. "I think what the Seeking Darrol is good for doesn't involve too much thinking."

Pol kept his mouth shut because he thought Darrol could hear the conversation.

"Did I explain everything?"

Pol shook his head. "You only gave us a summary. I could have listened to another two hours."

"You probably would have assumed the same position as Darrol soon enough. I'll talk to the Abbot and see if he'll let you sit in on my other discussions. Give-and-take makes it all the more interesting than a lecture."

Pol looked over at Kell, who gave him a dirty look. Pol didn't care. "I'd like that."

Akonai raised his eyebrows. "I've got to run."

"Is he gone?" Darrol said lifting his head from the table.

Pol laughed. "I didn't think you were asleep."

"I absorb everything better with my eyes closed. Anyway, I grew up in East Huffnya, close to Lake. I keep up enough to know a bit more than what Akonai talked about today."

After quizzing Darrol, Pol realized that his friend knew as much as he said. The room emptied out, and Darrol and Pol were the last ones to leave the classroom, passing much older acolytes coming in for a different course.

~ ~ ~

Chapter Five

~

"WHERE IS YOUR FRIEND?" Gorm said to Pol, just coming to bed.

"Paki?"

Gorm nodded. "The very one. He isn't on the grounds."

Pol hadn't seen him since the morning Seeker class. He shook his head.

"Probably gone to Deftnis Port," Gorm said. "I'll give you an hour to retrieve him. Acolytes aren't allowed to spend the night outside the monastery in the first year."

Pol knew that and wondered where his friend could be. "I'll find him."

He ran out of the dormitory and headed to the building where Darrol lived. Pol knocked on Darrol's door.

"I need your help."

Pol heard stirring in his room. Darrol looked like he had thrown on his robe, since Pol looked down to see bare feet on the stone floor.

"What?" Darrol yawned and rubbed his disheveled hair. He evidently had retired early.

"Paki is missing. Gorm seems to think he has gone down to Port Deftnis for fun and games."

Darrol shook his head. "I didn't think he was that stupid, but if he's gone, I have an idea where to find him. Give me a minute," he said.

Pol waited outside in the corridor. A few monks passed by him, giving him funny looks, but eventually Darrol came out, wearing boots this time. His hair had been dampened and combed back.

"Follow me."

Pol padded after Darrol to the stables. Pol took the time to check on his horse while Darrol looked around and frowned.

"I thought there would be a game of chance here, but I'm wrong. Perhaps we'll have to take a bit of a hike to the port."

The trip down from the monastery was uneventful. Darrol talked to Pol about the few places that would serve acolytes. They would find him, but getting back in an hour might be a close thing.

Pol followed silently behind Darrol as they began their search. Darrol knocked on the door of a tiny restaurant. Glimmers of candlelight edged drawn curtains.

The door opened. Pol could smell the liquor.

"Any acolytes tonight?"

"Darrol Netherfield? Haven't seen you in ages. Come in for a spot." A skinny, grizzled, gray-haired man ushered the two of them in.

Pol looked around at the bodies of snoring men and boys. Most wore the robes of the monastery, monks and acolytes both. He spied Paki, dressed in regular clothes, but behaving like the rest.

"Sorry, Billious, maybe another time. I've come to collect that one on the bench." Darrol pointed to Paki.

Bilious grunted. "Take him. He was one of the first to go beddy-bye tonight. The younger they are, the quicker they fall." The man cackled like an old woman.

Darrol bent over and lifted Paki over his shoulder. Once outside, Pol heard a bell pealing from the monastery. He doubted they could make it back on time.

"What was that place?"

"Billious is a shrewd tavern keeper. He sells monks alcohol for a bit more than other places, but lets the monks sleep it off in his establishment. Since fellow monks frequent the place, it's a bit more discreet than a tavern, albeit more expensive."

"Where did Paki get the money to spend?" Pol asked.

Darrol shook his head in the darkness. "He hasn't had the

opportunity to buy anything since he came. I imagine it's money he brought with him. You haven't spent any of yours, either, I suppose."

Pol hadn't, and he couldn't even think of wasting it on getting his head muddled. He worried about reaching the dormitory after the hour that Gorm had given Pol. Darrol grunted as he dumped Paki on his bed.

"Both of you will be punished tomorrow," Gorm said coming from his cell at the end of the dormitory. "You weren't supposed to leave the monastery, Pol."

"He was with me," Darrol said. "I showed him where Paki was and helped carry the lad all the way from the port. It takes longer getting up the hill."

Gorm shook his head, his face looked like carved granite. "You'll see the Abbot tomorrow, first thing."

"C'mon, Gorm. Pol wasn't doing anything wrong."

"Rules are rules," the monk said, looking defiantly at Darrol.

Darrol just pressed his lips tightly together and nodded to Pol before he stomped out of the dormitory.

"Go to sleep," Gorm said, already heading to his cell.

Pol couldn't shake off the feeling of unfairness and glared in Gorm's direction.

Pol shook Paki awake. "Hurry up. We're to meet the Abbot before breakfast," Pol said, clutching the message that Gorm had given him. Pol didn't like the look of satisfaction on the dormitory monk's face. He had never thought that Gorm disliked him, but that had ended last night.

"Wha—?" Paki said. He put his hand to his forehead. "I'm not feeling well."

"That's because you got drunk where you shouldn't have," Pol said.

"Where?"

"Billious? Remember the old man?"

Paki looked up at Pol, who threw his robe at him. "Put this on and straighten your hair. We have a disciplinary meeting with the Abbot as soon as we can get to his office, and I don't want to keep him waiting."

"Why you?"

"Because Darrol and I fetched you, and we didn't get back in time. Now I'm in just as much trouble as you are," Pol said.

Paki got up and began to stagger to the door. By the time he reached it, he walked normally. Pol followed him all the way to the Abbot's office.

The two desks in the clerks' room were empty. They were probably eating breakfast, Pol thought. He knocked on the door.

"Come in," the Abbot said.

Pol poked his head through the door, and then dragged Paki inside with him. He put his summons on the Abbot's desk. "We are here as instructed, sir," Pol said.

"Sit down, the both of you." The Abbot said, picking up the notice. "So you both went out to Port Deftnis last night. Is that true, Pakkingail?"

Paki nodded. It irked Pol that his friend didn't say a word.

"Pol?"

"Monk Gorm told me that Paki was missing just before I went to bed last night. He gave me an hour to find him. I asked Darrol Netherfield to help me, since he knows the monastery grounds better than I do."

The Abbot smiled, just a bit. "You mean he knows where young acolytes would likely get into mischief?"

Pol nodded. "We found Paki asleep at Billious's place. I don't know the formal name—"

"I know it, well enough," the Abbot said.

"By the time we returned the hour had passed, and Monk Gorm informed me that we were both subject to disciplinary action."

"That's it?"

Pol nodded.

"Pakkingail, do you have anything else to add?"

"I was asleep through it all, sir." Paki said, keeping his head down and his eyes on the floor.

"Gorm will expect punishment. He probably told you rules were not meant to be broken, or something to that effect."

"Rules are rules, sir," Pol said.

"Well, then let's not break them. You both will spend Sevenday brushing the muck from the main courtyard. For that, you each will receive a silver hen."

"Payment for punishment?" Paki said, his eyes rising to meet the Abbot's.

"Don't tell Gorm you're both getting paid. Paki, you realize what you did was wrong?"

"I was with two stable monks. They talked me into going, but it was me that decided to go."

"You'll have plenty of opportunity after your first year. Don't go without permission. We do allow first year acolytes occasional trips to Port Deftnis and Mancus, as well… in the daylight."

Paki nodded.

The Abbot stood. "I'm famished. Let us walk to the commissary together."

Pol rose faster than Paki, who seemed to still feel the effects of his actions the previous night.

They entered the commissary. Pol and Paki hurried to the food line, and the Abbot proceeded to sit at the high table to be waited on.

"What was that all about?" asked one of the other acolytes standing in front of them in line.

Paki groaned. "We were disciplined." He made a sorrowful face and kept it that way midway through the line.

Pol was just happy he wouldn't be put into a dungeon cell or expelled. Now he knew their infraction wasn't as serious as Gorm made it out to be.

They sat down, and Darrol joined them.

"We have to muck the courtyard on Sevenday," Paki said.

Darrol winced. "Not a nice job, but it could be worse, and you escaped physical punishment."

"Physical punishment?" Paki parroted.

Their friend nodded. "The maximum would be twenty strikes with a cane, but there are worse things than being caught late."

"But I was drunk," Paki said.

"So?" Darrol said. "Being drunk and sleeping isn't a violation of any Deftnis oath. If you caused damage, that would be a different story, but you didn't hurt anyone but yourself."

"It isn't fair to Pol."

Pol felt Paki's eyes on him and he looked up from his food. "I don't care. If it keeps Gorm off of me, I'm okay," Pol said.

Darrol nodded. "The Abbot doesn't want to overrule the dormitory monk very often. Gorm is a special case."

"He isn't a real monk?"

Darrol shrugged. "He's a real monk because the Abbot made him one, but he has an unfortunate history. I'll leave it at that. Don't blame him for who he is."

That was an interesting revelation, Pol thought. He had tried to develop a pattern for Gorm, but his behavior didn't quite match up. If Gorm had a history, perhaps there was more to the monk than what Pol could discern. Now he was a bit confused. Perhaps he was too hasty in assembling a pattern. The concept of improper patterns was significant. He would bring it up with Vactor, his magic tutor.

Pol was attentive enough in his Seeking class, and with Master Akonai he methodically took notes, but he couldn't wait for his magic lessons.

He arrived early in the classroom to find Vactor alone.

"It's just you. Sakwill and Coram are practicing with pattern masters today, trying to pick up the anticipation magic that you tried to teach them. Did you want to join in?"

Pol would have under other circumstances, but not today. He hadn't been able to thoroughly test his new endurance. He had been to the healers weekly, but he still felt like his strength wasn't near to normal.

"I have some questions about patterns."

Vactor smiled. "Good. It's always good to talk about patterns. It's what makes a good magician great. Go ahead."

Pol told him about his adventure the previous night, and the Abbot's judgment. He trusted Vactor enough to tell him the Abbot would pay.

Vactor chuckled and shook his head. "Gorm."

"It's Gorm's pattern that I wanted to talk about. I thought I understood him. I had a pattern crafted that might have worked, but Darrol said that Gorm had a background."

"And what does having a 'background' have to do with his

pattern?"

"Maybe nothing, maybe a lot," Pol said. "What happens if a magician senses a pattern and tweaks without fully understanding it? I know if you apply too much or too little force, you won't get the results you intend."

Vactor nodded. "Malden told you that magicians don't bother to tweak most patterns?"

"Something similar. He said that he rarely tweaked patterns, but he saw patterns everywhere, and he often didn't need to tweak them."

"Part of the reason is what you discovered today. Tweak a poorly understood pattern, with magic or influence or physical force or whatever, and you probably won't get what you expect. Magic is not omnipotence. Magicians aren't gods. They can make serious mistakes that backfire."

"So that's why Malden said that battle magicians are useless? I thought it was because of the unpredictability of a conflict."

"You answered your question. Malden is correct. What is the uncertainty of war, but a pattern not understood or not static enough to reliably tweak?"

Pol sat back. "Oh. I thought it had to do with changing conditions. It does, but now I know why."

"It's good that you do."

"Then why does Deftnis send out pattern-masters?"

Vactor leaned forward and clasped his hands on the table. "Because they are taught to restrict their actions to what they see. Anticipation magic doesn't make a swordsman unbeatable, but it helps well enough. It only works with a few opponents at a time. The more variables there are to anticipate, the harder it is to use."

Pol figured out how that could be true. "I used location magic in a fight in Tarida to place my knife throws. I sensed more than just one person, and I was successful."

"I read about that. Val reported on that fight. It showed us that you can think very quickly, but what if there were twice the number?"

'Oh, I see." Pol thought about his health. "I'm physically stronger than I was. Will that make me fight better?"

"Fight, yes. Anticipate? No. Pattern-masters need physical prowess, but their magic is based on quick thoughts and quick reactions, not strength. Magic augments what is already there. Personal patterns are a different thing. One doesn't try to manipulate a personal pattern without understanding the consequences."

Pol nodded. The answer meant Pol had to be very careful when he developed personal patterns. He now realized that he didn't know enough about people to make an accurate pattern.

"Shall we test how strong you are?" Vactor stood and walked away from the table.

"Move me about four feet in the air and turn my body around."

Finally, a test of his strength, Pol thought. He stood in front of Vactor and lifted him so that he looked at his face quite a ways up. Pol could feel the strain on his body. The next step involved turning Vactor, and he was able to get Vactor swiveled three-quarters around before his heart began to beat hard. He lowered Vactor while he still retained a bit of strength and staggered back to his seat.

Pol hunched over, struggling for breath, clutching the edges of the chair to stay upright.

"Better," Vactor said, walking over and putting his hand lightly on Pol's shoulder. "When you came here a month ago, you would have been out cold, wouldn't you?"

Pol couldn't speak, but he nodded his head. Vactor let him breathe for a bit. Pol's heart settled down.

"I'm not cured."

Vactor shook his head. "No, but you're not dead, are you?"

"I still could die before I'm an adult," Pol said. All the anxiety that he thought put away for good assaulted him again.

"You won't," Vactor said. "I have faith that you will find a way."

Pol didn't know what Vactor meant by that, but Pol didn't disagree with him. He didn't want to end up dying early like the father he had never known.

~ ~ ~

Chapter Six

~

FALL HAD ORDERED THE TREES TO DROP THEIR LEAVES, although on
Deftnis Isle, the weather was mild enough so many plants didn't
go dormant, and that kept the island green. His Seeker class stopped
when Jonness was called away from the monastery. No one mentioned
the reason, but the assistant monks decided it was a good opportunity
to teach horsemanship.

Pol found out that most acolytes did not have their own horse,
but the monastery had large stables. Pol had only been able to get bits
and snatches of time to ride his Shinkyan horse. He knew the horse
needed a name, and he finally came up with one. Pol remembered the
Sleeping God had a name, Demeron, or something similar to that. He
decided that Demeron, a god's name, was worthy of his mount.

The acolytes rode out the stable gate. Pol looked up as he passed
underneath the door and spotted a portcullis hanging within the stone
wall of the monastery. He couldn't imagine anyone invading Deftnis,
but someone designed it as a fortress, with every gate defensible.

Paki slipped by his side. "What do you think we are going to
learn?"

"Maybe we will learn how scouts take care of their mounts or how
to ride in cavalry formation." Pol didn't know and didn't care. All he
knew was that he enjoyed being on Demeron's back for more than the

few minutes he usually had to exercise his horse. He told Paki about the naming.

Paki laughed. "Trust you to come up with something so obscure." Paki had to look up at Pol sitting on the tall mount.

"I look down on you from my heavenly perch," Pol said, trying to make his voice sound low. He noticed that Paki's voice had begun to change.

"One of the Six Hells is more like it," Kell said from behind him. "My father told me that Shinkyan horses were devils."

"Jealous?" Paki said.

"Of something so evil?" Kell shook his head. Pol noticed that Kell rode his own horse, and it looked quite handsome. "Where does someone like you get something like that?"

"Pol grew up as a prince," Paki said.

That brought a scowl to Pol's face, and he nudged his riding crop into Paki's ribs.

"Right," Kell said.

"I was a prince," Pol said. Now that Paki had brought it up, Pol didn't want it discussed again. "I was disinherited."

"You were?" Kell's face looked a bit uncertain until he thought about it. "Both of you are pulling my leg. I can't believe you. Prince of what?"

"A country I'd rather not mention," Pol said. "My mother died, and I was not liked in the castle, so I petitioned for disinheritance."

"You volunteered?" Kell said in disbelief.

"I didn't want to be assassinated. That's why I came here." Pol turned back to the column of horses.

"A fairy tale." Kell paused. 'That's how you claim you got your horse? I guess that's a story to cover the fact that you stole it."

Pol didn't turn around. He didn't like Kell, or his accusations, or his disbelief. He continued to ignore his insults until they reached a turf plain on the far side of the island. The ground didn't look like it would be very fertile, but what did Pol know.

The two monks who accompanied the eighteen acolytes made them line up into two rows of ten. One of the monks stood in his stirrups and addressed the group.

"We will split into two groups. Those who are magicians go into my group on the left and those who aren't go to the right."

Paki and Pol headed left. Pol was relieved to see Kell mill around, but he ended up on the right.

"The others will learn how to ride using their knees to guide their horse. We will do that as well, but I'll also teach you some basic ways to guide your horse using magic. Have any of you ever tried?"

Pol raised his hand. "My horse bolted, not this one, and I stopped it by thickening the air in front of it."

"Never heard of that before." The monk wore a purple cord, tying up his robe, and that meant he rated a Level Five, two levels above Pol.

"I hadn't either, but I had to stop the horse, or else."

The monk nodded in agreement. "I've experienced 'or else'. Horses are sensitive to magic, so most of them can be 'nudged' by simple spells. I'll teach you the spells, and you are to tell your magic masters what they are. Except you." The monk looked at Pol. "You're the only Third Level here, so Vactor will assume you can do this."

Pol looked around, and the rest of the riders were First or Second Level magicians. He felt a little embarrassed by being pointed out, so he just nodded and kept quiet while the monk explained how to tweak a simple pattern projected towards the horse.

The large meadow became dotted with acolytes trying to guide their horses. Pol found the spell ridiculously easy, and Demeron followed his commands without fail. He leaned over and slapped the horse's head when he meant to pat it.

Not too hard.

What was that, a voice in his head? He withdrew his hand and looked at it. Pol reached over again and patted Demeron's head more gently.

Better.

Pol looked at his horse. "Are you talking to me?"

Who else?

No one had told him that horses could talk back.

"Do you know who I am?" Pol said.

My rider, Pol Cissert.

"I named you. Do you accept the name Demeron?"

Why did you name me that?

Pol told him.

That sounds like a name I can accept.

"What do you call yourself?"

Horse. No one named me after I became thoughtful.

So Demeron had come to him before he could think. He let the implications of a thinking horse soak into him.

"Do I treat you well?"

Good enough. I am fed. You exercise me. I get bored, but I can learn by listening in the stable.

A talking horse. No wonder Kell's father might have thought the Shinkyan horses were devil horses if magicians could talk to them. Pol knew about superstitions, and Kell's mention of the Six Hells told him that Kell was probably from Fen or Vento. There was a religion prevalent in the adjoining countries that preached the Six Heavens and the Six Hells.

Pol laughed to himself. He had never thought that his summer assignment of learning about the religions of the world would help him.

"Can you listen to me think?" Pol said.

A bit. I don't know what you thought about just now. I'm not very learned.

"So I'll have to be careful thinking around you?"

I don't think so. If you don't have me on your mind, I won't hear you in my mine.

That made sense to Pol, since he couldn't hear anything that Demeron didn't specifically direct his way.

"Why didn't you know to communicate with me sooner?"

You didn't think of me and use your power at the same time. I thought you didn't have any, but I'm happy that you do. You will teach me more?

Pol nodded his head. He laughed. Demeron couldn't see him from behind. "Yes. Let's see what we can do."

Demeron followed Pol's instructions perfectly as they practiced turning and going through various paces. Demeron was more talkative than Pol would have dreamed.

Pol dismounted, and Demeron walked away from him, and they

communicated to see how far their link extended. It seemed they could communicate for at least fifty paces.

Demeron pranced around the plain, jumping and dancing on the turf. Pol could feel the joy Demeron felt. His horse knew he would be three years old in the spring.

Pol called Demeron back and pulled a brush out from the saddlebag behind the saddle and groomed Demeron with the horse telling him where to brush a bit harder. Pol couldn't wipe the grin off his face. He had found a new friend in the unlikeliest of places.

The monk rode up to Pol.

"You have quite a rapport with your horse."

"I can feel his emotions," Pol said. It was as much as he dared tell the monk.

"A link? Very good. He is Shinkyan, after all. They are supposed to be the smartest horses in the world. I won't ask you how you came to own him."

"It's better left unsaid." Pol put the brush away and mounted Demeron again. "What else are we to do today?"

"Look at the others," the monk said. "We'll have to have a number of classes through winter to get everyone proficient."

Pol hadn't really noticed, but everyone else seemed to struggle with their mounts. Paki resorted to using the reins, and he noticed Kell's horse sort of ambled on its own, despite Kell's angry threats.

"Oh. I'll still come out and let Demeron get lots of exercise," Pol said.

"Demeron? Isn't that a Volian god somewhere?"

Pol nodded. "In Fassia. The Sleeping God, but my Demeron isn't sleepy, at least not today."

Demeron answered, but Pol didn't tell the monk that.

A few weeks later, Akonai's lectures finally arrived at the eastern side of the Empire. Pol knew quite a bit about Tarida. When Akonai began to talk about North Salvan, Pol's breathing quickened. He stopped taking notes when the monk began to describe the summer's events.

Pol wondered if Akonai got his information from Mistress Farthia.

Every word he said was accurate. He even included Pol's movements in his description, but he didn't reveal his name, since it had a bearing on the political outcome culminating in his mother's death and his flight from Borstall.

Tears welled in Pol's eyes. He wiped them on the sleeve of his robe and caught Akonai's reassuring smile. But Pol's tears turned to anger as Akonai moved to explain King Astor's role in disrupting North Salvan.

Pol hadn't realized, but if the monk's analysis was correct, then King Astor had pushed his daughter on King Colvin. Pol had thought it was the other way around. After putting this new information into the pattern that Pol had spent hours creating on the ride to Deftnis, it all clicked into place. His stepfather had been manipulated by the real villain, King Astor, aided and abetted by his daughter Bythia, recently installed as Queen of Listya.

Akonai now reviewed the Listyan situation that he hadn't spent much time on before. Pol expected the monk to forecast the possible joining of the two Salvans and Listya into one, and he knew why. The Emperor wouldn't stand for a kernel of opposition to grow in the East, especially one with a foothold in the West.

Darrol had filled a page with notes. "He's right on target," Darrol said. "Sorry you had to relive all that."

Pol shook his head. "I learned a lot today." What he really meant is that the uncertain parts of the pattern that Akonai had clarified had changed his perspective of the situation.

Akonai raised his hand to silence the students. "My time with you has ended. I hope you took good notes. Another monk will administer a written test tomorrow and the next day."

Acolytes grumbled about having to take a four-hour test. Pol didn't mind and looked forward to the experience as a way to reinforce the overall pattern of the Empire.

Akonai stepped up to Pol. "I'm sorry I reopened old wounds," he said. "Some of my information about South Salvan is recent, however. I hope that helped."

"As much as you probably know." Pol realized that Akonai wore a gray cord for a belt, the second highest level.

The monk nodded. "I'm sorry I wasn't allowed to let you join in the higher level discussions. I'll be back in two years, most likely, and I think the Abbot will demand that you attend by then."

Pol looked at Akonai's belt again. "What level was Malden?"

"Black, of course. You'll get there soon enough," Akonai said.

Pol still didn't expect to live that long, or if he did, gain the strength necessary to achieve the rating, so he just nodded.

"Any personal words to anyone in Yastan?"

"Tell Malden, Ranno, and Valiso Gasibli, if he's there, that I now know why they call Shinkyan horses 'devil horses.' Give my regards to Mistress Farthia, and tell her I continue to learn, thanks to you." Pol thought he might write a letter to Malden, with his impressions of his pattern of South Salvan.

Akonai put his hand on Pol's shoulder. "I will. Do well in Deftnis. The Empire needs you."

Pol couldn't help but laugh at the ridiculousness of his words, but then he nodded. "I will do my best."

Kell watched Pol from across the room and walked over after Akonai left to talk to a few other students. "You were that disinherited prince?"

"I still am. My mother was the Queen of North Salvan and should have been Queen of Listya."

"What was it like having a king for a father?"

Pol didn't see any friendliness in Kell's face. He responded with the literal truth, "I wouldn't know."

~ ~ ~

Chapter Seven

~

O N A BRIGHT WINTER'S DAY, POL AND DEMERON EXERCISED during another horsemanship session. Monks had set up hurdles around the little plain for the acolytes to practice jumping. Pol and Demeron had no problem negotiating all the jumps on their first try.

Pol didn't see the point of doing it again, so he took off Demeron's saddle and let the horse frolic in the open spaces.

One of the monks dismounted and sat next to Pol. "You are a remarkable horseman for one as young as you."

"Don't compliment me. Demeron did all the work. It was hard enough for me to hang on. He wanted a romp as a reward, so I gave it to him." Pol looked across the plain to see Demeron jumping and rearing up, and basically dancing in the coolish winter light. Pol put his hand to his heart. The healers had helped him gain some strength, but running through all the jumps had still made Pol's heart beat faster.

"Something wrong?"

"I have a heart condition."

The monk nodded. "I heard it's better now."

Pol was surprised that the monk knew his situation. He looked out at the field. "Better doesn't mean I'm healed."

"We used to have the master of Master Healers on the island."

"Searl? I've heard his name spoken a number of times. Why did he leave?"

The monk paused for a bit. "He came to like one of his herbal remedies too much. I was in my third year at the time. Maybe the Abbot knows exactly what it was, but whatever happened affected his ability to heal, and eventually Searl was strongly encouraged to leave, which he did."

"A monk on drugs?" Pol said, his mouth dropping open. It assaulted his perception of the Deftnis pattern.

The monk smiled, a bit too condescendingly in Pol's view. "We aren't the paragons of virtue that you may think. I seem to remember you had a run-in at Billious's? There are other avenues of pleasure or oblivion that monks take from time to time, if you understand, and that includes drugs."

Pol had a hard time thinking that monks would go to brothels, but the monk all but said that.

"If pursuit of such things doesn't affect the work of the monastery, no one cares, unless you are here in your first year." The monk smiled and looked at Pol sideways. "We aren't a sect of religious monks seeking solace in meditation and deprivation. But don't get me wrong, most of us would be considered very good men in today's world and wouldn't dream of disappointing a young idealistic ex-prince like you."

"So where is Master Searl?" Pol had no idea what dreams the monks of Deftnis actually had.

The monk shrugged and got back to his feet. "I heard he was still in The Dukedoms." He looked at a crowd of riders clustering around an acolyte. "It looks like I've got an injured student. Make sure you don't let your horse frolic so much he gets injured," he said as he mounted and left Pol in thought.

Although Darrol attended classes for Seeking, he didn't bring his horse out with the acolytes. Pol found him inspecting practice swords as usual.

"Did you ever know Master Searl?"

"Looking for a better healer than what's in the monastery? There are few better ones roaming the Empire. Searl was a special case. He did some experimenting with herbs and got himself addicted to minweed, of all things."

Pol didn't know what minweed was, but it must have been powerful to take a master healer. "My horse-riding instructor said he didn't know the details."

Darrol grunted. "I did. A friend of mine had taken a nasty slice to his body during practice and was under Searl's care. That was just before they kicked him out of Deftnis. Searl's mind was clear only for a few hours a day. Nearly killed my friend with his antics. I'm glad he left."

"He might still be in The Dukedoms," Pol said.

"What are you interested in an old healer for? Still worried about your health? You look fit enough to me. I can see you've even grown some since we arrived."

"I'm still not fully healthy. I'm better, but not good," Pol said. He left it at that. "Are you up to a little sparring?" Pol wanted to know how his improving swordsmanship would compare to a Deftnis-trained swordsman. They had rarely crossed swords after their trip to the monastery.

"Wooden swords, and," Darrol jabbed his index finger at Pol, "you wear a jerkin."

Pol laughed. "What about you?"

"Anything I get, I'll deserve."

Master Edgebare walked into the armory. "Ah, a Level Three versus a Level Two."

Pol had always wondered how much magic Darrol had command of since he wore leather rather than cord. Being a Second Level, Darrol didn't have enough capability to fight with anticipation magic.

"Show me what you have, boy," Edgebare said. He had only seen Pol working out with first years who didn't have much sword training and when Pol used the little practice room, he made sure he was never observed.

Pol selected a sword that was balanced well enough and walked out on the hard-packed dirt of the large indoor practice hall. A few monks stopped what they were doing to look on. Pol didn't see any acolytes, and that made him feel less uncomfortable about using his magic, but he also didn't want to get pummeled by the much larger and brawnier Darrol.

Darrol smiled and lifted his sword tip in the air and swooshed it down in a salute. Pol did the same and shook the tension out of his shoulders.

Darrol was going to rush him, so Pol, using sips of magic, stepped aside and let Darrol pass him by.

"You are faster, Pol."

Pol had no idea how fast he was to begin with, but he let Darrol come after him. His magic allowed him to elude Darrol's parries and thrusts. Pol just let Darrol come at him and played defense.

Darrol put his hand out to grab Pol's wrist and was rewarded with a loud slap on his own arm. Pol's opponent shook his hand in reaction. "That hurt!"

Pol had put a little magic into that slap to see if he could use magic to speed up his movements. He could feel his power drop. Sips didn't take anything out of him, but enhancing his speed taxed his overall strength.

In a flurry of slashes and thrusts that Pol had never encountered sparring with the acolytes, or with the thirteen-and-fourteen-year-old swordsmen last summer, Darrol succeeded in slipping the point of his sword into Pol's stomach.

Pol grunted and quickly shuffled backwards. His anticipation magic worked with single strokes and simple combinations, but not with something powerful like that.

"You've fought against real pattern-masters before," Pol said, waving his sword at Darrol, trying to get him to keep his distance while he caught his breath. A year ago, Pol would be gasping for air, but now, he was just getting winded.

"I have," Darrol said, grinning. He breathed heavily as well.

He approached again, giving Pol a chance to see what he had missed before when Darrol used the flurry technique. Pol took two deep breaths, since he was about to run out of breath and successfully countered Darrol the second time. When Darrol withdrew, Pol thrust his sword into Darrol's chest, right below his ribcage. His friend let out a gasp of air and fell on his behind. The monks in the armory clapped at Pol's victory.

That was enough sparring for Pol. He leaned over and grabbed his pants just above his knees as he bent over, out of breath.

Darrol put his hands out behind him and made a face. "That'll bruise," he said. "You were too quick to figure out my offense." Darrol said slowly, his chest heaved, and Pol could see Darrol was in pain.

"I didn't mean that to hurt."

Darrol raised a hand briefly and put it back behind him. "You'll pay for that."

Now Pol worried about losing his friend.

"I'll have to have that seen to by a healer."

Edgebare laughed. "Darrol tried harder than I expected him to," he said. "Although he gave you chances, you were tested, Pol, and came out a winner. I imagine you wouldn't have lasted much longer?"

Pol shook his head. "No, I had to put an end to the fight, or I would have been forced to yield."

"I've never seen such a judicious use of magic before," Edgebare said.

"Sips. That is what Malden called them. If I use too much magic, I wear myself out."

Darrol rose slowly to his feet. His hand held his midsection. "He can go much longer now," he said. "At Borstall, Pol was done in a minute or less. We went four or five minutes?"

"Closer to four, I would say," Edgebare said and patted Pol on the shoulder. "You still have some growing up to do, but I'll be looking forward to it." He turned around and walked away.

"I'll need you to lean on," Darrol said. "I wasn't joking about needing to see a healer. We learn in Deftnis that you can be injured without breaking the skin."

Pol thought of Siggon when Pol found him beaten. He had sent his son Paki back to the Emperor's tournament in Borstall last summer, but Siggon had died from internal injuries, as Malden had called them.

Darrol laid his heavy arm on Pol's shoulder as they walked slowly out of the armory, followed by the gaze of some entertained monks.

Darrol needed a day of rest, and the healers wanted to observe if there was any additional redness or swelling. Pol had winced at the sight of the bruise at the top of his friend's stomach.

After telling the healers about Pol's own stomach, they examined Pol's bruise, but said he wouldn't have to do anything special.

"Good thing we weren't using real swords," Darrol said as they walked down the steps from the infirmary wing on the other side of the armory.

"I wouldn't have done what I did with one."

"Even if I had armor?"

Pol looked at Darrol. "Would a thrust work if you had your belly covered with metal?"

"Not with your strength," Darrol said, giving Pol a grin. "But if you magically enhanced your thrust, you could put it through a breastplate."

Pol thought about that. "A pattern-master wouldn't be able to keep that up for very long before he lost strength, right?"

"Right. You found that out on your own?"

"I'm a Third Level, who doesn't know very much about Third Level things. It's just something I picked up listening to Sakwill and Coram. They are training with the higher levels, learning how to use anticipation magic."

"You probably know how to do it better than they do. Few pick up the aspects of control and magic versus strength, and I think you could be called a pattern-master once you get a bit of meat on you."

"With a little help from Malden."

Darrol nodded. "He was very good to you at Borstall."

The hourly bell rang in the courtyard. "He was. Speaking of magic, I have my class with Vactor coming up. Can you get to your cell okay?"

"I think I'll make it after a good night's sleep. Go on."

Pol hurried to the administrative building and slipped in the door just as Sakwill and Coram turned into the corridor from the other side.

"You are late," Vactor said to Pol, reading a page from a stack of papers. "They are later." The master looked up as Sakwill and Coram hurried to their seats.

"It is always better to be early to a class than late. Agreed?"

Pol nodded. Coram poked Sakwill in the ribs.

"Is there a story behind the nudge?" Vactor raised an eyebrow and looked at Coram.

"Nothing to report. I was in a healing class in the infirmary."

Pol knew that wasn't the truth since he just came from there. Why did Coram have to lie?

"How is your swordsmanship coming?" Vactor said.

"We are doing okay." Sakwill said, looking at Pol from the corner of his eye.

"And your anticipation magic?"

Sakwill grunted. "It slows me down, but I'm getting the hang of the technique. They said the speed will come."

Vactor glanced at Pol as if to make sure Pol listened. "Why does it slow you down, Sakwill?"

"You should know. Knowing what someone is going to do is quite different from being able to react to it. I like putting magic into my swings better."

"What does that strategy do when you rely on it alone during a match?"

Sakwill and Coram looked at Vactor for the answer.

"It saps your strength, and if a swordsman loses his strength, what happens?"

"He loses," Pol said. He knew that much from that morning's experience. He looked at the two acolytes and felt sorry that they hadn't accepted him as an instructor. It was obvious they hadn't learned to sip magic when they fought. Pol would save his question about using magic for a later time.

Vactor began an informal lecture on creating fire. "There is a difference between creating fire and creating light. Can any of you guess what it is?"

Pol thought back to Val's magic light and the fire that Malden had created at his mother's pyre. "Light is smaller and more controlled. I guess you make the pattern go into a sort of tight, chaotic spin. Fire is more expansive. It can't be as controlled, or it won't spread. There must be different kinds of fire, since I've seen at least two colors produced."

"What about either of you?"

Sakwill sat back with his arms folded. "I'll go with what Pol said. I haven't been able to create a light, but fire is easy."

Coram nodded.

"Fire is easy, why?" Vactor looked at Coram.

Coram cleared his throat. To Pol than meant a delaying tactic while the acolyte searched for an answer.

"It's easier to tweak, especially if you are tweaking something that burns easily."

Pol thought back to his fire-making experience with Kell. "The tweak must be similar to rubbing wood together to get the friction to make something hot."

"That's right. Fire is exciting the tweak. Light is creating friction from the air."

Pol couldn't fathom how air would create friction.

"Ah, Pol is confused," Sakwill said.

The acolyte irked Pol, so he concentrated on the problem. "I got it. When the wind blows it moves things, so air does have friction."

Vactor nodded. "Close, it has force and mass, although we never think if it that way. What would the tweak do?"

"Compress it so it makes light?" Pol said. He looked over at Sakwill and Coram who looked as perplexed as Pol just was.

"Right. Most First Levels can create fire, although it taxes them. Second Levels definitely can. Light is generally thought of as a Fourth Level spell, but a third of Level Threes can create something that will light their way. Shall we give it a try? Don't you boys want to get your red cord?"

Vactor placed a large ceramic plate on the table and put a wad of used paper on the center.

"Go ahead, Sakwill."

Sakwill furrowed his brow, and the paper began to smoke, but didn't burst into flame.

After Vactor brushed the embers into a metal container next to their table, he had Coram do the same.

Coram didn't need to furrow his brow, and with a squint, the paper burst into flames.

"Very good. Surprisingly good, Coram. Now Pol."

Pol wiped damp palms on his robe. He had never tried this tweak and wasn't quite sure how to visualize it. He eventually settled on visualizing the paper turned to ash.

"Are you ready?"

Pol nodded. "I've never tried this before, so you better stand back."

Vactor walked to the side, but Sakwill and Coram didn't move an inch.

Pol closed his eyes to visualize the tweak and poured his energy into it.

The next thing he knew, Pol opened his eyes, on the floor by his chair.

"Too much," he said. He looked over at Sakwill and Coram. Their hair was singed and their faces were blackened. The robes they wore were darker above table height.

"Too much is right."

Pol slowly crawled back to his chair. His strength was just about gone. So much for being in better shape, he thought. He looked at all the white ash scattered on the tabletop.

"I'm sorry," he said.

Vactor gave Pol half a smile. "That was a flash, not a fire. Did you visualize ashes?"

Pol nodded. "Is it wrong to do that?"

"It is, unless you mean to. Thinking of ash creates a flash. It is not an unnoticeable effect, as you can see. Do you want to try it again?"

Pol took a deep breath. "I only have a little bit of energy left."

"Try it again, but this time visualize a tiny flame, maybe something the size of a candlelight."

Vactor blew off the plate and returned it to the table. He crumpled up another piece of paper and put it on the plate. "Here."

Pol looked at the ball of paper and thought of a candlelight wavering in the darkness. That had to be easier. He opened his eyes and tweaked the flame. He fell into darkness again, for just a moment. He was able to extend his hand and keep from slipping off the chair.

A small flame burned on the paper, and Pol watched it spread naturally to engulf the ball.

Vactor put out the fire with a thought.

"I think that's enough fire spells," Vactor said. "I want you all to think about the demonstration today. What did you learn, Pol?"

"Control. A lack of it is the most dangerous thing about magic."

Pol knew he'd have to practice every tweak before he performed it, if at all possible. "There are some tweaks that affect no one, like enhancing one's hearing, but when you apply magic to something physical, you have to have control."

Vactor clapped slowly. "All three of you must remember what Pol just said. At the upper levels, some of what differentiates a blue from a gray, or a gray from a black is control. I think we've learned enough for today. I want you all to practice controlling fire. Create different sized flames for your ball. Your dormitory master should be able to provide you with used paper. We will talk about our results when we meet again on Oneday."

Pol didn't know if he wanted to practice fire, but he would have to demonstrate control. He would make very tiny fires. Pol didn't think he had the strength for a magic light and would consult the magic book that Malden had given him. Maybe it would talk about conserving personal energy.

~ ~ ~

Chapter Eight

~

"Where is it?" Paki asked, tearing out items from his locker.

Pol struggled to open his eyes. The waking bell hadn't rung yet, and his friend looked frantic. "What?"

"My Lions, they are gone."

"Lions?" one of the acolytes said. "You keep lions?"

"South Salvan Lions. They are tiny cubes of gold. Paki has two of them," Pol said. He went through the clothes and bags on Paki's bed. "Is it the thief, again? I thought that person stopped his stealing."

"They were in this leather pouch with the rest of my money," Paki said, holding out an empty bag. "I haven't played with them since I've been in Deftnis. They wouldn't have fallen out."

Gorm shouldered his way to the growing crowd of youth around Paki's bed. "What's all this?" The wake-up bell rang just as Gorm arrived.

"Someone stole two South Salvan Lions," Paki said.

"You had two Lions?" Gorm said. Pol could hear the doubt in Gorm's voice.

"One was his father's, and I gave him the second," Pol said.

"Report this to Jonness right after breakfast." Gorm shooed the other boys off and told them to get ready for the day.

Pol helped Paki go though all his things again, but the Lions had disappeared. "Did you lock your things up?" Pol asked. He looked at the lock on his own door. Vactor had taught his three Thirds how to immobilize a lock's mechanism, and Pol already had learned how to use magic to unlock. That bit of magic didn't affect Pol's strength very much.

Paki put his hand to his mouth. "I didn't."

Pol looked away. "That's the first thing Jonness will ask."

"It's not that I put a sign on my wardrobe, 'take me'."

Pol put his hand on Paki's shoulder. "I'll help you put this back and go with you to tell Master Jonness."

Paki nodded. Pol didn't say another word after he saw his friend's eyes well up a bit. Pol made sure his wardrobe was locked.

After a dismal breakfast, Paki and Pol went early to their Seeker class. Jonness sat at the desk up front shuffling through the written tests they had taken the day before.

"What brings you here so early?" Jonness said. His amiable expression faded when he looked at Paki's face. "What happened?"

"Another theft," Paki said. "My money was taken. I had two South Salvan Lions."

Jonness winced. "Did you lock up—"

"No," Paki said, interrupting Master Jonness.

"That will make it harder to find someone. You don't know when you were burgled?"

Paki looked at the far wall. "I haven't opened up my bag since the time Pol retrieved me from Billious's tavern."

"It's been a couple of months, sir," Pol said.

Jonness shook his head. "I'm sorry, boy. The trail could be weeks old. If the lock was found open this morning, we could have done something."

Paki shook his head and moaned.

"Don't worry about the money," Pol said, "I have enough to give you, even another two Lions."

Paki nodded, but Pol could tell his friend felt pretty numb at the theft.

"If you need anyone to help Seek out the thief, I'll volunteer," Pol said.

"We still need another solid lead before we can do that, Pol. I'll let you know when the thief strikes again."

Jonness had the boys sweep the practice yard outside the Seeker classroom while they waited for the other acolytes to arrive.

"This feels like punishment," Paki said.

"I think it's more like doing something to give you time to get over the theft. From what I can tell, Master Jonness has no active leads. I'll give you some of my money. Malden made sure I had a fat purse before I left Borstall. I don't need it any more than you do. We can share."

Paki smiled weakly, but without any emotion that Pol could detect. He didn't say another word until the acolytes began to gather.

Paki and Pol went inside and sat in the back. Jonness handed out the tests. Paki had scored well, but, as usual, Pol scored highest in the class. Kell and the three acolytes he now ran around with sneered at him. Pol tried to ignore Kell at the best of times, but the monks liked putting the two of them together for practices.

Jonness raised his hands to silence the chattering acolytes. "I have two announcements. First, Pakkingail Horstel is the latest victim of the monastery thief. I'd like to remind you all to keep your valuables locked securely in your wardrobes and check to make sure such things are secure regularly. Second, we will spend tomorrow morning in Deftnis Port on a field trip. I will give you clues, and I want you to find certain articles hidden around the village."

The acolytes cheered. Most of them had not been out of the monastery and the grounds since they arrived, except for the riding on the isle opposite the port.

After class, Pol hurried to his locker and unlocked the door to inspect his things. Nothing had been stolen. He felt very relieved and made sure that he spelled the lock shut before he left for lunch and then knife practice.

During his practice, the Abbot walked in with Malden Gastoria.

"Malden!" Pol ran and clasped the magician's hand with both of his. "It's so good to see you! How is Mistress Farthia?"

"She sends you her warmest regards," Malden said with a smile. "And how have you been?"

"Better," Pol said. "I've received treatments, and they've

strengthened me. I'm not normal, but I'm not as weak."

"Vactor has let me know how you've fared." Malden looked at the makeshift targets Pol had set up for his knife throwing. "Valiso would be happy to see this."

Pol could feel his face heat with a blush. "It's something I can do while others learn things I picked up from Mistress Farthia."

"Akonai Haleaku told me about his class. Did you enjoy it?"

Pol nodded. "I was tempted to write you about the South Salvan pattern. It finally clicked for me. Did you know of King Astor's actions when I was at Borstall?"

Malden shook his head. "They were possibilities. The pea shooter, of course, but some of the truth came out after you left." Malden looked at the Abbot. "I'll catch up with you later after I've spent some time with Pol, if you don't mind."

The Abbot smiled. "Take your time. I have plenty to do in my office." He waved as he left them.

"Landon took possession of Listya right after his marriage to Bythia. I'm afraid Listyans will not like their new rulers. Bythia..." Malden shook his head.

"She's not a nice person, right?" Pol said. "Everything tells me she's like her father, not Queen Ida."

"In that regard, our patterns match. No one is happy in Borstall. If you thought they would be gleefully dancing after you left, it didn't happen. Everyone now realizes that any one of the other siblings would do anything to improve their chances at King Colvin's throne. The castle has become a dark place, filled with distrust. I never realized how much light your mother brought." He sighed. "So I see they rated you a Third. Tell me what you've learned."

Pol thought for a moment. "I can produce fire, but magic light is beyond my power. I can collect the energy, but not enough to maintain it. My strength is much better, but that only means it takes longer before I faint."

"You have most of the knowledge of a Purple, but there are a number of spells a Purple should be able to handle that you can't. Your anticipation magic was already at a Purple level with little room for improvement."

Malden asked more questions, and Pol happily reported his progress.

"You got my message about Demeron?"

Malden looked confused. "Who?"

"My Shinkyan stallion."

The magician laughed. "Oh, the devil horse. How did you finally make contact?"

"Akonai actually conveyed my message. I didn't know if he would," Pol said. "Demeron and I went riding in the little plain on the south side of the island, and our instructor wanted us to use a bit of magic to steer our horses with it. I guess I connected with him when I did that. He's a nice, uh, thing to talk to. We can communicate when we are over fifty yards apart."

"Demeron?" Malden said. Pol nodded. "Demeron would have been wasted as Landon's horse. Both Val and I knew that you were suited to him. It takes a very powerful magician to link."

"We've done that, and it doesn't drain my energy. I asked him if he was bored, but he enjoys listening to the stable boys chatter. It has affected his vocabulary, though," Pol said, grinning.

"I can imagine. I wish I could stay longer, but I have other messages to deliver, and then I'll be returning to Yastan. Ranno has me jumping."

"So you're working for Ranno, too?"

"For now," Malden said. "I have something for you." He reached in his pocket and pulled out a large amulet. "This is the symbol for Deftnis. It's fallen into disuse these days, but as you can see, the outer circle is surrounded by a braid. That stands for the patterns of healing. The sword and flame are for arms and magic. You know how to handle both, and someday you'll learn about healing. Probably in another year or two."

Pol accepted the amulet from Malden. "I have a little one on my keys. This is too large to wear around like a necklace."

That brought a smile to Malden's face. "Any monk who achieves Master Level gets one of these when they leave Deftnis. It proves to other monks where you came from. This was mine, and I'm giving it to you in advance. Some monks mount it to a belt buckle; others put it on the end of their cord or hanging on the scabbard of their sword at formal occasions. Where you put it doesn't matter."

"But I'm not a master," Pol said.

"You are to me," Malden said. "I've never had a student pick up magic and patterns as fast as you. Have you ever heard of an acolyte creating a spell or devising a new pattern here?"

Pol had to shake his head.

"That's what masters do. I wouldn't flaunt it, but I've had your name magically etched on the back if someone disputes that it's yours."

After reversing the amulet, Pol saw his adopted name, Pol Cissert, shining in rainbow colors. "I don't know what to say."

"Thank you will do, as always. Keep it safe," Malden said. "I've got to get going. My carriage is waiting in Mancus to take me to my next stop. I sort of like being Ranno's messenger boy." He gave Pol a genuine smile. "The Emperor remembers you, as do the rest of us. Make us all proud."

He gave Pol a quick hug and left Pol alone with his knives and his new piece of jewelry, or whatever it was. The amulet shone with a silvery yellow, a gold alloy of some kind. It didn't have the mystery of the one he wore around his neck, and it was two or three times the size. It wouldn't do to flaunt it, but he'd have to ask the Abbot if Malden gave him the symbol of Deftnis with his approval.

Pol wrapped the amulet up with a handkerchief and put it in the little bag of knives he had brought from Borstall. He smiled, feeling good that his friends still remembered him. He had to discount what Malden said about the Emperor. Hazett had other things to worry about other than a sick boy far to the south of Yastan.

After practice, Pol took a wandering route to the stables to check on Demeron. This time he noticed the Deftnis symbol discreetly carved in at least four places. Pol had ignored such decorations after seeing a few during his first few days at Deftnis. Seeing them show up in unusual places, Pol now had something fun to do. He'd count how many devices he could find.

~~~

Chapter Nine

~

SIXTEEN ACOLYTES MOUNTED UP FOR THE RIDE down to Deftnis Port. Everyone seemed excited. More than a few talked about sneaking into a tavern for a drink, although ale was served at all meals in the monastery.

Pol had made sure that he had given Paki sufficient money to spend on something. Jonness and his two assistants called to the acolytes to move on. They would eat lunch in town and then get back up to the monastery for their afternoon classes.

A biting wind kicked up after they left the confines of the monastery, and some of the boys hadn't worn much clothing under their robes. When they complained, Jonness said they could buy something in town.

I like this side of the island better than the back side, Demeron said.

Pol could see his horse's point. There were trees to break the wind, and the landscape didn't look as forlorn or as wind-scoured as the other. He smiled. "You won't like the cobbles much longer." Pol saw that the monks rode on the side of the road. "Why don't you walk on the side?"

That sounds like a good idea. Pol picked up that Demeron was as happy about the field trip as he was.

They proceeded to the port, silently talking. Pol just responded to Demeron's observations.

After putting the horses in the large stables that belonged to the monastery, Jonness took his charges to the hall that the Deftnis monks used for remote classes.

The hall could probably seat half or more of the monastery, but Jonness had the acolytes gather in a corner along with their belongings.

"We will be breaking up into teams. As we gather here, my two assistants have been hiding eight objects around the town. They are all within the city limits and are out in the open. You will be given clues as to the object's whereabouts, and you'll be given two hours to find them. Once you are successful, come back here to report. Do not disturb any other items that you may come across. If you do, both of you will be disqualified. Am I understood?"

"Yes, sir," most of the acolytes said.

"I will call the pairs. Come up and get your clues. Say nothing to each other until you have left the building. You need to return no later than noon."

Pol waited for six pairs to leave before he heard his name called, and then Kell's name reached his ears. He groaned. Pol just didn't deserve a partner who hated him.

Kell reached Jonness before Pol. He tried to snatch the paper with their clues before Pol had a chance to look at it. His partner growled as Jonness gave the clues to Pol.

"You need to work together. If only one of you arrives with your find, you will both be disqualified. Understood?"

Both of them nodded, but Pol noticed that Jonness hadn't given that rule to any of the other pairs. He could picture Kell ignoring Pol for the entire exercise.

Pol memorized the clues and gave the paper to Kell who read it and jammed the clues in his pocket.

Pol walked outside. Kell took off towards the center of Port Deftnis.

"Shouldn't we puzzle out the clues?" Pol said, hurrying to Kell's side.

"You're so smart, why do you need me?"

Pol didn't know why Kell was so angry. "Because we are a team. Working as a pair is part of the exercise."

"It is?" Kell stopped. His eyebrows furrowed. "I thought the point was to find Jonness's little trinkets."

Pol shook his head. "The point is to use Seeking skills. It really does help to talk it out between us. I know."

"As if you've done it before."

Pol threw his hands up in exasperation. "I have. I solved two problems with an actual Seeker, Valiso Gasibli. I also had a scout for a tutor that made us practice finding objects, but not in a town."

Kell sputtered. "You know Valiso Gasibli, personally?"

Pol nodded. "He served as my bodyguard for my last days as prince. If I hadn't been so scared, playing Seeker would have been exciting. I did learn quite a bit."

Kell took a step back to gather his thoughts. "Well…"

"Well, what?"

"What should we do if you know so much?"

Pol could tell that Kell's reply was meant to mask his astonishment. But that only made Pol more surprised by Val's obvious reputation.

"Let's review the clues," Pol said, holding out his hand.

Kell grunted, but put the wadded-up paper into Pol's palm. After smoothing out the paper, Pol read the script out loud.

"Not by water, not by fish, not by grain or sainted wish
Look for something hanging high, but not a thing that you would buy
A script proclaims a partner's name
Failure to find will bring you shame"

"What is that supposed to mean?" Kell said.

Pol looked around at the village and looked back at the clues. "It tells us some places to disregard. What do you think not by water means?"

Kell looked towards the two docks that stretched into the ocean. "The waterfront is out. That's easy enough."

All of the clues were easy, but that didn't make the seeking simple. The clues only told them where not to look. "Why don't we go into a general store and see if they sell maps of the port."

"Why?" Kell's face brightened and snapped his fingers. "That might keep us from wandering all over town."

"Maybe," Pol said. "But I don't have a better idea. Finding our object involves figuring out the pattern. In this case, the places that are not included."

"Patterns?" Kell asked.

"We obviously haven't gotten to those yet in detection. It's a methodology that Seekers use to analyze what went on with the crime and helps determine how the criminals acted. We should get to patterns some time soon. Don't worry about it. We should be able to solve this without the use of patterns."

Kell shrugged as the two youths walked down towards the docks where there were more commercial establishments. Kell pointed out a general store, which they entered.

"How can I help you? Acolytes on a treasure hunt?"

Pol only nodded. Kell looked offended. "Do you have a map of Deftnis Port? We have to find an object, and don't want to wander all over the port."

"You're only the second pair who have come calling," the shopkeeper said. He turned around and pulled a sheet of paper from a drawer against the wall. "Here. No charge. The monastery had these printed up."

"Is it current?" Pol asked.

"Current enough. Do either of you need anything to snack on while you search? I've got some sweet rolls left over from my morning rush."

Pol hadn't thought to bring any money and shook his head.

"We'll take two," Kell said. He looked at Pol. "Not by grain means we won't be near a baker's shop."

Pol smiled. Finally, Kell did something nice. Pol put it down to a momentary miracle. "Can you include a scrap of charcoal or something else to mark up the map?"

The shopkeeper let the youths each choose a roll, and then presented a used pencil stub to Pol. "Is this good enough?"

"It is. Thank you!" Pol said.

They walked out of the store and sat on the raised wooden walkway that lined both sides of the street. Pol laid the map out between them.

"No bakers, fishmongers, restaurants that sell fish, and no churches or graveyards."

"Graveyards?" Kell said, furrowing his brow.

"Sainted wish. People of faith, living and dead. I don't know how people on the island dispose of the remains of those departed. In North Salvan cities, most people are cremated."

Kell nodded. "The map has labels on everything but homes."

They both went to work and began eliminating much of the village.

"So what hangs high, something that a man could fly?" Pol said.

"People don't fly, birds do." Kell groaned with frustration.

Pol wasn't ready to panic, but he leaned back against a post and closed his eyes.

"Find anything yet?" Paki said, walking down the street with his hands in the pocket of his robe.

Pol opened his eyes and could see by the way the pair stood that they hadn't been any more successful than he.

"Is that a map?" Paki said.

Kell put the map out of sight.

"The general store will probably give you one, if you ask," Pol said.

"Thanks," Paki's partner said. He tugged on Paki's sleeve, pulling him towards the store.

Kell narrowed his eyes at Pol. "Why did you tell them that?"

"Why not? Master Jonness didn't call this a competition. We shouldn't care if others succeed or fail. All I want to do is find our object. That's why it didn't matter if they saw our map. All the objects are different, right?"

Kell nodded and said, "You really are a smart one." Pol didn't know if the comment was sarcastic or not.

"When you're as scrawny as I am, you have to develop your mind to survive. Even then, I nearly didn't a few times."

After an awkward silence, Pol squinted. "So what can a man fly?"

Kell still didn't have a clue, if the expression on his face was any indication.

"A kite? Fly a kite?" Pol said.

"Oh," Kell said. "Fly a flag?"

Pol brightened. "That would work even better. Look for flags. One that has my name or your name on it. Oh, could this be so easy?"

"I hope so. Let's go looking."

Pol consulted the map. "Here are places we don't have to go," Pol said.

They wandered around the town, consulting their map for places that fit outside the pattern of the not water, not fish, not grain, and not a sainted wish.

They walked past a walled house and Kell spotted a flagpole. Someone's coat-of-arms flew above a crimson-trimmed white flag that had 'Digbee' scrawled on it.

"There it is," Kell said. He went to throw open the door embedded in the wall next to larger double doors.

Pol took Kell by the arm. "Not so fast. We can't just walk up and take it."

"Why not?"

"It's too easy, right?"

Kell nodded and smiled. "I think you are correct. But still a direct approach wasn't forbidden." He knocked on the door.

A wizened man dressed in servant's clothes opened the door after a long wait.

Kell towered over the man and looked down. Even Pol could feel the intimidation. "We'd like one of those flags," Kell said, pointing to the flagpole surrounded by a circle of winter flowers nearly overcome with weeds.

"I'll inquire of the master." The man bowed and closed the door. Pol heard a bolt slam shut.

"We'll just scale the wall then," Kell said.

Pol leaned back and folded his arms. "Do you own the property?"

"No."

Pol nodded. "Do you know the trespassing laws of Deftnis Port?"

Kell sneered. "Do you?" He went back to his Landon imitation.

"No. That's why we shouldn't scale the wall. If we are caught stealing the flag, then we might not be able to make Jonness's time limit, will we?"

Kell shook his head. "So we wait?"

"Let's just ask politely. Val said sometimes the easiest way is the best. If the owner doesn't let us have the flag, then we will have to come up with an alternative plan."

Kell shook his head again. "We'll try it your way, and then we will try mine."

"That works for me," Pol said. He'd rather be first than Kell.

Both of them stood straighter when they heard someone withdraw the bolt from the door.

"You may come in and speak to my master," the servant said. He held the door open for Kell and Pol and then shuffled slowly ahead, leading them into the house.

The sitting room was just off the foyer. The servant offered them seats. Kell looked around at the house and made an approving face.

"Maybe it's not your style, but I like it," Kell said.

Pol's rooms at Castle Borstall were fancier than the sitting room, but that was part of his past. He just sat with his hands gripping the side of the straight chair that he sat in. Kell had taken residence in an easy chair, and Pol thought that a bit presumptuous.

"So, what is it you want?" the owner said as he rushed in, adjusting the sleeves of his coat.

"Your flag," Kell said.

Pol shook his head and tightened his lips. Kell's upbringing obviously didn't include the deportment lessons that Pol's did, even if he had let his temper get in the way too often.

"Not your flag, sir." Pol stood. "As you may surmise, we are Deftnis acolytes on a training outing. One of our instructor's men had you raise a small flag underneath your own. We have come to recover it."

"And what will you give me in exchange?"

"What?" Kell said.

Pol pursed his lips. "Do you know what time it is?" he said.

"One hour to noon," the man said.

Pol thought for a moment. "We will weed the flagpole flower bed if you will give us the flag."

"Manual labor?"

Pol thought for a moment. "Your servant probably has a hard time getting down on his knees to weed, so we will be doing both you and him a service."

The man put his hand to his chin. "I thought you would want to pay me money, but I like your approach. Once the bed is weeded, you may retrieve your flag."

Pol felt it a bit odd in the way the man acquiesced and wondered if there would be another obstacle, but they had made an agreement. "We will get to it at once, if your man can provide us with a cart to dispose of the weeds."

"I can arrange that. Go to work, boys," the man said.

Pol dragged Kell out of the house before he said anything else. The man hadn't introduced himself, but the owner had to be highly placed in the village to have a nice house and yard. The device on the owner's flag was a coat of arms. He looked up and could see in one square of a shield the symbol of Deftnis, so the man had to have been an acolyte or a monk at some time.

Both of them went to work. Pol had to show Kell how to weed and minimize the damage to the flowers.

"How do you know how to do such menial work?"

"My friend Paki's dad was a Royal Gardener. I used to help them in the gardens in exchange for learning about scout methods."

"So that's how you knew how to do such a good job at making fires."

Kell had picked up that skill rather quickly, but Pol nodded. "I consider myself an experienced expert in weeding flower beds, too. It goes much quicker if two work and don't talk."

Kell didn't say another word, and in half-an-hour or so, their task was complete. The wheelbarrow that the servant had dropped by was filled with weeds, and Pol surveyed their work with a smile. It would take a while for the flowers to fill in, but they looked better than before.

Kell took the flag cord and tried to lower the flags. "It's stuck."

Pol looked up at the pulley at the top of the pole and wondered if the owner was a magician who tweaked a pattern to put another obstacle in their way. That would have fit what Pol felt about the man when he agreed to give them their flag.

"Let me try," Pol said.

"You? What strength do you have?"

"It isn't apparent, but I do have some, you know," Pol said. He looked up and closed his eyes. He opened them, but held them slightly out of focus as he concentrated on their flag and tweaked the ends that were knotted to the rope. After a few moments, the flag fluttered to Pol's outstretched hand.

"You could have retrieved the flag from outside the wall," Kell said. Pol didn't like the petulance, but thought Kell might not have been raised in a very polite, refined environment.

The owner walked out. "I see you were able to get the flag down magically. That should be an easy task for a Third. Why didn't you just do that in the first place?"

Pol looked at Kell and then at the man. "You must be a magician yourself."

The man nodded. "My name is Garryle Handson. I'm the Deftnis representative in the Port, so basically I'm the mayor. Jonness's message said that he was sending a good pair this time. He always sends the best magician in his class to me, and Jonness didn't disappoint. We didn't introduce ourselves before."

"I am Pol Cissert and this is—"

"Kell Digbee. My name is on the flag," Kell said, interrupting Pol.

"Well, I am glad you chose the higher path. I was prepared to retain you here until after noon, but now you are free to leave."

Pol turned around. "Is it impolite to ask you what level you attained at the monastery?"

Garryle smiled. "I am a Gray, and I still don my robes to teach upper-level magicians. Perhaps we will see each other again, Pol Cissert."

"Perhaps," Pol said. He bowed to Garryle, and both of the acolytes hurried to the Deftnis hall.

Jonness looked up from talking to his two assistants. "Ah, I expected to see you two here. Four of the teams won't be joining us at noon since they'll have their lunches in jail, and we think there will be three others coming. The question is will they make it on time?"

"Are all the teams given tasks with hidden teeth?"

Jonness grinned and nodded his head. "All of them."

After a lunch with half the acolytes, one of the assistants escorted the jailed acolytes back into the hall. They all rode back to the monastery, trading stories along the way.

Pol walked into the magic class, interrupting Vactor's conversation with the Abbot.

"I can wait outside," Pol said.

"No, no," the Abbot said. He took a seat next to Pol. "Your classmates won't be here today. How did you do with the Seekers this morning?"

Pol told them all about his adventure, which, admittedly, didn't take very long.

"Jonness stuck you with Garryle, eh? You'll see him when you advance. I'll bet he was rubbing his hands waiting for you to steal the flag. That's what most boys do."

"Most?" Pol said.

"Jonness uses much the same exercises for each class. Garryle is a gray, Seventh Level, as you might have found out, and just sits in his house when the search begins, locating anyone who ventures near. If you did anything questionable, shall we say, he would have frozen you on the spot and had you hauled off by the port constables, whom he directs."

"So we were lucky?"

"If you want to call it luck, Pol," Vactor said. "You did the right thing. I'm not a Seeker, but I know that in broad daylight, one doesn't just take things."

Pol thought back to the time in Borstall when Paki talked him into roaming around the festival grounds before the Emperor came. They were caught stealing candied apples. Pol discovered he could unlock doors, when things became desperate. He feared his father would discover him in a jail, and that gave him the motivation that he needed.

"I learned that lesson recently enough," Pol said.

The Abbot chuckled. "Malden wrote about it. I'll bet this was the first time you untied a flag above your head and had the flag fly into your hands, right? Garryle usually stops up the pulley."

Pol nodded. What hadn't Malden revealed about Pol's summer?

"That is good enough for your Fourth Level test," the Abbot looked over at Vactor who nodded in agreement. "Sakwill and Coram will be spending the rest of the winter learning anticipation magic with Edgebare's monks, so you can continue to see Vactor, who will provide you with individual training. You've missed some things along the way with your rapid learning this summer, but you've already shown that you are ready for a higher level of training." The Abbot slapped his knees. "Could you fill out the paperwork and see that Pol gets a red cord?"

Vactor grinned and nodded. "I will." The tutor looked at Pol. "Stay right where you are. Your course work won't be changing, since I've been preparing you for Fourth Level while the other two have been gone."

That suited Pol, although he didn't think he had done anything special to get a higher ranking. He felt that he knew so little, but Pol had to admit that he had already mastered all the spells and techniques in the little book on magic that Malden Gastoria had given him.

~ ~ ~

222

Chapter Ten

"What's that? A change in color?" Paki said, looking at his white cord, and then gazing at Pol's new red one that he cinched up just before breakfast.

"An unasked-for promotion," Pol said. "It doesn't change anything. I was already told that I was between Orange and Red when I arrived. I guess I finally learned enough to move up."

Paki looked around the dormitory. "No one else is a Red in here. Will they be giving you a cell?"

Pol shook his head. He didn't know what made magicians live in cells or in dormitories. "Not if I have any say about it. I'm still the youngest one here. I just had a head start, I guess."

"More than a head start. You've got tons of talent. I just learned how to create a tiny flame this week." Paki grinned. "To be honest, I was thrilled."

Pol felt relieved that his friend didn't feel any jealousy. He could imagine what Kell might do under similar circumstances. Kell had begun to acknowledge Pol's presence after their partnership at the port, but barely.

Pol tightened his belt and let the robe hang over much of the red color. He didn't want to show off his promotion. He took a deep breath, and they walked over to the commissary.

A few congratulatory words were spoken by some of his colleagues in the Seeker class, but then Sakwill and Coram approached Pol.

"So you are red now, are you?" Sakwill sneered. "Who is your sponsor, and how much did they have to pay the monastery to get the Abbot to let you wear that?"

Coram gave Pol a push.

"If you don't think I earned it, talk to the Abbott. He's the one who promoted me. I didn't ask for it," Pol said. He took a deep breath, trying not to let the confrontation get him upset. He remembered all the times his siblings at Borstall Castle had baited him. Pol wouldn't let that happen here.

"I challenge you to a duel," Sakwill said.

Pol looked at the older acolytes. "Can he do that?"

They all nodded back in the affirmative. Pol looked up at Sakwill. "Very well. I don't know the rules, but I'll fight," Pol said. He didn't want to fight an opponent even older than Landon, but looking around the commissary, he knew he couldn't reject Sakwill's challenge in front of so many people. Pol wondered what kind of foolish thing he had just done.

Edgebare sat Pol down in his office at the armory building. "You don't have to fight Sakwill if you don't want to."

"But I will lose face," Pol said.

"Better that than your life."

That made Pol blink, and he felt the beginnings of real fear. "Do they allow duels to the death here?"

Edgebare laughed. "No, of course not. But accidents have been known to happen." He looked sympathetically at Pol. "What questions do you have of me?"

"What are the rules?"

"For what kind of duel? You get to choose you know."

"I just assumed that we would be fighting with swords."

Edgebare shook his head. "You are in Deftnis. Do we just teach swordsmanship?"

"Magic?" Pol said.

The older man nodded. "Magic gives you an advantage. A Fourth versus a Third."

"But I don't have much stamina for more than a few spells."

Edgebare pulled at the long hair of his white eyebrows. "Think of something else."

Pol looked around Edgebare's office for inspiration. "Something that I can likely do better than Sakwill. If I was Paki's size, I could probably beat him with swords, since he's still learning to be a pattern-master, and I'm already adept at anticipation magic." Pol shook his head. "I can only defend for a short period of time against a full-grown man."

"I think you are better with a sword than Sakwill. He may have a tough road ahead to become a true pattern-master." Edgebare paused, and then smiled. "When you've fought full-grown men, as you say, how did you defeat them?"

"With a knife." Pol raised his eyebrows and slammed his fist into his other hand. "Are knives permitted?"

Edgebare nodded. "If you don't try to kill Sakwill, those will be permitted."

"I can do that. Do I pick the venue as well?"

"It comes with choosing the weapons."

Pol smiled. "Sakwill may regret his challenge." He felt confidence fill him. "Knives in the woods at nine hours after noon when it's dark."

"That's a specific challenge. It does give Sakwill an excuse to make a mistake and kill you since the duel can't be monitored closely."

"I can locate. I know the pattern of the woods, and I'm sure that I'm better with a knife than he is."

Edgebare put his hands on his desk palms down. "Then it is settled. If you close with each other, Sakwill has a huge advantage, you know that?"

Pol nodded. "I do. What are the magical limitations?"

The old man thought for a moment. "If a weapon is chosen, then no spells that are directly aimed at the other duelist, if my memory serves. That can be monitored over the course of the duel. Minor magic is permitted, lights, for example, and location spells, of course," Edgebare said. Pol liked the smile that appeared on Edgebare's face.

Edgebare and Pol talked about the specific details of the duel. When they finished, Pol felt he might just have a chance at coming out of this duel with his honor and his skin largely intact.

The duel had been quickly arranged for the next night. A number of monks and acolytes showed up in the Seeker's practice hall, which stood close to the gate that led out to the wood. A table had been set up.

"You will only use the knives on this table. Each of you will be given six. The challenger can choose which set," Jonness said to Pol and Sakwill, who stood an arm's length apart from each other. "The challenger will enter the wood and proceed to the left. The challenged will proceed to the right. A horn will blow when you are deemed far enough apart. The duel will last for thirty minutes, or until one of you is wounded, yields, or has used up all his weapons. Good luck to you both."

Sakwill scowled. "Trust a boy to come up with something so dishonorable. Knives." Sakwill snorted and picked up the set of knives that were new and shiny and trotted out into the rainy night.

Pol heard a peal of thunder and wondered how the poor weather might affect the duel. He smiled, getting the older knives. He had practiced with these. Edgebare was confident that Sakwill would assume that shiny and new was better than older and worn.

After Sakwill was out of sight, Pol shed his acolyte robes, revealing tighter clothes dyed dark. He pulled out a hat that he jammed over his silvery hair.

"That's not fair," Coram said. "Sakwill is wearing his robes." He stepped up close to Pol and glared down at him.

Jonness pushed the man aside. "You agreed to the terms. There were no requirements as to what the duelists could wear. Let Pol leave."

Pol had noticed that Sakwill wore something stiff under his robes. Probably a leather breastplate or something. It didn't matter to Pol. He wouldn't be throwing his knives to kill. He padded through the gate and into the wood. The monks and acolytes who decided to brave the rain followed him.

It didn't take long for Pol to find Sakwill, who had stopped not far from the entrance. Would he wait for the horn to sound? Pol ran further right, keeping trees between Sakwill and him. After a few moments, the horn sounded in the wood.

Pol tracked Sakwill's color, a green dot in his mind, moving quickly towards Pol. Suddenly, a magic light appeared in the distance, so Pol now knew exactly where Sakwill was. He ran back towards the gate, hugging the stone wall and circled to the back of Sakwill and past the spectators.

He began to walk silently towards the light and noticed that the green dot representing Sakwill was moving to where Pol had been. That brought a smile to Pol's face. He could imagine Sakwill cursing when he found Pol had gone somewhere else.

Pol moved deeper into the wood. Branches whipped against his face, and big drops plopped on his hat. The green dot began to move erratically on the right side of the wood and finally began to move to the middle.

There were other locators viewing them, so Pol didn't feel he could just hide for the half-hour that would produce a tie. He moved towards the gate into the monastery, intent on cutting off Sakwill.

He noticed a light to his left, and this time, he could see Sakwill carrying light in one hand and a sword in the other. Pol shook his head. Did the man want to be expelled from the monastery?

Pol approached him. It was time to end this.

"Really? A sword?" Pol said, with a knife in his throwing hand and two in his other.

Sakwill jerked towards Pol. "You!"

"Me," Pol said. "Do you want me to end this now, or should I give you time to bury your sword?"

Sakwill scowled. He extinguished his light and attacked.

Pol couldn't muster the energy for magic lights, so he just slipped past the charging Sakwill and picked up a branch that he nearly stumbled over. He poked Sakwill in the back with his knife. The acolyte did wear armor under his robe. Pol ran to Sakwill's left, and had to duck a bit to miss the edge of the swinging sword.

He stood behind a tree watching Sakwill swinging wildly in the dark.

"I'll give you one more chance, Sakwill. Bury the sword."

"Never!" he said. He lit another magic light and found Pol standing to his side.

What kind of thinking caused such desperation? Pol had ascribed better motives to those chosen to attend Deftnis. Kell was belligerent, but not like Sakwill. He would put an end to this and cocked his arm to throw his knife. Something kept him from throwing. Magic.

"Did you think I would let you defeat me?" Sakwill said. "Your arm is frozen. I thought that any Fourth would know how to defend against that spell, but it was worth a try. Good for me, bad for you."

Why did Sakwill hate him so? Pol at least understood why his siblings wanted him dead because he was a threat, but Pol didn't see himself as any kind of a challenger to Sakwill. It wasn't as if his opponent couldn't advance to Red because of Pol.

Sakwill stepped closer with his sword in front of him. Pol could barely move his arms, so he dropped the knives in his left hand.

"Why are you so angry?" Pol said. "I haven't done anything to you."

"I won't be shown up by a fifteen-year-old. I won't!"

Sakwill wasn't right. Pol could tell there was something else driving his opponent, but he couldn't tell what it was. Pol just didn't have the experience to know.

The sword was getting too close for Pol's comfort, so he closed his eyes and tried to tweak the immobilization spell. He succeeded in getting his left arm free which was just enough for Pol to flick the knife into Sakwill's thigh. Pol did add a little magical force to the throw.

His fight against the spell and enhancing the speed of the knife had finally exhausted all his strength. Pol gasped for air as weakness overtook him. A moment later, whatever spell held Pol dissipated.

"Healer! Here!" Pol called as he fell to the ground, out of breath and heart racing.

Sakwill wailed, clutching his leg with both hands while Pol rushed to bury Sakwill's sword in the leaves a few paces away.

Jonness arrived after a moment or two. He attended to Sakwill's injury.

"What happened?"

Pol just shrugged. "My knife ended the duel," he said. "I did win, didn't I?"

Jonness narrowed his eyes at Pol. "You prevailed." He worked on Sakwill for a bit until others came. Jonness handed Pol's knife to him. "Go to bed. We will talk later."

Pol nodded and left. He hoped his honor had remained intact, but the look in Jonness's eyes seemed to contradict that thought.

Jonness called Pol up to the front of the practice hall after Seeker training. Pol had worried all night about what Jonness would have to say about the duel.

He walked forward as if he were approaching a gallows. Pol bowed his head. "I am here."

"I can see that. Now, tell me exactly what happened and tell me the truth. If I suspect you aren't, I'll not hesitate to put you under a truth spell."

Pol could easily tell that Jonness meant what he said, so he described the duel with all of its warts. He cringed inside when he admitted that Sakwill carried a sword.

"Why did you hide the sword?"

Pol pressed his lips together. "I didn't want to get Sakwill expelled. Using a sword would do that, wouldn't it?"

Jonness nodded. "It wasn't your place to decide, but," Jonness sighed, "you did. It shows you don't hate him."

"Hating is something that I reserve for others," Pol said, thinking about King Colvin and his children. "Sakwill is just jealous, I guess. I know I wouldn't want to be shown up by an eight-year-old."

Jonness smiled, a bit too condescendingly for Pol. "I don't suppose you would. I'll talk to the Abbot. I'll only say that Sakwill didn't get away with using his sword. The knives were still bundled up in his pocket. I suppose that he intended on bloodying up a knife once he was done with his sword."

"Anticipation magic doesn't work with knives, I suppose."

"It does, Pol. You just haven't tried to use it yet."

That surprised Pol. Jonness was absolutely right. He hadn't attempted to use anticipation in any effort other than swords. He'd have to think on that.

"The Abbot will likely want to see you after dinner."

A monk put a note beside Pol's plate and walked off. Pol watched the man go and wondered if this was his summons to the Abbot. He read the note, and all it said was Abbot's Office right after dinner.

Pol looked up at the dais. The Abbot chatted amiably with a monk that Pol hadn't met. He returned to his meal, letting Paki do all the talking. At least his friend had finished talking about the duel.

The Abbot rose from his position and made eye contact with Pol. The man made a sign for Pol to follow. Pol watched the man leave the commissary, while he put his tray in the little window that led to the adjacent kitchens.

As Pol left the commissary, the Abbot tugged on Pol's robes. "A word, if you will, Acolyte Cissert."

Pol didn't know what the Abbot meant by using his last name.

"We can talk while you accompany me back to my office."

"Whatever you say, Abbot."

"Good. I had a talk with Jonness. It appears you fessed up to using attack magic to win the duel."

Attack magic? Pol had never even heard of the term before. "I don't know what attack magic is. You mean putting power into the knife, so it would sink into Sakwill's leg? He had me mostly immobilized."

"One of the rules of the duel was no magic applied physically to your opponent."

"He advanced with a sword in his hand and used a spell to freeze me. I couldn't think of anything else to do," Pol said. He ran the scene over in his head again and couldn't see an alternative action. "I did what I felt I had to do."

"To win?"

Pol shook his head. "To survive."

"You're rather good at that, aren't you?"

"I don't believe I think in those terms, Abbot, but perhaps that is correct."

The Abbot didn't say a word until they reached the administration building. "We will continue in my office."

The two of them walked in the twilight until they reached the Abbot's office. Books and scroll cubicles covered one side of the office. There were overstuffed leather chairs by the fire. Abbot offered Pol one of the leather chairs. That made their conversation more informal, Pol thought.

"Sakwill used a spell that is usually thought of as a Level Four spell. How do you suppose he learned it?"

Pol still had an incomplete grasp of what constituted a spell on any of the levels. Vactor had taught him only a few Level Four spells. The application of the tweak that Pol had used on Sakwill was the same kind of spell that Pol employed to increase the range and power of his knife throws. He had practiced it enough times back in Borstall to know the tweak sapped his strength, but he never knew the level of that particular spell.

"I've never learned how to freeze someone's body."

"But you have stopped a horse," the Abbot said.

"I did, but it's not a freeze spell. I patterned the air to act dense like water. I slowed the horse up until it stopped."

The Abbot furrowed his brow. "I must have misread what Val put in his report. You say you thickened the air?"

Pol nodded. "I wished that the horse had to run in water. That would slow it down. So I made thick air. I don't really know how I did it, but the horse itself wasn't frozen. Sakwill made it so my limbs wouldn't work. I barely had time to drop two of my knives."

The Abbot sat up. "You didn't have the use of your arms?"

"I didn't, sir, until I was able to free up my left arm."

After shaking his head in amazement, the Abbot stood. "And I thought you were a Level Four."

"I'm not?"

"You just haven't been thoroughly taught. I don't know what level you are. But let's leave you at Four, and with Vactor as your personal tutor, you will learn spells as they come. Now about Sakwill—"

"Don't expel him. I think someone pushed him. There was something wrong with the way he challenged me."

"He really doesn't like you, Pol. That has been thoroughly established," the Abbot said.

Pol thought for a moment. "If he used a Level Four spell, then someone had to have taught it to him, and that person might have used a little magic to persuade him to challenge me and convince Sakwill to use a sword and not his knives. Is that possible?"

"That fits the pattern better, doesn't it?" The Abbot chuckled. "I think you have the makings of an excellent Seeker. Jonness does, too. I'll talk to others about the possibility. For now, I'm going to make you clean out the main courtyard as punishment for violating the terms of your duel."

Pol didn't like the Abbot's solution. "I don't think that is fair, sir."

"Fair? I didn't tell you what Sakwill got as his punishment. You definitely wouldn't want to trade. But don't worry, I won't expel him."

Pol thanked the Abbot and went to the monastery's library to finish the day studying for his other classes.

~ ~ ~

Chapter Eleven

~

$\mathbf{P}$OL SPENT AN HOUR A WEEK AT THE INFIRMARY receiving treatment for his heart. As winter turned into spring, his stamina had increased, but still nothing near normal. He walked across the wet courtyard to the administration building to attend his classes with Vactor.

Vactor still taught mostly Third Level magic. The pair of them hadn't yet touched many Level Four spells since Vactor insisted on Pol learning more breadth. Pol agreed with his tutor. He was amazed at how narrow his knowledge had been.

Malden had had a different approach. The magician had challenged Pol to use higher-level spells without taking the time to present the wide variety of Level Two and Level Three magics. Patterns still remained the central core of what Pol learned, but even Pol's understanding of patterns began to expand under Vactor's new course of study.

Pol walked into the familiar training room.

"I have a letter for you." Vactor slid it across the table towards Pol.

"From Yastan?"

Vactor nodded.

Pol opened the envelope. He didn't recognize the writing.

Pol Cissert,

I love your new name. Akonai says you are doing well, as I expected. I hope you are enjoying winter in Deftnis. It's certainly milder in the Sand dukedom than Yastan.

I have some news. Your father has written the Emperor demanding that you return Landon's Shinkyan horse. Why he writes the Emperor is beyond me, but since he did, Hazett asked me to do something about it.

I sent a letter to King Colvin notifying him that his son shouldn't have been able to procure a Shinkyan horse. Therefore, the Emperor has seized it. It appears that Hazett has given it to you in compensation for obvious losses. You'll find a certificate of title for the horse signed by Hazett himself. It includes an Imperial dispensation, since our treaty with Shinkya generally forbids the possession of such a beast.

I also included an identity document in your new name. Congratulations! You are now an official citizen of the Baccusol Empire. I assume you already know the privileges of such a thing. It's not much, but it's all I can do for now.

Far and Malden send you their love. Akonai and Valiso sent you their regards. There is a difference.

You may show this to Abbot Pleagor, so he is aware of the formal ownership transfer and your new status as an Imperial citizen. I suggest that you get some copies certified by the Abbot and have him keep one set. There are those who would choose to ignore Imperial decrees.

Let me know how you are doing. I'll look forward to seeing you in Yastan when the time comes.

Stay Healthy,

Ranno Wissingbel
Instrument to the Emperor

Pol re-read the letter and the two documents that were nestled in the envelope with it. He handed it over to Vactor.

His magic tutor whistled. "You do travel in high company. I can give this to the Abbot, and he'll get the copies made. You do know what an Imperial citizen is?"

Pol nodded. "Mistress Farthia was one. You are not required to bow or give allegiance to any King or Duke. An Imperial citizen is quite a privilege."

"There are other legal advantages. The Emperor has done you a great service by recognizing you. What about the horse? I don't know much about them."

"Demeron, my Shinkyan stallion, and I can communicate. He can speak in my head. He's not particularly smart for a human, but for a horse…"

"Really? I'll have to research that. When did you learn you could do such a thing?"

"I used magic to guide him in Seeker training, and that seemed to set the link. He can get quite talkative. I try to exercise him as much as I can. He likes the stables, though." Pol grinned. "Do many magicians have animals that can speak with them?"

"Familiars like you read about in novels?" Vactor shook his head. "Nothing where words are spoken. It's not related specifically to levels, but even non-talented people can communicate with their animals. I think this is different. Are there other horses like him?"

Pol nodded. "There are, he told me. I think that's why the Shinkyans don't let the animals out of their country."

"Contraband," Vactor said. "And the Emperor just gave him to you with the legal right to own him."

"I suppose. I wondered if my stepfather would be requesting my brother Landon's horse back. I guess he knows I'm here."

Vactor nodded. "I'm sure he does. Sakwill was definitely influenced by someone from the outside, but whoever did it was very skillful to hide his manipulation. I can't think of any other reason why he would have challenged you. Your enemies definitely know you are here."

"So, I'm still an enemy?"

"You are until you find out that you aren't. I think the royal families of North and South Salvan have no love for Poldon Fairfield or Pol Cissert."

Pol returned to his bed after an intense evening studying in the library and found the lock on his wardrobe open. Pol knew he had left it secured. He didn't touch the mechanism and tried to see if magic had been applied. He thought he found traces of tweaking inside the lock, but he hadn't looked inside it before.

He sighed as he searched for the bag of jewels thrown in the back of his wardrobe when he first arrived. It was, of course, gone. The monastery thief had struck again. Pol wouldn't let the thief go. He looked around his bed and couldn't find any clues other than faint wet footprints drying on the flagstones. He quickly drew as accurate a picture as he could and followed the remnants to the door.

All he could surmise was that someone had walked directly to his bed, unlocked his wardrobe, and stolen his most precious possessions, other than the amulet that still hung around his neck. Pol shook his head and sighed again. He walked out into the dripping night to see Jonness.

The Seeker lived in a cell built next to the Seeker practice hall. Pol knocked on the monk's door. Jonness answered, dressed in normal clothes.

"Why do you bother me at this late hour? It had better be of great importance."

"The thief struck again. I found my wardrobe unlocked, and my mother's jewels were stolen."

"Mother's jewels?"

"The jewels and ornaments that she brought from Listya to North Salvan. I took them with me when I fled Borstall," Pol said. "Now someone has my mother's heirlooms, and they don't deserve them. I want to find the thief."

"You won't be finding him tonight. I'm going to bed."

"I'll talk to you tomorrow morning. I found a wet footprint drying by my bed. The thief came into and left the dormitory, so it likely isn't one of the fifteen acolytes I share space with. His foot is a little larger than normal. I was careful in drawing it."

Jonness rubbed his stubbled jaw. "Good work. You picked that up from Valiso?"

Pol nodded. "I did. It's not much to go on, but perhaps we can begin building patterns that we can sort monks and acolytes with tomorrow."

After a low chuckle, Jonness nodded. "We haven't gotten to any of that yet. It doesn't really come up in the first year. I'll have the entire class help us."

"Won't that tip off the thief?"

Jonness shook his head. "I'll talk to Garryle and have every monk and acolyte discreetly searched for contraband before they leave the island. So far, the thief hasn't been so greedy as to steal obvious heirlooms."

True to his word, Jonness seized upon the theft to talk to the class about solving a crime. Pol could tell that the subject didn't fit into what Jonness had been teaching up to now. He brought up patterns for the first time, giving an abbreviated explanation.

Jonness nodded and had his assistants bring out a slate board filled with notes. "We will try to make some sense of this," Jonness said.

The class spent the rest of the time mostly observing a conversation between Pol, Jonness, and the two assistants. At the end something struck Pol as odd. There seemed to be two thieves. The monastery thief followed a different pattern than the one who stole his jewels.

When the rest of the class left, Pol approached Jonness. "There are two thieves. The one who stole my things is not the monastery thief."

"Why?" Jonness said.

"The monastery thief stole in the night, after everyone was asleep. All the possessions were not secured, so he was opportunistic, an acolyte who was looking for an easy theft."

Jonness nodded. "An acolyte or a monk, but one who didn't have to break into anything to steal."

"The other used magic to break into my wardrobe." Pol looked at the board and tried to complete the pattern. "None of the other thefts involved magic at all, so the initial thief could easily be a swordsman rather than a magician."

"So, why do you think magic was used in your case?"

Pol thought for a bit. "Easier to perform. Faster with no destruction involved. I might not have noticed anything if Paki hadn't been a victim. I insisted that he always lock his wardrobe, so I've been doing the same myself."

"What if the thief had a key?"

Pol wondered about that. "If he had a key, and it was the same thief, then there would be a number of thefts that matched mine." That made perfect sense to Pol as he said it.

"I think you are right. So how should we proceed?"

Pol furrowed his brow. "Why are you asking me? I'm the youngest in the class."

Jonness smiled and leaned against the worktable. "You are the most experienced, trained well in a short time by the best Seeker in the Empire."

"Val?"

"Valiso Gasibli," Jonness corrected. "He used to be sent out by the Emperor to solve crimes that stumped local authorities. He has quite a reputation in the countries where he has worked."

"Kell knows who he is."

"See?" Jonness clapped his hand on Pol's shoulder.

Valiso had quite a reputation, but then Pol thought that as a prince, he had lived a sheltered life, even more sheltered before Mistress Farthia became his tutor. Pol straightened up. If Valiso took the time to train him, then Pol would use what he knew.

"We develop two patterns then. If we get the Seeker class to help solidify clues, then we can catch both the thieves," Pol said.

"That's the spirit. You have to get to your next class, but rather than your nightly study in the library for the next week, come here, and we'll work with my assistants to create the two patterns. In class, just observe your classmates. The first thief might be one of them. If you are right about the second thief, they know how to tweak inside a closed object. That means at least a good Third and maybe a Fourth Level magician."

"How high do you get when you aren't considered an acolyte? Could either thief be a monk?"

"Monks can be Thirds. One of my assistants is, but he is a good Seeker and a better teacher. Generally acolytes who are here four or five years can become monks. The only real difference is that monks are teachers. Acolytes who are here that long and don't want to teach or serve in the monastery in a specific capacity are encouraged to leave."

"Darrol Netherfield?"

Jonness nodded. "He's only here because you are. He became bored at Deftnis, but he seems to like his new assignments. I think he wants to stay with you."

Pol smiled. "He says he's my sworn man. I don't think disinherited princes can have sworn men."

"Anyone can have sworn men. It's the man, not always the title," Jonness said.

Pol became a little embarrassed where the conversation was heading. "I'll be back tonight?"

Jonness nodded. Pol heard him chuckle and call one of his assistants as he quickly left the practice hall.

Pol yawned while Jonness went over the conversation he had with Pol after class. The assistants only added to the questions Pol had asked, but the pattern didn't expand.

"When did the last theft occur, before mine, that is?" Pol said.

Jonness shuffled through the sheaf of papers that held all the information of the thefts.

"Three weeks ago."

Pol thought about those regular thefts and wondered if they should look at those first.

"Is there a pattern to those thefts?" Pol wondered if they could create a pattern to predict the next theft, ignoring his.

Pol looked down at the dates and times on the page that Jonness pushed over to him. "Does something happen on the days after these thefts? Could there be a reason they are timed as they are?"

One of the assistants shook his head. "Different days of the week and different intervals. How could that be a pattern?"

Jonness took the paper back from Pol and laughed. He threw it to the assistant who had just spoken. "Think a little harder."

The assistant looked at the paper and back at Jonness with a shrug. "I can't see it."

"I'll give you a hint. Mancus."

Jonness had said the name of the little town on the mainland across from the island. It meant nothing to Pol.

"Oh. It's not every week, is it?"

Jonness grinned and slapped Pol on the back. "The monastery occasionally lets monks and senior acolytes across for the day. I know for sure the last two trips coincide with the dates here. Am I right?"

The assistant turned red. "I go every time. It matches well enough. I'll talk to Garryle tomorrow and get the logbook."

"Logbook?" Pol said.

"We track monks coming and going from the monastery. We occasionally lose a monk or an acolyte, and it's an easy solution to find if someone is missing and we have to go looking for them."

"When is the next trip?" Pol asked.

"Three days from now. We will be prepared."

~ ~ ~

Chapter Twelve

There were only four monks and three acolytes who had made trips on all the days after the thefts. Pol stood at the dock along with one of Jonness's assistants registering the monks leaving for Mancus.

Pol looked across at the shore. The boat bobbed gently on the waves as it left the dock, heading for Mancus. He wished the waves had been as mild when he crossed six months ago.

"Two monks didn't make the trip," the assistant said, "and only one of the acolytes is headed over today."

They rode back to the monastery. Pol was happy to ride Demeron and catch up on the horse's life. Demeron found it interesting enough.

Jonness met them in the stables right after he dismissed the Seeker class that Pol should have been in that morning. "So perhaps we are down to three suspects. Let's head over to the administration building."

All four of them sat in a small room with a table littered with three files.

Jonness read the files, and the other three made notes. Pol couldn't find anything incriminating. None of them came from families in apparent need.

"Coming from a rich family may mean nothing. Right, Pol?" one of the assistants said.

Pol nodded. "Maybe the thief needs the money for something."

"Garryle has arranged to have the three of them followed. We will need more indication of a motive before we can do something definitive," Jonness said, and then looked at Pol. "What would a Seeker do in this situation? Our hands are somewhat tied by the rules of the monastery."

"Perhaps a Seeker would be in their rooms right now, going through their things to see if one had a motivation that fit into the thief's pattern?"

"Isn't it illegal to break into a person's house?" an assistant said.

Pol could sense these were questions meant to teach him. "It is. Do Seekers always follow the laws in a strict fashion?" He thought of Val sneaking around. Seekers wouldn't need stealth if they didn't push the limits of the law. "Guards are more restricted than Seekers, aren't they?"

The assistant looked at Jonness and nodded. "We generally don't get to that point with our initial trainees, but you are right. Valiso had you running around in the dark at Borstall?"

Pol nodded. "I did it a few times. Once successfully, to my regret, and another a bit more open, to a different kind of regret."

"You're a novice. It's easy to fail but hard to succeed, as you found out."

"I did. We can't search their cells, then?"

Jonness shook his head. "A truth spell can't be administered with the scanty evidence that we have. Without those rules, we could question everyone in the monastery to find the culprit who stole."

Paki wouldn't have any problem playing at the edges of legality, but it still bothered Pol, even though he saw the necessity of getting information any way one could. He could imagine Val doing all kinds of questionable things on the border with Tarida, getting information that helped keep the North Salvan border safe a few years ago when the Emperor assigned him to help King Colvin, his stepfather.

"I guess I'm a bit uncertain about when a Seeker works by the rules and when a Seeker ignores them," Pol said.

Jonness shrugged. "That is a judgment that every Seeker makes a little differently, something my two assistants have never had to make."

"It's why I'm still at Deftnis, Pol," one of them said. "I went out on a few Seeker missions for Ranno Wissingbel after I left here, and I couldn't make the right decisions. I love the concept of Seeking, but the actual thing…" the assistant shivered.

"Same here. I didn't have a problem with doing something on the other side of the rules, but I knew there would be decisions that would test me. It's safer teaching than doing, in my case."

Pol looked at Jonness. "I've done plenty of Seeking in my time," Jonness said, "but I eventually got tired of it. There aren't many old, active Seekers."

How much longer did Val have? He was much younger than Jonness, but he still looked older than Malden Gastoria. Pol remembered Val had traveled with somebody to Deftnis.

"Val escorted a person to Deftnis around mid-summer. What ever happened to him?"

Jonness laughed. "Whatever brought that to your mind?"

Pol felt his neck heat up. "I wondered how long Val would remain a Seeker."

"Oh, I think you mean Namion Threshell, who stayed for a month waiting for orders from Ranno Wissingbel. He and Val had just completed a mission on the Volian continent. I taught him a few advanced locating techniques. The orders came and he went," Jonness said. He stood up. "I've got to return these files. We will meet at the practice hall tomorrow morning and see what report we get from Mancus. There should be a report of another theft."

Pol had enough time to make it to the commissary for lunch and had plenty to think about until the next morning. He was upset that the thief had stolen his mother's jewels, but he knew someone other than Paki's thief had done the deed, and he didn't want to wait until they had found the original monastery thief.

Paki didn't join him for lunch, so Pol sat in a corner of the large room wondering what motivated the second thief to steal Pol's precious possessions. Could he create a pattern where he could evaluate all the possible reasons why someone would target him?

He felt the amulet under his robe and began to think. The person would likely have personal animosity towards him. Perhaps the thief had orders from North or South Salvan to retrieve the jewels. Pol nodded to himself as he took another bite of the mutton stew on his plate.

Kell didn't particularly like him, but he was from the other side of Eastril. Sakwill or Coram seemed to be the likeliest candidates. Pol didn't know of any who would have a motive. The solution might be much easier than capturing the monastery thief. He finished off his lunch and went to see Vactor or the Abbot.

The Abbot welcomed Pol into his office. "I haven't quite ordered your papers copied," the Abbot said.

"I didn't come to visit for that. It's about the theft of my mother's jewels. There are three acolytes who have some antipathy towards me."

The Abbot nodded and said, "Go on."

Pol's train of thought was interrupted for a moment. He was nervous enough anyway and took a moment to collect his thoughts. "Kell Digbee, Sakwill, and Coram."

"You think it might be one of them? Why?"

"Kell has been angry with me from the start. Sakwill and Coram were jealous of my becoming a Fourth Level. We both know about Sakwill, but I think Coram could have been the person who encouraged him. Sakwill had to have had some help."

The Abbott nodded. "Go on."

"I'd like to collect some evidence. I think I know where Kell is from, but I don't know the origins of Sakwill and Coram. There is a possibility that my step-father or King Astor might be supporting the thief."

"So you are doing some Seeking on your own. Why do you come to me, rather than Jonness?"

"He is busy with the monastery thief solution, and I don't want my mother's jewels to leave the island. I have nothing else to remember her by." That wasn't the full truth, but Pol didn't want much time to lapse.

"I see. I know where each has come from. Rather than let the youngest acolyte at Deftnis ruffle through other acolytes' files, I will answer your questions," the Abbot said. "Kell Digbee is from Fen. His father is the leader of the Merchant's Guild in the capital. Kell is jealous of you, I think, but not destructively jealous. In fact, I am sure all three are jealous of you to some extent. Sakwill is from the family of a minor noble in Boxall close to the border with North Salvan. I agree that someone must have provoked him to challenge you. I am sure that you will be eager to learn that Coram is a transfer from Tesna Monastery. He is in his second year at Deftnis. Does that help?"

"It can't be that easy, can it?" Pol said.

"I'm afraid it is," the Abbot said. "Tesna looks upon Deftnis as its rival. We have no secrets," the Abbot shrugged, "but they think we do. Coram is the likeliest to be your thief, although I expected more from a spy in our ranks. If Coram were fully Deftnis-trained, he would at least have realized that we would have our eyes on him. Jonness didn't put your theft on a priority because there is no mystery. We even know where your mother's jewels are hidden."

Pol sat back. "Why didn't you tell me sooner?"

"Have you learned anything looking for the original thief?"

Pol had to nod. "I have, more than just detection," he said. "I suppose you didn't think I'd be willing to participate in the investigation if I knew who stole my property?"

"Would you?"

That was a good question, and Pol had to admit that his own theft was a motivation. "I might not." That was as honest an answer as he could give the Abbot.

"Just tell Jonness that we had this talk when you see him next. Don't confront Coram. He's more experienced than you."

"I won't," Pol said.

"By the way, there was another theft reported at noon. It occurred last night. Jonness has updated me with your investigation. All four of you have done a good job." The Abbot looked down at the papers on his desk. "If you don't mind, I have other matters."

Pol rose from his chair and bowed to the Abbot. "I appreciate your candor," he said. "I'll try not to disappoint you."

The Abbot's face crinkled into a smile. "I don't expect you to. You'll have to hurry to your next class. Have a good day."

Pol felt a huge weight had been lifted from his shoulders. He smiled as he made his way to class. The rest of the day went well. Pol looked forward to dinner, but he wouldn't tell Paki anything until after his meeting with Jonness.

After his last class, Pol decided to visit Demeron. As he walked into the large stable yard, Coram had just mounted Pol's horse.

"Stop!" Pol said.

Coram urged Demeron right towards Pol.

Move to the side! Demeron said.

Pol felt the disappointment that his horse would desert him, but he didn't want the massive horse to run him down, so he stepped to his right.

Coram drew his sword and leaned forward, switching his sword to his left hand. He cocked his arm back for a sweeping stroke. Pol looked into Coram's eyes and couldn't summon a pattern. He was frozen to the spot, just as he had been when he fought Sakwill!

Pol could only move his eyes, and he shut them waiting for the killing blow. He expected to die, but his ears detected the sound of metal sliding on the cobbles. Pol instinctively tried to duck, but thought he was a dead acolyte. He heard a yelp.

Pol raised his eyelids to see Demeron's head not much higher than his own. He stood up to see Coram fly over his horse and roll along the cobbles. The sword clattered between Pol and the other acolyte. Free from the spell, Pol ran to the sword and picked it up. Stable hands and the monk in charge of the horses ran up.

Coram struggled to his feet and began to pose. Pol's mind filled with anger at the man and used his strength to push Coram's body fifty feet further into the main courtyard, where the man tried to rise up and then fell back.

Pol tossed the sword away while he collapsed on the pavement. His strength had deserted him, as usual.

"Here are your jewels," Jonness said, putting the familiar bag on the table. "Coram admitted under a truth spell to being the Teslan equivalent of a Fifth Level magician. Originally, King Astor put him into the monastery to learn our ways, but when he found out that you ended up here, Astor wanted him to retrieve the Listyan jewels for his daughter. She's the Queen of Listya, right?"

Pol nodded. "He coerced Sakwill to kill me, didn't he?"

It was Jonness's turn to nod. "He did. Coram had a South Salvan ship anchored just off Port Deftnis to retrieve your horse and the jewels. When he saw you in the stables, he probably thought fate had brought you to him."

"I'm not sorry to disappoint him," Pol said. "Demeron saved me."

"He did. A marvelous horse. I can see why your brother Landon wanted him."

Pol smiled. "But I can talk to him, and Landon can't. He told me to stand aside so he could quickly stop, bucking Coram over his head onto the pavement."

"Not that you didn't contribute to his injuries. I talked to eyewitnesses. You threw him a good long ways. Not a nice way to treat a fellow acolyte."

Pol refused to think of Coram as a 'fellow' anything. "He deserved what he got."

"Even if he wasn't judged?" Jonness said.

The words shocked Pol. He remembered Val's execution of the stable master who had been instrumental in the murder of Paki's father. What had he just done that was much different? He winced. "I had his sword in my hands and could have killed him right there."

Jonness squinted. "Or he could have blown you away before you did the same to him. He was a Purple, remember? Who knows what they teach Purples at Tesna?"

"Maybe that was why I did what I did." He looked at Jonness. "But I didn't seek his life. I was so frightened that he would kill me, that all I felt was anger looking at him on the ground and did what I did because I was mad."

"At least you're honest. Garryle didn't let the South Salvan ship land. I don't think your horse would have let them put him on a ship, anyway."

That thought brought a smile to his face. "He wouldn't."

"Now that we've settled that, let's get back to our thief." Jonness pushed the bag across the table to Pol and called for his two assistants to join them. He rubbed his hands together. "What do we have?"

"The acolyte and one of the monks have wives and family living in Mancus. The both have some family money, so that leaves us with a single monk."

"Just because they have family money, doesn't mean they don't need more," Jonness said. "What about the monk?"

"Harvell Crestglen. He's a pattern-master, sixth year."

"Should we bring in Master Edgebare?" one of the assistants said.

"Darrol Netherfield might know him, as well," Pol said.

"You trust Darrol?" Jonness said.

"I do, and he trusts me."

"So let's begin with two inquiries. Pol and I will visit Master Edgebare." Jonness got up. "You can start the class if we run a bit late," he said to his assistants.

On the walk to the armory, Jonness turned to Pol. "What is the disadvantage in interviewing someone you know well?"

Pol thought a bit. "I can't think of anything."

"Think harder. How would your presence change their pattern?"

The question rolled around Pol's brain for a bit, and then he nodded. "My presence can change the answer?"

"Why?"

"The questioner wants to please me? That's what servants would do. So that makes their answers less credible?" Pol said.

"Right. So you have to make sure when you interview Darrol that you make it plain that you seek the truth and nothing else."

"You want me to interview him?"

Jonness nodded as they walked through the door to the armory. "Edgebare first."

Edgebare ushered the both of them into his office. Pol had sat here once before. Jonness and Edgebare nattered on about gossip in the monastery. Pol had no idea what they were really talking about.

Jonness cleared his throat. "Now on to a little bit of business. Tell us about Harvell Crestglen."

Edgebare narrowed his eyes. "Why are you asking me that question?"

"His name has come up in something we've been working on in the Seeker class."

"Well, he's a decent enough teacher. Better swordsman than

magician. He's a Red, like Pol, here for magic and a Red belt for swords. Didn't like crossing swords for real. That happens often enough, but he fancies himself as a rather dashing fellow among the ladies, if you know what I mean."

"Is he a generous sort of man?" Jonness asked, looking sideways at Pol.

"Not particularly, I'd say. What is this about?"

"We will let you know, soon." Jonness got up. "Can we have a few words with Darrol Netherfield?"

"He's just finishing up his early morning class, but feel free." Edgebare gave Pol a stare, but it didn't strike Pol as unfriendly.

Jonness and Pol walked to a corner of the armory where a group of eight acolytes practiced basic forms with Darrol. None of the attendees were close to Pol's age, and none had anywhere near the expertise that Pol had quickly picked up with intensive training the summer before.

Darrol nodded at Pol and Jonness as he monitored the movements of each of his charges. Pol noticed that all of them were First Level magicians. He looked down and flipped an end of his red cord.

"That's enough for today. More drill tomorrow," Darrol said. He walked to a chair that had a damp towel draped across the back and used the towel to wipe his face while he walked up to Jonness and Pol. "I assume this isn't an offer to become a Seeker?" Darrol said.

Jonness bumped Pol.

"We are engaged in an investigation. A name came up and we wondered if you could answer a few of my questions," Pol said. He rubbed sweaty palms on his robe. He didn't want his discomfort showing, but he plowed ahead. "Do you know Harvell Crestglen?"

Darrol tried to keep from laughing, and that infuriated Pol. "Of course I do. He's one of my fellow instructors."

"Tell us about him?" Pol asked. He used the same question that Jonness had asked Master Edgebare.

"What do you want to know?"

Darrol answered a question with a question and that flustered Pol, but he had to continue to ask his friend more questions. "Uh, what kind of instructor is he?"

"Fair to middling. He has decent sword skills, and he can do anticipation magic, something that I can't. I don't think he connects to students very well."

"So he's aloof?"

"Yes."

Pol realized that his question wasn't a very good one. Edgebare was a better interviewee than Darrol.

"Does he have much of a life outside the monastery?" Pol said.

Darrol grinned. "That's a much better question, Pol. Yes, he does. He often goes over to Mancus to break hearts. He's boasted about his ability with the ladies, and there are more of them over there than in Port Deftnis, you know." A cloud seemed to pass over Darrol's face, but he shook it off. "I think he's a bit overconfident about his looks, though." Darrol looked across the armory. "There he is."

Pol turned to look. Monk Crestglen didn't strike Pol as the dashing type. He was tall and built well enough, but he sported an over-long nose and a scraggly beard that did little to make up for his balding head. Crestglen turned his head their way, causing Pol to turn back to Darrol. "That's him? A pattern-master?"

Darrol smiled, the tone of his voice lowered. "The gods make men in many images."

Pol thought furiously for another question. "Does he talk about buying gifts for his, uh, girls?"

"Women. Women who are usually bought, Pol. Yes, he does."

The revelation stopped Pol in his tracks. He looked pleadingly at Jonness.

"How often do you go to Mancus, Netherfield?"

"No more," Darrol said. "I learned my lesson."

Jonness finally turned to see Crestglen disappear through a door. "Has he learned his?"

"I can't say for sure, but probably not."

"Thank you, Netherfield. Pol thanks you as well." Jonness looked at Pol. "Time to go."

"I'll see you later," Darrol said.

Pol could only nod as he rushed to catch up to Jonness, who was already marching out of the armory.

Back in the Seeker practice hall, students had already begun to settle for class. Kell and Paki looked back at Pol, standing next to Jonness. Darrol nodded to both of them and slipped to the back.

Jonness waved to the assistant to get the class started and took Pol outside into the practice yard where they could talk by themselves.

"How do you think you did?"

"Badly," Pol said. 'Darrol didn't directly answer my questions, so I had to come up with more direct ones. I'm sorry."

"Why are you sorry?"

"I thought that you didn't want Master Edgebare or Darrol to know we were asking about the monastery thief."

Jonness looked out at the empty practice yard. "I didn't tell Edgebare we were looking for the thief. Did you?"

"No, sir."

Jonness shrugged. "You did fine for your first interrogation. Darrol has put in years as a guard and knew you were questioning him, so he played a bit of a game with you."

"I thought so."

"What is the other reason we shouldn't be interrogating our friends?"

"They don't take you seriously?"

"Right. Just like Darrol. You could have done worse, but you still verified what Edgebare told us. We'll have Garryle take it from here. There is still a week or more before he'll be heading back across to Mancus."

"We can't arrest him now?"

"We could, but I'll still have all three of them monitored. It would be easier to catch the culprit in the act of thievery, wouldn't it?"

Pol couldn't think why they wouldn't rush to grab him, but he just nodded. "What did Darrol do wrong in Mancus?"

"You ask him. Time for class."

~ ~ ~

Chapter Thirteen

IT SEEMED THAT ALL THE CLASSES DECIDED TO HAVE TESTS during the same week. Pol was walking quickly through the rain to the library, carrying a bag filled with notes, when Paki ran up to him.

"They caught the monastery thief."

"Crestglen?" Pol asked.

"The pattern-master?" Paki said. "No. It's an acolyte. The Mancus constables saw him at a dogfight and when confronted, he admitted that he had a gambling problem. He didn't want his wife to know, so he funded his habit with the funds he stole. One of Jonness's assistants caught him red-handed in a monk's cell the night before his next boat ride to Mancus."

Pol stopped in the rain. "Really?"

Paki nodded and then shrugged his shoulders with resignation. "I won't get my South Salvan Lions back, but at least he won't be stealing from other monks. I'll see you in the library after I retrieve my own things."

Pol watched Paki rush across the wet pavement. So all the evidence didn't point to Crestglen. Pol thought about the investigation as he continued to the library. Finding Coram to be a thief was easy, but Paki's news shocked Pol. With the information he had, Pol was certain Crestglen was the thief. He wondered how Jonness would talk about the seeking in the morning to the class. Pol felt embarrassed about his own conclusions, but then as he reviewed what Jonness had told him that morning in the practice yard, the Master Seeker had still intended to follow all three suspects.

Pol found a space at a table and set out his papers. While he waited for them to dry a bit, he sat back and thought. Should he be upset by Jonness questioning Edgebare and Darrol? But then he realized that Jonness probably regarded part of the investigation as a learning experience for him. He grabbed one of his blank sheets and began to write down a detailed description of the investigation, including Coram's story. The experience had been filled with lessons about Seeking.

He thought about Paki's Lions and decided to give him his own. Pol didn't need it, and it would still be a good reminder of Siggon, Paki's father.

"This is my personal report," Pol said, handing the account of his recent experiences finding the thieves to Master Jonness.

"I didn't assign you to do this." The Master Seeker quickly scanned the pages. "Good work, nevertheless. I'll give this to my assistants to review, as well. We have to document our actions for the Abbot's files anyway. There's no sense letting this good work go for naught."

Pol bowed to Jonness and took his place among the gathering students. Darrol sauntered in and sat next to him on the floor, as usual.

"I heard they caught the thief. Some married acolyte," Darrol said. "I had hoped it wouldn't have been Crestglen. I would be pressed into teaching his classes, and I don't know very much about anticipation magic."

"Sorry," Pol said.

"What for?"

"I didn't mean to accuse your friend."

Darrol gave Pol a little shove. "First of all, he's not my friend and second of all, you did a good job for your first time interviewing someone."

"You're not offended?"

Darrol shook his head. "Not at all. From my practical perspective, you've got to follow up on all your leads. Don't worry about it."

Pol did worry about it. In his mind he had decided that Crestglen was the villain, and that incorrect assumption might have led to further mistakes on his part.

Jonness called the class to order. "This morning we will talk about practical Seeking. As all of you know we have had a monastery thief in our midst for some time. Recently some extremely valuable possessions were stolen, so that increased the priority we placed on finding the criminal." Jonness proceeded to go through much the same thing that Pol had written in his report, except for the ending.

"So we ended up with two thieves. Our investigation led to an individual who, we thought, matched the pattern of the thief, but then as the investigation continued to a conclusion, new information was received. An individual's pattern matched the circumstances better with the additional information."

Jonness let the students talk for a bit, and then he raised his hands for silence. "Pol Cissert accompanied us during the investigation, since he was one of the victims. What did you learn from the experience?"

Pol stood up and twisted his fingers in his hands with embarrassment. "The biggest thing I learned is that sometimes it's easy to find a solution. It was in finding Coram guilty, once we realized that his actions didn't match the others. I thought it might be just as easy to find the monastery thief, but it wasn't. I came to a hasty conclusion that was wrong. Seeking isn't as easy as I thought, and there is more uncertainty, even if you think you've got someone who fits the pattern. Is that good enough?" Pol asked Jonness.

"It is, if you think it is."

Pol nodded and sat down.

"With this episode our class changes. We will be emphasizing scouting for the rest of the year and will leave Seeking behind us. Those of you that are here for Seeking only, please line up so we can help you find other courses. Seekers who want to learn more scouting techniques can leave for today and return with the rest of the scouting students tomorrow. There will be more advanced courses in Seeking next year."

Darrol stood up and stretched. "I guess I'm done here until next year. What about you, Pol?"

"I'm going to talk to Jonness."

Paki came up to Pol. "I'll be staying in the class. See you later."

Pol looked at the line of students already forming. He noticed that Kell was one of them. Pol couldn't picture Kell as a scout, anyway. He would want to mix it up in battle, he thought.

Pol sat back down. One of Jonness's assistants joined him.

"No scouting? You'd be a great one," he said.

Pol shook his head. "I learned a lot about scouting already this year, but I would rather learn more about Seeking. I can use the pattern practice."

"There are patterns in scouting."

Pol nodded. "There are, but…"

"I know what you mean. I tried my hand at Scouting just before I decided to return to Deftnis to teach. You need to have a certain attitude to like it."

Pol thought of Kolli and compared her to Val. He thought that Val would chafe at following orders all the time. Kolli seemed to be able to operate independently and still observe the chain of command.

He honestly didn't know what his preference was, but it seemed that Seeking required more brainpower. Magic and brainpower were his strengths, not the physical demands that scouting required.

"Can I help you decide what to do next?"

"I'll talk to Jonness."

"If you have any questions about scouting or Seeking along the way this year, don't wait to ask." The assistant clapped Pol on the shoulder and walked out of the practice hall.

Pol didn't know what to do, so he waited for the end of the line. He watched Kell go out, looking smug, as usual.

After the last student left, Pol rose and stood in front of Jonness, who was seated at the table.

"You don't want to be a scout?" Jonness asked. "I didn't think so." His eyes crinkled as he smiled. "So other than the specialty of Emperor, what would you like to be? You are currently training to be a magician with Vactor, so what else?"

"I don't know," Pol said.

"The healers are about to start herbal remedies, now that winter is about over. I sent your friend Kell over there. It might be a good thing to learn. We don't teach field medicine in the scouting program until the third year, so why don't you join him?"

Pol knew he didn't care much for Kell, but healing would be a nice diversion from the rest of his current courses.

The healing class wouldn't start for another week, so Pol took advantage of the break and took Demeron out for extended trips on the backside of the island. He fixed the broken jumps that had been neglected for much of late winter as best he could, and took the opportunity to find out what Demeron knew and what he didn't know.

They spent most mornings riding, and then while Demeron ate the new grass that was beginning to grow, Pol became a teacher to a willing student.

The interlude finally came to an end, and Pol walked into the infirmary for the beginning of his new morning class.

A monk ushered him to a greenhouse in the back. Seven acolytes sat on stools, with Kell making them eight. Pol took a stool across from Kell, who acknowledged Pol's presence with a grunt.

"We are embarking on a new phase of your healing class. There are two newcomers with us," a healer monk said. The man wore an orange cord. Pol looked around, and he was, again, the highest-ranked magician in the bunch, with most of the others sporting white or yellow-corded belts. To Pol's surprise, Kell had changed his tan belt for a white cord. He didn't think Kell had any talent.

"There is no magic in what we will be learning the rest of this year. I hope there are a few of you that have some gardening experience. This is more of a gardening class than a healing one."

Pol saw a few disappointed faces, but with his time spent working in the Royal Gardens at Borstall with Paki and his father, Pol knew a bit about cultivating plants.

Kell scowled as he walked out of the classroom. "I didn't think I'd be getting my hands dirty," he said.

"I've gotten my hands dirty, and they seem to clean up just fine. Besides, we've already benefitted from dirty hands," Pol said, showing Kell his hands. "Why are you taking this class anyway?"

They both walked down the steps from the infirmary. Kell looked back at the black stone. "My mother was a healer."

"Was?" Pol said.

Kell nodded. "She died a few years ago. We were caught in a storm between cities and had a carriage accident. No healers were available, so she died. You lost your mother, too, as I recall."

"I did. She had an excellent healer by her side, but the poison had acted quickly."

"Oh. The monk from Yastan didn't say she was poisoned."

He had, but Pol didn't think it was appropriate to dispute Kell's memory.

"So you are going to dabble in healing because of her?"

Kell nodded. "I told my father that I would, if I can get through this course. I don't have much magical talent, and I'm not excited about herbs, but…"

Pol looked at Kell. He felt a bit bad about his mother dying. Pol could certainly empathize with him. "Look, I can help you get through this if you need to. A lot of healing has nothing to do with magic. In fact, there is a good healer that I know, a very powerful magician, who told me that most of what magicians and healers do has nothing to do with magic."

"So I can learn," Kell said, almost to himself.

"It always helps to know how to do things on your own. If you are out in the countryside, a good knowledge of what plants might help various ailments can't do you any harm."

"I guess not," Kell said. "I have to hurry to exercise my horse during lunch." He ran off.

Pol looked at him hustle towards the stables. Perhaps Kell might not be the jerk that Pol thought him to be.

~ ~ ~

Chapter Fourteen

GORM SHOOK POL AWAKE. "Jonness told me to wake you. Coram has escaped from his cell and is currently on his way to Mancus. Jonness said you might want to accompany him."

Pol blinked sleep away from his eyes. All of the other acolytes were fast asleep. He was tempted to wake Paki, but decided he would go on his own. He threw his clothes on and placed some knives in strategic places. Coram's sword mastery might be significantly higher than what he demonstrated at the monastery. Jonness would bring others better than him.

By the time he made it to the stables, five monks were mounted. Darrol, Jonness, the two assistants and a monk Pol didn't really know.

"This is Master Hopken, a pattern-master. Hurry and get Demeron."

Pol ran into the stable and found his horse already saddled. He climbed up on Demeron's back and trotted out of the stable into the darkness of the yard. The party didn't waste any time heading out the gate and clattered on the cobbles as they sped towards Port Deftnis.

They galloped so fast that Pol didn't have an opportunity to talk to anyone. They reached the dock and put their horses on the barge. There wasn't much night wind, so four of the men joined two sailors in using sweeps to move the craft.

I don't like the water, Demeron said.

"I don't either," Pol admitted. He sought out Jonness working a sweep. "Why did you bring me along?"

Jonness grinned. "Don't you want to catch him? I would, so you could use the experience."

Pol looked at the others in the group. "Is this part of Seeking?"

The Master Seeker grunted. "It's a less glamorous part, unless there is a chase, and this time, I think there might be. At least the South Salvan ship wasn't hanging around when Coram broke the lock on his cell."

"Magic?"

Jonness nodded and took a few deep breaths. Pol wished he could join them, but he would only last a few minutes exerting himself at the same level as the rest. With the light wind, the water wasn't too bad for the horses and for Pol.

He walked back to Darrol. "Why are you here?"

"Volunteered. I heard them rousing Hopken, and since it was a South Salvan, I decided to join in. Jonness has taken a liking to you, lad. He thinks you'd make a great Seeker, so he's giving you this opportunity, even though you're not in his class any longer."

Pol could hear all the heavy breathing, so he decided he wouldn't wear anyone else out by talking to the rowers as they worked. Hopken stood at the bow looking towards the lights of Mancus in the distance. He took a place at his side and noticed the black leather belt that Hopken wore.

"I'm Pol Cissert."

Hopken snorted. "I know. You get around, don't you?"

What was that supposed to mean? Hopken looked at him sideways, and then turned back looking ahead.

"I don't know. I suppose."

"So we have the best swordsman in the monastery and the worst on the same boat," Hopken said.

"I'm not the worst. I can anticipate. I'm not a pattern-master, but I know how to discern the patterns."

That got a grunt from the unfriendly swordsman-monk.

"I'm pretty good throwing knives."

"A coward's talent...or an assassin's."

Pol tried to keep from getting mad at a Deftnis Master. "Knives have saved my life. I don't exactly have a long reach with a sword."

Hopken turned around and left Pol alone in the front of the barge without saying another word.

I heard that, Demeron said.

Pol looked around to find Demeron only a few paces away, tied up to a post in the front of the barge. "I didn't notice you there. It is dark you know, and you are a dark-haired horse."

My natural camouflage.

"Why do you think Hopken dislikes me?"

I can read your mind, but not his. Maybe he doesn't like boys. Demeron snorted and raised his head up and down. *I don't think he is an enemy.*

Pol and Demeron had talked about enemies and friends. Pol would have to trust Demeron's instincts more than his own.

The early morning began to wear on Pol, so he found a place to sit. The easy rolling of the boat put him to sleep.

He woke with a sharp pain in his side. Pol looked up into Hopken's face, and then he looked down at the pointed toe of his spurred boot. "Up, boy," the swordsman said, with derision filling his voice.

Pol rubbed his head, and then looked at Mancus rapidly get closer. They were nearly across the water. He stood next to Demeron, ready to lead him up to the dock, and then wait for the others.

Garryle's face was lit up by a magician's light inside a cage atop a pole.

"He had someone help him. The dockhand said two men got off the boat and headed to a stable to buy horses. I wasn't fast enough to catch them from Port Deftnis."

"Tesnan spies," Hopken said. He had reserved a more venomous voice for Coram. "Where did they head?"

"Probably the coast road to Finster."

"Then we are off!" Hopken began galloping out of the village.

Jonness stood there. "Pol, is 'probably' an adequate call to action for a Seeker?"

"No, sir, but we can't investigate while Coram puts more distance between us all."

"Then let us get out of this town."

They all mounted and followed Hopken, but at a slower pace. Once they were a few hundred paces past the last house, Jonness stopped.

"Are you going to look for tracks?" Pol said, remembering the investigation of Paki's beating back in Borstall.

"Right." Jonness said. Pol noticed a little surprise in his voice.

Pol jumped off his horse and walked forward in the darkness. They weren't far from where Pol first set his eyes on Deftnis Isle six months ago. "We should see fresh tracks of three horses."

"But there are only two fugitives," Darrol said.

"Plus the pattern-master," Pol said. He heard an unintelligible sound from his friend. Pol hadn't learned to keep a magic light from burning out his energy, so he waited for someone else to make one.

"What do you see, Pol?"

"Only one horse. Hopken's tracks are fresh, but none of the others are."

One of the assistants joined them. "How do you know that?" His voice indicated that he was testing Pol.

"The fresh tracks are darker. The ground is damp from the night. See here?" Pol sat on his haunches and pointed out to tracks close to another. "The fresh tracks are darker. I learned that from a tutor back in Borstall."

"Paki's father?" Darrol asked.

Pol merely nodded.

Hopken finally returned. "I saw your light. Why aren't you following me?"

"Pol read the tracks correctly, Hopken. Coram and his accomplice didn't take this road. Only you."

"You take the word of this boy?"

"I can see it for myself, man. Let's head back and hope we didn't miss them leaving this road."

As they just entered the town, Garryle, now mounted with two other men, not monks, met them. "We found a witness. They headed northeast."

"Lead on," Hopken said. Evidently, he had thought he had taken over the group, but Pol wouldn't follow him. He would only follow Jonness.

They rode through the early morning and into the dawn. Far ahead, Pol could see two riders silhouetted, going over the top of a rise by the lighter western sky.

"There they are!"

I can run faster than this, Demeron said.

"I'll catch them." Pol yelled to Jonness, and then he let Demeron go as fast as he wanted.

Pol had to hang on to Demeron, but the horse moved forcefully ahead, not like the time when the horse Pol rode bolted on him. Pol could feel the power of Demeron's muscles bunching and exploding as Pol gained on the other riders.

The others were far behind, and Pol began to wonder what he would do when he caught up to Coram and his accomplice. Pol began to think of how he could disable the horses. Perhaps he could throw a knife into the flank of each horse.

That will hurt, Demeron said, *but they won't slow down much. When a horse is running fast, they can ignore just about everything but moving forward.*

Pol didn't know that "So I should stop the riders, not the horses?"

Let me take care of the horses. Be prepared to defend yourself and hold on tight.

After grabbing hold of the reins, Pol hung on for his life. He went over where he had put his knives and which ones he could use the quickest. Pol could see both men were dressed in normal clothes. Perhaps the accomplice, whoever he was, didn't live in the monastery. Maybe he had been let ashore by the South Salvan ship and took residence in the port.

Demeron surged with speed and ran close to one of the horses and bit it on the rump. Pol looked into the face of Sakwill who was trying to come up with a pattern while his horse began to slow. Demeron forced his way ahead of them and slowed in the middle of the two horses and bumped Coram's horse, which struggled to stay upright, running on the side of the road, plodding through the edge of a freshly plowed field.

Sakwill's horse stopped. He drew a sword, but Pol had the answer to Sakwill and threw his knife, aided by a sip of magic to adjust its trajectory, and it sank into the magician's shoulder.

"That trick won't work with me," Coram said. "I'm no Third," he said. "And, soon enough, you won't be anything."

By now all three horses had come to a stop. Sakwill dropped to the ground, clutching his shoulder.

Coram's eyes glazed, but not before Pol spelled a gust of wind at him, using the still air in the field as a pattern, and tweaked. The gust nearly blew Coram off his horse. Coram's eyes cleared, so before the Tesnan could generate another spell, Pol quickly threw another knife at Coram and put every bit of magical energy into the throw.

Pol saw spots in front of his eyes and his heart pounded. His last view was of the knife intended for Coram's shoulder, deflect up and into the man's neck. Coram's eyes rolled up as Pol fell from Demeron.

Pol looked up at the sun blazing in his eyes. He laid at the edge of the road. A cart passed by.

"You're up?" Darrol said.

"I am." Pol sat up and looked around. "Where is everybody?"

"We're here," one of Jonness's assistants said. "Drink this."

Pol nearly spit out the watered wine, but after gagging for the first swallow, let the rest flow down his throat. He actually began to feel better.

"Jonness, Hopken, and the other assistant took the body with them back to Mancus."

"Did Sakwill say anything?"

Darrol laughed. "He complained quite a bit, but it didn't take a genius to realize that Coram still had Sakwill under compulsion."

"His condition didn't affect his memory," the assistant said. "Coram was heading back to Tesna. He boasted to Sakwill that they might even send a ship to sack the monastery and execute you."

"Why me? I'm disinherited."

"Pride? Jealousy? Vindictiveness?" Darrol said. "I'd like to see Tesna take us. Sakwill said that Coram was the only practitioner of anticipation magic that Tesna had. It seems he boasted about it to

Sakwill plenty of times."

Pol furrowed his brows. "How long did it take Jonness to find all of that out?"

"Hopken. He's adept at truth spells. Sakwill just sang and sang and sang. He's probably still singing," Darrol said. "Are you well enough to ride?"

Pol shooke his head. "Not too fast. Demeron will take care of me."

"Did your horse really stop the other two?"

Pol nodded his head. "He is wonderful."

I am, aren't I?

Pol looked around and found Demeron munching on some new spring grass behind him.

"You are. Can you take it easy going back?"

Demeron snorted and raised his head in reply.

"That's one smart horse," the assistant said. "And fast."

"He is that," Pol said as Darrol helped him up and onto Demeron. Pol leaned over and patted Demeron on his neck. "And the best part is we are good friends."

Indeed. That brought another shaking of Demeron's head.

This time Pol sat in a hard chair rather than the easy chair he used the last time Pol sat in the Abbot's office. Jonness sat on his right and Hopken on his left. Pol had no idea why he had been called into this meeting.

"That was a foolhardy thing to do," the Abbot said.

"Demeron suggested it. None of the other horses had the speed," Pol said.

"Or the ability to stop other horses, if Sakwill's description is true. He called Demeron, a 'devil horse'," Jonness said.

"He's sentient," Pol said, shrugging. "We can talk to each other and I just followed his lead."

Hopken snorted. "A treasure like the Shinkyan stallion belongs in the hands of a superior swordsman, and that's why we are here."

Pol looked at Hopken, and then at Jonness.

"Master Hopken wants your horse," the Abbot said. "You do not have to give it to him, for you possess the title signed by the Emperor."

"I'll call a full council, if you don't, boy," Hopken said. "You don't deserve him."

Pol didn't know what to say. How could he overcome the wishes of a magician warrior of the highest level? He felt more intimidated than he ever had around Val.

"And why not?" Jonness said. "I seem to recall that Pol, and his horse, stopped the escape and disabled both riders. He fulfilled our mission all on his own."

Hopken straightened his robe and cleared his throat. "He killed Coram, when we could have questioned him."

"Why didn't you question him when he was in his cell?" Pol said, getting a bit angry with Hopken. "He was getting ready to throw some kind of spell at me. I had to defend myself."

"With a coward's blade," Hopken said.

The Abbot stood up. "I'll have none of that! You know better, Master Hopken. I'd like you to call Valiso Gasibli a coward to his face."

Hopken looked taken aback by that retort.

The Abbot glared at Hopken. "What did you expect Pol to do, draw a sword and close on a magician several levels higher than himself? Just what kinds of acts qualify as honorable in self defense?"

Hopken's eyes bulged a bit. "But, but…"

The Abbot remained standing. "I was going to give you a reasonable hearing, Hopken, but no longer. You know our principles about arrogance. I think you need to reflect. It's quite clear that Pol holds an Imperial title to the horse signed by the Emperor himself. You are dismissed from my presence."

The master blinked a few times, turning red. Pol didn't know if it was from embarrassment or anger. Hopken's chair overturned when he stood, and he didn't turn back to set it right.

Pol did, as the Abbot returned to his seat. "You will forgive me, both of you." The Abbot pulled out a pocket square and dabbed at his forehead. "Hopken is a marvelous man and one of the best pattern-masters alive. It does not excuse what he just did."

"You gave him a hearing. He deserved one," Jonness said.

Pol wondered why the Master Seeker defended Hopken.

"But, arrogance makes a man blind," Jonness said, finishing his thought.

The Abbot nodded. It was obviously a saying at the monastery, Pol thought.

"You performed as we would expect," the Abbot said to Pol. "So Jonness said you devised some new spells?"

Pol shrugged. He had told Jonness every detail he could remember.

"A wind spell, inexpertly applied, so you admit, but an interesting tweak. It's been done many times, but not without being taught. And was this knife thrown differently than what you threw at Sakwill in your duel?"

Pol had to shake his head. "As before, but this time I tweaked a lot more force into the blade. Coram was throwing up some kind of shield. I didn't know they existed, so I used all my strength. It went though his shield, but it somehow deflected up and into his neck. I didn't intend to kill him, but his spell caused the blade to move."

"Unfortunate for him, but fortunate for you," the Abbot said. "I expect more from you and Demeron. Don't disappoint me."

~ ~ ~

Chapter Fifteen

After Coram's death, Pol began to have nightmares about Coram, with a knife in his neck, leading South Salvan soldiers in an attack on the monastery. Sometimes the pea-shooter from his time in Borstall joined the fray with Bythia, Landon's wife, armed with a spear.

He tried to shake the dreams off, but he couldn't help but look at others with a different eye. Who were enemies, who were friends? Pol found he didn't know. He was vaguely aware that he fell behind in his studies. He now dreaded to practice with his knives and kept away from Demeron. When he went to study, he could no longer concentrate and often woke up after having fallen asleep over his lessons.

Paki was on a completely different schedule, so he never saw his best friend, and that made Pol sad. He felt totally alone. The nightmares became real things in his mind, and he began to shrink from social contact.

One bright early spring day, Pol dragged himself to the herbalist class and sat by himself, tending the little plot that all of them had been tasked to cultivate. Pol knew the herbs should receive better care, but he didn't care if they grew or not.

Kell came up to him. "What's the matter with you?"

Pol struggled to make eye contact with him. "Nothing. I'm just tired, I guess." He poked around in his plot and stayed there when their tutor called them to gather.

He looked at the group and didn't want to join them, so he continued to run his finger through the soil. Pol wanted to bury himself in the dirt with the seeds. Maybe he could rise again bigger and stronger and not be looked down on by everybody. Maybe the nightmares that never ceased would be replaced by the dreams he could never quite remember.

He vaguely noticed Kell talking to his tutor, and then both of them looked at him. He put his elbow on the planter box and looked back at the soil.

Two monks lifted Pol up by his arms and led him into the infirmary. Pol didn't know why they were taking him away, but he found that he didn't care, as long as they found some way for him to avoid the nightmares.

They put him in a bed in a room of his own. Pol smiled at the memory of the little room in the Castle Borstall infirmary where he had visited so often. He didn't know private rooms existed at the monastery infirmary. They gave him something to drink and Pol started. Were they putting him to sleep?

He didn't want the nightmares, so he began struggling with the monks. "No. No. I don't want them coming back!"

"What?" a healer asked.

"The nightmares. I don't want Deftnis taken over by South Salvan." Pol seemed to think that's what he said, but now he couldn't remember for sure if the words actually came out. He tried to blink hard to keep from slipping away, back into the maelstrom of images that had been assaulting him. Finally he gave up, and pictured himself sinking into soft, rich soil warmed by the spring sun.

Pol's eyes flew wide open. What had happened? Had the invasion begun? He hadn't seen the vision of Deftnis' destruction in his dreams for a long time, it seemed. He sat up, alone in the tiny room he barely remembered.

He fell back into the pillow and put a hand to his head. What had happened? He struggled to remember where he was and why he was waking in the infirmary. A monk walked past the open door to the little room.

"You are awake?"

Pol nodded, still looking up at the ceiling. "I am. What happened?"

"I'll get the Master Healer."

Something bad must have occurred for the monk to get the Master. Pol sat up again, letting the pain in his head fully awaken him. He poured himself a cup of water from a pitcher left by his bedside and let the water flow down his parched throat.

The Master Healer walked into his room, followed by another monk. "You are finally back with us."

"How long have I slept?" Pol asked.

"A little more than three days."

That shocked Pol. "Why?"

"You can answer that question better than we can, although we've seen similar illnesses before."

"Illness? I was sick?"

The master nodded. "Your adventure catching the South Salvan magician was the trigger. We think that Hopken's demand for your horse added to it."

"I had nightmares," Pol said. "Coram returned to sack Deftnis Monastery with a South Salvan army. My knife was still in his throat…"

"That kept recurring?" the master said.

Pol nodded.

"We've seen it before. It comes from intense stress. The stress led to your losing touch with your surroundings. You were suffering from malnutrition when we brought you in, so you weren't even caring for yourself. We call the condition melancholia."

"Am I crazy?"

"Temporarily, you can call it that. It's an illness like anything else that can be treated. We'll prescribe medicine for you to take at night for the next two weeks and thereafter if the nightmares return. Do you think an invasion is imminent now?"

Pol thought for a moment and shook his head. "No. Deftnis is very defensible. In my nightmares it wasn't." He put his hand to his head. "I wasn't thinking very clearly."

"If you realize that, then you are well on your way to recovery. Your friend Kell told us you weren't acting right. You might want to thank him."

Kell, a friend? thought Pol. He'd have to talk to Paki and Demeron about his behavior…and Kell.

The monks let Pol return to the dormitory after lunch, armed with the powders to help him sleep later that night. He returned to his classes to find himself far behind in the classwork. Pol had been far enough ahead of the others in most of the classes that catching up wouldn't be too much of a trial.

He caught Paki between buildings at the end of the afternoon and asked if they could have dinner together.

"I wondered where you were," Paki said as they sat down with their trays of food. "I thought you might be off catching more criminals."

Paki laughed, but Pol couldn't. "I was sick in the head," he admitted. "The Master Healer said it was from stress."

Paki snorted. "I guess so. When have you ever not been under stress? I thought you would have broken last summer in Borstall. At least you held it off until we got here."

"You thought I would snap?"

Paki nodded. "My dad often worried about you. I'll bet the Court Magician and your tutor were concerned, too."

"Not Val," Pol said.

Paki took Pol's wrist. "He was. He told me how you stopped your horse with magic in the forest. Val wondered when you'd overdo it and not recover."

Pol sat back, holding his spoon up with the handle end on the table. "I never knew."

After taking a big mouthful of food, Paki said, "You do now. I'm not so sure a week's rest will be enough."

Some kind of breakdown, Pol thought. He'd heard about such things, but never thought anything like that could happen to him. He filled his spoon with stew and ate it, deep in thought. "We need to talk more often," Pol said. "I felt myself withdrawing."

Paki nodded grinning. "You did. I tried to talk to you, but towards the end, you just ignored me. I won't let that happen again."

"Don't," Pol said, shocked and ashamed at the same time. Despite his physical issues, Pol thought he was pretty infallible. Not all-knowing, but what he did know he felt he mastered. He remembered what Jonness had said in the Abbot's office, Arrogance makes a man blind. It made a fifteen-year-old boy blind, too.

~

The next morning Pol looked down at his herb garden. Some of the seeds had sprouted. He poked his finger in the moist soil. Someone had taken care of his planter box.

"I kept them going for you," Kell said, sitting down on his haunches next to Pol.

"Thank you. And thank you for noticing my condition. I wasn't really there for the last while, was I?"

Kell shook his head. "You are my first successful diagnosis. I had an uncle that came back from a border skirmish who turned out like you. His best friend had died at his side, and he never talked about it. He ended up killing himself. I remember that he had the same lost look on his face."

Pol looked at the shoots, not even remembering what he had planted. "I could have done that."

Kell clapped his hand on Pol's back. "But you didn't. Let that be a lesson to you, one that my uncle never learned." He got to his feet and went to his own plot.

Pol blinked back tears. Perhaps Kell was a friend, after all.

~

Vactor welcomed Pol back to his classes.

"I'm glad you are back," he said. "You've gotten little accomplished since the Coram incident."

"Maybe we could talk about what happened between Coram and me?"

"Are you up to it?"

Pol nodded. "I want to know what he did and what I might have done better." He took a deep breath. "I think I ran away in my mind for awhile."

"That's a good term for what you might have done. Such things happen to us all in one degree or another," Vactor said. "You said he was in the process of setting up some kind of a shield?"

Pol nodded. "It shifted the path of my knife."

"Ironic. So, he basically killed himself?"

"I hadn't thought of it that way," Pol said. "What was the shield, thickened air?"

Vactor smiled. "You are back. That might be one explanation. There are other tweaks that an experienced magician might employ. Sometimes a shield can be crafted to repel metal. That works for arrows and knives, but swords carry too much force. That's probably what his shield did. Your magically enhanced knife throw penetrated, but it was thrown off by Coram's defense. Thickened air would have slowed it down, or it might have even stuck in the shield."

"How can I learn to do such things?"

"You'll need to get stronger." Vactor raised his hand. "Everyone tells me that you are getting stronger from where you were before. But you fainted right after you tweaked the wind and added force to the knife—"

"Before I fell off Demeron."

Vactor nodded. "Your strength still remains something that might eventually hold you back."

Pol had to agree. "I know that I'm still limited."

"Give it some time, Pol. You're still a boy, only fifteen. Most magicians haven't felt a breath of talent at your age."

Pol had to restrain his comments. He recognized what he was about to say as arrogance and he wanted to avoid blindness as much as he could, so he changed the subject to something that he had wondered about.

"Why aren't their female magicians?"

Vactor blinked. "What brought that on? Who said there aren't?"

"The Emperor only tested males when he passed through North Salvan on his Processional."

"Oh, that. The Emperor looks for magicians as a lever of power. More male magicians means more pattern-masters, which means better Imperial forces. The Emperor and his predecessors all believed in having a more effective fighting force than the subject kingdoms and dukedoms to maintain their power."

"And women don't make better fighters?"

"Not with swords and pikes. They are simply smaller and less dense than men. We have nunneries for women, who generally gravitate to the healing arts or use their power for other things."

Pol didn't know if he believed that, and it must have shown to Vactor.

"The Emperor does have a school for women magicians in Yastan. Its focus is quite different from a nunnery. Women who can reach Level Four are taught additional arts."

"Like Seeking?"

Vactor nodded. "Most of the Emperor's scouts are female."

Pol wondered, not for the first time, if his mother had had any power. If Queen Molissa had, she hid it very well.

"Coram might have used a magnetic shield. Rather than hardened air, it relies on shifting the pattern of magnetism. You know what a magnet is?"

"Of course I do. I've studied basic navigation. Magnetism gives a ship direction."

"An indication of direction," Vactor said. "There are traces of magnetism all around us. That is the pattern. The tweak is drawing magnetism around you as a cloak. That is the shield for knives and arrows."

"Is it one-sided?"

"What?" Vactor said.

"King Colvin's father died because the Court Magician at the time set a shield facing one direction, and the enemy flanked the position."

"Oh. He might not have created a cloak, but a shield-shape. It depends on how you visualize your tweak," Vactor said. "What could penetrate a magnetic shield?"

Pol considered the question. "An arrow without a metal arrowhead? A glass knife?"

"Right and anything with sufficient force. I would guess that Coram used a magnetic shield, and your knife powered its way through, like a sword would. The deflection was a natural outcome of the formation of Coram's shield. Remember, every shield has a weakness. We can study shields after the next break."

~ ~ ~

Chapter Sixteen

THE BEST DEFENSE AGAINST RETURNING TO THE MELANCHOLIA that had afflicted him was focusing on his work. The herbs grew, and after they sprouted their second sets of leaves, the monks were able to help Pol identify what he had planted.

He had to laugh at his selection of herbs. Kell had moved his own planter box over next to his, and they worked on learning the herbs together.

As the monks taught them about the efficacy of various herbs, Pol wondered about Searl. One day they were drawing various plants for an herbal portfolio. He took a healer aside and asked him.

"Oh, you heard about Searl? A tragedy. He became addicted to minweed after a severe shoulder sprain. You should never try to treat yourself unless there is no one else to do it. Even Searl couldn't use his magic to take away the pain. It became so bad that the Abbot had to dismiss him. A few other monks occasionally get a short message from him. Searl probably wants to let people know that he is still alive."

"Could you let me know who they are?"

The monk nodded. "I'll ask them."

"What exactly is minweed?"

"Oh, it looks like mint, but the leaves are blue-green. Pounded and mixed with water, it doesn't take pain away as much as masks it in a dreamlike hallucination. It can be very addicting to some. It was to Searl."

It sounded like the opposite of melancholia, Pol thought. "Let me know. I might want to write to him."

"Why?"

"I have a heart condition, and I've been told that Searl might be the only one who can fix it."

The monk nodded his head. "So that is why you looked undersized for fifteen. I'll see what I can do."

Pol went back to drawing herbs and frowned. Pol looked at Kell's work and decided that Pol would never be able to make a living as an artist. After a while a familiar healer monk tapped him on the shoulder.

"Come with me."

Pol put his work on the table upside down and followed the monk to a small office.

"You asked about Searl?"

Pol nodded. "From what I can tell he's the only healer capable of fixing my heart. You've given me treatments before, haven't you?"

"It's time for another one, actually," the monk said. "Why don't you try to find him during the harvest break? In fact, I would imagine that the Abbot might give you the summer to find Searl. He refuses to see any of us, but a young man in need might be more persuasive." The monk's face turned into a frown before he recovered his smile.

"Why don't you just write him?"

The monk pulled a ragged piece of folded paper and handed it over to Pol. "Read."

Pol looked at the scribbles. He could hardly discern any of the words. "He wrote this under the influence of minweed?"

"No. He wrote this when he wasn't hallucinating. His mental state must be deteriorating. We would like him brought back to us to see if he's worth saving. He was a great teacher until he wrecked his shoulder and became an addict. Minweed isn't the worse addictive substance known to man, but it can still become a nasty habit that is reluctant to let go."

"If he wants help," Pol said. His hope of a quick recovery might not be so simple as locating Searl. Pol shrugged off negative feelings.

He vowed he would not sink into melancholia again. "I will find him, if I can take some friends along."

"Speak to the Abbot. He'll do what he can." The monk stood up. "How about a treatment right now?"

"Not yet, I have things to do. I'll come back in a few days."

~

"So you'd like permission to find Searl this summer?" the Abbot said.

Pol sat in the Abbot's office. The last time, Hopken had tried to steal Demeron from him, and that still made Pol a bit uncomfortable.

"I do. I will need some people to come with me. I was thinking of Paki and Darrol. It's best not to traipse into unknown lands by myself."

"I agree. Maybe you can think of another traveler, but I will give you my permission and will even fund your trip. The healers tell me that Searl likely needs some help, and I would do nearly anything to get him back into Deftnis transferring his unique skills."

"What makes him so unique?"

"He can reconstruct things rather than repair." The Abbot shrugged his shoulders. "I didn't deal with him as intimately as others. You might want to prepare for your trip by doing a little Seeking work before you go."

Pol smiled, buoyed up by the Abbot's encouragement. "I will. Thank you, Abbot. I'll talk to Jonness to get some pointers on doing that."

The Abbot stood and offered his hand to Pol.

"We were all worried about you for awhile," the Abbot said. "You're not the first to succumb to the pressures at Deftnis, nor will you be the last."

Pol grinned. "Thank you again." He bowed and shook the Abbot's hand and then left feeling better about everything.

~

"Get a profile of your target," Jonness said. "Learn what you can of him."

"You mean get as complete a pattern as possible, to increase my chances of locating him?"

The master nodded. "You've done it before. We use the same

techniques over and over again. It doesn't get boring because everyone's pattern is different. When were you planning to go?"

"Summer. Is there a break of some kind?"

Jonness nodded. "There is a change in instruction that starts the first Oneday after Summer and lasts until Harvest Break. If you want to find him quickly, the first Oneday of Summer would be best. Who is going with you?"

"Paki, Darrol, and maybe someone else."

"I wish I could part with one of my assistants, but that's not possible. One of them will be spending time in Mancus with his firstborn child, due about the same time. What about Kell? He's smart enough to help and could use the experience." Jonness chuckled. "Once Darrol knows about the trip, he will be thinking about it every waking hour."

"Kell. I hadn't thought of him. My impressions of Kell have changed a bit. I'll ask him."

Jonness nodded, and they continued to talk about possible monks that he knew were friendly with Searl before he left.

Pol arranged to skip his herb class for the treatment the healer had offered at the infirmary. The day was bright and filled with promise. He lay down on an examination table after removing his robe.

The Master Healer stood with the monk who knew Searl at his side. He started examining Pol's limbs, gradually moving to his trunk. He had been through this a number of times and just relaxed.

"What's this?" the Master Healer said.

Pol didn't like the concerned tone of his voice.

"Our work is breaking down," the other monk said.

"What's wrong?" Pol said.

"The strengthening that we did to your heart is showing signs of deterioration."

Pol made a fist and brought it up so he could see it. "I don't feel weaker." However, he remembered the utter exhaustion he had felt after fighting Coram.

"You will after a while," the Master Healer said. "I wouldn't be too concerned at this point."

He sounded too worried to give Pol any comfort.

"Maybe I shouldn't wait for summer to find Searl."

"Perhaps you shouldn't," the Master Healer said.

Pol jumped off the table. "I'll talk to the Abbot."

The shock of reverting back to the puny, weak, body he had had before he arrived at Deftnis nearly sent Pol back into a fit of melancholia, but he had a plan. He would find Searl, and he would do what he could to purge the monk's habit long enough to get healed.

The Abbot was just walking out of the administration building, so Pol caught him by his sleeve.

"Sir, my body is rejecting the monks' treatments. I have to find Searl as quickly as I can," Pol said.

"Is that right?" The Abbot looked concerned. "Get your companions together and see me tomorrow morning when you are all ready."

Pol ran towards the armory. Paki was there with Darrol. He explained his situation, and they thought they could be ready to go by dawn.

"Talk to anyone who knew Searl. We will need to find him," Pol said.

He walked back to the infirmary and found Kell. "I am leaving the monastery for awhile to find Searl, a master healer. Do you want to come with me? I don't know how much of an adventure it will be, but I'm sure we will do some Seeking."

Kell looked as if he had just been released from jail. "Anything to get away from all of these herbs. Count me in," Kell said.

"What did you say?" one of the tutors said. "You are going to find Searl?"

Pol nodded. "Do you know where he is?"

"Not exactly, but I know where minweed grows best, and that's on the north slope of the Wild Spines. I'd bet anything that Searl has a hut up there."

That was the best lead Pol could hope for. He knew where the Wild Spines were, but they stretched across The Dukedoms from east to west. "Do you have a map?"

The monk shrugged. "Not really, but that should narrow his location down to the north dukedoms."

"It does, thank you."

"Get prepared," Pol said. "I'm going to see Jonness."

Pol began to get a little winded from his running around on the monastery grounds, and that concerned him. He found Jonness reading letters in his office.

"Do you have any maps of the Wild Spines? A monk told me that minweed grows best on the northern side."

Jonness frowned and raised his eyebrows. "I didn't know that."

He rose and went to an open chest. Pol could see the tops of rolled up maps. Jonness pulls out two.

"This is a good map of the major northern road of The Dukedoms." He laid it out. There were cities, towns, and villages linked with lines, along with some topographical indications. "The Wild Spines go from here to here. It ends at the dukedom of Hardman and continues as another, lower range of hills splitting Listya and Daftine." He used his finger to trace the extent of the mountain range. "It's not easy going, and you'll have to watch out for bandits and unfriendly villagers. Some of the inhabitants are pretty remote. I imagine Searl will be one of them, if he's still alive."

"So the northern slope isn't as rugged?" Pol said, looking at the drawn-in hills.

"Not from this map, but this document might not be accurate." Jonness unrolled the second map, a longer document than The Dukedom map. "This map is only of the Wild Spines. I can't speak for its accuracy either, but it might be of some value. If you don't mind, feel free to mark up this map if you find anything of interest or any glaring mistakes. I expect you to return it to me."

Jonness rolled both maps together, and then pulled out a thin leather sheet that became a map case when rolled around the outside. He put out his hand.

"Good luck," Jonness said. "I thought you were waiting for summer."

"My health isn't responding to treatments, and I want to get better, quicker."

Jonness grunted. "That's a different attitude than a while ago."

"We are leaving early tomorrow," Pol said. "Thank you!"

Pol began to assemble his few possessions. He took out his

mother's jewels and hid a few small pieces that had no sentimental value on him before he took the rest of the Listyan jewels to the Abbot's office for safekeeping while he was gone. He scribbled on a piece of paper and handed it to one of the Abbot's clerks.

"This goes to Malden Gastoria if you don't return?" the clerk said.

Pol nodded. "It does. He'll know best how to use it, or his girlfriend will."

Armed with maps and a direction, Pol found his three companions, and they ate as much as they could at dinnertime while planning their first few days.

The Abbot came out of the administration building with Vactor when the four loaded horses were brought to the main courtyard.

"Please bring back Searl. It was a mistake to let him go," the Abbot said. "You have supplies, and here is a purse."

Pol accepted it and handed it to Darrol. "You guard our money," Pol said. "Is that all right?"

Darrol grinned. "It is, My Prince."

Pol winced at his old title, but Darrol just chuckled.

"Make sure you remember to observe patterns in as much of your surroundings as possible," Vactor said. "We will all be waiting for you to return."

"We'll be anxious to get back to Deftnis," Pol said.

Kell and Paki looked excited. Pol felt good about taking his destiny in his hands. He had waited long enough. He knew he could still die young like his father had, but Pol felt like he was in a race to save himself from the curse of his ancestors.

They mounted, and without further ceremony, the four of them headed out the Deftnis gates towards the port below. Pol looked out at the rolling ocean. Val wasn't with them to put Pol under for the trip. He only hoped he hadn't made a mistake by eating a hearty breakfast.

Chapter Seventeen

"I FEEL LIKE A FATHER," Darrol said. "The last time we traveled together Valiso Gasibli balanced out the group." He looked at Kell. "Although Kell is too old to be a son of mine, both of you two could be."

They all shared a table in a modest inn situated in the middle of a village that huddled against the edges of the road north to Palleton, the capital of the Dukedom of Sand. The road from Mancus to the mountains led them right through the capital city.

The food seemed acceptable to Darrol and Paki, but Pol could taste meat that was aged a bit too long, and Kell had refused to eat anything but bread and a few apples that had seen fresher days. They all ate their fill after losing their breakfasts on the voyage across the strait between the Isle of Deftnis and Mancus.

Paki laughed. "What restrictions are you going to put on us?"

"Not too much drinking, because we will be getting up early. I want to be able to get to the northern side of the Wild Spines in a week."

Pol pulled out the map. "See how the mountain range separates The Dukedoms? There is a reason for that, and it's because there aren't a lot of passes through the mountains. I read that they aren't tall mountains, but they are steep and treacherous."

Darrol bent over to trace a path. "We can take the Palleton road further north to get out of the dukedom of Sand, and then slip into

Terrifin to work our way westward on the north side."

"It will be slower going if we have to hug the mountains," Pol said. "I guess we better appreciate the inns while we can. I doubt if Searl lives in a village. It could take us weeks to find him, but find him we must."

Paki looked sideways at Pol. "You are sure he's alive?"

Pol nodded. "The last nearly unintelligible letter arrived after Winter's Day. It's a matter of finding him, but if he's a minweed addict, we probably just have to find where the best minweed grows. That's the pattern I'm going to follow."

~

Palleton was a bit of a disappointment. It was less than a quarter the size of Borstall, and actually not much bigger than Mancus if it had had a wall built around it. There were few admirable buildings in the town. If the dukedom of Sand had a distinctive architecture, Pol couldn't detect it.

They rode on through after they realized that they could get a couple more hours of travel time in. Darrol proclaimed the local produce not worth buying.

Pol spent the next two hours talking to Demeron, who had been silent through much of the first two days. When he became more talkative, Pol learned that Demeron had taken a while to recover from their rough crossing from Deftnis Isle. He had never thought of horses being under the weather before.

They were between villages and stopped well before night fell. The night was mild, so they decided to camp by a large pond in the midst of a small forest. Pol and Paki put out snares to see if they could catch some rabbits for breakfast.

Darrol brought out a packet of ham and vegetables, while Kell found the stream that fed the pond where he filled up water skins.

"We let it boil for awhile. You just can't trust the water unless it comes directly from a spring," Darrol said to Kell, just when Pol returned.

Pol found a big log, which enabled him to stand tall enough to more easily pull off Demeron's saddle.

You don't have to hobble the other horses. I'll keep them together at night.

"Okay, Demeron," Pol said.

"What did the horse say?" Kell asked.

"We won't have to secure the horses. Demeron will see that they are all here tomorrow," Pol said.

Darrol watched the pot boil. The three youths sat around an existing fire ring. The lake had obviously been a popular spot.

"We still keep watch," Darrol said. "Sand may be civilized, but bandits infest every country in the Baccusol Empire. I should know."

Paki sat down. "Do you have any juicy stories?"

"I do. You're just getting started moving about the countryside. You can always talk about how Valiso Gasibli saved you from an ambush in the midst of a battle, and then there was the time when we sneaked up on the pea shooter's assassins. Pol has even more."

"What's this ambush all about?" Kell said.

Paki puffed his chest up and recounted the trip Pol and he made north from Borstall to the Taridan border and the attack that Kolli, Pol's temporary bodyguard, Paki, and Pol had fought off and how Val finished it.

Pol had to wince at the embellishments. It looked like Kell didn't believe all of it, either.

"Darrol? What caused you to leave Deftnis?" Kell said.

An awkward silence came over the camp. Darrol threw the meat in to soak in the steaming pot.

"It's a sensitive subject," Pol said.

Darrol laughed. "Not that sensitive. My magic wasn't progressing, since I'm a Level Two and no higher. I made it to the green level in swordsmanship and would need to use more magic to progress since my sword work is good, but not great."

"Stuck in a rut?" Paki said.

Darrol smiled. "So I began to drink and carouse in Mancus more than I should have. One time, when I couldn't think straight, I found a willing woman. We dallied." Darrol sighed. "Her husband found us. It was awkward. He wanted to fight, but neither of us had swords, so we used our fists." Darrol shook his head. "I was drunk, and he was untrained. I killed him."

"You what?" Kell said.

Darrol raised his hand. "It was a fair fight. There were witnesses aplenty. Deftnis became a place tied to that ugly memory, so I left. I don't have any appetite for war, so I bounced around as a guard in enough places until I landed in Borstall."

Pol scratched his head. "But you returned to the monastery."

"The woman in question left Deftnis and went to live with her parents in Finster. I don't know what happened to her after that. Without her around, I didn't mind returning. I just hadn't had a reason. Now I do."

"Which is?" Kell asked.

"Pol saved my life. I pledged right there to be his man," Darrol said and shrugged. "When Pol leaves Deftnis, I suppose I will leave, too."

"Darrol is my one-man-army," Pol said.

Paki looked injured. "Hey, what about me?"

"You are my scouting force." Pol laughed at the thought.

Kell was silent for a while. "It's good to have true friends, I guess."

"You seem to have enough friends," Paki said.

"True friends are different from acquaintances. There is a big difference. I was upset when I first got here, and my anger drew me to acolytes who were mad like me, but they didn't share my reasons. We've pretty much gone different ways," Kell said.

Kell's words rang true. He had sensed Kell softening up, from how he had originally perceived him, but now he knew why. Kell was forced into the monastery, and the surliness he showed to Pol hadn't been really aimed at him, but a reaction to his dissatisfaction.

"Is Deftnis more palatable?"

Kell nodded. "I didn't think I had any magical talent, but the monks discovered that I have a bit."

"About like me," Paki said.

"Maybe more than you," Kell said. That brought laughter from Pol and Darrol. "I may end up like Darrol, qualified enough to be better than most in the world, but not at Deftnis," Kell said. "I'm fine with that, if I can learn a bit of healing and become good enough to be a Seeker."

"You don't need magic to work with patterns, only a good mind,"

Pol said. "Malden Gastoria always reminded me that magicians work with the patterns around them, but don't tweak them as much as others think. I have seen proof of that. We didn't need to tweak to find the flag, remember?"

Kell shook his head with a rueful grin on his face. "We needed to tweak the flag into your hands, if you recall."

Pol had to agree. "But we still solved our problem together." Pol looked at Darrol. "Are there Seeker teams? There has to be. I saw teamwork in action when we found the monastery thieves. Val had just worked with a younger seeker on Volia when I first met him."

Darrol shrugged. "That's a question better asked of Ranno Wissingbel or Val. It seems logical. You went out with Val a few times in Borstall, I heard."

"You heard right," Paki said. "Don't worry, Kell. Seekers don't always work alone."

That reminded Pol to use his locator skills when he was on watch.

Dinner was pretty dismal. It seemed that Darrol didn't bring much in the way of herbs and had woefully underestimated the amount of salt he should have packed. He vowed to buy some in the next village, but that didn't help the stew he had made.

Paki volunteered to take the first watch. Pol checked on Demeron, who scolded Pol for waking him up. Pol fell asleep only to be nudged awake by Paki.

"It's your turn."

Pol looked around the camp. Paki had kept the fire burning, but that would only ruin a watchman's night vision. He remembered Paki's father teaching them that in Borstall.

He looked out with his locator sense after he spread the fire a bit to stop the flames. He put his hand over the glowing coals and reached out with his locator sense. To his surprise he found six dots converging on them from different directions.

Pol tried to remain calm. He took a few deep breaths and rose to his feet and nudged Darrol.

"Visitors. Six coming from different directions except the lake."

"What?" Darrol rose up on his elbow. "Oh," he said in a quieter voice, while he put his boots on and slid his sheath from his baldric and quietly removed his sword. "You wake Paki, and I'll tell Kell.

Before Pol could get to Paki, the brigands attacked. Kell stood with his sword in his hand, in bare feet, while Paki was rising. Pol hadn't taken his boots off after his watch.

Pol stopped one brigand from attacking Paki, but two more faced him. A black shape rose from the darkness. Pol's stomach turned as the huge form slowly walked behind his opponents.

Demeron neighed and reared up, striking one man while Paki took care of the other. The stallion ran towards Darrol, confronted by two other men, and took care of them both, prompting Darrol to just back up out of the way. He turned to help Kell, trading sword blows with the last of the bandits.

Demeron paced up to Pol and bent his head down. *Are you all right?*

Pol nodded. "You didn't give me a chance to get into the fight."

The horse shook his head. *As intended. I've got to get back to my tiny herd or they might run away.*

Pol watched Demeron leave. He realized that his army was significantly larger than one.

"Devil horse," Kell said, breathing heavily, but then he smiled. "I like it when the devil is on my side."

Darrol grunted. "I do, too. Let's see if they're all dead."

Pol woke up as the light of dawn began to color the tops of the trees. He shivered under his blanket and walked over to the fire that Darrol had already begun coaxing back to life with a bit of magic.

"At least I can do this," Darrol said as the fire sprang back to life. "Let's go look at the brigands."

Darrol led Pol into the wood where the bodies of six bandits lay lined up in a row. Pol had seen death too many times in his young life to be overly affected by the dead bodies of men who had just sought to kill him.

"What do your Seeker skills tell you?" Darrol said.

"These were in their pockets?" Pol said, pointing to piles of possessions at the foot of each body.

"They were. I did that right after I dragged them here. It was a little easier to get them out then than now."

Pol nudged a stiff body with his foot and understood what Darrol meant. They were all a bit stiff.

"Anything about how these thieves are dressed?" Pol asked. He wouldn't be able to know what was normal or not. They all looked pretty much alike to him.

Darrol got down on his haunches and fingered their clothes, and then he shook his head.

Pol knelt down and began to go through the men's possessions. Some of the things were bloody, but Pol took a deep breath and sought out pieces that might be part of a pattern.

"Their weapons aren't of a high quality, so they might be hired swords," Pol said pulling a knife from a sheath. The money mostly came from Sand. "Maybe something is hidden in their boots."

Both of them began the grisly task of pulling off old shoes. There were two small knives, of the same mediocre quality, but there was a little, thick leather pouch wrapped in a piece of paper.

"What's this?" Darrol said, unwrapping the paper. He looked it over and gave it to Pol.

"Undersized fifteen-year-old with very light hair riding a large black stallion out from Deftnis," Pol said and gave the message back to Darrol. "These weren't brigands."

Kell made a disagreeable sound. "Shouldn't we bury them? I don't like dead people."

"You can get started," Darrol said. "There is a small shovel with my saddlebags."

"I have one, too," Paki said, scratching his head and yawning. "Find anything?"

"Assassins," Pol said. "You can thank Demeron that none of us were hurt last night. You two get the hole dug. We'll bury them all together. Darrol and I will find their horses. I don't want to leave them tied up forever." He looked over at Darrol. "If it's all right with you."

Darrol raised his hand. "You are doing fine, My acolyte." He grinned. "What's in the pouch?"

Pol knew before he even opened it, but he looked anyway. Six South Salvan Lions fell into his palm. "They really don't like me." Pol said. He tucked them back into the leather bag and gave it to Darrol. "For our travel fund."

"You keep them," Darrol said. "They were after you."

Pol examined all the other possessions and found nothing of consequence. The purses of the other men would be taken and split between Paki and Kell. The money wouldn't do the dead men any good, and they had no desire to find the bandits' relatives. Darrol thought it would be a good idea to take the weapons to the next village.

Demeron herded nine horses on the other side of the little lake. Pol called out. "Bring them over here." He hoped the Shinkyan stallion had heard him.

By the time the thieves were dragged into their shallow graves, Demeron brought the other horses into the camp.

"Can you talk to them?"

Horses don't talk, Demeron said.

Pol looked at his horse with narrowed eyes. "I think you do."

I'm not an ordinary horse. We have other ways of communicating, mostly gestures. They gladly followed me after I untied them. Demeron shook his head.

The four of them went through the saddlebags of the thieves and found little else of interest.

Darrol passed out stale bread that he had purchased from a street vendor in Palleton. Darrol split the six horses into strings of three. Kell and he led them as they left the clearing and got back up on the road that led north.

It took another two hours to reach the next village. Darrol insisted that Pol wear his hat. The fewer people that noticed his silvery hair, the better.

Along the way Pol wondered if he would ever get rid of assassins and the constant attacks. He had already removed himself from the lines of succession to Listya and North Salvan. What more could his enemies possibly want? Demeron? Pol didn't think he could ever give up the horse that had become such a good friend.

"Where is the law around here?" Darrol asked a shopkeeper sweeping the wooden porch in front of his brick store. Most of the other buildings along the street were made out of rough-cut stone.

"The Duke has a guard office two lanes up and to your right. What happened?"

"Brigands, but we took care of them. They won't be bothering any of you."

"Sand is a safe place. You say they are all dead?"

Pol nodded. "They are." He nodded to Darrol, and they left the shopkeeper staring at them as they passed.

Darrol dismounted his horse. "You can come in with me if you want, but it's better that you don't say anything. We aren't from Deftnis, right?"

Pol could see Darrol's point if there were others after him. He nodded. He followed Darrol into the guard building. The stone was cut much finer than any in the town, but the furniture looked rather worn and shabby. A bearded guard looked up from reading something on his desk.

"Can I help you?" The guard didn't seem very pleased to see someone upset his work from the tone of his voice.

"We came across six bandits in the wood a few hours to the south. We brought their weapons and their horses."

The guard looked out the door. "Where are the criminals?"

"They are dead."

The guard grunted and walked out to look at the horses. "The horses and saddles aren't worth much. I guess you buried the bodies?"

Darrol nodded. "I've never been along this road before, and we didn't want to ride hours with dead bodies strapped to the saddles. Their weapons are tied to their—"

"I can see. What do you want me to do? There's not much to investigate."

"Just find a home for the animals."

The guard checked the horse's mouths and hoofs. He grunted again. "They haven't been mistreated. I'll pay you ten Sand shillings for each."

Darrol pursed his lips. "A good horse and saddle would fetch a pound in the south."

"Is that where you're from?"

"Mancus," Kell said.

The guard looked at the four of them. "If you didn't have the two boys, I'd guess you were Deftnis monks. Mancus, eh?" He patted Demeron on the rump. "This guy is worth all of your horses together."

"And then some," Pol said. "He is a gift from a noble."

"A king, most likely." The guard eyed Demeron again.

"Five pounds, since up north we don't value horses so dearly."

Darrol nodded. "Done. We'll be on our way as soon as we pick up some supplies."

"Where are you headed? I am asking as a representative of the Duke."

"To the other side of the Wild Spines," Pol said.

Darrol cleared his throat. "We are on our way to Yastan."

The guard squinted his eyes. "Why are you headed to Yastan, lad?"

"We are going to see my uncle."

"Name?"

"Ranno Wissingbel. Heard of him?"

The guard's eyes widened. "The Emperor's Instrument? I daresay I have," the guard said. His attitude improved instantly. "You be on your way. I'll be back out with your money."

The guard counted out the five gold pound coins to Darrol. "Watch out. If you think six bandits are bad, the Spine crawls with them. Be warned, My Duke doesn't bother to exert his influence much past the foothills."

~ ~ ~

Chapter Eighteen

~

MUCH RICHER, THE FOUR RIDERS SPENT THE NEXT NIGHT in a village a bit smaller than the town where they had sold the horses.

Darrol came into Pol and Kell's room with a sack of supplies. He pulled out a packet. "Hair dye. It's generally for the ladies, but we need to darken your hair if we aren't to be noticed all the way to Searl, wherever he is."

"What about Demeron?"

Darrol shrugged. "A good magician can change a horse's color but…"

Pol didn't want to try something like that on Demeron without practicing. He submitted to the instructions cribbed on to the packet by the salesperson. They ruined one of the inn's towels, but Pol had to admit he looked different. He tried to arrange his hair in front of the tiny discolored mirror above the washbasin in the room, but it was so straight that it didn't want to cooperate.

The four of them walked into the common room of the inn. Paki kept giggling and poking at Pol. He ruffled Pol's hair once. At least Pol didn't share his room with Paki, who might be sniggering at him all night.

The food was the best of the trip so far. Darrol brought out the map of the Wild Spines.

"The foothills are here, and then we head into the Spines. There are villages along the way except for this stretch over the pass."

"We should be able to move from village to village in less than half a day," Kell said. "If there are criminals in the mountains, we won't want to stay out in the open."

Darrol nodded. "The guard gave us good advice on that, I'm sure. If there are bands roving the Spines we won't be fending off five or six, but we could face twenty or more."

The innkeeper walked up to them with another round of drinks. "Heading north, I see."

"We are," Paki said.

"Merchants generally form trains from Rocky Ridge, right here." He pointed to a town just before the foothills turned to mountains. "You'd have to pay some money to join them, but if you're good with weapons, you can probably get the fee reduced. That's what I recommend."

"That's what we'll do," Darrol said. "Thanks for the tip."

The man nodded in acknowledgement. "I don't get much repeat business from those that wind up dead in the Spines."

~

Pol never did like wearing hats, so he gladly let his brown hair tousle in the breeze. Two main roads joined theirs from the east and from the west as the traffic increased, heading towards one of the few passes up over the Wild Spines.

They arrived at Rocky Ridge no worse for wear. Demeron had appreciated stopping at inns as long as Pol had paid extra for feed grain rather than hay. The citizens of Rocky Ridge had decorated the town with green and yellow bunting.

There were three inns in the town, and they didn't find rooms until they reached the third one on the north side of town.

"What's the occasion?" Paki said, "A festival?"

"Summer's Come. It's the second best one of the year," the innkeeper said. She was an older woman. She looked severe, but Pol noticed the smile lines at the sides of her eyes. "Hinkeyites settled Rocky Ridge four hundred years ago. Their calendar—"

"Is a little strange," Pol said. "Even though it's mid-spring, this is the first day of Summer for them. They do the same thing for winter and their new year is a month and a half earlier than the rest of the Baccusol Empire. They followed the prophet Hinkey, who prophesied that the sun would turn blue at the end of the world."

"How did you know that, young man?" the innkeeper asked, her mouth open.

"I've made a study of most of the world's religions. I thought the Hinkeyites lived in Daftine?"

"Most of them are there, but there are sprinkles of them all along the southern slope of the Spines," the woman said. "Marvelous. You are one of the few who know us."

Pol bit his tongue. He was about to say something rude, but didn't. He saw a pattern in keeping his mouth shut to avoid embarrassment. Malden had told him about something to the same effect in Borstall, but Mistress Farthia would be pleased he remembered a bit of all the studying he had done with the big religion text that was his academic focus the previous summer.

"Does the whole town celebrate?" Darrol said.

The woman grinned. "And visitors are welcome. It's a celebration. Put off your travels for at least a day and enjoy Rocky Ridge."

Darrol looked at Pol, who shrugged.

"I don't think a day's rest will hurt us," Pol said. He looked at Kell and Paki, who was already bobbing his head up and down with encouragement.

"I'm all for it," Paki said, eyes gleaming.

Kell didn't look excited. "I suppose it wouldn't be an awful thing to do," he said. "If everyone else wants to, I'll go along."

"It's settled then. Two nights," Darrol said.

"With grain for our horses," Pol said.

The innkeeper's eyes flashed. "I can do that. Enjoy yourselves. The festival grounds are on the west side of town, in walking distance. I suggest you eat your evening meal there, while strolling around."

Darrol paid the woman, and they lugged their possessions up the stairs. Pol insisted on sharing his room with Darrol. All four of them joined others in the town walking west where Pol could already hear the sounds of music and cheers from the festival grounds.

"What else do the Hinkeyites do?" Darrol asked.

"They believe in three gods, one for good, one for evil and one for life, but other than that they have local pastors, rather than a hierarchical priesthood. No one has any idea when Hinkey's prophecies are supposed to come true." Pol thought for a bit. He tried not to get his religions mixed up. "They are very moral with strong families, and honesty is a prized practice. Except for…"

"Except for what?" Kell said.

"I think I read that they are purported to let their morals loosen a bit during the Summer and Winter festivals."

Paki whooped. "That's even better! Let's go see what loosened morals look like."

The light became brighter as they approached the festival grounds. This was nothing like the festival the King put on when the Emperor visited Borstall the previous summer. Pol didn't see any children, and not even many youths Paki's and his age.

Couples and groups of unattached people roamed past stalls selling clothing and trinkets. People were kissing in public and being uncomfortably intimate. His companions' eyes grew as they walked through the crowds.

A bandstand played instruments that were similar but still different from what Pol was used to at Castle Borstall. Locals danced on the large wooden floor that had been built over the leveled dirt of the field. The riotous behavior continued while the couples danced.

Pol could feel his face heat up with embarrassment. He looked at Paki, whose eyes just increased in size. Paki left them and found a youngish girl clapping to the tune, standing with what must have been her friends, and he took her out on the floor. His friend merged with the rest of the dancers.

Kell looked inside a gambling tent. He emptied out half of his purse in Darrol's hands. "I really like to wager," he said, "but take this so I don't lose it all." He rushed inside to play games of chance.

"What do you want to do, Darrol?"

"This is a little too much for me. Let's get some of the local flavor in our stomachs and head back to the inn. Kell and Paki can fend for themselves."

That sounded good to Pol, who turned down a lane of stalls that seemed to sell food. Soon Darrol and he were eating roasted turkey legs. Pol had never seen such a large drumstick. Even the cooks at Deftnis would have sliced the meat off the legs. He found a fruit juice stand, but soon realized that the juice was fortified with alcohol, so he turned away. He had no idea how strong it was & what effect it might have on him, besides, he had never understand the allure of pleasure to be found in dulled senses. Being alert & on guard had kept him alive. He & Darrol walked along the stalls one more time, then turned back to the dance floor, but could not see Paki anywhere. "The town isn't that big. He'll find his way back to the Inn," Darrol said indistinctly. Pol surmised that the tankard of ale and juice his friend had downed on an empty stomach were beginning to have an effect. "Let's head back to the inn", Pol suggested."Paki can take care of himself." By the time they made it back the inn, Darrol was noticeably unsteady on his feet & Pol had a bit of a struggle getting his larger friend up the stairs and back to their room. Depositing an extremely groggy Darrol on the bed, Pol shook his head in wonder. It had taken less than an hour for their party to separate and for Darrol to become incapacitated. How easy it was to succumb to the enticement of pleasure and how ironically tiring an evening of leisure turned out to be. Pol pulled the bar across the door to secure it and rolled contentedly into his own bed, hoping that Darrol's snoring wouldn't keep him awake. A shaft of light shone across Pol's face, causing him to stir. Though Darrol still snored, Pol had managed to sleep throughout the night. Rising & dressing quickly in the chilled morning air, Pol wondered if Paki had made it back to the inn or had spent the night burrowed into a hay pile in some barn. Curiosity got the best of him so he quietly left his room, went into the hall and tried the latch on Paki's door. It was unlocked. Silently he opened the door and stepped in. Kell's bed had not been slept in.

Paki lay sprawled fully clothed and still wearing his boots across his bed. Pol smelled that Paki had indulged too much before he saw the trail of it from the door to Paki's bed. Paki always enjoyed his pleasure to the fullest even though it almost always resulted in a mess of some sort. The spiked fruit juice must have been very potent Pol thought, suddenly glad that he had passed on it. Not wanting to risk crossing the filth coated floor, Pol hailed his friend from the doorway. "Paki!" A groaning Paki lifted an eyelid slowly and replied, "not now Pol, I'm not in the mood for morning."

"Mood for it or not, it has come. It seems you had a good time like Hinkeyite last night." Pol scoffed. "Do you even remember any of it though!?" "Alcohol and smoked something that made my head spin, might have been minweed. I don't even remember how I got back here. You should have seen the things people were doing last night, they're crazy !" Paki exclaimed. "You need a bath my friend, and you need to clean up this mess. Don't even think about leaving it for the poor inn keeper's daughter!" Pol chastised. As fond as he was of Paki, Pol found himself a little disappointed in his friend's choices and actions. As much as they had shared and as much as they were alike, they were just as much different, especially in the ways they enjoyed life's pleasures. While Paki began to get the room to rights, Darrol wandered into the room. Surveying it disgustedly he said "so I take it you had a good time last night?" "I think I did, I can't remember all of it but I have the impression of enjoying myself very much." "Where is Kell?" the former guard asked. Paki's eyebrows went up. "Isn't he with you? I thought perhaps he came in after I did but then got up early." "I haven't seen him", said Pol, shaking his head. "Perhaps he's downstairs breaking his fast." Paki half heartedly finished up cleaning the floor, & then the trio made their way to the tavern below. Not finding Kell, Pol ordered and ate a small meal quickly while his two friends avoided food altogether. Apparently last night's fun was this morning's woe. Soon they were heading out to the festival grounds, which looked more forlorn and much less festive. People were sleeping off their excess in stall corners here and there. An old man was cleaning up the inside of the wagering tent where they had last seen Kell enter. "We are looking for a blonde twenty year old man. A friend who didn't return to his room at the inn last night," Darrol announced. "His name is Kell Digbee." The toothless cleaner grimaced and spat a stream of brown liquid from the corner of his mouth."Don't know, no Kell." he said, shaking his head. "I just clean up here after they's all done." "Do you know who runs the tent?" Darrol inquired. The man chewed his gums together a minute before replying. "That'd be Clorence Noster. He runs *The Dainty lady*."

That sounded good to Pol, who turned down a lane of stalls that seemed to sell food. Soon Darrol and he were eating roasted turkey legs. Pol had never seen such a large drumstick. Even the cooks at Deftnis would have sliced the meat off of the legs.

He found a fruit juice stand, but soon realized that the juice was fortified with alcohol. They walked along the stalls one more time, returning to the dance floor, but this time Paki wasn't in sight.

"The town isn't that big. He'll find his way back to the inn," Darrol said. His voice was a little slurred from drinking a tankard of ale at a stall and finishing off most of Pol's juice.

Pol kept Darrol from staggering too badly as they reached the inn and made it into their room. There were only a few patrons sitting at tables in the inn, and their hostess was nowhere to be seen.

Darrol nearly fell into bed, and Pol sat on his for a bit to collect his wits. It took less than an hour for their party to separate, and that startled Pol. How easy it was for them to succumb to the enticement of such pleasure. Even he smiled at the thought of the huge drumstick, which he never did finish, before he finally went to sleep.

Pol lifted his eyes and sat up as the sun began to light up the thin curtains of their room. Darrol still snored, his back to Pol.

Pol rose and quickly dressed, wondering if Paki had made it back. He knocked on the door to their room and tried the latch. The door hadn't been locked. Pol could see that Kell's bed hadn't been slept in, but Paki seemed to have picked up a friend. Her hair fell on the outside part of the bed.

"Paki," Pol said quietly, tapping on his friend's shoulder. He leaned over a healthy-looking girl, dressed only in an under-shift. He now noticed their clothing strewn about the room.

"What?" Paki's eyes were red and took a bit to focus. They grew when he noticed he shared the mattress. He sat up.

The girl woke up. Her eyebrows rose with alarm.

Would she scream? Pol thought.

She jumped out of bed. Pol didn't get his eyes averted and he saw more of the girl than he had seen of any other while she slipped into her clothes. She bent over and kissed Paki on the lips. "Late for work," she said, winking at Pol on her way out.

Shocked, Pol sat on Kell's empty bed.

Paki held the covers to his bare chest. "I, uh..."

"You had a good time like a Hinkeyite, I suppose," Pol said.

"Alcohol and some kind of smoking drug. It might have even been minweed. I..." Paki shook his head. "These people are crazy."

"Did you..."

Paki nodded, not able to keep one side of his mouth from twitching up. "'Fraid so. My second time."

"I think you are supposed to take a bath after a time like this. I think my brothers did, Val told me, after I caught them with servants," Pol said. He tried to keep from getting upset, but he didn't know why he was upset...maybe more flustered. All he knew is that he wouldn't make a very good Hinkeyite at his age and with his physical condition.

Darrol walked in. "Did you have a good time, Paki?" The former guard grinned.

"I think I did. I can't remember all of it, but I seem to recall both of us did." Paki closed his eyes and smiled.

"Where's Kell?" Darrol asked.

Paki's eyebrows went up again. "Isn't he with you? I thought he might have slipped in, seeing that I was, uh, occupied, and then he went to your room."

Pol shook his head. "He's missing. Let's get something to eat if they are serving breakfast, and then go back to the waging tent."

The festival grounds looked a bit more forlorn in the morning. People were still sleeping in corners and out in the grassy field away from the stalls. An old man cleaned up the inside of the waging tent.

"We are looking for a blondish twenty-year-old. He didn't make it back to the inn last night," Darrol said.

The cleaner had lost all his teeth, and it looked like he had been chewing on bark or something when Pol walked up to him. "His name is Kell Digbee."

The man shook his head. "Don't know no Kell, no how. I just clean up here. Don't have no money for gambling anywho."

"Do you know who runs the tent? Who pays you to clean?"

The man moved his jaw a bit before speaking. "That be Clorence Noster. He runs *The Dainty Lady*."

"A pub?" Darrol asked.

"Partly," the man said, grinning, showing his gums.

Pol was already out of the tent. The three split up and made a quick tour of the festival grounds. No Kell.

"Let's get over to *The Dainty Lady* and hope they're open," Darrol said.

Pol didn't have a better idea, and after checking to make sure Kell's horse still stood in the stables, they asked directions and found the tavern near their inn.

Darrol led the two youths into the dark interior. The walls were painted to look like wallpaper. Too much red, Pol thought. A few women sat at a table eating breakfast. They must have been the other part of what made *The Dainty Lady* money. Pol was learning too much about life on his quest.

"Is Clorence Noster around?" Darrol asked one of the women. She had red-dyed hair and wore a simple cotton gown.

"Looking for a job? You look like you could handle a lot, sweetie. The boys are too young for guards and too old for…you know."

Pol quickly cleared his throat. Too much information, he thought.

"One of our party went missing from the gambling tent. We want to be on our way north."

"Did he have money?" one of the other women asked. "Bandits sometimes come and kidnap rich visitors. Once they wring all the money out of them, some of their victims are good for ransom bait."

"There are two or three victims each festival. The Duke of Sand's guard don't push much past Rocky Ridge, unless it is to protect the pass," the red-haired woman said.

"Where do they live, these bandits?" Darrol said.

"West into the Spines, of course. I think it's time you went on your way. Your friend is lost, unless you have more money than his kind do."

"I'd still like to see Clorence." Darrol looked at Pol and Paki, but Pol couldn't understand what his friend wanted them to know.

"Won't be back until tonight. You might want to spend a few coins in the gambling tent first. That would be the kindly thing to do."

"Thank you for your time, miss."

She giggled. "He called me miss." The women all laughed, rather coarsely in Pol's view.

Darrol led them outside into the cleaner morning air. "What do you think?"

Pol recalled what the woman had said and how she said it. "I think we find Clorence."

"Why?" Paki asked.

"Do you think the guard would let bandits just come in and take two or three visitors hostage every festival? I don't."

"Then we visit the guard." Darrol stopped a man passing by to get directions to the Duke's guard building, more towards the center of town.

The guard building was bigger than the last one they visited.

Darrol walked up to a man seated at a high desk in a lobby lined with chairs.

"What can I do for you?" This guard was no friendlier than the last one they visited.

"One of our party has gone missing," Darrol said.

"At the Festival? It happens." The guard didn't seem to be very alarmed by Kell's plight.

"I'd like to speak to your superior," Darrol said.

"He's unavailable right now." The guard waved Darrol away with his hand and looked down at his paperwork.

Pol couldn't believe a traveler would be treated so poorly by the Duke's guard. He spied a door that said Chief Guard, Dixtor Tildan on it. Another guard had just walked out of the Chief Guard's office.

"We need to see him now," Darrol said.

Pol walked over to the Chief's door and entered. "Are you the Chief Guard in Rocky Ridge?" he said to a man in a different uniform from the others.

"Who said you could enter?" Dixtor Tildan said.

"My friend is missing. He was gambling into the night and didn't return. He's not sleeping it off on the festival grounds, and we heard that bandits abduct rich gamblers for ransom."

"That's just a story to scare visitors," Tildan said.

Pol looked at the man. Tildan quickly developed a light sheen of sweat on his forehead and began to play with a penknife on his desk. That seemed to be a reaction to lying.

"I don't believe you."

The Chief Guard's eyes bulged. "You don't have to believe me, you sapling," he snapped.

Pol lifted the man up from his chair with his magic and put him down again. "I am a Fourth Level magician from Deftnis. My friend, indeed all of us, are on a mission for the monastery. We wanted to pass through here quietly and go on our way, but you are impeding our journey," Pol said, doing his best to imitate his stepfather, King Colvin. "Do you want another demonstration?" Pol leaned forward on the back of a sturdy chair in front of the Tildan's desk. His heart was beginning to pound. Any threats from here would be bluffs.

Darrol stormed in.

The Chief Guard looked at Darrol. "You are from Deftnis?"

Darrol pulled out the folded portfolio with the Abbot's note. "You can read. This will verify our mission." He tossed the folded parchment on the desk.

"Parchment, eh?" The man looked at Darrol with a trace of fear on his face. He unfolded the thick document and read. "I can't help you."

Pol could tell the man lied again. "Do you know Clorence Noster?"

"There are ten thousand people in Rocky Ridge right now. How could I know them all?"

"I would think you would be familiar with the owner of *The Dainty Lady* and the operator of the only gambling tent on the festival grounds," Darrol said, retrieving the Abbot's note.

The man put his finger around his collar. "Perhaps, I know him."

Pol was going to accuse him of being in league with Noster, but what little he had absorbed from the man's pattern, the man would only resist harder. The key was finding Clorence Noster, and the brothel owner would lead them to Kell.

Pol touched Darrol's elbow. "We must go," he said.

"It will go ill for you to get in our way," Darrol said.

Dixtor Tildan rose from his desk. "Are you threatening me?"

"No," Darrol said quietly. "I just want to remind you of your duty to the Duke of Sand." He turned and left with Pol. Paki stood at the doorway and followed them out.

"Brigands, my foot," Darrol said. "The biggest bandit sits behind that big desk."

"He was lying," Pol said.

"Of course he was. As soon as he didn't admit knowing Noster, that did it. He knows we are from Deftnis."

"I lifted him off his chair," Pol said.

Darrol grunted. "Good. He'll think we can all do that. Let's go talk to the innkeeper. I hope she's not in on this."

"What?" Paki said.

"Fleecing travelers." Darrol shook his head. "What lousy timing to come through here for some festival."

~ ~ ~

Chapter Nineteen

⁓

THE INNKEEPER SAT AT ONE OF HER COMMON ROOM TABLES, shuffling through bills, when the three of them sat at that same table. She gave them a big smile.

"Did you enjoy yourselves?"

"The big blond youth was abducted last night," Pol said. "His name is Kell, and we've already been to see the Chief Guard and have made a quick visit to *The Dainty Lady*.

The woman's smile disappeared. "You quickly found the rotten underbelly of Rocky Ridge. Clorence Noster and Chief Tildan have not done Rocky Ridge any favors," she said.

"Do you know where we can find Noster?" Darrol pushed the Abbot's documentation towards the innkeeper.

She accepted it and unfolded the parchment. Her eyebrows rose. "Magicians?"

"All of us are, at one level or another," Darrol said. "We even have a pattern-master amongst us."

"The young man missing?"

"I'd rather not say," Darrol said, his face calm.

"Modesty. It suits you," she said, with a smile back on her face. "How can I help you?"

"Are they keeping Kell in town? Kell Digbee is our friend's name," Pol said.

"No." She shook her head. "Never in town. They do this a few times a year, you know."

"We do," Darrol said.

She nodded. "I only know of rumors, but further west and then north into the Spines, Noster funds a band of brigands. Perhaps you can follow him. It has to be less than half a day away, because he can disappear in the mornings and return to host the activities at his brothel." She raised her hands. "Don't tell anyone I said a thing. I still have to live in this town. It's my home."

"We won't. Chief Tildan already knows we are Deftnis monks, so we'll get our horses and be heading out. Hopefully we'll be back tonight, but we won't be going to the festival, you understand."

She nodded and watched them leave the common room. Pol looked back to see her face. She still looked concerned, and Pol interpreted that as a good sign that she spoke the truth.

How much easier it would be if he knew a truth spell. He wondered how often Val employed his. From his impression, Val didn't resort to using magic to uncover the truth unless there were no alternatives. Was there a reason? Perhaps truth spells were rude and looked down on.

They took all their possessions with them, even though Darrol said they would be back. Paki loaded Kell's horse, and then they left Rocky Ridge, heading east, the opposite direction from where the innkeeper said the bandits lived. They rode out of sight of the town and then turned back, traveling west.

After an hour at a reasonable pace, Darrol turned them south. "What are we looking for?" he said, playing the tutor. That brought a smile to Pol's face, so he let Paki answer.

"Tracks. If Noster travels back and forth to the brigand hideout, he's sure to have worn some kind of path."

Pol thought back to the map. "There is a west road, so it's also possible that he takes the road and then heads north, if the hideout is in the Spines."

"Oh," Darrol said. He looked a bit deflated. "So we still head west?"

Pol nodded. Darrol hadn't gone to as many Seeking classes as Paki and Pol, but his instincts were right. "We will travel a little north of the road, if we can, and be alert for trails crossing our path. If we don't find any that look fresh, then we can take the road back, looking for paths heading south."

Pol rode along thinking of patterns. He talked to Demeron, who had little sense of the kind of patterns Pol was trying to create. Pol had to admit there were limitations in Demeron's thinking, but it helped pass the time.

They had ridden for another hour when Paki noticed the trail. "Hoof prints. They look fresh."

They dismounted. Demeron took the horses to the side, and they began munching on a patch of tall spring grass. Pol lowered to his haunches and used a twig to look at the impressions in the dirt.

"Five or more horses," Pol said. "There must have been a rain shower along here last night. These are the only prints, and it's clear none are heading back to the road. He looked northward at higher hills topped by glimpses of the vertical shards of rock that gave the Wild Spines their name. "Should we just follow these?"

Darrol shrugged. "You're the most experienced Seeker."

Pol smiled, but he had no humor behind it. "I'm not a scout or a tracker. Paki's done more of that than I."

Paki raised his hands. "I'm still just learning. After you left the class, we've been talking about battle strategies."

"And what kind of strategy should we follow here?"

Pol's friend put his hand to his chin and thought for a moment. "If we are outnumbered, it's better to flank your enemy. Surprise is on your side that way. A scout should always be on the lookout for opportunities to get past the enemy."

"Then that means we should have known the land better. We don't have the luxury of that," Pol said. "Unless it's dark. Then I have an advantage with my location spell." He thought for a bit. "First of al, let's follow this up, but let's not ride on this path. We'll make our own. They might see our own hoof prints."

Paki shook his head. "How do you come up with all this?"

"For me it's just common sense. I've been reading about battle strategies since I was ten years old," Pol said. He had to admit he had learned a lot since Mistress Farthia had come to teach him at that age.

"Then let's do it," Darrol said. "Your strategy sounds good to me."

They mounted again and rode fifty paces west, and then headed north again, into the Spines.

There is a man on a horse heading down the other path, Demeron told Pol about an hour and a half later.

"How do you know?"

Horses can see and smell better than humans.

Pol closed his eyes and reached out with his spell. He could see a colored dot, orange, moving south. "Someone is coming down the path. It's time to find some cover."

Since the hills had become steeper, jagged rocks now poked through the soil, making them ride around the stony clusters. Pol thought that they made great hiding places. The three of them dismounted and waited.

Pol sensed the man getting into sight range, and there he was, an older man, dressed rather well, ambling along with his horse down the trail. He suspected that was Clorence Noster.

"You stay here. Demeron and I will follow him down for a bit. I want to get a look at his face," Pol said.

"Don't waste too much time," Darrol said.

"I won't." Pol mounted Demeron, and they paralleled the rider for a few hundred yards until Pol nudged Demeron forward. He looked back at Noster and saw a man with a grizzled gray beard and narrowed eyes. He looked mean.

He was about to return when he noticed more men riding from the south. They would intercept Noster in a few moments. Pol dismounted. "Help me if I get into trouble."

Demeron shook his head, and Pol crept through the underbrush that led all the way to the trail. Dixtor Tildan, the Chief Guard of Rocky Ridge, rode into view with two guards.

"Three Deftnis monks are searching for you," Tildan said. "They figured out what we've been doing. It looks like they headed east of Rocky Ridge, but they might end up coming this way."

Noster laughed. 'What's three against my eight men? With you three that makes eleven against three."

"Where will you be?" Tildan said.

"I have to find another rich visitor or two. I won't let any monks ruin this summer's ransoms. Spend the day up at my camp. I'll make it worth your while," Noster said.

Pol was close enough to see the displeasure on Tildan's face. "I'll make sure that it is. There is a boy who is a powerful magician. He lifted me right up from my seat," Tilden said.

"Tricks are all magicians know," Noster said. "Go on up. You'll be just in time for lunch. I feed the men pretty good at festival time. If nothing has happened when I return tomorrow, you can return to Rocky Ridge."

Tilden nodded and motioned to his two men. They headed up the trail.

"Monks!" Noster muttered as he continued south towards the road.

Pol watched the man go and wondered if he shouldn't capture him. He decided against it. He had seen and heard enough. He let a few moments pass and headed back towards their hiding place.

After recounting the mid-trail discussion, they decided they could ride and soon headed along a narrow defile, surrounded on both sides by the rocks making up the Spines. Pol made sure his location spell was active to notify him of watchmen.

Eleven to three. He had to assume Kell couldn't help them. "Can we go against them?"

"Are you intending a battle or what? We can't just go in and grab Kell," Darrol said, "Right?"

Pol nodded. "So we can't sneak in? Should we wait for dark?"

"I would," Paki said. "That will make it easier to use Demeron."

Pol had forgotten about the very horse he rode.

"Are you up for that?" Pol asked.

I am. I'll see if I can persuade my fellows into helping.

"I didn't think you could talk to other horses."

Demeron didn't reply. Did Pol just learn that horses talked and could keep secrets? He wondered.

He sensed two men on watch up ahead, so they took a small trail to their right and led their horses through a narrow slice in the rock, which rubbed against Demeron's sides as he slipped through.

Can we come down the trail coming back? Please?

Pol patted Demeron's jaw as the trail opened up into a little valley. A trail of smoke wound up in the still afternoon from a stand of trees on the other side. There weren't any brigands close by, so they stopped to mount up and rode closer to the other side, moving along the forested edge so that they ended up behind the camp rather than in front of it. Darrol carved flashes in the bark in case they had to escape the way they had come.

"Flanking," Paki said, grinning.

"Right," Darrol said quietly. "Our easiest escape isn't through eleven armed men."

They dismounted. Paki volunteered to move closer to check out the camp, but Pol stopped him. "I can use my talent to see where the men are and where they are keeping Kell."

Pol took off, but not too quickly. He had to maintain his strength for any magic he would have to perform. He gnashed his teeth, wishing that this had happened after they found Searl and the monk had healed him. As if that would ever happen. He shook off the negative thought and slipped a little closer. Most of the men congregated on the south side of the camp facing the conventional entry to the valley.

He located ten spots. The other two were watching the trail and were out of Pol's range. So he could guess the one dot that had no one around it must be Kell.

The camp was permanent. There were four mud-walled buildings, all faced with a lime wash covering the thick sides. Pol didn't think Kell could break through the hardened mud. The roofs were made out of wooden shingles. There were two wooden outhouses and a large firepit/outdoor kitchen from which smoke trailed skyward.

No one guarded Kell in the small building. He crept closer, willing himself into invisibility, still not confident that the spell worked, and spied the sturdy iron lock keeping Kell in his prison.

Pol could see two tiny windows up towards the roof, but they were only a foot square, enough to let in a little light, but too small to crawl through, especially Kell. He looked towards the brigands. They were just serving lunch. Pol crept towards the little building and used his magic to open the lock.

"Who's there?" Kell said.

After putting his finger to his lips to quiet Kell, he released his spell. It obviously worked, and he couldn't help but grin. "Are you ready to run for it?"

Kell nodded. "I didn't know you could hide yourself," he said quietly.

"Wasn't sure myself." Pol looked around at the storage shed. Shelves lined the walls. Weapons, pots, pans, and other things littered one side, and the other held food stores.

"Can you make fire with your magic?" Pol said. "Fire drains my energy too much."

Kell shook his head.

"Then do you remember your lesson making fire? The materials are here," Pol said. "The floors are wooden rather than dirt so the whole place should burn."

"Why?"

"If we make it out of here, they might think you burned up in the shack, or maybe they'll spend more time putting the fire out rather than chasing us. We have to do something, since they outnumber us about three to one."

The two of them got to work. Kell had his set-up going before Pol. Then someone fiddled with the lock on the door. Pol was glad he had thought to lock it back up when he went in.

"Don't try nothin'. There's four of us here," the voice said on the other side of the door.

Pol could see that only one of the brigands spoke to them from the other side, so he spelled himself invisible. The door opened.

Kell had pushed their fire making tools behind him.

"Stay where you are," the bandit said. He set the food down on the floor and was backing out of the shed when Pol hit him over the head with a hammer from one of the shelves. He used a bit of magic to make the blow as hard as he could.

"Is he dead?" Pol asked, watching the floor turn red with the man's blood. He couldn't believe he had just killed a man. He took a deep breath and tried to convince himself that the brigands could have killed Kell at any time.

Kell nodded and seemed impressed with Pol's feat. "I didn't know you had it in you. Let's get the fire started and get going."

They went to it, and soon they had two small fires growing in the shed. Kell ran out and hid behind the building while Pol locked the door again. Maybe they would think that Kell had died in the blaze. The bandit's body might be confused for Kell's.

By the time they made their way to Darrol and Paki, another trail of smoke floated up over the hideout, and it grew thicker. Pol could hear excited voices. Even from their concealed vantage point, they could tell the shed was lost. The roof was burning fiercely, and the mud was beginning to crumble from the walls, leaving wooden slats to catch fire.

"Time to leave," Darrol said. "Let's hope it won't come to a fight."

Pol looked back and saw cinders from the roof catch on another building. None of the brigands or the guards even looked their way. They rode without haste through the woods and found the narrow passageway.

"Sorry, Demeron."

It is a small price to pay to keep everyone without injury.

"Including your fellows?"

Demeron nodded with his head while they all dismounted and led their horses through the tight trail.

When they finally reached the main track, an arrow shattered against a rock by Paki's head.

"They've found us!" Darrol said and urged his horse on. Pol let the others go ahead, while he spelled the magnetic shield that Vactor had taught him just before they left on their mission, and Demeron had to keep from running ahead of the others.

The arrows stopped. No one had been hurt, but Pol could barely hold onto Demeron as they continued their flight. Darrol led them onto their previous path that would lead them just north of Rocky Ridge. After a few minutes, he halted.

"A quick rest for the horses and a bite to eat," he said.

"I have no desire to spend another night in that town," Kell said. "I learned my lesson. They drugged me, and I woke up in that shack this morning."

Paki's mouth turned into a pout. "I was going to meet up with that girl tonight." He sighed. "I suppose my life is worth more—"

"Than a roll in the hay?" Darrol said, smirking.

"A bed is a lot more comfortable than hay," Paki said, sighing.

Demeron was ready to pick up the pace, now that Pol had forced down some awful-tasting trail bread and leather-like dried meat. He felt better after eating.

They were picking their way through a stretch of woods when Pol could sense six horses behind them.

"Four against six," Pol called out to the others. "They are catching up.

"We'll find a place to stand. I don't want to be dogged all the way through the pass to Terrifin." Darrol led them further to an outcropping of tall rocks, an edge of the Spines. They dismounted. Demeron took the other three horses around the rocks.

Paki and Darrol held swords. Kell had pulled his bow from his saddle and plunged ten arrows into the dirt in front of him. Pol kept his sword in its scabbard and held two knives in his left hand and another in his right. He had three more on him.

They stood, ready for action, in front of a twenty-foot high curtain of rock.

All six riders pulled up, led by the Chief Guard. They had no choice but to dismount.

Kell drew an arrow and pierced one of the guards in the neck.

"You'll pay for that," Dixtor Tildan said.

Kell shot one of the brigands in the thigh. He went down. "That makes it four to four," he said.

"Get them!" Tildan said, running towards the four of them.

"Two more coming up in the woods!" Pol said as an arrow hit Darrol in the side of his shoulder.

"Six to three, now." Tildan laughed as he approached Paki.

Tildan wore armor, but Pol's throw accurately took care of the man as he approached Darrol, down on the ground.

"Three to Five," a brigand said, taking up the scoring.

Shouts rang out in the forest, turning into screams.

"Three to three," Paki said as he clashed with the last guard.

Kell tossed his bow aside and drew his sword as he took on a brigand.

That left Pol fighting against another bandit. He took deep breaths as the man slammed his sword at Pol's. His anticipation magic didn't work quite as well with an undisciplined fighter. He had learned that back when he fought Grostin, his stepbrother in Borstall.

The man backed Pol up to the rock. He stumbled, giving Pol time to draw another knife, but not enough time to use it.

The man began to methodically hack, and rhythm was what Pol needed to effectively use his magic. He finally sensed an opening and sliced the man's clothing on his left side, not getting much skin, but that was enough to back his opponent up. The man took the luxury of pausing to breathe, and Pol lunged, using more than a sip of magic to plunge his sword into the man's stomach. Pol jumped back, ready to defend himself, but gasped when he noticed Paki in distress. Blood ran down his friend's arm, and Paki's eyes exposed the panic that he must have felt.

Pol threw the knife left-handed at the guard, whose armor left his side exposed. The knife went in hilt-deep, aided by another big sip of magic. Pol fell to his knees, done for the fight. He watched as Kell finally took care of his opponent.

"Eight defeated by four," Kell said.

Demeron led eleven horses. They ringed the small battleground. Eight to eight. If Demeron could smile, he would.

Two brigands survived the fight. Horses had killed the two archers in the woods.

Darrol and Paki needed attention, and Kell could use a few cuts sewn shut. Pol was, as usual, drained of energy, but he sat until he recovered enough to put all the bodies on the horses. Kell tied them securely before he bound the two injured brigands and helped them mount.

Darrol had lost some blood, but the arrow had pierced the top of his shoulder all the way, so they cut to remove the arrowhead and bound the wound tightly. It took them just over an hour to reach Rocky Ridge. Despite their previous intentions, they stopped at the inn.

The innkeeper ran out to view the carnage. "Dixtor Tildan?"

"He is in league with Clorence Noster. From what we could tell, Noster directed the Chief Guard, not the other way around."

Townspeople gathered around the horses.

Two guards came running up, swords drawn.

Darrol put up his good arm. "We haven't come to fight you. These men attacked us in the Spines. They abducted our friend." Darrol pointed at Kell. He recognized a guard. "You saw us in your office this morning."

The guard nodded. "We knew the Chief was on the take."

"Get some reinforcements from Palleton," Darrol said. "These two should recover from their wounds. They should confirm who their boss is. There is a hidden valley a few hours from here where there are a few more bandits. Noster ran a kidnapping operation as part of the gambling tent. I'd shut that down, if I were you. We're going to get some medical treatment and head out first thing in the morning." Darrol struggled to get his Deftnis document out from his clothes and showed it to the guard. "We are from Deftnis on a mission for the Abbot."

That brought some noise from the growing crowd. So much for maintaining a low profile, Pol thought. At least he still had brown hair.

~ ~ ~

Chapter Twenty

~

THE FOUR RIDERS MADE IT TO THE TOP OF THE PASS, and looked into Terrifin, letting the five merchant wagons in their makeshift caravan roll past. Pol was very glad to see Rocky Ridge behind them. Clorence Noster was jailed, along with the remaining five of his brigands. Pol wondered if the residents would wait for word from Palleton before they took care of the blight on their town.

Paki was the only one who had taken advantage of the second night of Summer's Come. Paki was still smiling about his two blissful nights. Evidently, his girl was very impressed by Paki's part in fighting the bandits. Kell amiably agreed to sleep on the floor of Darrol and Pol's room.

They continued their trip down to the Great West Road that led all the way to Alsador, Listya's capital city. They had decided to ride up into the Spine at intervals, rather than trying to ride west along the steeper slopes. They verified that they could use inns along the Western Road as a base. Darrol still needed the attention of healers and wouldn't be accompanying them into the actual Spines for another few days or so, but he could ride between the inns on the smoother road.

They learned that a Deftnis-trained healer lived in the town where they stopped on the third night.

Kell stayed behind in their rooms to write a letter to his parents, while Paki, Pol, and Darrol found the healer's clinic on the main street of town.

They walked into a full waiting room and had to wait two hours before their turn arrived. The sign on the counter in the front said 'Healer Willmont'.

"I hope Kell had a lot to write about," Paki said. He worried at his bandages. "I hope the stitches are ready to come out."

Darrol shook his head. "I wish that was all I needed. I told you I could snip those off. I've done it often enough, and I didn't hear Kell whine about my work, although we aren't quite done yet."

Paki pulled away from Darrol. "You won't be pulling stitches out of my body," he said.

An older man with a fringe of white hair walked up to them. He didn't wear the monk's robes that Pol expected. "Do all of you need help?"

"These two," Pol said. "We ran into some difficulties some days ago in Sand."

"Come on back. I'll see you all at one time."

Pol and Paki sat while the healer started with Darrol, who had to take his shirt off.

"What happened here? An arrow?"

Darrol grunted as Willmont touched and prodded. "It's one of our difficulties," Darrol said drily, looking at Pol.

"We ran into some brigands," Paki said.

The healer's eyes lost a little focus. "Ah, you need a bit of additional help here."

"That's why we came to a Deftnis healer," Darrol said.

"You've had some magical healing in the past?"

"We all have," Pol said. "We came from Deftnis Isle." Pol decided it was time to break the ice in regards to Searl.

"I would have guessed, except you two boys seem a bit young for acolytes."

Paki nodded. "We are. Pol is a special case, and I tagged along."

"A special case?" Willmont said.

"I wear a red cord," Pol said. His comment was a test for the healer.

"Level Four, at your age? Impressive. What brings you north of the Spines?"

Darrol looked at Pol and nodded.

"Searl. We are looking for Searl. Do you know him?"

The man sighed. "Who hasn't heard his story? Just a minute." He laid hands on Darrol and closed his eyes.

Darrol hissed. "That's a magical touch, all right," he said.

"And it's good that it is. You might have lost the use of your shoulder at some point. You are a monk?"

"Second Level Magic, Third Level Sword. I'm at Deftnis as Pol's sworn man," Darrol said.

Healer Willmont raised his eyebrows, but the placid look never left his face. "Sworn man. Pol must be important." The healer turned his gaze to Pol.

"I was a prince."

"Was?"

"He's a disinherited prince."

"North Salvan?"

Pol nodded.

"I heard of you. I keep my ears and eyes open and send an occasional message to Abbot Pleagor. I trust he's been doing well?"

Darrol nodded.

"So you are looking for Searl. Why would you do that? He was cast out of Deftnis years ago."

Pol worried with his hands and decided to tell all. "I have a condition. He is the only one who might be able to cure it."

"I could guess. Heart? You are a bit undersized for your age. Fifteen? I'm sure Searl could have done what you want before he was taken."

"Taken?" Pol said, quite alarmed with the term.

"Taken by minweed. He's an addict, you know."

Pol nodded. "He is my only chance to get really well that I know of."

The healer closed his eyes again, and Darrol winced one more time. "There. Take it easy for another week. No more 'difficulties'?"

Darrol nodded.

"You next, young man."

Paki took Darrol's place and took his shirt off. The healer unwound

Paki's bandage. "It looks like a local healer didn't do too badly here. Not like your friend." He sent a pulse of healing power into Paki's arm. "Time to take the stitches out."

Paki jammed his eyes tight as the healer used tiny scissors and a knife along with tweezers to remove every thread.

"That hurt more than the cut."

"They nearly always do, if the sword is sharp. But now that pain is only a memory."

The placid exterior of the healer astounded Pol. The man was so calm.

"Now you," the healer said to Pol. "I'm no Searl, but I've no lack of talent. I wore the gray cord."

Pol took his shirt off and Willmont instructed Pol to lie down.

The healer sent a warm surge of magic through Pol. It felt just like the treatments he received at the infirmary. "You have a unique heart. If I didn't know better, I'd say it wasn't quite human."

"It isn't."

Pol heard Darrol and Paki gasp.

"I am one of the last descendants of a non-human race. My hair is actually nearly silver."

The healer bent over and parted Pol's hair. "Indeed. Go on."

"The male offspring between humans always have or had bad hearts. My real father died not long after he turned twenty."

"What about King Colvin?" Paki said.

"He's not my father."

"Good for you," Darrol said. "I never liked your stepdad."

Willmont put his ear to Pol's chest. "A murmur like I've never heard. I can't help you other than to give you a bit of strength, but you've had such help before at Deftnis?"

"I have, but my heart is beginning to reject the treatments," Pol said. "The healers said Searl could do more than give me a treatment."

"He could," the healer said.

"Do you know where he is?"

Willmont gave Pol his shirt. "He's not in Terrifin or in Asfall, the next dukedom to the west. Minweed grows best in Lawster and Hardman. I would guess he's got a place there surrounded by the stuff, if he still lives."

"He sent a letter to Deftnis this winter. It was hardly intelligible."

"Minweed does that. The addiction can be powerful. It hit Searl badly. We talked about it when he first left Deftnis. He came through here and told me that he had given himself over to the stuff."

"He's my last chance. My heart is beginning to fail," Pol said.

"I know," Willmont said. "I wish you well. Tell him that you visited me and I'm am still doing exactly what I wanted to."

"You could teach at Deftnis, if you wanted to?" Darrol asked.

"But that isn't really healing the way it's supposed to be done. It's like being a pattern-master with no one to fight, except those who want to learn to be a pattern-master. In a sense, it is the sign of a job unfinished, to put it charitably."

"Pol's a pattern-master," Paki said.

"Have you put it to use?"

Pol snorted. "I have, but I can't fight for very long."

"Of course, you can't." The healer walked over to a pitcher and poured water over each of his hands in succession and dried them off with a towel. "I wish you well."

"How much for the treatment?" Darrol said, pulling out his purse.

"I treat the Deftnis-trained for free," Willmont said with a calm smile.

"Then a contribution to your clinic?" Pol said. He pulled out his purse and gave a South Salvan Lion to Willmont.

"I don't deserve this."

"Think of it as recognition for healing the way it's supposed to be done," Pol said.

The healer bowed. "I will put this to good use." He smiled and ushered them out through his still-full waiting room. "I wish you luck. Again, give my best to Searl. If you can free him from the addiction, the world will be a much better place."

~

Pol looked at the same landscape. Every dukedom seemed a little different from the others. The guards wore different colored uniforms, although the people looked much alike. Asfallians tended to like their buildings whitewashed, where the fine citizens of Goste must have had large stone deposits of light yellow stone, since they built most of their houses out of the stuff.

He looked forward to Lawster. Whenever they asked about minweed or Searl, every piece of the pattern seemed to point them to the dukedoms of Lawster and Hardman as the prime sources of the drug. The healer had to be in the western part of the Spines.

Paki and Darrol had recovered from their wounds. Kell had Darrol remove the last of his stitches along the way. They still traveled the Great West Road, which wound around the foothills of the northern slopes of the Wild Spines. Although they traveled in relative peace, they were all ready for 'difficulties', as Darrol had referenced their adventures to Willmont back in the dukedom of Terrifin.

Pol expected more danger to arise when they plunged south into the foothills and into the Spines. Everyone they talked to warned them of the 'wild lands of the Wild Spines' that seemed similar to the situation they confronted in Rocky Ridge, but they never ran into bandits, and no one had heard of Searl.

"We will visit Senaton, the ducal capital of Lawster," Darrol said. "I think we can splurge on a nice inn before we begin heading south into the Spines."

"Sounds good to me," Kell said. "We won't have to practice our swordplay in the middle of a city, will we?"

Darrol laughed. "Did I overtax your ability to learn? I thought we could all use practice while on the road." His hand went to his shoulder. "I needed to work out the injury. You did too, Kell. Don't you feel like you've improved? I think both Paki and you have."

Pol remembered the last six days of stopping by the side of the road and spending an hour or more with their weapons. Pol sparred for half the time and spent the rest working on throwing knives. He felt that all four of them had become more comfortable fighting with one another, and that would prepare them for anything that came their way in the Spines.

They had all fought well outside of Rocky Ridge, and that experience had made them more of a group. A bit of seasoning, Pol had thought of it. Still, he had to admit he looked forward to a night in nicer surroundings.

The Great West Road curved to the north to intersect the ducal seat of Lawster. In an hour, the spires of Senaton rose above a plain just below the foothills. Many of the fields displayed a shimmer of green growth as the crops began to poke their way into the world of sunlight and rain.

The Senaton city wall shot up fifty feet from the ground. The stone was pale, but as they got closer, Pol noticed mottled tans of various shades against a basic white. The Lawsterians liked spires. They rose up from behind the walls. There must have been thirty or forty of them making the city's skyline look like a box of pikes.

The Duke of Lawster ran an orderly city, and that included a visitor tax of a silver guilder. That was what the inhabitants called their silver coinage. Darrol paid the equivalent and extra for information about exceptional inns in Senaton. As expected, the best shops, marketplaces, and inns clustered around the ducal palace. The Duke of Lawster didn't live in a castle, although it looked enough like one to Pol.

Darrol stopped a local merchant and decided on an inn popular with visiting merchants. "If we stay where nobles might frequent, I'm afraid we won't enjoy it as much. Merchants are more tolerant of fellow travelers," Darrol said. "At least in my limited experience in staying at nice places."

That fit a definite pattern, Pol thought, so he didn't object to Darrol's decision, not that any of them would. The day was about to end, and everyone was tired, even Demeron complained about walking on the uneven cobbles of the city and looked forward to resting in a good stable.

The four of them found the inn and soon sat at a table covered with an actual tablecloth. They wore their cleanest clothes. Pol looked around. There were enough other travelers dressed in a similar fashion, now that they had left their weapons in their rooms.

"Traveled far?" the young serving maid said. She gave all of them ale except for the fruit juice she gave Pol. She held the tray to her and gave them a warm smile.

"Deftnis," Paki said.

Her demeanor cooled. "Please don't say that again in Senaton. The Duke of Lawster is not a friend of Deftnis. There were some, uh, disagreements with the Emperor two years ago. His chamberlain did not survive. I don't know any of the details, but please keep your travel plans to yourselves." She curtseyed and hurried away.

"What do you think?" Paki said. "I thought we were out of danger, and now we're spending the night in hostile territory."

Darrol grunted after he took a sip of ale. "It's not hostile at this point. Let's enjoy a good night's rest and be on our way tomorrow." He glared at Paki. "That will happen as long as our lips are sealed." Darrol ran his finger along his mouth.

"Don't worry about me," Paki said, but he looked guilty.

"No, you just announced to the whole room where we were from," Kell said. "As for me, I'm going to enjoy a good meal and a soft bed."

Pol just kept quiet. He had assumed that Deftnis was universally respected as a place of learning, but now he knew it was tightly associated with the Emperor. Val and Malden were from Deftnis. Could Ranno have been trained there, too? He wanted to ask Darrol, but knew he shouldn't mention it in the dining room.

"This is the best food we've had, so far," Kell said. He called the serving maid over to ask for another plate. "It's okay, Darrol?"

Darrol waved his hand. "Enjoy yourself."

A squad of six guards and an officer entered the dining room.

"Who owns the big black horse that came in this afternoon?" the officer asked.

Pol stood. "That's probably Demeron. He's mine."

"Shinkyan horses are forbidden by treaty. The Duke hereby confiscates him."

"You can't do that," Pol said.

"Take it up with the Duke tomorrow, if he will permit an audience."

Pol clenched his fists. His arms and the arms of his friends were up in their rooms. Darrol clasped his wrist.

"Not now," Darrol said quietly.

Pol shook off his hand and followed the guards out the door to the stable.

Two guards stood outside the stall by two others, nursing wounds on the ground.

"Easy, Demeron," Pol said. "I'll be visiting the Duke of Lawster tomorrow morning to retrieve you. Don't make a pest of yourself or they will hurt you, and I don't want to see you hurt.

Neither do I. If you know of this abduction, I will go with enough spirit to let them know I am not theirs.

"Keep calm as much as possible. Do it for me?"

Demeron shook his head. *I will.*

"It's like he understood you," the officer said.

Pol nodded. "He's smarter than most people. Treat him decently and he won't resist you. He does like to eat grain. A lot of grain."

"The Duke wouldn't think of mistreating a treasure like him."

Treasure? Pol thought. That would make it harder for them to convince the Duke to let Demeron go.

Pol watched Demeron pull the two guards leading him this way and that, but didn't attack the guards as he could have done. He said farewell to Demeron in his mind and his horse reminded him to come quickly tomorrow morning.

He returned to their table.

"That was quick," Darrol said. "Someone high up must have spotted Demeron while we rode through the city and told the Duke."

"Confiscate? More like steal," Paki said.

"Watch your tongue," Darrol said. "We aren't necessarily among friends in Senaton."

"I have my proof of ownership."

"And who signed it, Pol?" Kell said between bites.

"You know who. Oh. That might not be enough."

"We'll see tomorrow morning," Darrol said.

The serving maid came to take the plates from the table. "I'm sorry."

"Does the Duke take what he wants from travelers?" Pol asked.

"It's been known to happen. His chamberlain was worse, but…" She just shook her head and left them.

"So is this a Seeker opportunity?" Paki said.

Pol nodded. "It will be, but I don't know where we will get good enough information to build a working pattern." Pol looked at the serving maid serving tables and picking up dishes. "I'm going to talk to her."

He rose from the table and followed the serving maid into the kitchen.

"We are travelers who don't know Lawster very well."

"I know where you are from." Her voice lowered. "Are you magicians?"

Pol noticed the looks from the kitchen staff. He realized that the girl wasn't much older than he was. "We are not without talent. Do you know of anyone we could ask how best to approach your Duke?"

"Who are you?" the innkeeper walked up to Pol. "We are not a brothel, so leave my daughter alone."

The serving maid looked up at the innkeeper. "There is nothing untoward going on. These travelers are from the South, and the Duke has taken their finest horse."

The innkeeper sighed. "I thought that kind of thing was stopped." He looked exasperated. Pol took that as a positive sign. "Sanctioned thievery, if you ask me."

"Sir, I came back here to see if your daughter knew anyone who could give us information about how best to approach your Duke, so I can retrieve my horse. He's rather special to me."

"I've seen two Shinkyan horses before, both mares. That horse of yours is huge. Do you realize how valuable he is?"

Pol shook his head. "He was a gift." In a matter of speaking, Pol thought.

"Do you have any papers for him?"

Pol nodded. "I do." He took a deep breath. "Signed by the Emperor."

"The Emperor of Baccusol?" The innkeeper's eyes widened.

"I can show the title to you, if you wish."

The man nodded. "Come down to my office just off the lobby in two hours. Now let my daughter get back to work."

~~~

Chapter Twenty-One

DARROL AND POL KNOCKED ON THE DOORFRAME. The innkeeper counted money in his office.

"You do that out in the open?"

The innkeeper shrugged and pulled up a small hand crossbow from behind the desk. "I do. Senaton is generally a peaceful city. Sit down and give me a moment."

There were three chairs arranged in front of the innkeeper's desk.

Darrol and Pol looked at each other and sat down. The innkeeper had a stack of envelopes on his desk and slid counted money into them. He slipped the last of the coins into one and scribbled on the outside. After ringing a bell at his desk, he clasped his hands and laid them on the desk.

"Tell me your story," He said. "First of all, my name is Okren Moss. You can call me Oak."

"I'm Pol Cissert, and this is Darrol Netherfield."

Pol heard steps enter the room and the door close. "And I am Deena Moss. Father agreed to let me listen in." The serving maid walked into view and sat in the third chair on Darrol's side. Pol noticed that she was actually pretty with her dark hair down, but why did she join them?

Pol took a deep breath to ignore the distraction of the girl. Darrol and he had decided that Pol would do the talking.

"We are on a mission for the Abbot of Deftnis. Darrol is a monk, and the others are acolytes."

"It hardly seems appropriate for your Abbot to send boys on a mission."

Pol pressed his lips together. "Well, it's my own personal quest. I am searching for a former healer that left the monastery. He, alone, can heal a malady that I have had from birth. The monk lives in the Wild Spines. We believe he is in Lawster or the Duchy of Hardman."

Oak rubbed his lips together. "What did he do develop an addiction to minweed? That's the only draw that I know of in the northern side of the Spines. The cursed plant only grows well where you seek him."

"He is taken by a minweed habit," Pol said. "You know your land well."

"Minweed is a scourge. You'll find out when you meet your monk. He won't be worth much. But what is this with your horse?"

Pol nodded and pulled out the Emperor's ownership certificate. He gave it to Oak, who examined it.

"You are known to the Emperor?"

Pol nodded again. "I am. He seems to have taken a liking to me."

"What is so special about you?"

"I'm a disinherited prince. It happened late last summer, and to a very minor extent, I have been offered his protection. I don't want my horse confiscated. He is special—"

"As is any Shinkyan. They are magnificent animals. I wish I would have walked out and taken a look at him."

""What we need is information that can help me get him back. Will my certificate be enough? Is the Duke honorable enough to accept this?"

Oak shook his head. "There isn't much love between our beloved Emperor and our beloved Duke. My daughter told you about his Chamberlain's death?"

"She did. What happened?"

"Theon had an unsavory habit of sending the guard out to raid wealthy merchants as they left the city. Merchants complained, but the Duke silenced their threats. I have many customers who live outside

Lawster, and they complained to the Emperor."

"Oh. Ranno Wissingbel took care of the complaints?" Pol said.

"You know him, too?" Oak looked impressed.

Pol nodded. "His daughter was my tutor for nearly five years in North Salvan."

"You know the new King of Listya then?"

"He is my stepbrother."

Oak sat back. "You do get around. Well, don't advertise any of that in this city."

"I won't," Pol said. "But I want Demeron back."

"Be at the palace gate by dawn and be prepared to wait. I will help you draw up a petition. You will need to produce the owner's certificate. Does the horse obey your instructions?"

That brought a grin to Pol's face. "He's a very, very, smart horse, and you might say we have bonded well."

"You may be called upon to demonstrate. I'm not saying you will succeed, but that is what you should do." Oak scribbled on two documents and handed them to Pol. "It will be hard for the Duke to ignore an Imperial title."

"This is your petition, and this is a note to Bester. He's likely to be your gatekeeper. It's from me to him recommending you. Don't show this to anyone else."

"What about my friends?"

"I suggest that they leave the city. The Duke can be unpredictable. The chamberlain didn't act alone, if you understand."

Darrol nodded. "I do. Is there a road south into the Spines?"

Oak pulled out another paper and sketched a crude map twice, and then ripped the paper in two. "Here you go." He gave one to Darrol and another to Pol.

"You are taking a risk. I can procure a serviceable horse, if you wish to just leave Senaton."

Pol shook his head. "I'll go by myself. Demeron and I can make it out together, and my friends will be close enough if the Duke sends men to hunt me down."

"Very well. I have another question to ask. Are you a magician?"

Pol said. "I am one of sorts. I can't blow down Senaton's walls, but I'm not without resources."

Oak stood up. "There is a price."

Pol shifted uncomfortably in his chair. He expected there would be a cost for the information.

"My daughter has magical talent and a good mind. She's wasted waiting on tables in my inn, and although her mother and I would like her to stay by our sides, I'd like her trained in the best possible place."

Deena flashed them a smile. "I would, if you could help me."

"I'll write to Ranno Wissingbel," Pol said, thinking of the Emperor's magical school for women. "Can I borrow some paper and ink? Will that be sufficient? I can't promise you more. You can send it to Yastan from here."

Pol rubbed damp palms on the legs of his trousers as he waited and waited. It had already been nearly three hours, but he didn't wait alone in the long hall. People lined both sides, both sitting and standing. Bester had helped him, just as Oak had promised.

He thought of the men he had killed on his mission. Unfortunately, the deaths meant less to him as they traveled. He regretted killing the bandit with a hammer. That was foul play, in his mind, and the deed still bothered him. The others had attacked Pol and his group and those were more easily dismissed, but Pol had fought for his life then.

The line between killing casually and killing to defend oneself was blurring, and Pol had to accept that it was.

"Pol Cissert!"

He stood at the sound of his name and followed a fancily-dressed guard into a small ornate throne room. The Duke of Lawster sat on a large gilded chair. The man was surprisingly small, almost waif-like to Pol's perception. He might even be just Pol's height. His graying hair took away any impression of youth.

The Duke waved Pol's petition in his hand. "This claims you are the rightful owner of a Shinkyan stallion. The Emperor has outlawed their possession in the Empire through treaty, and yet you show up with one. You're just a boy."

"I have an ownership certificate from the Emperor. You will note that I have received an imperial dispensation to own my horse."

Pol handed the certificate over.

The Duke read the document and gnashed his teeth. "I am

stunned that Hazett would entrust such a marvelous beast to a peasant such as you."

"Less than a year ago, I was a prince, but I lost my inheritance. As compensation, perhaps, the Emperor provided me with Demeron, my Shinkyan stallion."

"What proof do you have that you are the same Pol Cissert that owns the beast?"

"Demeron does tricks at my command. He won't do the same, even with your Master of Horse." If the Duke even retained one, Pol thought.

"Very well." The Duke rose from his throne. "We will put your lies to the test right now. If you lie, you will spend a few years in a Senaton cell."

They walked out through a few grand corridors that would put Borstall Castle to shame and descended steps to a large practice yard. Pol noticed a barracks and an armory of a more modest size than his old home. He could see the stable down a lane between the two buildings.

Two guards ran into the stables, and four men held ropes attached to Demeron's bridle. Demeron shook his massive head, making it difficult for the handlers to control him.

Pol raised his hand. "I have come for you. Calm yourself."

Only for you. The beasts in the stable walk on two legs. They didn't even remove your saddle.

Demeron's balkiness instantly ceased as he nearly dragged the men towards Pol. The horse bowed his head and nuzzled his dripping chin on Pol's hair.

"Stop that," Pol said. He could resist smiling, while he tried to wipe the slobber off his hair.

I want to show you my undying affection.

I'll agree with the undying part, Pol said in his mind, and then he turned to the Duke. "What would you like to see Demeron do?"

"Can you make him count?" the Duke said.

"Demeron, how many guards are standing in the shade of this practice field?

The oldest of the handlers sputtered. "A horse can't actually count like that."

"Is this your Master of Horse?"

"He is," the Duke said.

Pol turned to the older man. "Do you want to try?"

The man shook his head and muttered, "Impossible."

"Demeron?"

The horse looked towards the shady side of the field and then turned to Pol. He clapped his hoof on the dirt fourteen times.

"I think he is right!" the Master of Horse said.

"Bow to the Master," Pol said.

Demeron bowed.

"I am the master around here," the Duke said.

The horse just turned his head and stared at the Duke, who shook his head and addressed the Master of Horse. "Is there any possibility that I can learn to do what this boy did?"

Pol noticed the derisiveness in the Duke's pronunciation of 'boy'.

"I don't think so, My Duke."

The Duke let the Imperial certificate drift to the ground. "Pick it up and take the horse, but leave my city immediately."

Pol didn't see the man's expression soften. Once Pol left the city, guardsmen would certainly follow.

"I will. The Emperor will be pleased that you honored his wishes," Pol said, as he spelled the paper into his hands.

"You, a magician?"

"I know a few tricks, for a boy," Pol said. He mounted Demeron and bowed with a flourish to the Duke. "I thank you for your time. I will get my things and take leave of your fine city."

Pol didn't waste any time leaving the practice field for the palace courtyard. Demeron moved as quickly as he could through the morning crowds, and the pair of them finally made it through the gates and back onto the Great West Road.

He hoped the guards would head to Okren Moss's Inn before they continued their pursuit. Pol let Demeron take him to the little copse on the map where he happily rendezvoused with his three companions.

Pol only had enough time to throw his saddlebags on Demeron and arm himself when he sensed fast moving riders at the far range of his senses.

"Here they come," Pol said.

Demeron took the lead as they headed back east towards Goste. Pol wished there was a cornfield to hide in, but there wouldn't be any cornfields in Lawster for a few months.

Looking behind him, Pol could see the riders now that both groups were riding hard. Pol directed Demeron off the road, barely missing a group of merchants crowding the way with their wagons. They rode through plowed fields. Pol chanced to look back and couldn't tell whether the Duke's guards had followed.

They turned right along another stretch of woods and entered, heading back west. They found another track heading south in the woods. Pol couldn't locate the riders.

"I think we lost them," Paki said.

Darrol shook his head. "It all depends on how determined they are. We will have to continue to take this trail and head towards the Spines."

Pol looked south at the jagged line of the Wild Spines, hoping that somewhere along that horizon he would reach his goal.

~ ~ ~

Chapter Twenty-Two

THE PURSUIT DIDN'T REACH THEM. They spent the next few nights out in the open. At least Deena Moss had provided Darrol with a generous amount of food and skins. Pol didn't usually think of girls, but he thought he would have liked to know the girl better. Perhaps if Ranno could help Deena, Pol might get a chance to see her again when he was cured and a few years older.

The characteristic rocks of the foothills began to thicken as they got closer to the actual spines. They stopped at a village of woodcutters and furniture makers on the third night. The inn wasn't much more than a watering hole for the locals, but they had a few rooms in the back for the odd merchant and the carters that carried wood and furniture north to the rest of Lawster.

Pol stayed in his room while the other three asked about any local healers that could help Pol's aching back from a fictitious riding accident. They returned. Kell helped himself to some of the pack food.

"That was some vile stuff," Kell said. He shook his head at Pol. "Be glad you didn't join us. The tavern serves swill instead of ale."

"I didn't think it was that bad," Paki said. Pol knew Paki didn't have the cultivated pallet that Kell did.

Darrol finally entered Pol's room. "No male healers about. Minweed doesn't grow very well around here, but it grows best in

Hardman at the west end of the Wild Spines. The best weed grows where the hardwood trees begin to give way to the pines."

"That means we could have gone along the south end and come north. It would have saved us days of travel."

Darrol laughed. "But think of the adventure. What would our lives be like without dear memories of Rocky Ridge?"

The rest of them groaned, except for Paki.

"We haven't found Searl yet. Maybe we have already passed him."

Darrol shook his head. "No. He wouldn't be satisfied with anything but the best of any medicinal herbs and potions. We will find him in the Duchy of Hardman, and then it will be a quick trip home along the Coast Road all the way to Mancus."

In a week or two, Pol would be healed and heading back to Deftnis to really learn. The thought kept him up during the night, but he felt the time spent thinking of such things a decent start to the day.

~

As they headed further west, the Wild Spines became a bit less wild. The mountains began to lose their height. Pol felt a surge of relief when they passed a marker between the duchies of Lawster and Hardman.

They still plied the trails that ran west through the foothills. They found a few inns to spend the nights, but the fare wasn't much better than the woodcutters' village. At last the lay of the land forced them to turn north and down to the edge of the foothills.

Finally they reached a town that boasted three inns. Darrol led them to the nicest one. The stable boys let them care for their own horses.

Demeron appreciated a good brushing and a bucket of grain. Pol smiled at their conversation as he finally finished up after the others. Demeron had a lot more skin to brush than the other horses.

Pol even ate two helpings of the evening meal after their meager rations on the road. It seemed there wasn't a decent cook in the foothills.

Darrol tried the same ploy he had used at every inn along the way, and this time he asked the man who waited on them.

"Healer? There is a hermit that was a healer, a day or two to the west. He used to come into the town to help the folks around here every three or four months. I don't remember seeing him around for a year or more."

Pol felt his heart beat a little faster. "Did he use minweed?"

"That's what makes a hermit a hermit in these parts. The best minweed in all of Baccusol, maybe the world, is grown on the slopes around here. There are unsavory types in the hills who make a lot of money harvesting and transporting it. Some countries of the Empire have outlawed it. In fact, minweed is not allowed in this town."

"Why is that?" Paki said.

"Once we outlawed it, the vagrants up and left. Made our town a better place to live."

The next day, they bought fresh supplies and headed west, finding trails up and down the foothills. They found the locals weren't very friendly; in fact, most of them were males and looked more like criminals. What if someone had taken over Searl's land and killed him?

He hadn't been seen in the town for a year, and perhaps the letter that arrived in Deftnis had been sent months before. Pol wouldn't know until they found Searl or his remains.

The skies began to lower on their second day from the town, and then it started to drizzle. The trail became slippery, and the euphoria of being close to Searl was diluted by the miserable weather.

Kell's horse slipped, and in the process of getting its legs underneath her, the mare threw Kell against a tree.

Paki quickly dismounted. "Kell's head is bleeding."

Pol jumped off Demeron and wrapped it with bandages that he had brought along. "He's still unconscious."

"We'll have to find a place to stop," Darrol said. "Can you look ahead, Pol? Your locating skills stand a better chance of finding some shelter. We shouldn't move him until we have to."

Pol nodded and climbed back on Demeron, and he rode along the trail for half an hour or so until he came to a track recently used by a single rider dragging a sledge of some kind. Perhaps a woodcutter lived around here.

He followed the trail to a clearing. A large cottage overlooked a tiny pond with a stream running in and another stream running out. The place had a forlorn quality to it.

A sorry-looking horse stood underneath a lean-to, munching on hay piled in a trough at the back. The sledge he had tracked still carried a partial hay bale. Pol didn't see any wood-making tools, but he did note a spring garden with leafy vegetables, overgrown with weeds.

Smoke curled up into the drizzle. Pol approached the building. It had seen better days, but as he got closer, he realized that it wasn't as old as it looked. He dismounted and knocked on the door.

An old man answered the door. His hair stuck out on all sides and a beard covered his chest. Looking at Pol with glazed eyes, he said, "What do you want? Turn around and go back down the hill. I don't need any of what you're selling, and that includes my land."

He slammed the door in Pol's face, but then he opened it up again and looked at Demeron.

"Is that a Shinkyan?"

"He's mine, and his name is Demeron."

"I assume you named him after the sleeping god, Demron, who sleeps in Fassia," the man said, blinking as if trying to remember the details. "You're not a peddler, then?"

"I'm a traveler. One of our party hit his head and is about half an hour to the east on a trail. We were wondering if we could camp in this meadow tonight? There aren't many flat spots in these hills."

The man squinted at Pol. "No, there aren't. You don't look like a weeder. If you let me ride your horse, I'll do it."

Pol struggled to help the old man into the saddle at which time the man began to flail the reins and kick the stirrups.

"He won't move without my permission."

"You can talk to him?"

"And he to me," Pol said. "I'll still give you a ride."

They found the trail, and Pol located the three dots of his friends, surrounded by four other dots. "It appears they have attracted company," Pol said.

"Weeders. Curse of the Spines, they are," the man said. "Don't worry. I know most of them around here. Let's go meet them."

This had to be Searl, but Pol didn't ask the man anything. Only an educated man would recognize the source of Demeron's name and his breed.

They approached Darrol, standing with his sword out along with Paki.

"Settle down boys," the old man said. He squinted at Darrol. "Netherfield?"

"Searl. It's been awhile," Darrol said.

"Indeed it has." Searl wiped his eyes. "It is you, isn't it? My mind likes to play lots of games, these days."

Pol bet it did. He guessed that Searl was still in the thrall of a recent dose of the minweed.

"They's trespassing on our land," one of the men said. "Gotta pay the toll. You stay outta this, Searl."

"This one is a friend of mine, and I imagine the others will soon be. Leave them, if you want to preserve your health." Searl pulled a handful of weeds out of his pocket and stuffed it into his mouth.

Pol could feel tension in the air. He sensed one of the dots moving through the woods, coming up behind Searl. He jumped off Demeron and threw his knife just as the man attacked.

He turned and saw another dot approaching from where Kell lay and threw another knife, this time using his magic to enhance his aim and strength of his throw. Two weeders were down.

The one who had confronted Darrol and knew Searl ran down the path slipping in the mud a few times before disappearing from view.

"There is still one out there," Pol pointed to where the dot was.

"A locator and a pattern master?" Searl said. "You are another Deftnis monk! I didn't know. You should be too young to have learned those techniques."

Pol noted the location dot turn and leave their vicinity.

"That was too easy for you," Searl said, weaving in the saddle. "Ah, it's taking effect." His eyes glazed even more and he threw his arms out before he fell into Darrol's arms.

"He is still an addict. Lucky we caught him just as he had chewed a dose. It hadn't gotten to him yet. Can you find your way back to his place?"

Pol nodded.

Darrol and Paki draped Searl over Demeron and tied Kell to his own horse with his head tucked underneath some wadded up clothing on his horse's neck.

"Want to keep the head elevated, and that's the best we can do," Darrol said.

"He recognized you," Pol said.

Darrol nodded. "Searl was an exceptionally smart man before his habit overcame him."

"I could tell. He knew how I had come up with Demeron's name and that he was a Shinkyan stallion." Pol walked in front of Demeron, who didn't need to be led. They didn't move any slower than Demeron had walked in the bad conditions.

Eventually they made it to Searl's place. There was barely enough room underneath the long lean-to for all five horses. Demeron let Pol know that he would take care of his friends.

Searl's cabin was a mess inside, but it looked like it had been tidied up from time to time, so it didn't take long to find a place for Kell. They just dumped Searl on his bed. He thought that Searl might be living in filth, but his cabin seemed to be merely disorderly.

Pol looked around. Herbs hung in bunches from the ceiling and vegetables were in hand-carved wooden bowls. A large bowl held a fresh batch of bluish leaves. They reminded Pol of mint leaves with the jagged edges.

"Minweed?"

Darrol nodded. "This is fresh. I'll bet it grows all over the place up here. Let's build up the fire and look around, if the drizzle hasn't returned."

A few minutes later, Paki, Darrol, and Pol walked up to the vegetable patch. Bluish green weeds wound their way through all of the vegetables. Searl must have more lucid moments since the vegetable plot had spring plants in varying stages of growth.

"I've never seen minweed like this. I saw dried leaves before, but not fresh, and it grows in abundance," Darrol said. "It's an addict's dream."

"So, Searl is dreaming his dream," Paki said.

Pol checked Demeron to see if the horses needed any water, but was told they'd had enough for the day.

The three of them walked back into Searl's cabin. It looked big enough for a large family, and maybe there was at one time. Pol climbed up into the loft. It hadn't been touched for quite a while, but it was dry and warm now that a fire heated the cabin.

Paki and Pol cleaned up the loft as best they could while Darrol watched over Kell.

"He's still out, but he looks okay." Darrol said, once the pair of them had lugged Darrol's things up into the loft along with theirs. Kell's belongings stayed on the main floor.

Searl started and sat up. "Where is the fire?"

"In the fireplace," Darrol said.

The disgraced monk looked towards the hearth and the fire abruptly stopped burning. Smoke funneled up from the hearth and the cabin started to cool off.

"I see why he'd want to be alone. Are we safe tonight?" Paki said.

"Until the old man wakes up," Darrol said.

Pol didn't like the trace of fear in Darrol's words.

~ ~ ~

Chapter Twenty-Three

⁓

THE FORMER MONK SLEPT while Pol and his two companions continued to clean up the cabin, and then moved outside after putting some order into Searl's place.

"We should be on alert. We killed two men yesterday. Their friends might seek revenge," Darrol said as they rested on the rickety porch tacked in front of the cottage.

"Don't be," Searl said, walking out into the sunlight. He looked towards the sun and stretched. "The weeders have a rule against robbing travelers. It will bring the Duke of Hardman's forces into the hills and put a temporary halt to their activities."

Searl walked over to his well and drew a bucket of water and threw it over him, clothes and all.

"We stayed the night," Darrol said. "I hope you don't mind."

Searl shook his head. "I don't like company, but the boy inside will need to stay for a week or so." He looked around at his yard. "I see you've already started to pay me back. I've got some other chores for you."

"Have you taken a look at Kell?"

Searl nodded. "Not much I can do but stop a bit of the internal bleeding. His body will have to do the rest. He'll be out for another day or so. As long as he's not moved, he'll recover." Searl grimaced, and then closed his eyes, wavering on his feet.

"Is something wrong?" Pol asked.

The monk gave Pol a funny look. "Something is always wrong. Why do you think I'm up here? You all know you're at risk staying with me."

Darrol barked out a laugh. "As long as you kill the fire and not me."

"Kill the fire?" Searl said.

Paki looked at Pol and then at the monk. "You woke up and saw the fire burning. You snuffed out the flame with a look."

Searl laughed, a little painfully in Pol's view. "Sleep out of my sight, then."

"We did," Darrol said. "The loft is a bit more habitable now."

The monk nodded. He looked longingly at the vegetable patch. "I'll write out a list of supplies for you to get at Hill Creek, the closest village. You can get whatever you want there. The weeders won't follow you if you take the west path." He pointed to a break in the bushes where the trail must have begun.

Searl walked over to the vegetable patch and pulled up a stalk of bluish leaves. Minweed, Pol concluded, and, after tearing off the roots, stuffed it whole into his mouth. Without another word he returned to the cabin.

Pol followed him in.

"I'll be gone for most of the day, but I've got some minutes until I am back in the arms of my addiction." He gave Pol a mirthless laugh and scribbled out a list.

Pol had to ask him what some of the words were. He recognized the illegible handwriting from the letter Searl had written the Abbot in the wintertime.

"Do you think Paki will be safe?" Pol asked.

Darrol chuckled. "If Searl is in his cabin, where do you think Paki will be?"

"Outside."

"He'll be fine."

They continued to ride westward and descended into a cultivated valley. A village sat at the far end. The path followed one side of a large, meandering stream. Crops and orchards dotted the valley floor. It seemed like an idyllic place to live, but Pol thought it might be a bit claustrophobic for him.

"Hill Creek," Darrol said.

The village reminded Pol of the one he had visited during his trip with the North Salvan army last summer. The streets weren't cobbled, and the previous day's rain had turned the streets into mud. Demeron's large hoofs made loud squishing sounds as he plodded along. The village was a busy place with other horses, carts, and even a carriage traveling up and down the main street.

"Jadekin's General Store," Pol said, looking at the script, and then at the sign. "Here we are."

They tied their horses up outside the store and walked in. It was clear the style of clothes in Hill Creek didn't match their own. Pol endured the stares and realized there might not be too many visitors that came this way.

"What do you need?" the clerk asked. He looked like the owner with his thinning sandy hair and the wide flat nose. It looked like it had been broken at some time.

"Supplies. We're staying close by, up in the hills," Pol said. This far west, the Spines jutted further out from lower hills than the mountains to the east.

"We don't serve weeders here," the man said.

Pol wondered if the thugs that tried to attack Darrol dressed differently than these people, but he hadn't paused to notice.

"Not weeders. There is a healer that we're with."

"Searl? He's hardly a healer anymore. What business do you have with that hermit?"

Darrol put his hand on the counter. "He's an old friend. I knew him before he, uh, became what he is."

"You a monk, too?"

Darrol nodded. "I am."

The man's demeanor softened a bit. "See if you can get him sober enough to make more trips to the village. We've never had a healer do what he can do, even under the influence of minweed, especially when he first arrived. I'm afraid he's gotten worse."

"I know," Darrol said. "We have his list." He looked at Pol.

"I can go over this with you. I'm afraid his writing isn't very legible," Pol said.

They bought their supplies.

Pol looked over at the clothes racks. "Do you mind if I buy some clothes?"

The man's face crinkled into a smile. "That's what I'm here for. It looks like you two have been on the road for awhile."

"Weeks," Darrol said.

Pol used some of his money to buy new clothes for them all. The men of Hill Creek wore looser shirts and tight vests. The trousers were fuller in the thigh and thinner in the leg to fit into tall boots.

He treated Darrol to new boots and two shirts, since the repairs they had made to the clothes they brought with them from Deftnis weren't the best.

"You didn't have to buy these," Darrol said, on their way back to Searl's.

What did you get me? Demeron asked.

"Everyone needs a reward for getting me to Searl. The horses will enjoy the grain," Pol said, satisfying both comments.

The clouds began to build up for another round of rain that threatened just as they rode into Searl's yard. Pol felt that something was wrong.

He looked towards the lean-to and realized that the horses were gone.

Pol jumped off Demeron, head immediately down, looking for clues before the skies burst and any tracks washed away.

"Check inside the cabin," Pol said.

"I'll take our supplies in, so they won't get wet."

While Darrol hurried, Pol walked through the yard. He didn't see any blood darkening the ground, so that gave him a measure of relief. With their arrival the previous day, Pol had to sift through the footprints and find a pattern of those on the top layer.

He couldn't tell how many men came, but he detected both mounted and unmounted. Weeders had finally chosen to make Searl pay for the thugs' deaths yesterday. Pol couldn't help but feel guilty. If Searl was hurt, it was all due to Pol.

"All stowed," Darrol said. "We'd best get going. Which way?"

Pol could answer that question. "That way," he pointed towards another trail, not the one they had used to get to Searl's. His yard seemed to be a crossroads of sorts. He ran into the cabin and grabbed all his knives.

The heavens finally let go, and the journey became sloppy. Until the trail branched, they didn't need to do much looking down at the tracks. The trail intersected a rough dirt road. Pol could see the tracks led upward. It didn't take any Seeking skill to see the wagon ruts.

"This is miserable," Darrol said.

"If we are miserable, they are, too," Pol said, guilt still assaulting his mind as they rode. "We can pick up our pace on this road." He didn't say he would be using his locating spell as they went, but Pol would use any advantage he could.

They didn't travel far until they passed little meadows filled with bluish green plants. The weeders' crops. Not long after the meadows appeared, Pol picked up three colored dots.

"Sentries," Pol said.

"We can't ride any further," Darrol said.

"I'll leave you here, Demeron. Follow once I beckon."

Demeron nodded with his head.

The mud squished on the road, but Pol led them off into the forest that was drier beneath the leaves. Most of the trees were hardwoods, their leaves just out. The forest floor was soft and damp, allowing Pol and Darrol to advance quietly.

Pol led them past the first sentry, and then they circled back. Darrol hit the back of the weeder's head with the hilt of his sword. The man crumpled soundlessly to the ground.

With his heart beating faster, Pol pressed his lips together and concentrated on relaxing. He couldn't let his poor physical condition keep him from saving Paki and Kell, not to mention Searl and his promise of a future.

They made it through the next two sentries without a mishap. The men were obviously looking for riders. Being on foot disrupted the weeders' own perceptions of the pattern. Pol nodded at the realization, and then called Demeron to come forward.

"Halt any retreat, but watch for archers. I don't want to find out if Searl is an animal healer," Pol said.

You can rely on me to protect Darrol's mount and myself.

Pol continued up the road, but moved to just inside the trees.

"It helps to have a horse that follows instructions," Darrol said.

Pol shook his head. "It's not a matter of following instructions. He's one of us in this fight," Pol said. "He helps us willingly."

Indeed I do. Demeron said.

Pol just smiled to himself and walked forward.

About one hundred yards further up the road, the weeder's camp came into view. Pol noticed a large barn and two other buildings, one large and another smaller. It reminded Pol of the brigands of Rocky Ridge. They slipped closer.

"There are eight people ahead. That means five against two with Demeron as a backup."

Pol heard a noise behind him and looked back at Demeron. "Follows instructions? No."

Darrol chuckled. "It's time for a little retrieval."

With Kell and Searl out of the fight, they could only hope that Paki would be able to help.

All the dots were in the big cabin. Pol crept closer and peeked over the windowsill. Men littered the floor, as if they had all fallen asleep. Since Pol didn't recognize any of them, it appeared all the weeders were taken care of.

He stood up and looked again. Searl smiled at them. Pol got the sense that the monk would have waved, if the weeders hadn't tied Searl up.

Pol walked through the front door, beckoning Darrol to follow.

"Ah. You have arrived in time to free us," Searl said.

Paki was gagged and placed in a corner. Both Kell and Paki had their feet and hands bound.

Darrol untied Paki.

"I fell asleep before they crept up," Paki said once the gag had been removed. "I didn't stand a chance. Searl was asleep." Paki glared at the monk. "And Kell was still unconscious. The weeders have been out for less than a quarter hour, I figure."

"Couldn't have been long," Darrol said. "There were three sentries."

"Were?" Paki began to untie his feet.

"They are knocked out, but we didn't use magic," Pol said.

Searl stood and stretched. "I'm too old to stay in the same position for too long, unless…"

"Unless under the influence of your best friend," Darrol said, the disapproval plain on his face.

Searl nodded. "My best friend, indeed."

"How long will they be out?" Darrol asked.

"Another hour or more. Can you write a note? I'm afraid my handwriting isn't what it once was. We have our disagreements from time to time, and I'd rather deal with these morons than a newer, rougher bunch."

Pol looked at Searl in shock. "But they just abducted you! It's a wonder you are still alive!"

"Bound until dinnertime, then I would share a meal with them and return to my home. It's happened before. Evidently one of your victims was the cousin of Morfess, their leader. He had to do something. We're still friends, enough. I put them to sleep, knowing that you two would find us. I didn't want anything violent to happen," Searl said, too sanguinely for Pol.

"Then let's get going," Darrol said.

Since Searl was in a more lucid state, Darrol suggested that he make sure the three sentries were all right. After he applied a bit of his healing to two of them, they returned to Searl's cabin.

The rain had stopped, and Searl allowed them a fire. Darrol cooked a dinner of sorts with the meat that he had purchased in Hill Creek and leafy vegetables and carrots that Searl plucked out of his garden.

"I made sure there's no minweed in my stew," Darrol announced.

Searl smiled and took a handful of minweed from the basket in his cabin and threw it in his own portion. "I missed my afternoon dose." He began to eat more quickly.

"Why are you rushing?"

"Ah, the minweed puts me to sleep," Searl said. "If I take my time, I won't finish my meal."

The rest just ate, and by the time they were done, Searl snored with his head on the table. At least his bowl was empty and his stomach full.

"He said dose," Pol said.

"I told you he had a shoulder injury. Maybe he's still ailing. I wasn't that close with the man," Darrol said.

Pol and Paki lugged Searl to his bed.

"Where am I?" Kell said, holding onto his head. They had laid him out on some blankets on the floor with a pillow made out of his clothes propping up his head.

"Searl's cabin," Paki said. "Is there any stew left?"

"None for you." Darrol poured the rest of the stew into his own bowl and took it over to Kell.

"Hungry?"

Kell nodded.

Searl didn't wake until later the next day, and he checked on Kell before he stuffed another handful of minweed down his mouth.

"Your friend is no worse from his visit to my neighbors," Searl said, his voice already slurring.

Pol walked outside and said hello to Demeron before he began exploring the woods around Searl's place. He found minweed growing in little clearings. The plant seemed to like the sun and the proximity to the woods, but it didn't grow in the shady parts of the forest. Pol noted the pattern.

Paki caught up to him. "He's got little plantings of the stuff all through the woods?"

"He does. I don't know if he'll be sober enough to help me."

"We came all this way. You'll find something that will help."

Pol wasn't so sure, so he kept walking. The forest seemed to teem with minweed. He began to pull the plants out. They came up easily enough.

"Help me," Pol said.

Soon they had weeded three of the clearings. "We'll do more while we can," Paki said.

"I don't want Searl to get too upset yet, so let's find the outside extent of these patches and work our way back towards Searl's cabin."

Searl called them from their slumbers in the middle of the night. "I'm afraid I'm going to have to ask you all to leave."

"Why?" Pol said.

"The weeders know I'm entertaining capable men," he looked at Paki and Pol, "and boys. They might feel threatened. For my safety and yours, I suggest that you leave. I don't know why you're here anyway."

Pol climbed down from the loft and looked at a lucid Searl. "I have a unique heart condition, and you are my only hope to get cured."

"Unique. Not so. Every heart looks pretty much the same to me."

"Then look at mine."

Searl snorted and poured himself a cup of water. "Lay down on my bed after you take off your shirt.

Pol complied.

Searl leaned over and his eyes took on the characteristic glaze. He moved his hand over Pol's chest, and then moved down over his stomach. "I'll be damned by whatever gods you choose," Searl said. "That's no malformation. Your heart was designed to be defective."

"Designed?" Pol hadn't heard the term applied to a body before.

"Designed, pre-planned, meant to be. There are tiny little strings in every cell of your body that determine how you grow, blue eyes, brown hair, height, sex, whatever. Your heart and a couple of your other organs have developed defectively, but defective on purpose."

"You can see that?"

Searl nodded. "That's why Deftnis wouldn't mind me returning. I never taught anyone else how to do what I can do. I discovered it on my own, and then," he shrugged, "I had to leave."

"Can you cure me?"

Searl stood up, looking down at Pol. "I can't fix the programming, but I could fix your body, if I was sober for a few weeks."

"Weeks?"

Searl nodded. "I have to rebuild your heart, your spleen, and I haven't looked at your head yet."

"Rebuild. Can a healer do that?"

"I can, but your friends will have to agree to leave. I can't have them poking around up here with a bunch of skittish weeders looking on. I want another promise."

"I'll commit to nearly anything," Pol said. Hope burned in his chest.

"I want to find my daughter and her husband. I'll go with you, but I can't trust myself to go on my own."

"But my friends will have to return to Deftnis?"

Searl nodded. "If they don't, the weeders will return with a much larger force. Morfess is the boss in this area, but he reports to others. The minweed business is very big, and profits go to the highest level in Hardman."

"The Duke?"

Searl put his finger to Pol's lips. "I didn't say him."

He didn't need to.

"Give me an answer in the morning. I won't take as much medicine tonight." Searl took less than a handful of leaves from the bowl. They had wilted a bit, but he still munched on them.

~ ~ ~

Chapter Twenty-Four

POL LED HIS FRIENDS OUT OF THE CABIN. "Searl and I talked last night."

"I heard," Darrol said. "I don't know if I can leave you here by yourself."

"What?" Paki said.

"Searl took a look at my insides and said they are a mess. It will take weeks to fix, and he's uneasy that four men at his place might spook the weeders."

Darrol nodded. "It's a valid point. Maybe we could stay in Hill Creek while he's fixing you up."

Pol looked at Kell and Paki. "No, that's too unfair. If you go to the south, you can be in Deftnis before Searl is finished, and I don't think he can stay sober for that long. It will likely take longer. Kell and Paki can learn a lot at the monastery in a month or more."

"But what about you?" Kell asked.

"He is a black cord, isn't he, Darrol?"

Darrol pressed his lips together. "He is."

"I can learn a lot from him, so don't worry about me. I've always had a head start at the afternoon subjects anyway."

"Mistress Farthia Wissingbel," Paki said.

Pol smiled. "That's right. You head back. If I'm cured, I will join you in a month or less. If I'm not cured, I don't think I'll be lasting more than a few years to hear the healers at Deftnis talk. Their treatments have ended up only accelerating my heart's deterioration."

"It has?" Paki looked concerned.

Pol put his hand on his friend's shoulder. "I didn't want to tell you, but that is why we traveled in the spring rather than waiting for harvest break."

"Ah. You did say you didn't want to wait," Paki said.

"That's why."

"Then we will leave as soon as Searl says Kell is ready to travel," Darrol said. "Are you up to it?"

Kell nodded. "The further we travel away from the Wild Spines, the safer we will be. I wish you well, Pol."

They all went back inside for breakfast. Searl finally awoke.

"Decision made?" he asked of Pol.

"My friends will leave as soon as you say Kell can go."

Searl folded his arms. "You are safer leaving here than trying to fight off another wave of weeders. Sooner the better. The best road south is two hours or so west of Hill Creek. Go all the way to the coast, and then it's easy to get back to Deftnis."

Pol didn't want to see his three friends leave, but they were ready to go right after a hearty midday meal. Pol distributed their new clothes, and Darrol gave Pol a bit more of their funds.

He watched them take the path towards Hill Creek and went back inside Searl's cabin. The monk had already fallen asleep after taking his latest dose. Pol watched the monk's gaping mouth as he snored away the afternoon.

Had Pol done the right thing? He had just sent his protection away, or had he? Pol walked out to visit Demeron.

"Have I done the right thing?"

We will get through this together, and you will grow strong, as long as you can keep your monk friend upright and awake. Can you do me a favor?

"Whatever you want."

Groom Searl's horse. The poor guy has got some tiny friends that need brushing out. The monk isn't the only one we horses have to live with.

At long last, Pol began receiving the treatments he needed to survive. Unfortunately, Searl never was awake very long. After a long week, waiting for Searl to emerge sober, Pol sat the monk down for a serious talk.

"What kind of progress are we making?" Pol asked.

"Slow. These things come slowly. It may take weeks or months."

Pol caught Searl's eyes going to the fresh bowl of minweed that the monk harvested before Pol awoke.

"We will never be able to find your daughter at this rate."

Searl looked away from Pol. "Perhaps that's not so important."

"It was a week ago." Pol tried to keep from getting angry. He took a deep breath and fought off anger. The pattern to dealing with Searl indicated projecting calm and reassurance, Pol thought.

The monk put his head in his hands. "It's the pain," he said.

"Then teach me to spell it away. There must be a pattern I can tweak that will put your shoulder right."

Searl blinked. "What?"

"I'm a magician, Master Searl."

The monk looked away. "I'm no master," he said in a small voice.

"Teach me. I wear the red cord. Teach me patience and control. Turn me into an instrument of relief," Pol said. His words became part of the pattern. Pol had never experienced what he was doing. It was like being a pattern-master with words. "We will find your daughter, and you can approach life anew."

"No!" Searl said. His hands clenched into fists, and he put them against his temples. "You can't learn."

"Teach me," Pol repeated.

Searl's gaze finally met his. He straightened up. "It took me years to acquire the expertise to look deep within."

"I don't need to learn all your technique, just enough to take the physical pain away. You'll have to face your minweed habit, if you want to meet your daughter again."

Searl bit his lower lip and tears welled in his eyes as he nodded his assent. "We can get started when I wake up this evening."

"No," Pol said. "We start now. Before you take your dose of

minweed, we will spend an hour preparing me to alleviate your pain."

The monk shook his head from side to side. "I need my dose."

"You'll get your dose. We are doing this for you, for me, and for your daughter."

Searl nodded. "My daughter, yes." He took a deep breath and began his first lecture on healing.

Surprisingly, healing was much the same as any other tweaking. Find the pattern and use that knowledge to change the pattern through an expert tweak. The more intense the malady or injury, the more precision was required.

They spent the next four days, with Searl giving Pol a summary of how bodies worked. Pol knew the basic parts, but Searl gave him reasons why blood was red and taught him about the mysterious force that communicated instructions from the brain through the nerves.

Pol's pile of notes began to grow until Searl didn't wake at his normal time.

"Wake up," Pol said, as calmly as he could to Searl's slumbering form. He turned the monk over to see a remnant of a minweed leaf stuck to Searl's lower lip.

Pol sighed. The man had taken an extra dose when Pol slept. Pol couldn't wait for something to happen that wouldn't on its own, so he threw out all the minweed in the house.

Searl woke, and after their afternoon session, he asked Pol to fill the little cistern above the sink that gave them running water.

"What have you done?" Searl said accusingly when Pol walked in with two buckets of water.

Pol didn't respond until he had filled the cistern. "I threw out your minweed. You took an extra dose last night. That's against our agreement."

Searl's face turned red. "We don't have an agreement like that."

"Then we should," Pol said. "I'll give you a fresh dose at the end of every good session."

Searl gnashed his teeth. "Pour me some water, and let's see if you've learned anything."

Other than Searl's nasty attitude, Pol felt like smiling at the thought of doing something practical.

"We've talked about shrinking blood vessels to remove inflammation, and expanding blood vessels to alleviate pain. I'll let you use a tiny measure of magic on my shoulder. Remember the pattern we talked about. The arteries branch smaller and smaller, like the limbs and branches of a tree. Don't think of closing them, or you will not get the result you want."

"I always felt a flush of heat when Malden healed me."

"Malden? You know Malden Gastoria?"

"My father's Court Magician."

Searl furrowed his brow as this brought up some memories. "He left after teaching a magic course just as I was expelled. He learned a bit of my technique, but Malden didn't want to be a healer." Searl looked at Pol with new eyes. "You didn't tell me you were a prince."

"Disinherited. Presently I am less a prince than you are a monk."

"We'll have to talk about that another time. Right now we focus on your giving me a bit of relief before I can get a proper dose of minweed."

"A slight constriction of the blood vessels," Pol said.

"Try it. You might want to lay your hands on my shoulder. It isn't necessary, but it may help you to concentrate. No more than ten counts."

Pol took a deep breath and put his hands on Searl's left shoulder. He thought of the veins he could see in his palm and then the branches of a leafless tree. The pattern grew in his mind. Pol could tell his eyes looked inward, so he tweaked the vessels in Searl's shoulder to constrict just a bit while he counted.

He opened his eyes as Searl opened his. "Tolerable for a first try," he said.

Pol put one of his hands on the table, to steady himself. "That was exhausting." He downed the water left in the cup that he had given Searl.

"A pity." Searl raised his arm and then winced.

Pol started. "Are you all right?"

Searl shook his head. "Of course not, but I can feel a tiny bit of relief. So that took a lot out of you?"

"It did. Perhaps I can do more with practice. It has worked in the past."

Searl grunted. "A fine pair we are. I can't stay awake long enough to heal you, and you can't manage to tweak long enough to make me better. Perhaps you are right. We will have to work harder."

~

Pol woke, still sleeping in the loft, when the cabin door flew open.

"Searl!" a voice called from down below.

"Wha?" Searl's voice was groggy, as it always was after a large dose. Pol had let Searl consume more minweed in the evenings for the past week.

"Are those soldiers still with you?" Pol recognized Morfess, the weeder leader. Pol had never seen the man awake and was struck by the man's dominating presence.

Pol threw on his clothes and looked over the railing, his throwing knives now tucked in his boots.

"Only me," Pol said.

"You are the one with the big horse?"

"I am."

Searl sat up, scratching his beard. "He has become an assistant. He's learning a bit of healing from me."

"Good. Get dressed. I have an injured man outside. Heal him, and I can set aside our recent differences."

Pol could see the constant give and take that Searl had talked about. Morfess's anger seemed to be an act, or perhaps part of a game the two men played.

He clambered down the ladder and helped Searl get some bread in him. He had found that food would revive Searl, if he hadn't yet thrown a handful of minweed down his throat.

The three of them walked out into the yard. A man lay on a travois. A wagon wouldn't make it along any of the paths to Searl's cabin from the weeders' compound.

"What do you make of him, student?" Searl asked. He narrowed his eyes as he made eye contact with the monk. This was a serious event. There were four men in front of him, and he could detect another ten hidden in the woods, close enough to view what Pol did. Maybe this wasn't quite a game to the weeders.

Searl had taught him to detect heat within a person, likely caused by infection or inflammation. That part of healing didn't take too much out of him, since it was similar in concept to the location spell that Pol used.

Pol felt heat close to the man's back. "Turn him over," Pol said.

Morfess's face looked grim. He nodded to one of his men.

Blood covered the man's back.

Searl nodded at his student to proceed.

Pol took a knife from his boot, which surprised the weeders, and proceeded to cut the rays of a star in the fabric above the wound. He peeled back the cloth, revealing an inch slit in the man's upper back.

"Knife wound?" Pol looked up at Morfess.

"He made the mistake of going to Hill Creek for some fun," the weeder said. "They don't like us much."

Pol was convinced there was more to the story, but he just concentrated on the injured weeder. "I need a few supplies," Pol said.

"I'll go." Searl made a move towards the cabin.

Pol grabbed his hand. "I think you should check my diagnosis. I'll be right back." Pol didn't trust Searl not to touch minweed in a crisis, and they just might be facing one.

He ran into the cabin and grabbed his bandages and filled a washpan with water.

"It has the beginnings of infection," Searl said.

Pol knelt by the wounded weeder and cleaned the wound. The edges appeared angry and hot. He looked with magical sight and could see the redness was indeed hot, and it extended into the wound.

"This is beyond me," Pol said. "I haven't learned how to handle infection, and this wound is in the process of going bad."

Morfess swore, and then said, "Any fool can see that."

The weeder made Pol angry. "I detected it when he was on his back, didn't I?"

"You did," Searl said. "I'll take it from here." Searl's eyes glazed and Pol could now feel his healing power work on a pattern or patterns that Pol hadn't yet learned.

"How have I done?" Searl looked at Pol. "Look deeply."

Pol sought out a pattern of purity and could see where the wound had disrupted that. He saw the integrity of the man's wound and the vestiges of something Pol didn't know how to interpret.

"The infection has retreated?" Pol looked a bit more. "You've tweaked the good flesh to encroach on the bad?"

"That's good enough," Searl said. "Bandage him as best you can."

Pol made a pad of cloth and then wound another length around the man's torso, sideways and then across. He'd seen similar bandages at both the Deftnis infirmary and at Borstall.

Searl looked up at the weeder leader. "Change the bandage every day. Give the man lots of water to drink, but boil it, and let it cool first. He can survive, but only if you follow my instructions. You've done it often enough in the past."

"We have," Morfess said. The weeder eyed Pol. "I guess you can stay."

Pol didn't know whether to thank the man or not, so he merely gave Morfess a quick bow of his head.

The weeders left the yard with Searl and Pol standing in the middle. Pol followed the monk back into the cabin.

"It could have been worse," Searl said. "At least I didn't have to resort to using magic as a defense. Morfess hates that."

"There were ten more men hidden in the woods."

Searl smiled. "They only think they were hidden. We can both locate. You did well under pressure."

He could see the sheen of sweat on Searl's brow. The man must have been very scared, as scared as Pol.

"Remember, a magician can only do so much. We were surrounded and could have been easily executed," Searl said.

Pol realized that the monk had accurately read the situation, and Pol hadn't. He had always assumed they had the upper hand, even with ten men hidden away. He gulped when he realized how close he had been to losing his temper in front of the weeders. He had to change the subject.

"Is part of the pattern purification?" Pol asked.

Searl put both his hands on his knees and took a deep breath. "You see it as purification, but that's not quite right. I was peeling back putrefaction. Just the opposite."

"Oh, right, the tweak wasn't making the bad flesh good, but extending the good flesh into the bad."

"You noticed? Good. I also worked on strengthening the healing that had already begun."

"Healing? I thought he was infected."

"Just because there is infection doesn't mean there isn't healing going on at the same time. The body fights infection, but it's not a one-dimensional battle. Healing goes on, but think of the infection as an invasion. If left on its own, the infection soldiers, to put it in a military context, begin overwhelming the body's defenses with sheer numbers. It's the body that does the heating to kill the soldiers, the infection."

Pol tried to find a pattern that fit the situation. "Fighting the enemy soldiers with fire?"

"Right. Now, please, please permit me some minweed. It has been a taxing morning."

Pol reluctantly relented and let Searl sleep until the afternoon.

~ ~ ~

Chapter Twenty-Five

Searl began to start hiding minweed around the cabin. Pol found the stashes and destroyed them. For a while, everything proceeded as Pol hoped. He learned more about healing and began giving Searl treatments for his shoulder, which the monk admitted were working.

"Why didn't you let the other monks treat you like this?" Pol said when Searl woke up as evening approached.

Searl stayed silent for a bit. "I traveled to Orkal, the duchy on the western border with Sand, to heal a wealthy merchant who had once studied at Deftnis. My horse shied for some reason I'll never know and threw me to the ground. A woodcutter brought me to his house, not knowing who I was. I was unconscious, you see. A concussion to match my damaged shoulder. His wife knew some folk remedies, and she gave me minweed to alleviate the pain."

"But you could have just stopped taking it," Pol said.

Searl looked away. "You haven't learned a lot about healing, but people react differently to medicine. Overall, a potion works the same, but for some, there are more violent reactions. My body instantly developed a craving for minweed. I've not stopped wanting it since that horrid day."

"So you use your shoulder as an excuse?"

The monk shrugged. "I told the monks about my shoulder, but

my body craved the minweed, so I didn't let them heal me. My injury was always my excuse. I couldn't eliminate the excuse, could I? After all this time, you have learned to tame it," Searl said.

"But your addiction remains?"

Searl gave Pol a sorrowful look. "I am afraid so, but my excuse is going away."

This would never do, Pol thought. "You made a deal with me."

"I did, and I am fulfilling it. I think I have done well enough teaching you to heal that I can move on to repairing your body."

Pol had to admit he had taken to healing better than he had expected. Unfortunately, one could do little to heal oneself other than closing a wound and now Pol knew how to do that.

"I don't want to wait," Pol said.

Searl scowled. "Don't be petulant, boy."

"Don't be an addict, old man," Pol said. He lost a bit of control and bit his lip to regain it. "I don't want to spend the rest of a truncated life having you play around with my insides for a few minutes a day. Do you want my help in finding your daughter, or doesn't she really mean anything to you?" Pol thought about his words. "I'm sorry I had to say that."

After raising his hand in mock surrender, Searl said, "It's how you feel, isn't it? I know you're only fifteen, but you are correct. I'm an addict. What shall we do? Do you want me to dismiss you?"

"I don't want to leave. To leave is to die," Pol said.

"Fine, then what do we do?"

"Let's say I want to be cured in two weeks. How much time would you have to spend working on me?"

Searl twisted his mouth in thought. "Two hours a day, most likely.

"Then why don't you commit to two hours of your lucid time? We started at an hour a day, and it has dwindled to half or less than that," Pol said.

"I know. My life is—"

"...what it is because you made it that way. The problem only rests within you, right?"

"Who taught you to think that way?"

Pol shook his head. "I had to fight for my life continually last year.

My tutor and Malden tried to help me cope with the pressure. They did it skillfully, but it all revolved around my doing all I could to solve my problems, not looking for others to do it for me."

"That is an admirable life lesson. One that I can't follow."

Pol thought for a bit. "I had a case of melancholia after I killed a man. The tension must have gotten to me. I was nearly to the point where I wouldn't mind if I killed myself. I could have given up and just faded away. I wanted to, but I just didn't have the energy to do it. Kell noticed my change, and the healers intervened. I pulled myself out of a deep, deep hole. You can, too."

"As I said, it's a path that I can't follow," Searl said.

"Can't follow, or won't follow? You have a physical addiction, but not everyone is a minweed addict."

"They would be," Searl said, "if given a large enough dose."

"What if I took a large dose of minweed? Would I end up as an addict?"

"You wouldn't know unless you tried."

"If I take a large dose of minweed, will you go without, or with small amounts until I'm cured?" Pol had no idea if he could withstand the temptation of minweed, but he had to try something.

"That is quite a risk."

"My life is somewhat of a risk," Pol said.

"All right, I'll agree."

"In writing. I know you can violate the agreement at any time, but let's at least formalize our bet."

Searl pulled out a piece of paper.

"I'll do the writing," Pol said.

Once he had finished the agreement, both of them signed it. Searl left with an empty bowl and returned with it filled with minweed, fresh-picked from the garden. "Fresher is better," he said as he put the bowl in front of Pol.

"What does it taste like?" Pol said, not really wanting to hear the answer.

"Food from the gods," Searl said. "You will be transported to a better place."

Pol looked at the bowl and at the agreement set out to the side.

He had to do something, but what if he became addicted? At least the two of them could live in mutual oblivion. It was highly likely that Searl would even outlive Pol.

The alternative was a commitment that Pol would ensure the monk would follow. He took a deep breath and began shoving the weed in his mouth. It tasted like bitter lettuce, but he noticed a mint-like tang, which, coupled with its appearance, likely led to its name.

He needed a drink of water before he could finish and finally downed the entire bowl.

Searl grinned as if he had pulled something over on Pol, and he worried that Searl might win the bet.

Nothing happened while Pol sat at the table. Searl functioned for some time before he fell asleep. Pol rose to put the bowl at the sink and his legs began to wobble. He put his hand to his head and felt the floor begin to buckle, twist, and whirl.

His legs collapsed beneath him, and he fell to the floor. He looked over at Searl's face, which began to wobble, expand, and contract. When he shut his eyes, strange colored patterns began to appear and then began to whirl around and shift.

Pol's mind focused on the colors swirling and pulsating and creating patterns that repeated, but didn't make any sense.

Snoring broke into Pol's dreamless sleep. He opened his eyes and looked at the ceiling of Searl's cabin. After bringing his hand in front of his eyes, Pol could tell he was back to normal. His eyes ached, of all things.

He walked outside, surprised that he didn't stagger like he had the previous evening. After dumping a bucket of water over his head, Pol blinked away the drips and drifted over to the vegetable garden. He stood looking at the minweed, growing abundantly between the other plants.

Pol felt no urge to stuff his mouth with the weed. In fact, he sighed with deep relief when he found that minweed held as little attraction for him this morning as it had yesterday afternoon.

He thought about his agreement with Searl and realized how stupid he had been. Darrol would have never let him take such a risk, but now that was behind him. Pol knew he had won a small victory. The trick would be getting Searl to abide by his commitment, and that was no sure thing.

After walking into the woods, Pol found more minweed growing in the patches where Paki and he had removed the plants. They grew like weeds, malicious weeds. He bent over and continued to pull.

He went back and found a shovel in the lean-to.

What did you do last night? I caught that you were anxious about a risk, Demeron said.

"I made an ill-advised bet with Searl. I hope I won."

You don't trust him?

Pol considered what trust was. "I can't trust a man who doesn't control his own soul. I hope to remedy that, but I'm not sure how."

Remove the person or thing that controls him. That's what I would do if I had rider that wasn't nice. You've seen me do that.

Demeron had bucked Coram off of him.

"I'll be back to take you both out for some exercise later."

Do that for my sake and for his. Demeron moved his head towards Searl's horse. The animal lifted its head up and neighed. He patted Demeron and poured some grain out for him and the other horse. He groomed their coats and then took the shovel into the woods.

How could Pol remove minweed when it was so ubiquitous? He began to dig, alarmed that the familiar beating of his heart and shortness of breath had returned. Pol put his head on the handle of the shovel. His strength had begun to deteriorate. He looked over the small patch and felt discouraged. It would take him years to destroy the local minweed, and at the rate he was going, he'd be gone before he completed the task.

Pol returned to the cabin, fixed some lunch, and sat holding a cup of tea. He had to sniff it to make sure it was minweed-free, now that he knew its taste. Searl still snored and likely would for another hour.

He looked over the agreement they had decided on the previous day and made a copy. One for Searl and one for him. He signed it and left the copy out for Searl. Pol had fulfilled his bargain, but he didn't know if Searl would honor his or not. It wasn't as if he could force the monk to do anything. You really couldn't threaten the man who you depended on to heal you.

Some time later Searl began to stir. Pol reheated the tea and brought out some stale bread for dipping.

"You're alive?" Searl said, chuckling. "Want more?"

Pol shook his head and waited for the monk to get up and sit at the table.

"I guess I'm not the kind to get addicted. I must admit that I took a wild ride, but I'm not sad to say, it will be a one-time experience.

Searl looked disappointed. "You are going to hold me to that?" He looked at the agreement.

"It's the most important agreement of my life," Pol said.

The monk didn't say anything for a bit and dipped his bread into the tea.

He looked at the tealeaves in the bottom of his mug. "I'll cure you," he said, his voice nearly a whisper. "I'm sorry."

"Sorry?"

"I shouldn't have agreed to take on your dare. It wasn't very noble of me."

Pol laughed without humor. "Noble? What is noble about serving only yourself? You were noble when you used to travel around here and heal. Why did you stop?"

Searl didn't respond. He finished his breakfast and went outside to wash. He came back not much later with his hair wet. Pol was afraid he had taken a detour to the vegetable patch.

"Will an hour work this morning and an hour in the evening?"

"With a dose in between?"

Searl nodded, and for the first time he actually looked ashamed.

Pol agreed. "I'll head to Hill Creek for some more supplies while you sleep. I'd like some fresher bread."

"Fine," Searl said. He toweled off his wet hair with a rag that might have been part of his monk's robe.

"Lay down on my bed. Be prepared to feel some discomfort."

Pol straightened out the covers and did as he was told.

Searl pulled up a chair, and then put his hand out, leaning with the other on the bed frame. "Heart first. I hope you don't mind my babbling as I go. It helps me concentrate."

Pol shook his head. "I don't mind. Concentration is good."

Searl spent time with his eyes closed, and then Pol felt little surges of heat in his chest. He cried out as the heat turned into real pain.

"You have to endure it. I am remaking your heart. There will be a lot of this. Are you willing to endure it?"

Pol blinked tears from his eyes. "Please continue," he croaked.

After what seemed like ages, Searl sat back and patted Pol on his shoulder. "As you can imagine, I must change the pattern of your heart bit by little bit. It is a slow, slow process, and you will have to endure more. It takes a lot of my strength, too, but I'm glad to see, I haven't lost the knack. I thought that I would, you know."

Pol nodded. "Maybe I won't be heading to Hill Creek today." He felt like a washerwoman had wrung him out.

"Out of my bed. It's time for my dose, and I need it."

Pol twisted around and sat up while Searl gathered his mind salad outside. He felt rugged, as if someone had scraped the insides of his chest. Maybe that was Searl's technique. Pol had just been reminded that magical healing was not without its price.

He rose and climbed gingerly up the ladder to the loft and lay down.

Pol woke up to Searl calling to him. "Get up, it's time for your next treatment," Searl said.

Pol felt better, but his insides still were uncomfortable. He made it down to the main level and found that Searl had laid another blanket over his bed.

"Are you ready?"

Pol just grunted. "I will do whatever it takes."

The second session was a repeat of the first, but Pol felt worse.

"I don't think I can handle this tomorrow," he said. "I need to recover."

"You do indeed. I've done more than I normally would."

Was Searl punishing him? Pol wasn't in a position to know, but he did need to recover.

Pol rode Demeron down to Hill Creek in the afternoon of the next day. Searl was asleep, or whatever the minweed did to him most of the day after he and Pol had come up with a list of provisions.

Searl's horse followed behind carrying two sets of saddlebags, with Demeron leading while the other horse faithfully followed.

"I thought you fellas left Searl's place," said the clerk Pol had met before at Jerkin's General Store.

"Three of us did. I stayed behind for a while. I'm trying to help out Searl."

"We could still use his help from time to time."

Pol handed over his list and waited while the clerk filled the order. Both of them filled the saddlebags, and the grain sacks were slung over the saddle of Searl's horse. Pol had hoped Searl would be awake when he returned, but the monk disappointed him.

For the next three weeks, Pol received two treatments every other day.

He lay down, and Searl began to work on a spot just underneath his left rib.

"What are you doing?"

"Working on your spleen and then your liver."

Pol blinked through the pain. "What about my heart?"

"It needs another few days to heal, and we'll see if we are done there."

"Done?" Pol couldn't believe it. "My heart is fixed?"

Searl nodded, trying to suppress a smile. "We will see. I've never had to rebuild a heart quite like yours before, but it should be better than new. Your lungs will work fine with a stronger heart."

"My body won't reverse your work?"

Searl shook his head. "There is always a possibility, but I use a different technique than the monks at Deftnis did."

Pol didn't know what a new heart would feel like, but he could withstand the pain to improve the rest of his system.

"What with my spleen and liver?"

"They are undersized and need to be rebuilt as well. I've had plenty of practice on livers. Alcohol and livers are not friends, and I've improved more than a few. Spleens are not much different, but they are more fragile. It's not unusual to remove spleens rather than rebuild them, but in your case, I think I can rebuild it better than it is. The spleen is important in protecting against infection. Remember we talked about infection being a battle. The spleen is part of the body's defense."

"I will trust your judgment. When will I feel the effects on my heart?"

"Try some magic in a week. There is still some natural healing to do before you should exercise it," Searl said.

Pol wouldn't dare try sooner. He had waited a long time to be unaffected by his heart.

The treatments continued, but the spleen and the liver took much less time.

A week had transpired, but Searl told Pol to wait a bit more.

"I'll do a bit of work on your lungs, after all. You could use more capacity," the monk said.

Pol finally sat up. "That's the last?"

Searl nodded. "I didn't think you'd get me to stay sober long enough to cure you. You helped me stay that way. I admit I didn't give you much in the way of cooperation, but you made me prevail." He grinned. "Now do something that exhausted your strength before."

Pol stood and lifted the table up to the ceiling. He tweaked a twirl and brought it back down. He could feel a slight drain on his energy, but he lost less than he usually did performing a locating spell. He couldn't help but grin.

Then he went outside with his throwing knives and threw them into a tree trunk fifty paces away. He could never throw one that far using a sip of magic, and this time he added more than a sip into the flight. The grin didn't leave his face.

Pol held out his palm and tweaked a magic light out of air. He shouted with excitement. He was cured! Pol went over to Demeron, who stood looking.

You seem very happy. Your magic is easier?

Pol smiled and then laughed. "It is, isn't it?" He looked across the yard at Searl and ran towards him. His lungs hurt, and his heart hurt, but it didn't beat in his ears. "I guess I overdid it," Pol said.

"You'll need to build up by exercising. Come on inside and we'll work out a plan. You need to be in better shape when we head north to find my daughter."

Pol looked forward to improving his physical self. He followed Searl into the cabin.

"Run until your heart starts to hurt, just a bit. Your heart will be hurting more than your lungs for a while, and then it will be the reverse. You'll need to buy more food since your body will be burning more food," Searl said.

"It's a virtuous cycle, eat, exercise, rest, eat, exercise, rest. If you eat and don't exercise or don't rest, the cycle isn't virtuous. To build your strength, lift as much as you can stand. Lift until your muscles hurt.

"You do a little damage to the fibers and your body responds when it heals tiny tears by increasing your muscle mass and making you stronger. That's the theory."

"Now it's my turn," Pol said, while he put his hands on Searl's shoulder.

After the treatment, Searl sat back and worked his shoulder. "It's nearly good enough to stop taking minweed." He walked to the sink and plucked a large handful and chomped on it. "Nearly enough."

~~~

Chapter Twenty-Six

AT SEARL'S INSISTENCE, POL SPENT MORE MONEY on meat and milk. Pol had to drink the milk in a day or so, before it spoiled, and he found himself making more trips into Hill Creek. Each trip, Pol would run next to Demeron for a bit, instead of ride. He continued to feel stronger. He could feel his body respond to a stronger heart and bigger lungs.

Pol had always felt scrawny, but his ribs were starting to disappear, replaced by a layer of muscle. Now that he felt better, it was time to work on Searl's habit. If they were to leave the foothills and travel north to Dasalt, where Searl last heard from his daughter, Pol didn't think they could make it letting the monk sleep eight hours during the day.

After Pol had returned from one of his trips, he woke Searl up.

"It's time for you to clean up," Pol said.

"I'm clean enough."

"No. We can't travel to your daughter and have you awake for only a few hours a day. You have to wean yourself. Let's say one dose at night before you go to bed."

"My shoulder."

"I can treat your shoulder, even better now," Pol said.

Searl looked a bit afraid. "Maybe I can leave my daughter alone. She might not want to see her addict father."

"I think it is her father who doesn't want his daughter to see the addict," Pol said. He knew he was out of line talking to Searl like that, especially since he had no idea of what he could do to cure Searl.

"I can take bushels of minweed with us," Searl said.

"It's not the minweed," Pol said. "It's your ingestion of it. Let's reduce your ingestion and try keeping you sober for a day."

Pol could see the shine of sweat on Searl's forehead. Pol had to summon the courage to help a magician at the black level.

"You can teach me higher-level magic now that I won't faint every time I try something new. That can keep us busy while you aren't sleeping under the influence," Pol said.

Searl looked serious. "I can but try." He didn't smile or look encouraged. He walked over to his bowl of minweed and took a handful. "We begin tomorrow."

Pol would have rather had Searl start at that moment, but he didn't want to force Searl anymore than he had to.

Searl collapsed onto his bed after eating some food. He wouldn't wake until morning.

Pol took the shovel out of the lean-to and began to hack away at Searl's supply. With new strength, he began to root out the minweed patches in the forest. Not only did he maintain his heart rate, but he also could feel the muscles in his arms respond.

Pol took care of three patches and returned to the cabin. Searl still snored away in oblivion as Pol made himself a hearty stew.

In the evening, he took both horses for a ride towards Hill Creek and back, not wanting to wander around on unfamiliar trails. He didn't want another encounter with the weeders.

When he returned, Pol still felt unsettled, so he found his sword and began to practice forms. His anticipation magic didn't need to be used to put precision into his moves like it had before. Now he could actually incorporate the forms that he had not been able to handle for any length of time.

Pol could feel new power in his strokes. He knew he still lacked the strength of a full-grown man, but he maintained his practice for far longer than he ever had before. He began to enhance the power of his swings with sips of magic, and Pol felt a smoothness in his forms that didn't exist before.

He laughed, knowing that until he sparred with a known opponent, he wouldn't know how much progress he had made, but still, the practice did him a great deal of good. While he left Searl sleeping in the cabin, he came out at night and practiced his swordsmanship and his knife throwing.

Searl woke early the next morning. Pol had already fixed breakfast and filled the inside cistern.

"Good morning," Pol said.

The monk covered his face with his hands. "I don't know if I can do this."

"You aren't doing it on your own," Pol said, thinking back to the support that Mistress Farthia, Malden, and Val had given him in Borstall. "I am here to help."

Searl snorted. "Such words coming from a fifteen-year-old?"

Pol stood a little straighter. "I am a well-educated prince and a very quick study. I relieved the pain in your shoulder, didn't I?"

The monk waved Pol's comment away. "And I am a better educated Eighth Level magician."

Pol bowed to Searl. "I yield most things to your wisdom and experience."

"I caught that 'most,' lad." Searl went to the sink and emptied some water from the cistern into a bowl. He splashed water on his face and rubbed it hard with a scrap of towel.

They ate in silence. After Pol cleared the dishes, Searl stood and began to walk out the door.

"No. Today you will stay inside."

"Nature calls," Searl said.

"Then I will accompany you," Pol said.

Searl grunted and stomped through the door. He walked back to the outhouse and slammed the door shut. When he was finished, he exited and slammed the door shut again.

Pol dutifully followed him back into the cabin. He got out a paper and pen. "Let's write out a list of lessons. It might be better to have short goals, and I will document our activities."

"In case I leave and never return?" Searl said.

Pol nodded. "To show Vactor what I've learned."

"Vactor is teaching Level Fours? What a waste."

"He was teaching me when I was a Level Three."

Searl grunted and brushed the back of his hand on the bearded underside of his chin. "Write this down…" Pol stopped Searl at ten lessons. "If I pass these ten, we will leave. Okay?"

Searl nodded and let Pol see the hint of a grin. Did Searl not think Pol could learn the spells?

He didn't want to stay at the cabin forever. Pol itched to return to Deftnis, and if Searl truly did learn to control his habit, then he was still weeks away from returning. It would most certainly be summer before they arrived at the monastery.

After the first session, Searl walked to the vegetable patch and gathered a bowlful of minweed, without saying anything, and returned to the cabin.

Pol watched the monk settle down on his bed. He waited to hear Searl's snores before he grabbed the shovel and began to eliminate more of Searl's local supply of minweed. There were little patches all around Searl's cabin, but Pol committed to eradicating it about the time he intended to head north to find Searl's daughter.

He worked until the sun brushed the tops of the trees as it prepared to set in the west. Searl hadn't awakened, so Pol wrote notes on what he had learned earlier in the day and compared it to Searl's list. The monk hadn't taught him anything related to the items on the list.

Pol wished he could trust Searl, but he couldn't. The man was under the nasty influence of minweed, and that probably affected all he did.

Searl's list didn't seem that far off from some of the things he had seen around the monastery, so Pol decided he might try to puzzle out some of the techniques, using what he knew as a base. Vactor had always told him that the difference between levels was more of the ability to control tweaking.

Pol could see it was more involved than that, but he would do his best. He memorized the ten spells and decided to ask Searl related questions that would help him learn the techniques listed.

The lessons became a battle between Searl teaching Pol nonrelated techniques and Pol getting the answers that he needed to learn the ten techniques on his own. As the days wore on, Pol was learning much more than he expected. He had progressed to mastering eight of the ten items on Searl's list, plus whatever Searl taught him.

The first day of summer had come, and Pol had finished tearing out all of Searl's surrounding minweed patches. All that remained grew among the vegetable patch, now sporting summer vegetables.

Pol had puzzled out the ten techniques as Searl had begun another round of teaching him healing. Pol had to complain, but Searl just ignored him. The time had come to show Searl his progress and get out of the cabin and out on the road.

Demeron and Searl's horse were well-groomed, fed, and exercised. Pol had practiced pattern-mastering and could even throw his sword and guide it with his power for a short distance, while he had extended his knife throwing out to twenty-five feet or more with good penetrating power.

Pol was prepared to leave, so he sat Searl down before he started his next lesson, this one on how hands were constructed. Anatomy had nothing to do with the ten objectives.

"I am ready to be tested on the ten techniques you wrote down twenty days ago."

Searl narrowed his eyes. "We haven't even gotten to those yet."

"Yes, we have," Pol said. "I have learned them on my own with your guidance."

The monk put his hand to his chest. "My guidance? No, no, no, no."

"Test me."

"Very well." Searl took Pol outside where the monk ran Pol through each of the ten techniques.

"I passed."

Searl sat back against the post of the porch. "You have. How did I guide you? I am still mystified." He looked confused.

"The common thread through all magic is manipulating patterns. The trick is to discover what the true pattern is and how to tweak it to get the desired result. I was stumped on each of these until I asked you the questions that I needed."

"Oh," Searl shook his head. "I thought you were just off track."

"I was on my track," Pol said. "It's time to go."

Searl's eyes grew a bit with a tinge of panic. "It can't be. I can't leave here."

"Let's start with a trip to Hill Creek. You haven't been there for a long time."

"I have to, don't I?"

Pol nodded.

"Tomorrow. I need a dose."

The monk looked shocked enough that Pol would let him get one more in before Searl re-entered the world. Searl grabbed a bowl and filled it with the plant.

While Searl slept, Pol ripped out all of the minweed in the monk's garden except for a fringe that covered up the destruction that Pol had made of the minweed. He roamed the woods removing any traces of the weed, he returned to fix Searl dinner.

Pol noticed the bowl only half-consumed and would make sure that Searl didn't leave the cabin.

Searl rose and left the cabin for the outhouse. He didn't look in the direction of the garden before he returned. Pol breathed a sigh of relief.

"What do you want to do in Hill Creek?" Pol asked.

"I don't know. It's your trip."

Pol smiled. "Okay, we'll find something to do," he said.

They left early. "We'll get a cooked breakfast in Hill Creek," Pol said. "You're probably sick of my cooking."

"No, luckily, your cooking didn't make me sick," Searl said, with the ghost of a grin on his face.

Humor, thought Pol. Perhaps there was hope for his host.

They mounted and headed down to Hill Creek, an hour and a half ride to the north. The day had blossomed hot and the heat increased when they reached the valley. Pol hadn't been to the village for two weeks, and the fields had turned much greener.

People scurried about on their own business. The village's one restaurant was attached to the best inn. Pol and Searl walked in.

A man approached them. "Searl, it's been a year or more since you visited us."

"It might have been. This is my protégé, Pol Cissert."

The man tried to hide a smile. "Protégé in what?"

Pol felt the obvious undercurrents of the man's jest.

"I'm a magician. Master Searl has been tutoring me."

"Magician? Show me," the man said.

Pol looked at a small table surrounded by a chair on each side. He lifted them all up at once to the ceiling and back down again into the same place.

Searl gave Pol a sideways glance. Multiple object movement was one of the ten tests. Pol had used an assortment of tools at the cabin.

"Well, I suppose you are," their host said, his attitude changed.

"Serve us some breakfast, Harloy. What have you got that's fresh?"

Pol and Searl walked into Jadekin's General Store.

"I heard you were in town," the clerk said to Searl.

"My student dragged me here, Jadekin."

The clerk beamed. "I'm so glad to see you. Do you have time for a bit of healing? There are some in the village who could use your help."

Searl was about to say no, but Pol interrupted. "He will. I'm learning a bit of healing from him, so I can observe and help in my own small way."

The monk grunted and nodded his head. "Not for too long," Searl said.

Jadekin sent another clerk out, and by the time their order was filled, a space in the store had been cleared out, a padded table and chairs had been placed in a back corner of the store.

Since it was noon, someone brought in lunch for Searl and Pol while people began to line up.

"I can't cure everything," Searl announced to the crowd, "but I will do my best for two hours."

Patients were brought in. Searl talked to Pol while he worked, telling him what he did and what patterns he looked for.

Most of them had colds or flu, and Searl gave them common remedies and referred them to Jadekin for various potions and tonics.

A boy sat down with broken finger. "You can fix this," Searl said to Pol.

"Me?"

Searl nodded. "We've already gone over this. To knit a bone, you look into the finger and knit the ends together. For a simple break, you are tweaking the fracture back to its original shape. The proper pattern exists on both good sides of the bone, and you tweak the bone to knit. It will take some power, but now you have enough."

Pol couldn't imagine joining a bone, but he figured that Searl could repair a mistake. He looked with his magic into the wound. It was like locating in the dark, except there were no dots. He actually could see the insides of the finger, like he could see the insides of a lock. Pol wouldn't have thought to do such a thing until Searl worked with him. He had looked into his own body, but Searl had told him that a magician couldn't heal himself. The power couldn't transfer since it already ran through his body.

He saw the break. Pol had imagined a clean break, but the bone was mostly intact with shards of bone floating inside the finger. He located the pattern at both sides and applied his power to restore the bone and attach the chips.

"Ow, that's hot," the boy said.

"It takes heat to heal." Pol proceeded a bit more slowly in hopes that would help. He examined his work and brought his focus outside.

"Very good, Pol," Searl said. The monk hadn't done much complimenting, but his words sounded sincere.

"It is still tender, so don't get it bumped for a few days," Searl told the boy's mother.

"I didn't think I'd ever be able to do that."

"Malden Gastoria learned," Searl said. "He'd be pleased to know you did, too."

Pol nodded.

A woman came in clutching her stomach. Searl put his hands on her. "I will help you a bit," he said. "Get a digestive from Jadekin. You'll be fine in a few days."

Pol restrained a smile. "Constipation?"

Searl nodded with a straight face. "Most remedies are simple. You just need to know how to diagnose. Someone with the same stomachache might have something more serious. That is what takes a healer a long time to learn. Bones are easy, softer tissue issues are harder."

"What about infections?"

"You've seen me treat that before, but we'll talk more about that whenever we leave."

Whenever? Pol thought. Searl still hadn't really committed to leave.

The patients were still lined up, so Searl talked to each one, and most of them left to buy some more medicine from Jadekin. They ended up spending over three hours in the store.

"I need my beard trimmed," Searl said. He nodded to Jadekin, who thanked them profusely. Not only had Searl treated a large number of villagers, but also Jadekin had sold an awful lot of product during their session.

After a trip to the barber, Searl looked quite different. He had his hair trimmed, and his beard removed. His skin looked sensitive, but he looked years younger. They returned to Jadekin's store and loaded up their provisions.

The day was about over, and when they reached Searl's cabin they stopped in disbelief. Fifteen men were in the process of throwing Searl's belongings out of his home.

"What's going on here?" Searl said.

An angry man stood next to Morfess, shorter, but somewhat better dressed. "You had an agreement with Morfess," he said. "The minweed patches around your property were ours."

Pol's stomach dropped. He had destroyed all of the minweed for hundreds of feet around Searl's cabin.

"What?" Searl said.

"Death is the payment for such a violation."

"Noobel is right," Morfess said. The local supervisor didn't look as confident as his boss did.

"The minweed will grow back, soon enough," Pol said.

Searl's eyes grew. "You destroyed the patches?"

Pol nodded. "It's the only way to get you to leave this place."

"You did this?" Noobel said. His eyes were dead. Pol didn't expect any pity from such a criminal.

"You can leave right now," Pol said.

Noobel laughed. "An old man and a boy against fifteen?"

Pol used his locating spell. There weren't any men in the woods.

"We are magicians. Searl is a Level Eight and I'm a Level—"

"Blue." Searl nodded to Pol. "He's a Blue and a pattern-master."

"You are all charlatans."

Morfess plucked at Noobel's sleeve. "Searl is no charlatan, and neither is the boy."

Noobel glared at Searl. "Kill them."

Pol whipped out three knives from his boot. He pointed to Noobel. "Neither Searl or I will heal you from your wounds. Attack us, and you will die where you stand."

The men advanced drawing weapons. "You won't stop?" Pol said.

"Didn't I say 'kill them'?" Noobel said.

Pol threw his first knife and it went to the hilt on the left side of Noobel's chest. The man keeled over immediately.

"Who else would like to die?" Pol said, putting as much menace into his words as he could.

Another two men advanced, and Pol used his magic to blow them against the back wall of the lean-to. They crumpled to the ground.

A few men began to back up, and more ran into the woods.

Morfess stood over Noobel's body. "Go, both of you. Never come back." He shook his head with a sorrowful look on his face. "I'm sorry, Searl. I can't cover you on this." He turned and walked into the woods, followed by the rest of the men. Some of them dragged away the two weeders in the lean-to, but no one bothered to touch Noobel's body.

~ ~ ~

Chapter Twenty-Seven

~

"THAT IS A HECK OF A WAY TO GET ME TO LEAVE MY HOME!" Searl said with more than a bit of anger in his voice. "We have no choice but to get out of here as soon as we can."

Pol stood looking at Noobel's body, and then looked around at Searl's place. "I didn't mean—"

"Mean what? To rip me from my home so you can feel good about yourself? Save me from your being sorry." Searl turned around, head drooping. He turned around, his eyes wet. "My minweed. You've won." He trudged into the house.

Pol followed.

"You help me figure out what I need to take. You've seen my sledge. I can't take any more that what we can put on that."

"I have plenty of money to replace what you've lost."

"You'll keep me dosed up the rest of my life?" Searl shook his head. "Not likely." He sat down heavily on a chair. "We have to leave as soon as we can. I don't trust Morfess to keep his superiors at bay. Not now."

"Noobel was going to kill us."

Searl stood. "Because of you! Who told you to destroy all those patches of minweed? I didn't cultivate them, the weeders did. They didn't bother me, and I didn't bother them until you came around."

Pol escapted by climbing up the ladder to the loft and looking around. He didn't see anything worth keeping of Searl's possession. There were broken chairs and empty sacks, just junk. He gathered his things, such as they were, and began to stuff his saddlebags.

Searl still rummaged around, looking through the furniture, clothes, and the rest of the contents of his cottage. Pol could tell that most everything was replaceable.

"How can I help?"

Searl turned around and snarled. "You've already done enough."

Pol could see papers and things strewn over his bed. He slipped over to the table and folded up the ten-point test and put it in his bags.

"I'll gather some cooking gear and stay outside until I can help load everything up."

Pol found the sledge and checked the bindings. He hitched it up to Searl's horse and began to unload Demeron and pack their supplies for travel.

"We'll be leaving," Pol said.

I can see that. I am looking forward to being on the road again, and so is my friend.

"Are horses friends?"

Demeron snorted. *Not the same as human friends. The bonding is different. You and I are friends in the human sense, but Searl's horse will follow us without fail.*

Pol was done packing and wondered where Searl was. He stepped back inside the cabin and found him asleep. A cup of sludge was on the table. Pol sniffed it. Minweed. He shook his head.

Pol couldn't wait for Searl to wake up, so he gathered everything that looked like it had value and took it outside. Then he searched the cabin again. Tucked away in the corner of a shelf was Searl's black cord belt and the large Deftnis amulet, shaped just like the one Malden gave him. He reluctantly took a sack of dried minweed along, in case of an emergency. Pol dreaded packing it, but he stuffed in the bottom of his bags.

Pol looked under the bed, and gathered what remained, and he threw the bags over Searl's saddle. He picked up Searl underneath his arms and dragged him onto the sledge, after he had put plenty of blankets to pad the carrier.

After a third look, Pol closed the door and tied Searl to the sledge and left the clearing as the sun began to set. Noobel's body still lay in the middle of the yard. He didn't need light to travel, but he'd only go as far as Hill Creek.

"Make sure your friend follows, Demeron," Pol said as they entered the path downhill.

His horse snorted.

Pol located a single colored dot up ahead. He drew a knife and palmed it in his hand.

The figure stood in front of the pathway.

"Morfess wanted Searl to get his cut of the minweed earnings."

Pol's eyebrows rose. "Searl was part of your group?"

The man shook his head. "Not really. He helped us, healing and all, and Morfess thought he deserved this. Searl's not to tell no one about it." He looked at Pol. "You don't either."

"He won't, and I won't," Pol said. He accepted the purse as compensation for getting expelled from the mountainside.

Nothing happened on the way to Hill Creek. Pol took them to the inn where they had had breakfast the day before. The innkeeper helped Pol take Searl up to a shared room.

Pol looked down at the monk. Feelings swirled around in his head. Searl was likely to break his promise, of that Pol was certain, but still Pol didn't know who really owned the minweed he had destroyed. The act didn't backfire, but Pol hadn't wanted it to cost a man's life, even a criminal named Noobel.

His mind went over everything, and Pol caught himself rationalizing his actions. He could make up all kinds of reasons why everything turned out for the better, but the means weren't particularly honorable. He felt a bit diminished after it all. What would Val have thought of the outcome?

The next morning, Searl struggled to sit up. He put his hands on his knees and looked over at Pol.

"You messed up my life," Searl said.

"It seemed pretty messed up when I first met you."

Searl nodded. "Indeed, but I was comfortable with my life."

"As long as you could get a dose."

The monk shook his head. "I could use my magic to kill you."

"Could a former healer do that?"

Searl looked out the window at the roofs of Hill Creek. "No," he admitted. "It sounded menacing, though didn't it?" Searl broke into half a smile.

Pol hadn't expected the humor.

"We should leave Hill Creek after breakfast. I don't suppose we need any supplies."

"No. It's not as if we are roaming the hills. Desalt is civilized with lots of villages and inns, I suppose."

The monk nodded. "I'm hungry, and I need to tell you about what a withdrawal is."

They walked down the stairs. Villagers nodded to Searl with respect, those that recognized him without his beard.

Breakfast was included with the room. Pol had opened the purse from Morfess and was surprised to find more gold coins than silver and none of copper or iron. The denominations came from all over Baccusol.

"Morfess gave you a little going away present," Pol said. He pulled out the fat purse and handed it over. "I paid for our rooms out of it. I hope you don't mind."

Searl poked his head in the bag and snorted. "For a weeder, Morfess was a good man and honorable in his own way."

"I suppose. He didn't have his men attack us."

The monk sighed. "There is that. I met Noobel once before. He was a weasel and an awful man in his own way." He echoed his own comment.

Where did this humor come from? Pol had to keep from smiling.

"You said something about withdrawal?"

Searl nodded. "I'm going to have to teach you a little more healing, an extension of the treatments you are going to have to continue on my shoulder. Minweed is an addiction, and my body is not going to appreciate going without its favorite drug."

"Oh. Like a hangover?"

"But worse, much worse. I won't be a very amiable traveling companion."

Pol wanted to leave the Spines and find Searl's daughter, so he could put up with anything.

"Damn you to every hell on Phairoon!" Searl yelled from the sledge.

Pol kept cringing from the more colorful curses to come from the monk's mouth. It had only been three days since they left Hill Creek, but it felt more like three months.

Searl had barely taught Pol how to care for him during his withdrawal before the monk began to shiver. Before the end of the day, Searl had been tied to the sledge, since he couldn't stay up on his horse. The cursing began shortly thereafter.

The monk had told him he would have to be tied up for four or five days, and then the shivers and shakes would end, and the pain would begin. Searl had taught Pol how to put him under, but not until the pain began to overwhelm him.

The process of putting Searl to sleep exhausted Pol. The spell only lasted for two or three hours. Pol hadn't thought much about Malden putting Paki and Siggon to sleep in the Borstall castle infirmary, but it had to have drained him. He didn't know if he could ride for long after he started keeping Searl unconscious.

Pol rode up to a signpost. The right hand road led back into Lawster before another road would take them into Desalt. Pol pulled out a map that he had bought at a village and was tempted to risk going through Lawster, but decided to travel for two days longer over the eastern tip of Listya and then east to Desalt's capital, where Searl's daughter lived.

Two days later, they rode into a town that stood on the duchy of Hardman side of the border with Listya. He had put the monk under while he traveled through the town. Pol managed to find a modest inn with the intent to stay in one place while Searl went through his pain stage. Pol needed to rest while keeping Searl totally under.

"My friend is sick, but he isn't contagious. Do you have a more remote room? He's in a lot of pain and might be crying out during the evenings. I'll happily pay extra."

"I have an overflow room on the other side of the bath house. Give me a few minutes while we clear some of our supplies out," the innkeeper said.

Pol waited, and then the innkeeper arrived with a few of her larger stable hands to help Pol take the comatose Searl to the room. It was perfect for what Pol needed. He had the men come back after Pol got things settled, and help Searl bathe. He was a mess, being tied up for over four days.

Pol had never known how difficult it was to bathe an unconscious person. He ended up supporting Searl while the stable hands did the washing and scrubbing. He gave the two men big tips. Pol, as drenched as Searl had been, finally looked at the monk sleeping in a bed with clean sheets and fresh clothes.

The monk twitched and moaned in his induced sleep. Pol had a meal in the dining room and then brought broth into their room and dripped it into Searl's mouth for minutes at a time.

Time seemed to stand still for Pol while he monitored Searl and continually applied spell after spell, but finally the twitching stopped. That was the sign that the pain had ended.

Pol let Searl come out of his sleep.

The monk moaned as he opened his eyes and then covered them with a hand.

"I feel sick," he said. Searl looked at Pol. "How many days?"

Pol held up seven fingers. "We've been seven days from Hill Creek and are on the border with Listya. You were under for three of those."

Searl grunted, and then his eyes bulged. "I need a bucket!"

Searl had told him there would be intermittent nausea, and Pol was prepared. At least the monk had precisely described what to expect. Searl didn't have much in his stomach.

"Have you been through withdrawal for minweed before?" Pol asked.

Searl shook his head. "I've been the caregiver more than a few times." He spit into the bucket.

The monk fell back on the bed. "I'm just about through with this," he said. "Another day, and we can continue."

"Good. Demeron and I can only talk about so much on the road. He's extremely intelligent for a horse, but…"

That got an unexpected chuckle from Searl.

They took another day in the border town. Pol helped Searl

exercise by walking around the area close to the inn and climbing up and down stairs.

"I have one other thing to teach you before we go on the road. Since your hair isn't a living part of your body, you can change your own hair color. It's something I used to teach Seekers. You've got silvery roots showing, you know. I never realized that you had such light-colored hair."

Pol hadn't noticed, but he looked in a mirror and pulled up his hair to reveal what Searl described.

"The color will grow out, or you can change it back."

Searl discussed what kind of pattern Pol should think of, and Searl suggested that he needed to have a good idea of what color he wanted. He tried the technique and looked in the mirror. No person he had ever seen had the purplish hair that Pol now sported.

"Here." Searl pulled off his belt. "Try to emulate this."

Pol changed his hair color again and found that he would need an example when he tried it again. "I like this. It's sneaky."

Searl smiled and nodded. "It is that. I could use it to color my gray hair, but I'm too old to be vain like that. The highest level seekers can change their facial features, too."

"You could get rich in Yastan or some other big city coloring women's hair," Pol said.

"I could, I guess. It takes a Seventh Level to color one's own hair. If you are that high of a level, there are other ways to make money."

"Does that mean I'm a Seventh, a gray? Vactor is a gray."

Searl nodded. "Amazingly enough, you are getting there. You have the power and control, but not the breadth of learning."

On the morning of their fifth day at the inn, they both climbed on their horses and left the duchy of Hardman. Pol hoped that Searl had left his minweed addiction behind. He was more sober than Pol had ever seen him, and he enjoyed watching Searl's humorous side begin to emerge.

Pol hadn't been to Listya for seven years, since he was eight. He sighed, remembering bits and pieces of that trip. Time had softened most of his memories, but a few impressions had remained. Rolling hills dotted with woods and fields made up the eastern edge of the kingdom where Pol had once held the right to rule.

He never had imagined himself as king. The prospect of dying by the time he was twenty had eliminated any political ambitions. Now that he was cured of the malady that weakened him, Pol looked at the land with a different eye. He wondered how his life would have been different had he not been sickly.

Unfortunately, he would have represented an even greater threat to his older siblings and would have probably joined his mother in death. The bright, early summer day cast away depressing thoughts as they rode through the placid countryside. There were similar places in his home country of North Salvan, although the air was warmer and seemed more humid than in Borstall.

Searl began to tell stories while they rode. They related to his healing experiences, and then he turned to recounting old scandals at the monastery. Searl had seen many monks and acolytes come and go and described how the feel of the monastery changed as personalities shifted.

Some years were more raucous that others. Pol told him of his experiences at Deftnis.

"You seem to have an unnatural talent for attracting trouble," Searl said.

Pol noted the good nature in his comment. "I think anyone does when they are unique. My poor health offset my talent, which I worked hard to cultivate, and that irritated others, including Kell."

"But Kell seemed to be a friend of yours, right along with your other two companions."

"It took a long time to get to be companions, along with some shared experiences," Pol said.

Searl shook his head. "We've shared some experiences."

"Have they been good?"

The monk looked ahead and thought for a bit. "Taken together, they have. I haven't felt so free in years, but it came at a cost. I lost a lot of honor among the weeders."

Searl's comment shocked Pol. "What did it matter what the weeders thought?"

"I made a commitment to those men. I healed them, and those

that stayed with Morfess were, in a strange way, family. When you live close to anyone, relationships are created, and your lives, in a sense, intertwine. You destroyed that link when you removed the minweed patches."

"But Noobel was going to kill us," Pol said.

"For what? If the patches had remained, do you think he would have attacked?"

Pol knew the answer and he didn't like it. "He might not have."

"He wouldn't. Morfess would have been more likely to stop him. Once the minweed disappeared, Morfess couldn't protect me, but what is done is done. I'm glad I'm heading to see my daughter with a clearer head. That wouldn't have happened if you hadn't shown up on my doorstep."

Pol thought that Searl had a better idea of what had happened than he did, but it seemed that overall, both of them had benefitted by Pol's hasty action. Noobel had died, but if the man hadn't ordered their deaths, twice, Pol wouldn't have attacked in self-defense.

He sensed himself rationalizing his behavior again, and decided to change the subject. He had to accept that he had killed the man and not dwell on if it was justified.

"When was the last time you heard from your daughter?"

Searl looked up at the sky in thought. "Three years ago, after she married. When my wife died about ten years ago, Anna went to live with my wife's sister in Desalt. I was too far gone to attend the wedding."

"I'm sorry," Pol said.

"Not your problem."

~ ~ ~

Chapter Twenty-Eight

DESALT'S CAPITAL CITY SAT IN THE NORTHWESTERN CORNER of the dukedom, and served as the only port on a tiny sliver of land on the coast. Searl and Pol found an inn close to the address that the monk's daughter had given.

They ate a mid-afternoon meal and then walked to the address.

"The pair you're looking for left half a year ago," a mother said, with two small children peeking around her skirts at the two strange men on the doorstep.

"Do you know where they went?"

"Let's see. Alsador. Her husband was looking for a job as a decorative blacksmith. I think he makes fancy grills and doors for the nobles."

Searl nodded. "That's them."

"Sorry to have bothered you," Pol said.

"Do I get some compensation?"

Pol wanted to ask what for, but he managed to give the woman a Lawster guilder. The fewer Lawster coins Pol had in his purse, the better he'd feel.

They turned to walk back to the inn.

"There's an eruption of the Spines between Daftine and Listya," Searl said. "Do you want to go sightseeing?"

Pol nodded. "It makes up the border, but they aren't as tall as the Wild Spines, as I recall." One place that Pol didn't want to visit was Alsador. King Landon and Queen Bythia ruled Listya and their presence had taken away any desire to visit his mother's home. He hoped they would quickly find Searl's daughter, so Pol could run back to Deftnis. Why did she have to move? Pol lamented, yet again, that his life just couldn't be easy.

"If you're thinking of your brother, he won't recognize you. You've grown, put on weight, and you've got your dark brown hair."

Pol thought of Demeron, but then he smiled.

"I can change the color of Demeron's coat, can't I?"

Searl grinned. "I suppose so. What would suit him, orange? Green?"

"Something less noticeable. I can put a star on his forehead and boots on his legs. Landon wouldn't recognize him as the same horse." He looked away from Searl. "I'm uneasy about going to Alsador."

"Other than your horse being one of the few Shinkyan stallions in the Baccusol Empire. Didn't you mention you ran into a little trouble in Lawster? Did that scare you? Are you thinking of reneging on our agreement?"

Pol pursed his lips. "I gave you my commitment. I'll go with you."

"And I'll hold you to it," Searl said. "I didn't go through minweed withdrawal to face my daughter all on my own."

Pol tried to understand what Searl meant by that. He shrugged off the comment, and they continued on to the inn.

Pol changed into his Hill Creek clothes that seemed to better match Listyan styles. The next day, after Pol had changed Demeron's coloring, they purchased some fresh supplies and headed due west for Alsador.

"We could go by ship, you know," Pol said.

Searl shook his head. "I'm still a bit queasy from time to time. A ship?" Searl continued to shake his head. "No, no, no, no, no. I know my stomach well. You don't know how many times I rode the waves from Deftnis to Mancus."

Pol could understand.

I'd rather walk than ride a boat, Demeron said. *Searl, his mount, and I are of the same mind.*

'Well, that settles it then. I hope Listya has an excellent coast road."

They set out on what was billed as the Coast Highway. The cobbled surface stood three feet or more above the surrounding ground. Pol didn't mind all of the traffic, since that meant a number of inns along the way.

A town stood on the border between Listya and Desalt. Pol and Searl stopped in the afternoon for a cooked meal, and passing by a deserted border station, they entered back into Listya.

The Coast Road ended at the border, and a wide dirt track continued, rutted and washed out. The easy riding all the way to Alsador had evaporated like the outgoing fog.

They had to travel a fair distance into the night to arrive at an inn that looked over a fishing village on the shore. Pol hoped the inn still had some fresh fish to serve them.

"Two rooms for two men riding two horses," Searl said to the female innkeeper. This one was slight, only coming up to Pol's shoulders.

"Dinner?"

Searl nodded enthusiastically. Evidently his sensitive stomach was better at the moment.

"And two dinners," she said, smiling and writing their names down in a thick ledger.

"Breakfast is early around here and ends one hour after sun-up. Four fish extra if you want grain for the horses."

"Fish?" Searl said, looking slightly confused.

"That's what the Listyans call their smallest copper coin," Pol said.

"Oh." Searl pulled out his purse and paid for their stay. "What's for dinner?"

"Fish." The innkeeper laughed, and it took a moment for Searl to get her little joke, but he laughed heartily.

Pol just smiled.

After stowing their gear, Pol and Searl walked down from their rooms into the common room. A young man served them steaming bowls of a light fish soup with onions, strings of spinach and the white of egg swirling around the surface. He returned with light ale and bread and butter.

The bread might have been fresh earlier in the day, but it had hardened a bit. Pol dipped his in the soup, while Searl buttered his and crunched his way through a slice.

Pol looked at the ale. "I've never had ale before," he said.

"You haven't, have you? You only drank heavily-watered wine or fruit juice, as I recall."

"With my new constitution, I'll try it tonight."

Searl's eyes glazed over. "My work looks like it's permanent. You have your healer's permission to drink a mug or two." The monk took a sip and closed his eyes to savor the ale. "This is well-crafted. It seems light, but there is a good dose of alcohol."

"As long as it isn't minweed," Pol said, smiling.

Searl's face became solemn. "No, it's not."

"Sorry," Pol said.

"No need to be sorry. I'm getting to the point where I want my life back. My addiction wasn't the best of times."

Pol didn't bring up the subject again. The innkeeper sauntered between the tables. Most of the other patrons were there for drinking.

"Where are you headed?" she asked.

"Alsador," Pol said.

She made a face. "It's never been a happy place since the old king and queen died, and now the new king is terrible."

"Oh?" Pol said.

The innkeeper shook her head in disgust. "Taxes are going up, and for what? To line the royal coffers. We were promised a proper Coast Highway by the regent a few years ago, and the prospect of that went away as soon as King Landon arrived. Now there are suspicious characters poking their nose into other people's business in the name of the crown."

"Do you remember the old king and queen?" Pol asked.

"I do. I was a young thing, then." She smiled as she reminisced. "I can see the bright, shiny face of Princess Molissa riding with her parents. The future of Listya was filled with promise." She sighed. "And then they were both were taken by the Little Plague."

"Ah," Searl said. "I remember that. I was in training, and the healers didn't know what to do."

"And didn't find out until one-fourth of Listya and the rest of southeast Baccusol had died. I lost an uncle, aunt, and their only son." She shook her head, but then she brightened.

"Now that I know where you are going, where are you from?"

"Sand," Searl said.

"North Salvan," Pol said.

Searl furrowed his brow. Pol knew the monk well enough to know that he had misspoken.

"North Salvan originally, but we met up in Sand."

"So you're not related? I thought you might be grandsire and grandson."

"Close enough, but not by blood," Searl said. "What is the road like all the way to Alsador?"

"Oh. It will take you three days or a little more, depending on how hard you press your horses. There are plenty of fishing villages along the way and a few small ports. The road isn't bad for horses, but there are hells to pay for carriages." She shivered. "Have a good night." She patted Pol on the shoulder and joked around with a table of what must have been regulars before she disappeared into the kitchen.

"It sounds like my stepfather's regent didn't win the hearts of the people," Pol said quietly.

"And it's only gotten worse with King Landon."

Pol wondered how his mother might have ruled. He thought she would have done a good job of it. She used to give alms regularly, so she had a genuine interest in her subjects, and now Landon sat on the throne, making a mess of it, just as Pol had always thought he would.

They finished their stew, and Pol felt a glow from the mug of ale as he climbed the stairs. He quickly fell asleep when he lay down, fully clothed.

In the morning they bought a meal to take from the inn and mounted their horses. A man dressed as a merchant led his horse out into the stable yard.

"The innkeeper said you were headed to Alsador. Mind if I join you? My name is Carlon Winters."

Pol looked at the shorter man. He looked familiar somehow,

but he couldn't figure out whom he looked like. "We are heading for Alsador."

Winters smiled. "So the innkeeper told me. The road isn't particularly dangerous, I understand, but I wouldn't mind riding with two others, if you don't mind."

Pol turned to Searl, who shrugged his shoulders. "It's fine with us."

As the three of them rode along the Coast Highway, Winters began to talk.

"I'm from Yastan. My factor in Alsador died, and I have to hire another. I could take a ship from Dasalt or Hertz, but my stomach is a tender thing." The man smiled, but somehow it didn't reach his eyes. Pol didn't know if he trusted Winters, but so far he didn't need to.

"We are from Sand," Searl said. "My daughter moved to Alsador about six months ago, so we are hoping for a happy reunion."

"Not everyone is happy in Alsador. There are rumors that the new King and Queen are hell-bent on ruining the country. I heard this very road was to be paved by the regent, but Queen Bythia put a quick halt to the project."

Pol nodded. "We heard much the same thing from the innkeeper."

Winters laughed. Again, it seemed forced, rather than natural. "Keep your eyes and ears open when you reach the capital. You may learn more than you wished about Alsador, but it may save your lives."

"That's a dire warning for one traveling to the capital," Searl said.

"I didn't come to Alsador to seek out what stirs in the capital. There are those in Yastan that have a good idea of what ails Listya."

Pol thought Winters held back on his information, but the man quickly changed the subject.

~~~

Chapter Twenty-Nine

~

ALSADOR LOOKED IMPRESSIVE FROM A DISTANCE. It rose from a plain, greening up with crops, as the patchwork of fields promised a harvest at the end of summer. The stonework looked white in the morning sun, enhanced by the thinning mist that Winters, Searl, and Pol had ridden through since early morning.

The ocean disappeared behind a bank of misty clouds not far offshore. Pol didn't remember this view, but he might have been sleeping in the carriage as they approached Alsador seven years ago.

He took a deep breath as they moved ahead in the line of merchants, farmers, and others seeking entrance through the eastern gate and into the city. The guards demanded two Listyan silver foxes as payment to enter. No other city had asked as much, even the capital city of Lawster. His stepfather, King Colvin, had never charged visitors for entrance into Borstall.

Pol had been through capital cities large and small in the last few months, and Alsador seemed larger than them all, he thought as they rode underneath the main gate, and then approached another, smaller gate one hundred yards in. Farmers worked the fields in between the two walls that circled the city. He looked at the tops of the walls, and crenellations were evident, then he realized that he currently rode through a killing field, as Mistress Farthia would call it. In a conflict, the farmland would be plowed under and invaders could be attacked from both sides.

They continued on into the city proper. Listya's poorer sections hugged the real city wall just like in most cities.

Searl stopped a merchant heading out of Alsador and asked about a suitable inn to stay for a few weeks. Pol didn't hear most of the conversation since he continued to look around at the city of his mother's birth. The district was still poor, and Pol could smell the familiar stench of less-than-fastidious human habitation.

"I will take my leave," Carlon Winters said. "Perhaps we will meet again before you leave Alsador." He nodded to both of them and headed in a different direction.

"A strange man," Pol said.

Searl watched Winters thread his way through the crowds. "He is more than he seems, I'm sure. The man wore a disguise."

"He did?" Pol said.

"The man is a magician. He changed his hair and his features. With a little practice, you'll be able to do the same. When you learn, you can sense a disguise. His was well-done, but then I'm a Black. I think he is, too."

"You didn't call him on it," Pol said.

Searl snorted. "If he wanted to introduce us to his real self, he would have." The monk shook his head. "I'd not push a high-level magician too far." He looked at Pol, who nodded that he had understood the message between the words.

The inn was another mile in towards the center of the city where the castle stood on a man-made hill. Pol remembered the towers poking above the streets, but little else. People thronged among them and clogged the thoroughfare. The carts and carriages moved slowly through the crowds.

They finally reached the inn. It looked 'serviceable,' as Val might have described it. Pol followed Searl into the stable yard. Two stable boys took their horses, and two more ran up to carry their saddlebags.

"Grain for both of them," Pol said.

The boys looked at Searl for confirmation. The monk nodded and followed the porters into the inn.

The Turning Wheel Inn was much better than the one he used during Searl's last stages of minweed withdrawal. He looked around at the carpets beneath his feet. The main floor held a common room and a dining room much like the inn at Hill Creek, but much larger.

"We'll have to share a room," Searl said. "Prices are high in Alsador, and taxes have been raised recently." He shook his head. "What a burden King Landon has placed on the visitors to his city."

Pol nodded. He would've liked to say more, but there were too many people coming and going at the inn.

The room was larger than Pol expected, but they were all the way up on the fourth floor. The monastery's buildings didn't go higher than three stories. The two beds were on opposite sides of a sitting area. Good-sized windows looked out onto the roof of the next building. That gave them a good view of the castle towers poking above the roofs.

Pol stood at the windowsill, looking at the castle, wondering how Landon spent his day. Part of him wanted to find out, and another part abhorred being in Listya's capital city. Would have, could have, should have. Fate had spun a different path for Pol to follow. He examined his clenched fist. The blood that coursed through his hand was the same as always, but the heart that pumped it was different, repaired.

He felt that his new life hadn't begun yet and wouldn't until he returned to Deftnis.

"Looking at the castle that might have been yours?" Searl asked.

"It never was mine," Pol said, turning around and sitting on the simple couch that sat against one wall between beds. "How do you want to proceed? This might become a Seeking exercise."

Searl smiled. "I know it will. Alsador is big enough to swallow a craftsman up without any way to find him."

"He is an ironmonger? Decorative grills?"

"That's what he did in Dasalt. I don't know what he would do here."

"Both Dasalt and Listya are hot enough countries. People want their windows open during the day and at night. That's why iron grills are popular. Why would he change professions?" Pol said.

Searl shrugged. "Some countries have guilds that protect local craftsmen."

"Then we Seek. I think we should start out that way. You're looking for your daughter, there's no reason to be subtle."

"And what name will you have? King Landon will probably know that you are calling yourself Pol Cissert, since your South Salvan enemies know."

"How about Kell Digbee?"

Searl shook his head. "Think."

Pol quickly found the pattern. "He is associated with me. Fen is relatively close by, and his merchant father might have done business in Alsador."

"Good. I was just thinking about his association with you. Why don't you make up a name that might sound like you came from Hill Creek? You know that village well enough."

"Aron Morfess?"

Searl laughed. "That is as good as any and that's not Morfess's first name, but no one will know or probably care."

"Aron Morfess," Pol said to himself. He looked up at Searl. "Demeron knows he won't be exercised for the next two weeks, so I won't be associated with a big warhorse riding through Alsador."

"If one of us needs a horse, we'll take mine."

"And you will be a healer looking for his daughter."

"Yes, using my real name, Searl Hogton. My great-great grandfather came from Hogtown in the kingdom of Lake and liked the name. My father changed it from Hogtown to Hogton, but I never liked using it, so I am Searl."

"You sure are," Pol said, somewhat disrespectfully. Searl smiled, nevertheless.

The next morning, they set out seeking ironmongers who built decorative grills.

"I'm looking for my son-in-law, Mansen Lassler," Searl said to the first one they encountered.

The man at the counter shook his head. "Can't say I've heard the name."

"Is there an ironmonger's guild or some other guild that manages those who craft with iron?" Pol asked.

The man shook his head. "I wish. Everybody wants to sell to the nobility and make lots of money working with iron. The fact of the matter is there is little new construction in Alsador, and those that need grills on their windows can't afford them. I'd be surprised if he found any work at all. Sorry," he said. A customer walked in and the man moved away from them.

"Not what I wanted to hear," Searl said. "I wonder if my daughter has taken up healing."

"Is she as good as you?"

Searl laughed. "Can anybody be as good as me? No, to be honest she has a little power, but not enough to peer into a body like you can. She can stop bleeding and seal wounds well enough. I taught her quite a bit when she was younger and if she's kept practicing, she's probably as good as most non-talented healers. Even though she can't see into a person's body, she can even do some operations and knows how to keep things clean to fend off infection."

"Maybe we should split off. I can look for Mansen, and you can look for your daughter."

Searl pursed his lips. "This isn't going to be as simple as I thought."

"What is?" Pol said. He had never found things to be as easy as he thought. He had found Searl quickly, but he went through a long, arduous effort to get the monk sober

The next few days proved fruitless for Pol. He had gotten names of other ironmongers from the first and his list kept expanding for a while until he began to cover all the craftsmen in Alsador.

A few might have heard of Mansen's name but didn't know where he might possibly be. Searl's son-in-law definitely wasn't working as an ironmonger making grills.

"I don't know what to do," Searl said after their fourth day in Alsador, over an early dinner. They took their meal in the emptier common room. It would fill up later in the evening. "There are a number of healers that just set up shop in the streets and treat passersby. I've never seen anything like it in my life. Alsador must have the healthiest people in Baccusol, if you count health as the number of healers in the capital. However, I've observed a few, and most barely know how to bandage an injury. The better ones know how to sew wounds and can prescribe a few herbal remedies, but little else."

"Your daughter can do more than that."

Searl nodded. His eyebrows rose. "I just got an idea. What if we became street healers ourselves? I can do a little more teaching, and you could use it no matter where your magic takes you."

Pol thought it over while he chewed on a bite of roast beef. The inn had better food than Deftnis. That was for sure. "We could stay a day or two in a certain spot, and then move. People who might know your daughter would be coming to us. Is that your thought?"

Searl smiled. "And we can both do a little good along the way while we get information. It's been too long since I've done healing."

"You helped in Hill Creek."

"Two or three hours in a year or more? I can do better than that."

Pol took another bite, pleased at Searl's outlook. "What do we need?" he said with him mouth full.

"I passed a store that sold traveling goods. They had a collapsible cot, and we could also buy two chairs. An apothecary will have bandages, salves, potions, and other medicines. I'm not going to overtly use too much magic. Not out in the open in a strange city."

"Alsador seems a little strange, doesn't it? People are closed up and don't like talking. Do you think it's because of Landon?" Pol said.

"I don't know how life was in Listya before the regent from North Salvan arrived. If Landon behaved as you think, that would account for the change. We can find out while we offer healing from place to place."

Even though Pol thought people were offish, they had no shortage of patients. Most of them wanted free care, but Searl had monitored a few of the street healers and they all charged something for their services, and it looked like the quality of the patients' clothing had more to do with the fee than what malady the healers treated.

Searl encouraged Pol to help with the clientele and made sure that Pol kept notes of the treatments. "If we get back to Deftnis, I'll be able to give you credit for much more than a truncated herb gardening class," Searl said.

That was fine with Pol. He felt time had slipped away. While others learned from the monks at Deftnis, he had been fencing Searl with his wits.

"Another boil," a woman said, coming to the head of the line.

"Where?" Searl said.

"In a sensitive place."

"Where you sit down?"

The woman nodded. "Can you help me without taking all my clothes off in public?"

"If you allow me to touch the spot through your clothing," Searl said.

The woman's eyes grew. "Out here? Certainly not."

"Come tomorrow. We will fashion a screen."

The woman left to the laughter of waiting patients.

Searl gave Pol a look. "Go back to the travel shop and see if you can get a tent of some kind that we can put up in the street. Maybe something that wouldn't require tent pegs. She's not the only person who we've turned away because we didn't have any privacy. Other street healers must have some kind of contrivance."

"Don't leave."

Searl lifted one side of his mouth in a half smile. "I need you to help me lug all of this stuff back to the inn."

Pol ran through the streets of Alsador and entered the travelers' shop. The clerk looked up from straightening goods on a table. "You're back. Did something break?"

"No. My master is a healer, and we bought items to heal people in the streets. We need some kind of a tent we can set up and maybe a cart to carry out things."

"I can do that!" the clerk smiled. "I have to go into the back."

Pol watched the curtain for some minutes, but the clerk walked through the front door.

"Another shop has a small tent he rents out to merchants from out of town to erect in one of Alsador's many marketplaces, which are cobbled. The cart came with it. You can even hitch it to a horse, if you need to."

Pol followed the clerk out of the shop to examine the conveyance. The cart had two wheels that were four feet high and the pulling bar had a strut that lowered to keep the cart's bed level. Pol could see how a horse could be hitched to the cart by removing dowels and re-positioning the large pulling bar. They wouldn't use either of their horses in Alsador's streets, but they both could pull the cart wherever they wished.

The clerk gave Pol cursory instructions on how to erect the tent.

"Honestly, I've never put one of these up, so you can figure it out better than I just told you."

"How much?"

"To buy? These aren't cheap. A dolphin, I'm afraid."

Pol knew that a Listyan dolphin was a small gold coin. It would be equivalent to a South Salvan lion, a square block of gold. Pol pulled out his purse and brought out the square tube that held six lions stacked on top of each other.

"Will you accept this?"

"Hmm. A lion. I see these more often with the people our new queen has brought to Alsador. You don't look like you're from there."

"Hardly. My mother was a Listyan, but I am Aron Morfess from Hill Creek. That's in the Hardman foothills of the Spines. I've been traveling for awhile and picked this one up in a card game."

The clerk looked like he didn't believe Pol. Pol wouldn't believe that story either, but it would have to do. Putting the Lion in the clerk's hand smoothed any lingering questions.

"It's yours. Let me draw up a bill of sale, so my source doesn't think you've taken one of his rentals."

Pol appreciated the large spoked wheels while he trudged through the Alsadoran streets. Searl only had a few patients left to treat. The sun had dipped behind most of the buildings, and the crowds had thinned while Pol made his way to the monk.

"What is that?"

"Our portable infirmary," Pol said. "The cart carries the tent, plus we'll have enough room for our collapsible furniture and our supplies. We'll both have to pull it, though."

"Better that than lugging everything all over Alsador." Searl looked over the tent, which still took over a good portion of the cart's bed. "Shall we give it a try once I have taken care of these three fine souls?"

"I'll start while you treat."

Pol dragged the tent frame out of the cart and looked at it for a while before he began to set the tent up. It didn't take him long to realize that the wooden frame had been cracked.

He ran his hands along the wood and used the same pattern for fixing bones to fix the cracks. He could feel his strength diminish, but he had developed a better sense of when he might overdo his spells. Pol pushed it a bit, but the frame was whole again.

His success surprised him. He put the frame in place and fashioned the cross bars on the top. Then he draped the light tenting over the frame. Inside the tent, he inspected the cloth and found a few rips and holes in it. He had paid a gold lion for this? Even in the expensive city of Alsador, he knew he had been taken advantage of, but with a judicious use of tweaking here and there, the rips and tears were magically repaired.

He stepped outside. Searl had started to collapse the chairs.

"That was a pretty bold use of magic, but no one walking by would know, unless they were a magician themselves," Searl said, looking up at the tent. "Eight feet square. That's not large by tent standards, it will fit two chairs and the cot inside."

"We take up that much space in the street, anyway. The cart can carry our supplies."

Searl ran his hand along the cart's rail and smiled, inspecting Pol's work. "This will get us more customers."

"I don't want to spend the rest of my life learning healing on the streets of Alsador," Pol said.

Searl grinned, a heartening sight. "Lighten up. You're much too serious, lad. You don't have to behave as if every day is your last, at least not in a morose way. Enjoy life, now that it's been lengthened." Searl put his arms out and extended his hands. "There are people to meet, food to eat, and learning, so sweet."

The little verse made Pol smile. "I'll do my best."

"Best is good enough," Searl said, nodding, as he returned to breaking down their mobile clinic.

~ ~ ~

Chapter Thirty

"Y<small>OU ARE DOING JUST FINE</small>," Searl said during a lull in the second day's work with their new setup. "Magic is better suited to injuries than to illnesses. Remember the lady innkeeper at our first stop in Listya who talked about the Little Plague that killed your grandparents?"

"I do."

"The plague was caused by insect bites. Do you know what kind of magic saved the most people?"

Pol shook his head.

"Mosquitos were the culprits. Somehow they had been imported on a ship or ships from the southern part of the Volian continent, maybe The Shards, but no one really knows. No one suspected the little demons. The summer was hot and wet, and the insects thrived in all the puddles in Listya, Daftine, and the Dukedoms. A Seeker of all people discovered that mosquito bites caused the illness. Healers went around giving salve to everyone and told them to cover their arms and legs with clothing."

"No magic?"

Searl frowned. "Tragic, eh? The Emperor at the time, Hazett's father, brought in his troops and emptied every vessel of standing water. Black oil was poured on stagnant ponds and lit, burning the eggs."

"Magic healers could have destroyed the patterns in the eggs," Pol said.

"Do you know how many magicians there are in the empire?"

"Ten or twenty thousand?"

"With the power to destroy insect eggs? Maybe two or three hundred."

"But there are that many acolytes in Deftnis."

"It was tried, but it took a Level Three to kill the eggs in any quantity, and not all of them could do it. There were a number of magicians at the time who wouldn't dare expose themselves. Not one Teslan magician traveled to southwestern Eastril, for example. We called out for any magician. One didn't need to be a healer, of course."

"What did you do?"

"I prescribed the salve and long sleeves and long pants. The salve we had formulated repelled the mosquitos. Not all people died. A majority of those bitten had a natural immunity, and those that survived after contracting the disease developed their own. I also spent a lot of time scouting out ponds in the Dukedoms on the southern side of the Wild Spines."

"What happened to the mosquitos?"

Searl shrugged. "The little plague lasted two summers. We had a very cold winter after the second summer, and that killed most of the mosquitos, we think."

"Has the plague returned?"

Searl nodded his head. "It has, but never as badly. Healers know what to do. The outbreaks are localized. My wife died from an outbreak, just like your grandparents, but my daughter and I made it through. You might be surprised what a little hygiene and isolation can do to stop an epidemic."

A few patients showed up, and Searl continued to show Pol how to clean and dress wounds and remove surface infections.

"What causes disease?"

"Tiny little things. You can call them critters or tiny, tiny animals, but when they grow in a person's body, you can see clumps of them with your magic sight. Healers have different names for them. Some call them bad humors. Remember the dot board that Malden probably used to test you?"

"I do." Pol remembered all the colored dots on the board and how he had to relax his mind to see a pattern in the dots.

"To see them you have to do the same thing except the dots are incredibly tiny. Infection is caused by the body trying to kill the tiny things. That is often what causes fever. The body is trying to burn the things out."

"I remember talking about that before," Pol said.

"I know. It takes a skilled and controlled magician-healer to attempt to kill infection in the blood stream, rather than in a wound."

"Can I learn to do that?"

"You could, but I don't think you have the right temperament to be a healer. Come to think of it, I don't either, but I've become so adept at healing the inner workings of a body, that I can't imagine doing anything else."

Pol wanted to mention his addiction, but kept his mouth shut. More patients arrived, and the line began to grow, stopping their conversation, but the learning went on.

After each patient, Searl or Pol would ask about new healers in town, especially from Dasalt. They picked up a lot of information about healers, which Pol documented. In a few days, he would be out talking to the daughter's competition.

Towards the end of the day, a squad of guards sauntered up to their tent.

"Permit?"

Pol looked at Searl, wondering what to do. The monk just waved his hand. Pol took the gesture to mean stay calm.

"No one has told me I needed a permit to heal in Alsador's streets," Searl said.

The lead guard looked sympathetic. "The edict was signed yesterday by King Landon."

"How much?"

"How much do you have? The fine is forty dolphins."

"You must be filling up your prisons," Searl said. "We wouldn't make that much in six months."

"We are, but I'm going to have to ask you and your friend for your purses."

"And we still have to come along?"

"One of you, I don't care which, will head to the city jail," the guard said. "The other has to get your cart off the streets."

Pol handed over the purse that he had used to gather their fees. Searl's purse wasn't much larger than Pol's fee purse, since they both didn't want to possess too much money as healers in the streets.

The lead guard peeked in both and weighed them in his hand. "The penalty is two weeks in jail, then. No more healing from now on, unless you practice from a shop and pay for a license from the new Healer's Guild."

"Healer's Guild? I've never heard of such a thing before," Searl said.

"An innovation of Queen Bythia's," the guard said. "She will also set the fees that healers can charge."

"And the crown gets a percentage of the fees?" Searl asked.

The guard nodded, looking surprised. "That seems to be the new rules. Get used to them. There are a number of new guilds."

Searl just smiled. "It's up to you to find a suitable place for our cart, Pol, now that we are destitute. Keep it off the streets. Am I right, sir?"

The guard nodded. "Another new rule. If the cart is left on the street at night, it becomes the property of the crown."

"Is this another project of Queen Bythia?" Pol asked.

"Of course. She is interested in the beautification of Alsador," the guard said evenly. "I suggest that you watch what you say, young man. The King and Queen of Listya are in the process of making their mark on the city, and then they will do more to create a new Listya."

"Are you from Alsador?" Searl asked.

The guard shook his head. "I've recently arrived from South Salvan to help Queen Bythia make Listya more like her beloved home."

"Where is the jail?" Pol asked.

The lead guard looked at one of the other men in the squad. Evidently he didn't even know the plan of the city.

"At Hawker's Cross. Are you new to Alsador?" a shorter guard asked.

Pol nodded. "We've recently arrived after spending some time in Hill Creek in Hardman. Can I bring meals to my grandfather?"

"A good idea," the squad member said grinning. "Visiting hours are the two hours around noon."

"I'll see you tomorrow then, Grandfather. I'll find some way to scrape up enough for something good for you to eat."

"You do that, Aron," Searl said as the guards took him away. Pol wanted to save the monk, but he only had a few knives on his body, and there were too many guards and other citizens wandering around wearing swords.

Pol suddenly had a lot more to do before he would retrieve Searl. First, he would have to find Searl's daughter, while the monk sat in his prison cell. Pol wheeled the cart around town to make sure he wasn't being followed before he headed back to their inn.

Evidently there were guards out all over Alsador confiscating purses and imprisoning all kinds of street craftsman. The men and women in the common room of the inn argued and shouted in anger. Some supported the crown, but most were anxious to leave Alsador before Queen Bythia had levied some other tax, hidden or overt on the citizens.

The innkeeper walked over to Pol. "You two were healing in the streets, weren't you?"

Pol nodded.

"Your grandfather was taken?"

Pol made a face. "He was. Has our room rate gone up? We paid two weeks in advance, luckily."

"Not yet. It might happen. I heard they were confiscating purses. Are you without funds?"

Pol didn't know what position the innkeeper had in regards to the new regulations. "We have some laid aside that the guards didn't take. I'll pay you for another week's stay plus stable fees for our cart. It should fit in one of your stalls. My grandfather has to stay in jail for two weeks, and then we will likely leave Alsador shortly after that."

"I might be able to find a place for you to practice healing in town," the innkeeper said.

"Once I pay for our room and board, I'll be out of money. The Queen's guild will require a membership fee."

The innkeeper thought for a bit. "Let's see what happens. Edicts have a habit of being modified over time. It took the North Salvan regent a few years to understand us in Listya. I imagine the same will happen with the new royal family."

"I'll bear that in mind. Do you have any odd jobs I can do?" Pol asked.

"What can you do, other than heal?"

"I know how to care for horses and gardens. I'm also educated if anyone needs a tutor."

The innkeeper raised an eyebrow. "How old are you?"

"Fifteen."

"You can read and write?"

Pol nodded. "And do sums. I know my geography and history better than most." In his mind 'most' meant his stepsiblings.

"I can use a secretary to help me with my paperwork. It's mostly nighttime work. Can you handle it? I can give you credit on your room, but the stable fees still come from your payment."

"I accept your offer," Pol said. "When do I start?"

"We'll give you a tryout tonight. See that door off the lobby?"

Pol looked and noticed a door with a sign. He couldn't read the sign from where he sat in the common room. He nodded to the innkeeper.

"Eight hours after noon. Will that work?"

Pol smiled. "I won't disappoint you."

The innkeeper didn't show up until closer to nine. He didn't comment on the fact that he was late, so Pol kept his mouth shut.

After the innkeeper opened his office with a key, he let Pol in. The man's desk was piled high with paperwork. Bills, receipts, and letters were stacked haphazardly. "If the crown wants an accounting of my business, I'll soon join your grandfather." He pulled a key from the desk drawer. "You can come in and work during the day, too, if you like, while you get things organized. Sort everything by dollar value for bills and receipts. A separate pile for my daily tallies. Letters sort from oldest to newest. When you get that done...if you get it done...find me. Your work will tell me if you are good enough to be hired. Don't go looking for money. I don't keep any in my office."

Pol didn't believe that, but he let the innkeeper's comment pass. "I'll work on this for a few hours tonight."

"I'll want it all sorted by dinnertime tomorrow."

Pol nodded and went to work.

"Make sure you lock the door on your way out."

Pol nodded again and went to work. He had thought the lessons

Mistress Farthia had taught him about paperwork and logistics at Borstall Castle would never be put to use, but now he had that opportunity. Everything was familiar enough.

After sorting through all of the various shapes and sizes of paper, Pol finally could recognize patterns in the papers. Receipts were generally half-sized paper and bills would be a full-sized paper. Letters didn't have lists of numbers, and he had finished before the twelfth hour.

The sorting was only a first step. Since the inn seemed prosperous enough, Pol guessed that the daily tallies of cash in and cash out would be more accurate than adding receipts and bills and figuring out the inn's financial situation from those stacks.

It wasn't how Pol had been taught, but he could see how the innkeeper could keep the inn working without any kind of system, until the cash ran out, of course.

When the innkeeper inspected the office the next morning, Pol had impressed him enough that he allowed Pol to summarize the bills, receipts, and tallies. The letters were put into folders by date and placed in a locked drawer in the desk for the innkeeper's attention at a later time.

"I will give you three days to make the summaries. You said you wanted to take food to your grandfather, so go to the kitchen and take what you want. Any dishes or pots will have to be returned, or you'll have to pay for them."

Pol spent another hour in the office reorganizing the tally sheets and left to visit Searl. He had to prepare Searl's food in the kitchens, now that he was an employee of the inn.

Hawker's Cross wasn't too far from the inn. Pol looked up at the grim building. Somehow they had found an ugly, black stone for the guard headquarters and jail, where most of the rest of Alsador used a paler stone, although now that Pol walked the city's streets, he had noticed that some buildings were cleaner than others.

"I'm here to see Searl Hogton. He's my grandfather, and I've brought him food."

"Brought him food, eh?" the old guard behind the desk in the busy lobby laughed. After looking at a logbook, he pointed to Pol's left. "Take the first stairs you come to. The jail takes up the basement floor." The man gave Pol a blue-painted token. "Give this to the guard at the bottom of the stairs."

Pol did as he was told. The guard at the bottom looked over Searl's food and helped himself to a piece of bread. Pol kept quiet. All this was quite beyond his experience.

"Aisle Seven, Cell Three. There is a guard every two aisles."

Pol walked to the right and saw the corridor extend the entire distance beneath the guard building. Windows set in the edges of the ceilings brought light to the corridor. There were signs every so often from One to Ten. Pol walked past alcoves between each aisle. Just past Aisle Seven, he stood at the guard station. The man who sat at the desk was talking to the guard one desk down. He looked at Pol before he sauntered back.

"I've come to see my grandfather, Searl Hogton. He's in Cell Three on Aisle Seven."

"Is that food?" Pol nodded. "Good. We've been a bit hungry today. You can leave that here. Visiting hours end in twenty minutes."

Pol looked as the guard began to dig into Searl's food. "I brought that for grandfather."

"So?" the guard said, his mouth already full.

Pol sighed. "I have to take the pot and utensil back."

"They will be waiting."

There were four or five other people visiting inmates. Oil lamps lit each aisle with a dim light. The smells reminded Pol of his last visit with his mother to the poorest section of Borstall. Searl sat in a corner examining his hands when Pol called out to him.

Searl brightened and walked to the bars. "I suppose it could be worse. I imagine they could beat me on a regular basis."

Pol looked at Searl's face. "Should I produce a light?"

Searl's face looked shocked. "Don't do that! It would make everything worse. All I have to do is endure this for two weeks, and we can collect my daughter and be on our way. Have you made any progress today?"

Pol shook his head. "I've got a new job as the innkeeper's secretary.

He needs one. I offered to work in his stables, but I told him I can write."

"So you haven't found my daughter, yet?"

"No, but I have this afternoon off and a list of healers. They can't all be in here, can they?"

"There are four in this cell, alone."

Pol quickly counted seven men of various ages joining Searl. "Evidently Queen Bythia is starting to assert herself. The healers aren't the only ones."

Searl twisted his lips. "I know. It is less than useless to talk about it, especially here where there are many ears."

Pol knew the significance of Searl's statement. "I brought food, but the guards took it."

Searl smiled without humor. "The guard who took me was able to get an additional meal for his friends."

"I'll continue to bring them." Pol looked back and saw three other guards, taking care of what he had brought Searl. "Do you get anything to eat?"

"Enough to survive. At least we can all heal each other."

Pol looked at the other healers. "Are they all as good as you?"

"We all have our unique styles of healing," Searl said.

That was a polite way of saying no. Pol really didn't have anything else to say. "I'll return tomorrow."

Pol went back to the street and pulled out the list of healers. Any who would have an address might know where Searl's daughter was healing. He hoped she hadn't tried to practice on the streets.

All of the walking exhausted Pol. It took him three hours to visit four healers. He hadn't brought a map, so he ended up wasting a lot of time in unnecessary travel. None had heard of either of the Lasslers.

Pol walked into a bookstore and asked the clerk for a map of the city. He looked about the shop and decided to ask him about Searl's kin.

"I'm looking for a healer from Dasalt. Her husband is an ironmonger. I've been talking to other healers, but I found myself walking back and forth without any plan."

"A healer you say? Is she any good?"

Pol didn't know if Searl meant that his daughter was proficient. "I think so."

"Have you checked the Royal Infirmary?" the clerk said. His long thin fingers caressed the spine of an old leather book.

"No, is she injured?"

He looked at Pol with narrowed eyes, but with a sly smile. "Are you joking with me?" he giggled, and then continued. "The Queen wanted a female for her personal healer, and the infirmary didn't have the right kind of person. The Queen recently installed a woman as her healer. If she is good, she might be the one. Perhaps she was given an offer she couldn't refuse."

Pol furrowed his brow. "Does that happen here?"

"It has since the Royal couple arrived last fall. Things are changing in Alsador very quickly." The man waved his fingers. "Ask me no more. It is dangerous to talk. Even you might be related to the Royal Couple." The man laughed at his little quip. Pol nearly shocked him with the truth, but he stayed quiet since he had finally gotten what he wanted.

"How much for the map? I think I'll be using it a lot."

"A silver fox will do. It's a bit old, but most of the streets are accurate."

Pol paid him the right coin and left the bookstore. He had to be careful about his information. If Searl had been in the royal dungeons, Pol might have a better chance of enquiring about the Lasslers.

~ ~ ~

Chapter Thirty-One

Pol THOUGHT HE MIGHT TRY TO GET A JOB ON THE CASTLE GROUNDS. He returned to his rooms and changed into his most worn clothes and hiked up to the castle.

As expected, guards stopped him at the gate.

"I'm looking for work. I'm an experienced gardener," Pol said. "I can tend stables, as well. Do you have any openings here?"

The four men laughed at him. "Do you think any beggar can walk into the castle and get a job?"

"I'm not a beggar. I can handle a sword, too." He looked at the guards, trying to behave like his friend Paki would have in a similar situation.

"That we can test," one of them said, chuckling. "Here, you fight him." The guard pointed at another.

"Not me. I don't want to bring tears to his mother's eyes." The guard pulled his sword and offered it to Pol.

Pol took the sword and tested the balance. "Come on, gentleman. A single, bloodless touch. If I win, I get inside. If I lose, I'll go back to begging. What do you say?" He grinned at them, again playing the role of Paki.

The beefiest of the guards took off his tabard and handed it to one of the others. "I'll teach you a quick lesson." The guard swept his sword back and forth. He certainly didn't lack for power.

Pol could move faster than he with his own sword, but the thing they had given him was heavy and unwieldy. He'd have to act the part of a pattern-master as well to get inside the castle.

A crowd grew on both sides of the gate.

One of the guards raised his hand. "We are teaching this urchin a lesson, here. It won't take long."

The dismissiveness of the man's tone irked Pol. He ran through a quick warm-up trying to get a feel of the sword and found its pattern. Confidence didn't exactly flow from him, but Pol had nothing to lose.

The two of them stood off right in the middle of the gate. They saluted each other. Pol did the vertical position and the swoosh to the side. The guard just held his blade out.

"First touch, no blood if you can help it," one of the guards said.

Pol wanted this done quickly, but he still didn't trust his new strength and played defense, using sips of magic to move the sword more quickly. The guard was good enough to keep Pol occupied, and the match extended longer than Pol wanted.

The guard became frustrated and began to use more force. That gave Pol more holes, so he quickly slapped the flat part of his sword against the guard's elbow after one of his more wild swipes. The guard's sword clattered to the cobbles.

Pol backed away, breathing hard, but his heart hardly beat. He couldn't help but smile, but the guard glared at Pol and threw a punch, which Pol hadn't expected, as his jaw exploded in pain. Then the guard hit with his other fist, right in his cheek, and that put Pol on the ground. The guard continued to punch him until other guards pulled him up.

The guard stood over Pol with fists clenched. Pol couldn't get up as his vision began to whirl before he blacked out.

"Oh, you are awake."

Pol looked up at a woman dressed in a white healer's robe. "I am," he said, mumbling through a swollen jaw.

The healer smiled.

"Did you really beat a guard?"

"He wasn't happy about it." Every word hurt. "Then he beat me."

Pol put his hand up to his cheek. He couldn't see well out of his right eye. The lower left side of his face seemed to be numb. "Is my face swollen?"

The healer giggled. "You might say that. Your own mother wouldn't recognize you."

"I think I have a concussion, don't I?"

That stopped the healer's giggle. "You know what a concussion is?"

"I do. I've been injured before."

"And did healers treat you? You aren't an urchin, are you?"

"No. May I ask what your name is?"

"Yes." The woman smiled at her little joke.

Pol rolled his eyes, but the pain in his right eye stopped him. "What is your name?"

"Anna Lassler. I am the Queen's personal healer, but she doesn't need healing most days, so I spend the rest of my time treating adolescents who fight the King's Guards."

"What is Mansen doing these days?" Pol said. He couldn't quite keep the giddiness out of his voice. If he had to get his face pulverized to find Searl's daughter, it was well worth it…once.

Pol smiled at the shock in Anna's face. "Who are you?" she asked.

"A friend of Searl Hogton. I tried to get a job in the castle to see if you were here."

Pol heard a commotion enter the room. Bythia rushed in with four ladies-in-waiting right behind her. His breathing stopped. He looked for an exit but couldn't find one. His eyes locked with Bythia, his brother's wife. How would he ever survive? Pol was totally defenseless.

Bythia's eyes shifted from his to Searl's daughter. "Anna, I don't like you treating other patients. I've told you that before." Bythia looked at Pol, again. "You are treating riff-raff? How did that thing get in here? You are not to touch another patient other than me from here on out. Come with me." Bythia left the room without hearing Anna's response.

"Where can Mansen find you?" she whispered to Pol.

"*The Turning Wheel Inn.*" Pol said to Anna before she hurried out.

Another healer told Pol to leave the Infirmary. "Sorry, the Queen's orders," he said.

Pol understood. He had a new understanding of the kind of person his brother had married. She had not exhibited this kind of abominable behavior when he had first met her in Borstall Castle. He was never so happy that his features were unrecognizable.

The healer gave him some pain powders as he walked out. "Take it easy for a few days," he said.

Pol nodded and made his way to the gate.

The guards' attitude had changed when Pol left the castle. They smiled at him, and one of the guards walked up to Pol. "Our Captain would like to meet you." He shoved a message in Pol's hands. "Ossie shouldn't have beat you with his fists."

Pol mumbled his thanks and continued on towards the inn. He told the innkeeper he would have to have the day off. Pol went into the kitchen and asked for an early dinner to take up to his room.

He sat down and put his head on the table. He remembered the medicine and took it before he unfolded the message the guard had given him.

Bring this message to my office in the castle when you've recovered.
I might have use for a boy who can swing a sword.

Regent Tamio
Captain of the Guard

Pol held onto the message for a moment. He had a safe job with the innkeeper, but he wondered what good that would do him now that he had located Searl's daughter. She lived in the castle, under the tight watch of Bythia. Anna seemed to be as much a prisoner as her father. If he could get on with the Guard, Pol stood a chance of seeing her again.

It hurt to chew, but Pol managed as best he could. The numbness in his jaw began to wear off, despite the medicine. He lay down, prepared to spend a fitful night.

Pol stayed in bed for much of the next day. In the evening he worked on the innkeeper's files.

Someone knocked on the office door. It couldn't be the innkeeper, since he would just walk in. Pol got up from the desk to see who was there.

"You know my Anna?" a good-sized man with big hands said.

"Mansen Lassler?"

"I am."

"I am a friend of Searl's. Come in. My name is Po—, I mean Aron Morfess."

Mansen poked his head in the door and looked at the office. "You work for the innkeeper?"

"For now," Pol said.

"How did you find us?" Mansen said as he sat down on a visitor's chair.

"You really want to know? We went to—"

Mansen's eyes grew large. "Searl is here? How did that happen?"

Pol sat back. "Maybe I can answer one question at a time."

The big man smiled. "Go ahead."

We went to your old house in Dasalt and learned you had come here. That didn't work out very well, did it?"

Mansen shook his head. "I took some bad advice. Alsador already has too many people in my line of work."

"We found that out. So Searl thought we'd become street healers and get information about Anna. If you weren't working, then she would likely be earning some money healing."

"My Anna did too well. After a few weeks, she gathered a good number of patients. Most of the street healers in Alsador are charlatans. Queen Bythia wanted her own personal healer and took her right off the streets. She finally got a message out to me, and now we both work for Listya. I'm working in the royal blacksmith's as an apprentice, after being a journeyman."

"So why don't you come with Searl and me back to Deftnis?"

"His addiction. They won't let him back," Mansen said.

"He threw it off a few weeks ago," Pol said. "That's why he made the trip. It gave him a goal to get sober."

"If you were the one to help him, may the gods bless you. He's to be a grandfather, you know."

"Searl? He didn't tell me."

"He has no idea. My Anna just found out last week. Where is Searl?"

Pol ran his tongue against his cheek. "He's in the Hawker's Cross jail. They imprisoned him for healing on the streets."

"Oh, that. It's part of King Landon's money grab," Mansen said. "Can I visit him?"

"Visiting hours are the two hours around noon."

Mansen clutched his fists. "I'll make some time and see him tomorrow."

"Good. I won't be showing up until the day after. My face..."

Mansen smiled. "Anna told me." He pulled out a bag and gave it to Pol. "This is better pain medicine than what the healers would have given you at the infirmary." Mansen rose to his feet. "I have to get back."

"How can we get in touch with you?"

"Send any messages to me in care of the royal blacksmiths, for now. Anything sent to Anna will just get read by the Queen's creatures. She has plenty of them. Most of the leadership of the City Guard are South Salvans."

"What about Regent Tamio?"

"Except for him. Tamio is legendary in Listya; the people wouldn't stand for a new man in his position. He's a pattern-master."

Pol waited for visiting hours to start. His face had begun to look more normal, but large purple splotches still dominated his shrinking features.

He brought food again, and, like last time, it didn't make it to Searl. When the monk appeared at the bars, Pol brought out a waxed-paper packet containing a small, fresh loaf of bread that was buttered.

"Did Mansen come?"

Searl nodded with his mouth full.

"He told you how I found Anna?"

Another nod.

Pol told the monk his complete tale, including the encounter with the bookseller.

Searl swallowed. "That was foolish of you. What if the guard skewered you right there?"

"With forty or fifty people looking on?" Pol shook his head. "He didn't hesitate to make me pay for the privilege of getting the first touch.

"Let me—"

"No. This acts as a disguise," Pol said. "Have you ever heard of Regent Tamio?"

Searl nodded, his mouth full again.

"He's the popular Captain of the Guard at the castle. He wrote a note. He wants to talk to me."

"Are you going to do it?" Searl managed to say with his mouth full. "Sorry, this is the best thing I've eaten down here."

Pol looked back up the aisle at the light coming from the main corridor. "We need to find the best way to rescue your daughter and son-in-law. She can only treat the Queen and no one else."

"You were told you couldn't get a position in the stables?"

"Maybe I can work in their armory or something. If Tamio has integrity, then perhaps he will help us."

"Don't plan on anyone helping us. Who knows what relative he has had to sell to maintain his position," Searl said. "What about me?"

"You have another ten days?"

Searl looked away. "Some people, who were supposed to be here for days, have been locked up here for months. It's like they put you down here and forget that you exist."

"I'll find a way to handle that when the time comes," Pol said. Searl must also know how to manipulate a lock. The problem would be getting through a corridor full of guards.

"Thank you, Aron," Searl said. "I wouldn't have known I'm to be a grandaddy without you. I didn't care about anyone but myself for so long."

"Well, think of yourself a little longer. We aren't in the clear yet."

Pol couldn't help but wonder if everyone couldn't be in worse shape. Searl was in prison and his daughter was held captive, albeit in better surroundings. Pol had been beaten but might have an opportunity to work in the castle, after all. Perhaps their fortune had bottomed out.

～～～

Chapter Thirty-Two

~

SEARL SEEMED THRILLED ABOUT THE PROSPECTS OF A GRANDCHILD. That made Pol smile as he walked back to the inn.

The innkeeper came out at him waving his fists. "Your horse just about destroyed my stables!"

"What?"

"The city guard came by for their monthly inspection and seized the big horse. They said that he couldn't be your property and took him to the Royal stables."

The innkeeper took Pol to survey the damage. Half of Demeron's stall had been crushed.

"Was anyone hurt?" Pol asked.

"That was the miraculous part. For all of the horse's wild frenzy, he struck no one."

Good, thought Pol. Now he had one more reason to go to the castle.

"I'll pay for the damage."

"You'd better." The innkeeper's amiability disappeared. "I want your double room to rent. I've got a small room for you, since you are an employee."

"But I'm paid up for another two weeks."

"Take it or leave it."

Pol ground his teeth, trying to keep his anger in check. "I'll take the small room. I'll pay for the stable damage, but I still want to board my grandfather's horse and keep my cart."

"Everything must be paid for in advance."

Actually, most of it was already paid for, and the small room wouldn't cost as much as the large one that Pol and Searl shared.

"Fine. I'll move our belongings now."

The innkeeper followed Pol to his rooms. "Two dolphins, and we are paid up for the next three weeks."

"Will South Salvan lions do?" Pol said.

"They will." The innkeeper's lips nearly smiled. They would, since the fee was outrageous.

Pol pulled out his purse and gave the two lions to the man. "I will fill out my own receipt at work tonight." His six lions were now down to three, but between the weeder's money and Pol's, they could still live a long time in Alsador if they needed to. Pol shuddered at the thought.

After quickly shoving their most valuable belongings into two saddlebags, Pol followed the innkeeper down to the first floor. He led him past the bathing rooms and past the corridor outside the kitchen to a set of four doors. He opened one of them with his master key.

A small window lit up the dismal room. Two cots hugged the walls with three feet between them and with blankets and a pillow at one end. The storage room where Pol nursed Searl back to sobriety was larger. He put the saddlebags on one of the cots.

"Where is the key?" Pol asked.

"Come with me," the innkeeper said.

Pol used his magic to move the lock. The weeder money was on the other side of that door. He followed the innkeeper to his office where he gave Pol a key. Pol looked on the familiar desk and saw a receipt for the sale of one large warhorse. On his way back, the innkeeper looked nervous and for good reason. The man had betrayed Pol.

So much for the progress Searl and he had made in Alsador. Pol went to their old room and bagged up all their possessions and returned downstairs.

Now alerted to danger, Pol used his locator spell, there were four men hiding in one of the small rooms. The lock on the door of his tiny room showed new scratches. Some had tried to get in.

Pol quickly entered his room and buckled on his sword and hid his knives. Now it was apparent the innkeeper moved him down here in order to rob him of all his goods. He wondered why the man hadn't just cleaned out their rooms, but perhaps Pol's extra attention to the door locks had been enough to thwart him.

He opened the door and saw the four men, thugs from the streets.

"I'm giving you fair warning. If you fight me, I won't hold back."

The biggest of them laughed. "With a face like that? Did your mother beat you bloody, little tot?"

"No, a guard did after I beat him in a duel."

One of the other ruffians touched the big man on the shoulder. "He must be the one who bested a castle guard."

"Don't matter." The big man rushed Pol, who thrust out his hand and blew all the men down.

Pol took a deep breath, wondering if he would join them on the ground, but his strength held up. He began to slash at the men as they stood, and in the close quarters, he suffered two cuts, but the others lay still on the floor.

He didn't want to kill the men while they were down, but what was done was done. Pol bound his wounds as best he could, changed his clothes, and then took the side door out to the stable yard. He made quick work of pulling out the cart and hitching it to Searl's horse. He loaded al their things, including Demeron's big saddle, and left the stable and *The Turning Wheel Inn*.

Once he had ridden a few blocks, Pol pulled out the old map and found the location of a boarding stable not too far away. Now he was homeless, and his job at the inn had ended. Demeron was at the castle, but Pol still had his proof of ownership signed by the Emperor.

Pol buried most of his money in the filthy dirt of the stall where he slipped the cart. He carved a little line in one of the boards opposite of the burial place of his little hoard, thinking of what kind of pattern Val might create to protect himself in a hostile city.

Pol had no choice but to head to the castle for a meeting with the 'legendary' Regent Tamio.

The guards at the gate recognized Pol. He gave them the message from their superior. One of them grunted and took him towards a castle outbuilding, where they walked up the steps. Pol could see a practice yard through a window at the back of the building.

He followed the guard and went through a set of double doors to an office area. Guards sat behind three desks, busy filling out paperwork or reading orders or receipts. They seemed more efficient than the innkeeper.

"Sit," his escort said before he spoke quietly to one of the clerks, giving him the message from Tamio. They both looked at Pol with distrust, but the guard left Pol sitting by himself.

Pol sat for an hour and a half before a tall, straight-backed man walked purposefully through the offices and disappeared behind the Chief Guard's door. He presumed that was Regent Tamio.

A few minutes later, the man exited and went to one of the desks. He looked up and noticed Pol.

"You are the boy who bested one of my guards?"

Pol stood up straight. "I am."

"Come with me," he turned and went back into his office with a parchment in his hand. He sat at his desk. "Close the door and have a seat."

Pol dutifully did as he was told. What a difference between Kelso Beastwell, the bearlike Chief Guard at Borstall Castle and Tamio. The Alsador Chief Guard was a cobra compared to Kelso.

"Name?"

"Aron Morfess of Hill Creek in Hardman."

"Why are you in Alsador?"

"My grandfather and I came to town. He's a healer. He was picked up—"

Tamio impatiently waved his hand. "I know about the new regulations."

"I needed work, and I thought they would pay better at the castle."

"Pay better for what?"

"I've done gardening, and I know my way around horses."

"You were staying at *The Turning Wheel*?"

That bit of information surprised Pol. "Yes."

"That Shinkyan Stallion is yours?"

Pol began to get hot. How much could he tell this man? "Yes."

"Did you steal him?"

"No." Pol didn't know what to do or say at this point. He went with the truth. "I have an Imperial dispensation to own the horse."

That brought Tamio's eyes up. "Let me see it."

Pol took the leather carrier from within his shirt. He pulled out the document and handed it over. "My real name is Pol Cissert."

"Hmpf," Tamio said. He stared at Pol over the document before examining it.

"You are from Deftnis, of course."

How could Tamio know all of this?

"I am."

"Who is your 'grandfather'?"

"Searl Hogton."

"I know of Searl. A great healer gone sour. You met him in Hardman?"

Pol nodded. "Near Hill Creek."

"Why is he here?"

"It's his own personal business."

"And that personal business got him in jail for an indeterminate length of time."

Pol sat with his hands together. This man was so far ahead of him that Pol had nothing to say.

"You're a bit young for a pattern-master, aren't you?"

Pol shook his head. "I'm no pattern-master. I know how to anticipate, but that is only part of it."

That got another grunt from Tamio. "Level?"

"I was a Red when I left the monastery."

How old are you? Fourteen? Fifteen?"

"Fifteen."

"I want to test you, of course. I'm surprised they let you go."

"Personal reasons, sir." Pol thought he'd throw in the 'sir'. "I'm welcome to return."

Another grunt.

"You'll tell me if it's important. I need someone for a unique position. I may be able to get your horse back to you as repayment. Are you interested?"

"Can you free Searl?"

"I don't run the city guard, Pol or Aron."

"Call me Aron, please."

"Aron, then. You'll have to find a way of getting him out on your own, or the guards might want to clear out their cells and let him go. They are rather capricious these days. I was originally trained at Deftnis. I had a falling out with the Abbot and chose to leave. Let's go down to the practice hall. We have a private room where we can use our arts more freely."

Tamio got up and didn't even ask Pol to follow, so Pol had to scramble after him. He opened a wide door into a room about twenty feet on a side. The ceiling was twelve feet or so high. Swords and long knives were mounted on a wall along with other weapons. A long table held knives and small shields.

"Pads?"

Pol still nursed the cuts he had received not long ago. "Pads."

"Good. You should be able to find a jerkin that fits."

They faced each other. Tamio asked for Pol to choose a thinner blade. After trying a few out, he found one that wasn't too bad.

"You choose well. You can't have been at Deftnis long. I'm surprised they accepted someone as young as you."

Pol took a long knife along with the sword.

"Why the long knife?" Tamio asked.

"It helps me to parry against a larger opponent."

"And all of your opponents are larger." Tamio said it as a statement. "Very well."

"I started last fall."

"And a Fourth Level? You are a prodigy." Tamio shook his head. "I don't know how you got in, but evidently you have connections."

"I admit that I do," Pol said, "but I did earn my level."

Tamio nodded. "Let's find out."

They both used a Deftnis-style salute. Pol didn't know how well of a fight he'd put for a genuine pattern-master.

For the first few moments, both of them warmed up on each

other, then Pol could see Tamio about to take more than a sip of magic. It was an obvious move. He thrust, which Pol successfully parried with his sword alone, but then Tamio used his power to withdraw his sword faster than normal and then slapped Pol on the shoulder.

Pol nodded.

"Did you see what I just did?" Tamio said, a little surprised.

"I didn't think to speed up moving the blade back."

Tamio smiled for the first time. "Good." He nodded and then turned his face to stone once more.

The sparring took longer than Pol had ever been able to last. Tamio was a much superior swordsman and it showed; however, Pol was able to get two touches in during the session.

"That is enough. What else can you do?"

"I'm good with knives."

Tamio nodded. "Show me," pointing to a worn wooden shield hung on the wall.

"Where do you want me to hit it?"

Tamio looked at the shield with his hand holding his chin. "Throw five knives around the edge."

Pol walked over to the table and took six throwing knives. He didn't take long to throw five of the knives along the left hand edge and then the sixth in the center.

"You use sips to do that?"

Pol nodded. "Mostly to strengthen the throw. I can transport a blade, but it takes too much magical strength." Pol took a seventh knife, the last one and held it in his hand, point out. He magically transported the knife next to the knife in the center.

"I've never seen that before."

Pol could feel his magical strength diminish with the last throw, but he didn't feel weak.

"With good reason. I'm about out of strength."

Tamio nodded and looked at the knives for a while.

"How do you feel about the Royal Couple?"

"I'd rather not say, sir," Pol said.

"Then don't. I need you to protect me."

That request took Pol by surprise. "You don't seem to need any protecting."

"Oh, I do. I don't serve at the Royal Couple's command, but by the people and my allies in government. The Queen—"

"Is putting South Salvans in leadership positions."

"Yes. They currently run the city guard," Tamio said.

"Does Landon know?"

"King Landon?" Tamio corrected.

"Does he?"

"I don't believe he does," Tamio said.

Pol had no choice but to trust the Chief Guard. If Coram was the only pattern-master in Tesna, and Searl had heard of Tamio, then perhaps he had found an ally.

"Then I pity the King. I've met the Queen."

Another surprised look decorated Tamio's face. "After your guard put me in the infirmary, a nice lady looked after me, but Queen Bythia showed up and took her away."

"Anna Lassler. The Queen has turned the woman into her own pet healer," Tamio said.

"I guessed as much," Pol said. He took a breath and looked up at Tamio. "What do you want me to do?"

"We can talk about it during lunch in my office."

~

Pol took the time to look around Regent Tamio's surroundings. He noticed a black leather belt intertwined with a gray cord sitting on a shelf. That would be Tamio's Deftnis ratings. The man must have played with him, even to let him get two touches in.

"I see you've noticed my little play to vanity," Tamio said, his expression back to less emotion than Valiso Gasibli.

"Did you teach at Deftnis?"

"For less than a year. Some are given to teach, others to perform. I perform. Who taught you anticipation magic?"

"Malden Gastoria."

"Impressive. You have combined magic in your fighting. I didn't learn that until my last few years at Deftnis. Malden wouldn't have taught you that."

Did everyone know the North Salvan Court Magician? Pol was amazed that Malden had accepted the position in his stepfather's castle.

"I picked that up on my own," Pol said. "I'm not very strong, and used to be weaker than I am now. My knives wouldn't penetrate wood, so I learned to give them a sip of magic in order to move faster. It works with swords as well."

"But you never saw anyone pull back using magic before. Interesting. That verifies that you are self-taught. Not many magicians are, since most lack the power to experiment."

"I lacked stamina. I used to faint after one big spell."

A guard knocked and brought in soup, which Pol thought an odd choice at the beginning of summer. Tamio directed Pol to sit at the conference table in the room. The soup was cold and fruity, something that he had never tasted before.

"I brought the recipe from my homeland in Volia."

"You know Valiso Gasibli, then?"

Tamio nodded. "I do. He used to be a friend."

"Used to be?"

"Val is not the warmest of companions," Tamio said.

Pol thought Tamio wasn't either. "I understand."

"You might be one of the few who do." Tamio played with the spoon for a while. "You are the disinherited prince, aren't you? Poldon Fairfield?"

With all the mutual acquaintances, Pol had fallen into the trap of mentioning them. If Tamio knew his story, and he might from the Royal Couple, then it wouldn't be too hard to figure out. What had he done?

"Your story is safe with me, and we might do something useful together. My loyalty is to my adopted country of Listya. I came here twenty-one years ago, fresh from the monastery to work with your grandfather. I knew Molissa, a beautiful woman. I've met you once before when you visited some years ago when you were younger."

"I don't remember you," Pol said.

"You probably don't remember any of those who introduced themselves to you."

Tamio was right.

"What put me off was your brown hair, and I always thought you were smaller and frail."

Pol took a sip of the soup. It actually tasted really good after their sparring. "I colored my hair, and Master Searl has cured me."

Tamio sat forward. "Really, cured you? I didn't know you had a malady other than being a weakling. Do you want your throne back?"

Pol sat back and thought for a moment. The prospects of sitting on the Listyan throne had intruded into his mind often enough, but his health had always made him stifle such notions. "No. I don't think I'm meant to rule. I know how it's done, but I don't like the politics."

Tamio smiled. There was little mirth behind that smile. "There is politics everywhere. You can't have ignored the politics rife in the monastery."

"I didn't, but I wasn't the Abbot, either."

Tamio didn't look convinced. "Think of all the money in the Royal Treasury."

"For a good ruler, the money carries a responsibility. I'm not ready for such things, if ever."

"Well. Let's set that aside. It doesn't change what I want from you."

Pol waited for Tamio to say something, but he just ate some of his soup, so Pol did the same, looking up at the Chief Guard from time to time.

"Did Val teach you to be a Seeker? He must have, looking at your knife-throwing skills. For now, I just want you to be a messenger boy."

Pol made to object.

"No messages to the King or Queen. I need someone who will blend in and know enough to listen. The person I want will be my personal messenger. You fit the bill nicely. You can even visit your horse, if you are careful."

"Do I live in the castle?"

Tamio nodded. "I'll let you live in a small cell in this building, nothing fancy, but it will suit you just fine. You wouldn't stand a chance among the guards. Some would protect you and others would live to give you a hard time. When can you start?"

"Will today work? I don't have a place to stay."

"Ah. The innkeeper at *The Turning Wheel* cast you out, eh? When one of Bythia's officers bought the Shinkyan stallion from him, I figured the innkeeper would have you put away."

"He tried."

"Did you have to kill anyone?"

"Four."

"How did you do it?"

Pol guessed this was another test of fitness, so he told Tamio of his fight and flight from *The Turning Wheel Inn*.

"Location spells, too. Valiso has made a good little Seeker out of you. No wonder you don't want to rule. It wouldn't be as much fun. Well, you'll be my little Seeker for awhile."

Pol hadn't viewed Seeking as fun, but Tamio made him think about his own motivations. He didn't want to rule because of his terrible upbringing and the casual death of his mother, but he wouldn't share that with Tamio.

Tamio went to his desk and wrote out some orders. "Take this to the first desk on your right. They will prepare the cell while you retrieve your things. This letter contains your personal orders, and when you return, give this to the desk guard in the main lobby. I think we will get along, Aron."

Tamio put an emphasis on his assumed name, and the Chief Guard had written his travel name on the orders but misspelled Morfess. It didn't matter. Pol didn't know if he should salute or what, so he just bowed to Tamio and left.

~~~

Chapter Thirty-Three

~

$\mathbf{T}$HE ONE PLACE THAT POL WANTED TO AVOID while in Alsador was now his home. He looked around at the tiny room. At least it was bigger than the place The Turning Wheel Inn had offered him, and it sported an empty wardrobe for his clothes.

He wondered what Searl would think, but it didn't matter. Pol was now in a position to do something, where organizing the innkeeper's papers didn't accomplish anything towards his goal of contacting Anna Lassler and getting her out of the castle. Pol was given clothes to wear, a uniform somewhat different from the rest of the guard. His was less military, more like a dress uniform than anything else. The clothes were a little big, but Pol used his magic to make them fit a little better.

His strength had definitely improved, but his position might become more dangerous than it was in Borstall if Landon or Bythia knew he lived within the castle's walls.

The guard building had bells that rang on the hour, and Pol had to report for his first assignment at Tamio's office. It was just evening on the same day that he had entered the castle to meet with Tamio, and already he had work.

One of the clerks gave Pol a map and a leather letter-case.

"Deliver this to Lord Greenhill. His offices are here." The guard pointed to a spot on the map.

Pol nodded, but before he left, Tamio called him in.

"That fits well enough. Don't wear a cap in the castle proper. Your dark hair color is part of your disguise, right? For now, I want you to keep your ears and eyes open. Use the extra desk out front to write a report to me after every delivery. Give it to the clerk who wrote your orders."

"Do I salute? All I really know how to do is bow."

Tamio thought. "Bowing is good enough for now. Everyone knows you are new." Tamio brushed him away with his hand. "Get on with you." The Chief Guard looked down at the paperwork on his desk. Pol took that as a dismissal.

Pol stood in front of the door to the kitchens. He took out his map and found a route that would take him far from the Royal Quarters.

"New around here?" a cook asked. She reminded Pol of Paki's mother, a cook at Borstall Castle.

"Just started today. I'm running messages for Regent Tamio."

"Oh. Well good for you."

"Is there an extra bite to eat? I've got to hurry, but I'm hungry," Pol said. He smiled at her. Pol liked cooks, but he also knew the servants knew more than nobles thought. "I have to deliver this to Lord Greenhill."

The cook made a face while she sliced a chunk off of a roast beef that was on the spit. "Here you go. Don't spend a lot of time with Greenhill. He thinks a great deal of himself, and I don't trust those kind of folks."

Pol thanked her. "Can you tell me what to expect from the rest of those in the castle?"

"I'd be happy to. Just drop by with a smile, and perhaps, share a tidbit of your own."

"I will, and thank you for the food."

"Any time, if you're satisfied with bits and pieces of what we're serving others."

Pol picked up the meat. "I am," He bowed to her and made his way through the kitchens with his unexpected bonus. He had seen Paki do similar things in Borstall, and now he knew why. The meat was a bit rare, but that was how Pol liked it.

He hurried through his circuitous route to Lord Greenhill's office. The entry was from an alcove. A clerk sat at his desk, examining his fingernails.

"I have a dispatch from Regent Tamio."

The clerk squinted at Pol. The man must have been nearsighted. "You're new, aren't you?"

Pol nodded. "This is my first day on the job."

"Do better than the last messenger boy. He disappeared."

Pol couldn't keep his eyebrows from rising. "I'll make sure I don't. I want to do a good job."

"See that you do. The Lord is currently in conference. You can give the message to me."

Pol stood wondering what to do. "I'll leave it, if you give me a receipt that you accepted it. I don't want Chief Guard Tamio to fire me on my first day."

The clerk looked up at Pol with a languid expression. "Very well. He scribbled on a scrap of paper.

Pol looked it over and compared the signature to the name placard on the desk. "This isn't your name."

"You can read, eh?"

Pol nodded. "My mother saw to my education. It is comprehensive." At least that wasn't a lie, Pol thought. "Change it, or I will wait."

"Just knock and you can go in," the clerk said. He leaned back to look at his nails again.

What a warm welcome. Pol shook his head in disgust, but only mentally. "Thank you." He gave the clerk a bow, which the clerk didn't acknowledge.

Pol entered after he heard the office occupant instruct him to come inside.

"You made it through the gauntlet?"

Pol must have looked perplexed.

"Cirrul, my clerk. He guards my door," Greenhill said drily.

"I'm delivering a message from Chief Guard Tamio."

"Call him Lord Regent. He loves to hear it. Here." Greenhill extended his hand for the document.

"Should I wait for a reply?"

"How astute of you, but no. This is my friend Regent's expenses for the week. I do my bit managing the Royal Treasury."

"I'll be leaving, then," Pol said.

"See that you do." Greenhill waved his hand dismissing Pol.

When Pol lived in Borstall Castle, his stepfather's courtiers were always courteous, so Pol never felt threatened, but now that he was just a messenger boy, he could feel the intimidation that he never experienced before. Greenhill seemed to be mocking him from the start. The perspective wasn't welcome, but Pol knew that he would benefit from his experience.

The trip was marred by the unexpected rushing of footsteps in the corridor just ahead. Pol slipped into an alcove and made himself invisible. Landon walked past, surrounded by courtiers and guards. The first thought Pol had was that Landon loved being escorted by an entourage. His stepbrother had always liked the pomp that surrounded his stepfather.

Pol returned to Tamio's office and sat down to make his observations, giving them to the clerk he had dealt with before.

"Lord Greenhill told me to call Regent Tamio, Lord Regent."

The clerk laughed silently. "Greenhill is a trickster. Lord Tamio will work, but using 'Lord Regent' will get you punishments. I'm sure Greenhill knew that."

"I'll put that in my report."

"Do," the clerk said. "When you're done, Lord Tamio would like you to practice your swordsmanship with the other guards. He told me to warn you not to get them riled up."

"I won't. Do I wear these?"

The clerk shook his head. "Better-fitting clothes were delivered to your rooms this morning."

Pol nodded and left for his cell once he had submitted his report. Four sets of clothes were folded neatly on his bed. An even dressier version of the uniform that he wore accompanied a duplicate. The third stack intrigued Pol. There were black trousers, shirt, jerkin and a black knit hat that had a hole in the side. The fourth set of clothes consisted of a regular guard uniform complete with a sword enclosed in a polished metal scabbard.

Pol put the hat on and found that the hole was large enough for his eyes. A pair of soft leather shoes, also black, filled out the wardrobe. Was this Seeker's gear? An assassin's uniform? He put it at the bottom of the wardrobe. He used hangers for his uniforms and donned the guard uniform for weapons practice. Pol didn't know how the guards practiced. He'd find out soon.

He found his way to the practice field and could smell the Royal Stables that had to be on the other side of the far wall. A few guards were practicing, and Pol recognized the guard who had knocked him down.

The man saw Pol and walked up to him. "Sorry about the end of our fight," the man said. "I've never been bested by a kid before and I lost my head. It looks like you're one of us. If Tamio chooses you, that's good enough for me."

The man extended his hand, but Pol, using a bit of anticipation magic could tell the big guard was going to throw him.

"No need. Teach me what you know. That will be good enough," Pol said.

"What?" the guard looked perplexed, his hand still extended.

"I said teach me how to fight after a match. I've never had to defend myself with my fists before, and you seem handy enough."

"You want me to teach you? In your dreams." The guard grunted and walked away.

Pol watched him return to his buddies.

"Did you know he was going to throw you?" a guard walked up. He was a little older and a little slimmer than some of the rest.

Pol nodded. "He stood funny."

"Indeed he did. I'm Wilf Yarrow, the weapons master. You must be Tamio's new messenger boy."

Pol stood a little straighter. "I am. Aron Morfess, sir."

"Good. I heard about your fight with Ossie. What would you have done if you expected him to pulverize your face? It's still pretty mottled."

"I would have withdrawn. I can probably run faster than he can."

"And if you can't run?"

"I would have raised my sword. He was unarmed, but still

dangerous."

"Indeed," Wilf said smiling.

"What other weapons can you handle?"

"I haven't had any training on heavy weapons. I know swords, knives, and a little archery. I can throw knives rather well."

"Not something encouraged by the guard," Wilf said. "But it's always good to practice what you know best. Regent said you were particularly adept with the blade for your age. Care to spar?"

Pol shrugged. "That's what I'm here for." Pol took off his guard jacket and loosened his sleeves. "What are the rules?"

"No blood. If you can't control your blade, then we will fight with wooden practice swords. No hand fighting, no kicking or shoving unless you have closed and are pushing away your opponent. We go until each touch and then stop and start anew until one of us is too tired or beaten up to continue. Simple?"

Pol nodded. "I'm not known for my stamina."

"That's a fair warning. I'll pay attention."

A few guards gathered to watch Pol perform. He didn't know if he should go all out or let Wilf win.

They touched blades in the style that the guard had used at the gate and began. Pol backed up a few steps, ready for a flurry of attacks, but Wilf did the same. He grinned. "We think alike." He bowed and they touched swords again. This time Wilf did attack, and the man was fast, for an unassisted swordsman. Pol had to use sips of magic to both anticipate Wilf's attacks and augment his own enough to parry the man's powerful strokes.

"You fight like Regent," Wilf said after touching Pol on the shoulder.

"I do?"

"I think you know what I mean," Wilf said.

They closed again, and Pol knew more what to expect. He got the touch on the next exchange, a slap on the hip. That brought a few surprised cries from the guards. Pol knew enough to let Wilf win the rest of the touches, but not without a decent fight.

"Let us go over our match," Wilf said. He steered Pol to the edge of the practice ground. "I've never seen a pattern-master as young as you. Your fighting technique is still rough, but your use of magic is better than Regent's. Even I can tell he uses too much, and you are judicious. If he hadn't told me that you were from Deftnis, I probably wouldn't have noticed."

"Thank you. Can you teach me to fight better?"

Wilf shook his head. "I would if I could, but you won't be here long."

"Why not?"

Wilf looked around. "Regent recruits a certain type of boy for the Emperor. You are a perfect example of what he looks for. The last boy was good, but you are much, much better."

"I'm not going to Yastan," Pol said. "I've got my own purpose in Alsador and will be heading back to Deftnis when I've done."

"He said you might not, but he still doesn't expect you to be here long."

"That makes three of us," Pol said. "I'll learn what I can from you, though."

Wilf nodded. "I have another match. If you will excuse me, guard." Pol noticed the smile on Wilf's face.

Pol wandered to the other side of the practice field. "Demeron?"

You found me! I wondered when you would.

"I've been detained for a bit. I can't get you out yet, so be patient."

I will. They have excellent grain here and let me exercise. The King has even been by to see me. He looked a little disappointed, for a human.

"You used to be his. I took you from him, and the Emperor gave me permission to keep you."

I know. I didn't forget the King's smell. He has no magic and can't talk to me.

"Be patient, I'll be back to talk to you."

Come see me, too.

"I'll try."

Pol returned to his quarters and changed back into his messenger uniform. He returned to Tamio's office and addressed the clerk. "What do I do when I'm ready to be sent out?"

"Wait at your desk. You participated in sword practice?"

Pol nodded. "I sparred with Wilf Yarrow. How do I wash my

clothes, and where do I eat?"

The clerk told him. Tamio stuck his head out of his office.

"Morfess, inside."

Pol nodded to the clerk and sat down across the desk from the Chief Guard.

"Good work. I like the bit about the cook. Go ahead and make friends. You never know when you'll get unexpected information. I see you didn't like Lord Greenhill."

"No, sir. He's not a serious man for having financial responsibilities."

"Your ruling lessons are taking over. He does well enough, as long as you understand him. You handled the delivery of the message better than I would have thought. I have an errand outside the castle. There is another envelope for something I'd like you to try tonight after dinner, long after dinner."

Pol made another delivery, this time to the Royal Weapons maker who had a large shop outside the castle. He never thought he'd be leaving the grounds. Perhaps he could see Searl tomorrow, he thought. One of the sword makers gave Pol two new swords in shiny scabbards to return to Lord Tamio.

Pol felt someone tap him on the shoulder.

"Aron," Mansen said quietly. "I didn't expect to see you in the King's uniform."

"I'm just a messenger at present. Have you been reassigned?"

Mansen shook his head. "I work here three days a week and at the stable forge for the rest. I had a hand in making that one." He tapped on one of the swords that Pol held.

"Good. I've got to get back, but now you know where I can be found. Did you get a chance to visit Searl?"

"Twice. He said you stopped by."

"I'll try to talk to him tomorrow. I need to tell him that I am working for Regent Tamio."

"The Chief Guard knows him? I will let Searl know."

Pol waved to Mansen on his way out. He didn't like the look on Mansen's face when Pol dropped Tamio's name. Pol felt like he struggled in a political web again, except there were three lives at stake, not just his mother's. He felt a pang from her loss, like he always did when he thought of Queen Molissa. He wondered what she would think of him, playing guard in her father's castle.

He returned the swords to the clerk's desk and noted that the other two desks were empty. "Dinner time?" He asked the remaining clerk.

"You better get some. If you haven't read the assignment that Lord Tamio gave you, do so before you eat."

Pol rushed to his room and took his assignment out of the envelope. He read it and sighed. He was to sneak into the castle and remove the document that he had given to Lord Greenhill earlier in the day at two in the morning.

Now he was expected to be Tamio's burglar. Pol wondered what kind of game Tamio played. This had to be a test. Pol would have to pass it, because he would probably need an ally in the castle.

~ ~ ~

Chapter Thirty-Four

WHEN THE MIDNIGHT BELL RANG, Pol put on his black clothes, and then stood in the middle of the room trying to discern a pattern. Did Tamio want Pol caught? If he did, wearing the black outfit would point him out as an interloper in the castle, so he changed into the darker gray of the dress uniform. He would also go at the edge of a respectable hour to be about the castle corridors.

He walked out of his cell and proceeded into the castle, just as if he belonged there, and in a sense, he did as much as anyone. He found the circuitous route he had traveled before pretty empty. It wouldn't matter to see a messenger walking purposefully through the castle's corridors at any time of the night.

He spied a light underneath Lord Greenhill's office door and expanded the pattern of sound so he could hear.

Tamio's voice came through loud and clear. "The boy should show up in a few hours. Have your men stationed in your office. It won't hurt for the prince to feel a little fear."

"He's no prince," Greenhill said. "I know you like your projects, but this is a dangerous line you tread."

"And with the boy, I will cross it sooner than later. Get your men stationed before much longer," Tamio said.

The door opened. Pol shrunk into the shadows, willing his body to match the pattern of the office. One of them extinguished a light, and Greenhill locked the door. Tamio turned and looked towards Pol, but he didn't focus on him. Pol wondered if a magician could sense another working magic. He held his breath for as long as possible, until Tamio shook his head and walked away.

Using his location magic, Pol determined that no one occupied the office. The locked door didn't impede Pol. He walked in and created a small magician's light and levitated it above the desk. Greenhill had placed the leather portfolio in the second drawer amidst other files. Pol opened the paper and saw a list of numbers and descriptions, so that must be the right document.

He put it inside his coat and extinguished his light. He crept to the door and used his location sense to see if anyone approached. Not seeing anyone, he looked harder for any magician cloaking his presence. Nothing.

Pol re-locked the door and walked away, just as if he was delivering a message. He passed a few guards and other late-night wanderers in the castle, and then exhaled once he was outside on castle grounds. The night was crisp for early summer, and that cooled the sweat that Pol hadn't noticed while he was out on his mission.

Tamio's office was lit, so he knocked on the Chief Guard's door. "Enter."

Pol opened the door and slipped inside. "Here is the expense portfolio," Pol said, pulling the leather case out from his coat.

Tamio looked surprised, and Pol didn't think he faked his expression. "When did you take this?"

"I came straight here. There were two men in Greenhill's office. I couldn't make out who they were since the lighting is a bit sparse in that part of the castle at this time of night. When they left, I unlocked the door and slipped in."

"You're not wearing your black outfit. Why?"

"This one is dark enough. I thought if I left a few hours early, no one would notice a messenger boy, but they would stop a black-clad thief."

Tamio smiled thinly and bobbed his head. "Good thinking. You don't lack for initiative."

"Thank you, sir."

"Report back in the morning. I'm sure I will have more dispatches for you to deliver."

Pol bowed. He still hadn't had any kind of orientation on being a guard, and he had thought that odd before his foray, but not now. For any number of reasons, Pol agreed with Tamio that he wouldn't be a messenger for long.

He reached his rooms. Pol had to talk to Searl about Tamio. Anything the monk could remember would help him deal with the Chief Guard. The man intimidated Pol, to say the least, and he might, or might not, be an enemy.

Pol remembered his mother's words about trusting no one.

The cook remembered Pol and gave him a large lunch to take to Searl. After putting on street clothes, Pol visited Searl in the jail. As expected, the food didn't make it down the aisle to Searl.

"Pol, Mansen has visited. He says you are in the castle. Is that right?"

Pol nodded. "I'm a messenger for the Castle Guard. That's why it's important for me to visit. Do you know Regent Tamio?"

"He is the Chief Guard, still?" Searl said.

"I work directly for him. Can I trust him?"

Searl shook his head. "He was one of the best pattern-masters Deftnis ever produced, and he knows it. Tamio was smooth and ambitious. That ambition burned so bright, and it must still motivate him. I can't recommend him as trustworthy, only because I remember him being ruled by his own thoughts and not by anyone else. He left Deftnis not long after he earned his black swordsman's belt."

Pol knew what ambition did to a man. He had personally experienced it with his step-father and his siblings. He would have to add Searl's impression to the pattern developing on the Chief Guard. It only made Pol more wary of his situation.

"He got me into the castle, and he'll, willingly or not, help me get Demeron and Anna out."

"You play a dangerous game," Searl said. "What if your brother or his wife recognizes you?"

"Does royalty ever notice lowly servants? That is my primary disguise."

"But Tamio must surely know who you are."

Pol nodded. "He easily got it out of me, and he has told at least one other as well, but if the pattern holds up as I am beginning to picture, my identity won't be learned by Landon."

"Don't be naive, Pol. Tamio will use you for his own ends."

"If I am captured or killed, you can still live in Alsador after you are released and see your daughter." Pol told Searl where he had hidden their money.

Pol's meeting with Searl didn't go the way he wanted, and that disappointed him. He couldn't afford to react to other patterns, he needed to continue to create one of his own. Pol needed to talk out his plans, but Searl didn't seem to want to listen, so he took to the practice field and sought out Demeron in his thoughts.

I'm still here, Demeron said.

"I need to come up with a way to free you and Searl's family."

Demeron didn't respond immediately. *I can't help you. Even though we can talk, from where I stand, there is only so much I can do.*

The horse's response was a surprise, and Pol realized that Demeron, for all his magnificence, always reminded him of his mental limitations. "If I ask you to break out of your stall and come to me, can you do that?"

I could ever since they put me here, but where would I go? Demeron said.

"I will let you know when to come to me, and we will escape from Alsador."

I would like that.

"We'll be gone from here in days, not weeks," Pol said. His vow to Demeron sounded bold, but as Pol walked through the practice yard, he knew he would have to make it happen. He felt lonely and isolated now that he had no one he could trust in the castle. He stopped and realized that lonely and isolated were things he had to avoid. Pol dreaded falling back into the depressed state he had experienced in Deftnis. He straightened his uniform and lifted his chin. He would make something happen. If he waited weeks, so much could go wrong.

For now, Pol still had his anonymity until Tamio and Lord Greenhill decided to let others know, but he couldn't see broadcasting his presence would benefit either man, if they hadn't already. Pol thought that Tamio had big things in mind, and Pol's role in those big things had to be kept quiet, for now.

The capture he avoided the previous evening seemed to have been concocted to scare him. Tamio was looking to control him. Pol admitted that he was afraid, but he had been living in constant fear for a good portion of his life. He knew he could function while afraid.

Alone, but with a firm mission in mind, Pol decided that he would frame his dilemma as a Seeker would. Regardless of his reluctance to engage his stepbrother, he would gather information, so that if a confrontation happened, Pol would have an idea how to act.

The clerk didn't send Pol out for any messages in the afternoon but instructed him to practice his swordsmanship. Pol found a few willing guards. He fought them enough to make the experience exercise, but he let them win.

~ ~ ~

Chapter Thirty-Five

T HE NEXT MORNING, POL TOOK HIS PLACE BEHIND THE DESK waiting for his next assignment.

Tamio poked his head out of his office. "Aron, inside."

Pol rose and entered Tamio's office. "Three messages for you."

After checking his map, Pol nodded and was about to leave. "Lord Greenhill has a message for you after you've taken these."

"Are you expecting a reply for any of the deliveries?"

Tamio shook his head. "No. There will be more when you return. I'll be keeping you busy this afternoon, as well."

Pol bowed and left the Chief Guard's office. He checked with one of the clerks to note his destinations on the map and left on his deliveries.

He had to slow down as he was catching up to three women. One was Bythia. He stayed as far behind her as he could and still maintain his pace. The women stopped at a functionary's office. Two of them proceeded onward, but Bythia remained and stepped inside.

Pol checked his map and confirmed that she had gone into the office of one of his later deliveries. He stood in the middle of the corridor. What would Val do? Pol knew the answer. He took a seat outside the office door and sat with his face away, should Bythia come out the door unexpectedly.

Using his hearing spell, Pol listened in on their conversation.

"…get Landon to think that the Shinkyan horse is his to keep," Bythia said. "Can you color the feet and the diamond so it looks like someone disguised it?"

"My Queen, I will have it done. Only the gods know how dense your husband is. He's already enamored of the beast enough as it is and visits it every day."

"Anything to keep his little mind occupied while I solidify South Salvan's control of Listya," she said.

"We are close enough as it is, although it is too soon to carry out our plan. More officers should arrive within the month. The regent kept the local lords on his side, and it might be wise to continue to placate them for a bit longer."

"What do we need Listyan lords for? They will eventually get in our way. I won't let Father's plans be delayed by the local gentry. They are little better than commoners."

"They do not think so, My Queen."

"You are too presumptuous, sir. Father appointed you as my chief advisor, but once Landon is eliminated, if you do not suit me, you will be sent packing, or worse."

"As you wish, My Queen."

Pol bent over and began coughing as he heard her footsteps get closer.

"Do something about your coughing, boy," she said.

Boy? Bythia wasn't all that older than he was. Pol made as if he cleared his throat and mumbled apologies as he heard her rush down the hall away from him.

He stood and knocked on the door. On it was a plate with a large 'W'.

"Lord Wibon? A message from Lord Tamio," he said through the door.

"Come in."

Pol walked into an ornate office. Every book was ordered on the shelves. The paper and parchment on the man's desk was set just so. The first thought Pol had was that the man had little to do other than to scheme in behalf of Bythia and her father.

"You are new here?"

Pol nodded. "I started yesterday. I'm still finding my way around the castle."

"There will be some changes soon. I'm sure you've noticed some already out in the city. Do a good job and you can find yourself in an ideal position."

Pol bowed. "Do you have a reply?"

Wibon looked up at Pol and then back down at the letter. "Oh, this is from Regent? No, no. These are guard assignments." The man tucked the letter into a thick portfolio that he took from a close-by shelf, and then he straightened all the pages before he put it back. Wibon made sure the portfolio wasn't any further in or out of the shelf in comparison with the others.

"That is all. Remember what I said."

Pol bowed again. "I will, sir."

"Lord, if you please."

"Of course," Pol tried to look flustered. "Lord Wibon." He bowed again and left the office.

After delivering the letter, Pol consulted with his map and made his way to the other assignments. The walking gave him time to calm down after this closest call with the royal couple, yet. He didn't know if he could be more careful, but with the new information, Pol knew that Bythia wouldn't wait very long before doing something drastic.

He furiously digested the disturbing information. Bythia had no love for Landon. That was plain. Indeed, it appeared she had little love for anyone, and he had once thought his oldest stepsister, Honna, couldn't be exceeded in that category. Now he had something sinister to add to Bythia's pattern.

Each of the other two recipients of Lord Tamio's messages were also South Salvans. One worked for the Chamberlain in hiring castle staff and the other was an assistant to the Royal Surveyor. Where did these men fit into Bythia's own pattern? He would have to ponder their roles in a South Salvan-led rule.

Pol smoothed his hair as he approached Lord Greenhill's office. What test would this be? He stood at the snotty clerk's desk.

"I came to pick up a message for Lord Tamio."

The snide man curled his lip. "You mean Lord Regent?" He giggled. "Knock and enter. My lord is expecting you."

Pol quickly looked away from the sneering face and knocked. "Enter."

Greenhill stood looking out his window. Rain pattered on the glass, and that meant Pol would be getting wet when he crossed over the castle grounds to the Guard's headquarters.

"Ah, the messenger boy. Have a seat."

"I just came to pick up a letter, My Lord."

"Must I plead?" Greenhill said. Mockery filled his voice.

Pol didn't seem to have a choice. He sat and folded his hands in front of him.

"Tamio speaks highly of you. Do you have a lofty opinion of yourself?"

Pol looked up at Greenhill. "Not particularly. I know I have some good points and some faults, just like everyone."

Greenhill sat down and looked across the desk, examining his fingernails. "What are your faults?"

Pol could feel his face get hot. The man intimidated him, and Pol could do nothing about it. "I have a temper that I sometimes cannot control, and I am naive, even for a fifteen-year-old."

The lord leaned over his desk towards Pol. "Naive? That is precocious self-knowledge, boy. Just how are you naive?"

"I trust others too easily." Pol had just about eliminated that tendency, "and I am not one for drinking nor am I comfortable around girls."

That brought laughter to Greenhill, and he sat back again. "I would say that you could easily be led astray, then. Do you agree?"

"I'm only fifteen, sir." Pol said.

"I know some fifteen-year-olds…" Greenhill waved the comment away before he finished it.

"What do you know about the political situation in Alsador?"

"Truth be told, I've only been in the capital for a few weeks, sir."

"And caught the attention of Lord Regent in such a short time?"

Pol had nearly been flustered until he realized that was what Greenhill intended. He took a breath. "I had my reasons, My Lord."

"I'll bet you did. Is one of them a certain healer rotting in the city jail?"

"That is one of them, My Lord."

Greenhill narrowed his eyes as if judging the balance of a sword. "That is all."

"The message to Lord Tamio, My Lord?" Pol said, now standing.

"Tell him that you will do."

"With what, My Lord?"

"Just relay my words. That will suffice. Be gone, young man."

After changing out of his soggy uniform, Pol wrote out his observations on his foray into the castle. He relayed Greenhill's conversation, nearly word for word, but left out what he learned behind Lord Wibon's closed-door session with the Queen, although he did mention the South Salvan's talk of changes occurring soon.

After lunch, Tamio walked into the office, and Pol stood at attention along with the other clerks. Tamio threw off his cape with a flourish and shook it before opening his door. He cast a glance at Pol.

"Report?"

Pol lifted up his papers. "Here, My Lord."

Tamio plucked them out of Pol's hand and took them into his office.

Some moments later, Tamio called for Pol through his door.

"Yes, My Lord?" Pol said after closing the door behind him.

"Good observations. I'm aware of the South Salvans placed within our midst. They already have control of the city guard. Does it trouble you?"

"It does, Lord Tamio. King Astor is likely seeking to solidify his hold on Listya. At some point in time, he will invade North Salvan and depose my stepfather. It is rather clear, isn't it?"

"That is a possibility, at the least. Would your brother ally with King Astor to the detriment of your father?"

Pol had to think back. "I don't think so. He and his father are close." And now Tamio probably knew that Landon was a target of the South Salvan King, if he hadn't before.

"Where do you stand on such a schism?"

"I am sure the Emperor is aware of the possibility," Pol said, "and an overt move by South Salvan in Listya will likely provoke an Imperial intervention."

"You are well-spoken for a churlish messenger boy...My Prince."

"I am not a prince," Pol said.

"You didn't answer my question."

"I don't support the schism. My preference is for South Salvan to remain South Salvan and my stepfather to continue as king in Borstall Castle."

"And what about Listya? Do you support what the royal couple is doing to Listya?"

Pol broke out in a sweat. Tamio was trying to pin Pol down, and if he did, would he accuse Pol of treason?

"I don't support anything that would be against the Emperor's wishes and that wouldn't benefit the integrity of Listya," Pol said. He wouldn't say anything specific against Bythia or Landon to either Greenhill or Tamio.

"Very well," Tamio said. "I have another two messages and a Seeker mission."

Pol felt like he was a ball thrown back and forth between Tamio and Greenhill. He took the two messages and looked up at Tamio.

"I want to know what the Queen thinks about her husband. You knew both of them in Borstall. Has anything changed?"

Pol sucked in his breath. "You are asking a question that is dangerous to answer." Pol could answer it immediately, but would Tamio even believe him?

Tamio looked annoyed. "Find out what you can tonight."

"Is this another test?"

"Test?" Tamio said.

"Yes. Like delivering the first message to Lord Greenhill. That was a test."

"You knew?"

Pol nodded. "I may be young, but I'm not an idiot," he said. Pol chided himself for sounding so arrogant. "I'm sorry."

"No need. This is no test. I will be out and about myself tonight. Do not wear your uniform this time. That is an order."

Pol sensed a trap, but he had no alternative but to nod his head. He still worked for Tamio and was duty-bound to obey.

"Is that all?"

"Isn't it enough?" Tamio said with the hint of a smile.

~

The first letter delivered in the afternoon went to the Chief Healer. Pol found his way to the infirmary. He'd been there once before, but he only knew the way out the castle gate.

A woman dressed in white sat at the receiving desk. A few patients waited in the lobby. Poll waited after telling the woman at the desk that he had a message for the Chief Healer. He wouldn't leave the message for anyone to pick up.

"Boy?"

Pol stood up and followed a man wearing a white healer's robe into the infirmary. They didn't walk far before the healer showed Pol into a waiting room.

An older woman walked into the room. She wore a purple belt, but Pol didn't know what that might mean.

"Excuse me. Are you a magical healer?"

The woman batted her eyelashes. "I am. Why do you ask?"

"Why aren't you the Queen's healer?"

The woman narrowed her eyes at Pol. "Are you being impertinent?"

"I don't think so. I met Anna Lassler. She treated me here a few days ago."

"You are the boy that the guard beat up, aren't you?"

Pol nodded. "I know her father."

"Searl Hogton?"

"He is in Alsador, in the city jail."

The woman's face registered a touch of alarm.

"Tamio didn't tell me that." She put her hand to her lips. "I didn't say anything." She shook her head trying to will away her words.

"Lord Tamio doesn't really have me delivering messages, does he?"

"I can't say about other duties you have. He wanted me to meet you."

"Here I am. I'll answer any questions you might have if you answer one of mine."

The healer rubbed her hands. "I know who you really are."

Pol just nodded again.

"You are Deftnis-trained."

"Not even a year, and I'm a year younger than the youngest," Pol said.

"And a budding pattern-master?"

That brought an involuntary groan from Pol's lips. Did Tamio keep no secrets?

"What will you do when you take the throne of Listya?"

Pol felt deflated. "I've already told Lord Tamio that I gave all that up. I'm disinherited. I have no desire to rule for reasons of my own."

"Would you take it if offered?"

The woman wasn't very discreet, but she was quickly filling in possible aspects of the pattern.

Pol thought for a moment. He decided to give a non-answer. "I would have to decide such a thing if the opportunity actually arose. I'm inclined to say no."

The woman actually giggled. "You'll agree. Tell Tamio that you pass."

"My turn," Pol said.

"What?" The woman tensed up.

"My question. Where can I find Anna Lassler?"

She let out a breath. "She lives in the room next to the Queen's quarters. Anna is under guard. Queen Bythia wants a non-magical healer to attend to her health."

"That's ironic," Pol said. "I think Anna uses magic in her work."

"You are an astute boy," the woman said, but then she bowed her head, "My Prince."

"I'm not a prince, anymore," Pol said. If they put him on the throne, he'd be a king, anyway. "If you will excuse me, I'm not finished with my duties."

The healer stood up. "Of course, of course."

Pol dreaded having another interview. Tamio's pattern was pretty clear. Greenhill and he were parading Pol around to show him off as a possible replacement for Landon. From what little he could tell, there would be a clash between the two men for who would be the real power. He didn't see Tamio bowing down as a loyal subject.

He shook his head in dismay. Would he ever rid himself of being embroiled in these squabbles? His mood hadn't brightened by the time he found his other destination. This was the second in command of the Listyan military.

General Donton let Pol into his office.

"You have a document from Lord Tamio?" the General said a little too loudly as he shut the door. "Sit, let us talk. I'm sure you are tired from all your running around for the Chief Guard."

"Thank you," Pol said.

"Have you had any military experience?"

Pol blinked with surprise. "I'm only fifteen, My General."

"Tamio heard that you accompanied a campaign."

Pol looked off at the General's bookshelf, filled with portfolio cases.

"I did, once. I just about got myself killed. Do you wish to ask about military history? I know a fair amount. The general order of battle? I know that. Logistics?"

"I didn't mean to offend," General Donton said.

"Lord Tamio hasn't kept my secret very well."

"No, he has. There are only five of us who know your pedigree. You really do know what you mentioned?"

Pol nodded, and the General peppered Pol with general questions on strategy and important Imperial battles. Pol knew most of the answers.

"You know as much or more than my staff," Donton said.

"I was taught by Ranno Wissingbel's daughter. She was a very good tutor, and I was, at the time, a very willing student," Pol said.

"And now?"

"I'll be a very willing student in Deftnis, when I return."

"But you are sidetracked in Alsador."

The questioning wore Pol out. "I am sidetracked and I am unsure of what my future holds."

"It's all good, your future," General Donton said. "Tell Tamio that you are more than I expected."

Pol stood first this time. "I will, General. Thank you for your time."

If Pol did anything that night, he would be talking to Anna Lassler, guards or no guards. He had Tamio's mission to fulfill, but more important, he had his own.

~ ~ ~

Chapter Thirty-Six

⁓

DINNER WAS A LONELY AFFAIR, but that allowed Pol more time to define the Seeking patterns that he needed to tweak. Talking to Anna was his prime mission since he already had the information on Bythia that Tamio needed.

After dinner, Pol went through his possessions. He dumped all the old clothes out of his saddlebags onto his bed. Something still remained at the bottom. Pol pulled out a worn cloth sack and couldn't remember what was inside.

He opened the sack and smelled the mint essence of minweed. He had never had to prepare the stuff during Searl's withdrawal. Could he use this in some way? Pol repacked his bags. He didn't know what would happen, but he had to be prepared to leave the castle at any time. Demeron was ready.

He had to retrieve Searl, Anna, and Mansen, and then find a way out of Alsador without the shred of a plan. He'd have to craft one as circumstances dictated. Pol thought he'd have to improvise like he did with anticipation magic, acting and reacting and anticipating as circumstances unfolded around him. Pol felt a reluctance to creep around the Royal Quarters. He knew he didn't know what he was doing, and it made him anxious, more anxious than he'd ever been.

Waiting wasn't an easy thing to do, but Pol heard the bell ring the eleventh hour. He wouldn't learn anything if he went out too late. Pol pulled his gray uniform jacket over his black outfit, despite Tamio's orders, and walked across the grounds into the castle. He carried a leather message portfolio as cover, and no one challenged him.

He continued to make his way past various guards, servants, and courtiers to the royal chambers, and then slipped into an alcove to review the map and calm his nerves. He felt his breathing quicken and his heartbeat rise, but his body wasn't about to let him down as it had before Searl had cured him. Perhaps this was what normal anxiety felt like.

Pol moved past the final set of guards and crept up the last stairway to the Royal Quarters. He had been here once before with his mother, but he only recalled vague impressions. Anna's room must be around the next corner. Pol made himself invisible to the pattern and poked out his head and noticed that there were no guards next to her room.

He quickly slipped along the corridor, hugging the wall, and opened the door to Anna's room. She turned her head at the opening of the door, but pinched her brow a bit when no one entered. Pol closed the door and appeared.

"Quiet, please."

Anna's hand shot to her mouth, but then she must have recognized Pol, as she nodded. She must be as afraid as Pol was.

"You are Searl's friend?"

Pol nodded. "My goal is to rescue you."

"The guard will return."

That alarmed Pol. "Why is he gone?"

"She." Anna said, shaking her hair out of her face. "Not a bad person really."

Pol heard the despair in her voice.

"What is happening?"

"Queen Bythia is going to poison King Landon tonight, and my guard has gone to attend the Queen. She forced me to prepare a quick-acting poison."

"I didn't think she would strike so soon," Pol said.

Anna's eyes grew. "You knew?"

Pol nodded his head again. "She wants to rule by herself as a proxy for her father, King Astor. Is she going to do it now?"

Anna's expression told him that Bythia would.

"Where is Landon?"

"In his study. It's on—"

"I know where it is," Pol said. "I hope to be back. Don't scream if I intrude again."

"This is much too dangerous for you," she said.

"I can't say I'm calm about any of this. If I'm injured, Searl and you can patch me up." Pol gave her the ghost of a grin and slipped out without another word.

He spelled himself invisible and crept towards the King's study. A female guard stood outside. Pol touched her, putting her to sleep like Searl had taught him. She collapsed to the floor, but Pol caught her before she made much of a sound.

He opened the door slowly and slipped inside, closing it silently behind him and hugging the wall. He could feel pressure on his chest and his heart beat as loudly as ever, but Pol didn't succumb to his old weakness. His better condition hadn't removed the discomfort that he currently felt.

Bythia stood massaging Landon's shoulders, while his stepbrother complained about not getting much respect from the castle guard. Pol could see the malevolence on her face while Landon looked away from her at the small fire in the massive fireplace.

"That should be enough. Now for some wine to relax you." She said. Bythia patted Landon's shoulders and walked past Pol, not seeing him at all, towards a sideboard.

"Pour one for yourself," Landon said.

"I don't need any."

"Please do, my love. We scarcely spend time together anymore."

She gave Landon's back a look of distaste. "Very well." Her voice was brighter than her expression.

After she poured the wine, she took a small envelope from her bodice and opened it. Bythia tapped the powder into one of the pewter goblets and used a silver rod to stir the wine. She put Landon's wine in the center of a round tray and her own on the edge.

She walked over to him and put the tray down. Landon pulled

her onto his lap. He laughed and kissed her cheek. She resisted at first, but then it looked to Pol that she forced herself to relax, and slapped his face, lightly.

"That's no way to treat a queen."

"Ah, but it is quite proper to kiss one's wife."

He pulled her forward. Pol could tell she resisted, but she forced herself to kiss the man she was about to kill.

Pol walked forward to put her to sleep, like the guard. He bumped into a chair.

"Who's there?" Landon said getting up.

Pol appeared.

"Who are you?" Bythia asked in her harshest voice.

"I am Poldon."

"You?" Landon narrowed his eyes as he drew his sword from the scabbard that lay on his desk. "It is you. What are you doing here?"

"Seeing what it would be like to walk the halls of my mother's castle," he said. Pol could barely breathe confronting these two people who hated him so.

"Your mother is dead, and you gave up your right to the throne," Bythia said, the harshness in her voice grated. "Efron!"

"The guard's name? She's asleep," Pol said. "I've learned how to sneak around a bit."

She snorted. "Leave us."

Landon stepped closer with his sword pointed towards Pol. "Tie him up, Bythia."

Pol locked eyes with Landon. "Listen to me, brother."

"You are no brother of mine!"

Bythia detached two drapery tiebacks, and Pol let her tie his hands and feet. She pushed him onto a chair.

"She is going to poison you tonight," Pol said, looking at Landon

"Bythia?" Landon laughed, oblivious to his wife's designs. "That would never happen." He looked down at Pol, who let Landon slap his face.

Pol tasted blood. He had often enough in the past, and the hatred and meanness of his siblings came back into focus.

Bythia slapped him even harder. "Do you miss your mommy?" she said, mockingly. "I talked Amonna into giving your mother a nightcap. She didn't even know it contained poison." Bythia laughed. "However, the next morning she saw the wisdom of her actions."

Landon's eyes brightened. "That means the Shinkyan stallion in the stables really is my horse!"

Pol shook his head. "The Emperor gave me title to him. He's mine, not yours."

"He's mine!" Landon slapped Pol again. Pol's head began to hurt.

"Gods, I need my wine," Landon said.

"Someone comes!" Pol said.

"What?" Bythia said as both of them looked towards the door.

Pol used his magic to switch the wine cups while Landon opened the door and looked down at the sleeping guard.

"Fool," Bythia said.

Landon put his sword across the arms of another chair and picked up the cup on the side of the tray.

"No!" Bythia said. "Drink from my hand, husband."

Landon grinned. "That's more like it." He put the wine down and sat, adjusting his clothes. "Watch how devoted my wife is," he said. Pol hated the smug expression on his stepbrother's face.

Bythia took the wine from Landon's hand and picked up the goblet in the center. She put it to his lips. "It's sweeter this way, isn't it?"

Pol couldn't believe the audacity of the woman, killing her own husband, but then she was the Queen, and she probably felt that she could do anything she wanted to.

"Drink it all, darling."

Landon let her drain the cup into his mouth. Wine overflowed from his mouth and dribbled down his chin.

"Now I'll do the same for you."

Bythia's eyes widened, but then Pol could see her smooth her face. "Of course."

Landon, heedless of Pol watching on, took the other goblet and laughed as Bythia drank from the cup he held. He looked over at Pol, obviously proud of himself.

Bythia moved Landon and the goblet. She wiped her chin and put her hands on her hips.

"He dies, and you will, too," Bythia said, grabbing onto Landon's sword.

"What?" Landon said.

"You're a dead man. I poisoned the wine." The cold smile directed at her husband chilled Pol.

"No, he's not," Pol said. "I used my magic to switch the cups. I wanted you to know that before you began to feel the effects of the poison. I find it ironic that you poisoned my mother through a Fairfield, and I poisoned you through a Fairfield."

She dropped the sword and clutched her throat.

Landon looked totally lost. "What's happening, Poldon?"

"Her father wants Listya for himself, and they were going to kill you tonight. She's already put South Salvan guards in high positions. Then I suppose King Astor's next step would be a takeover of North Salvan."

"No!" Landon stood. "You lie!"

"Why would she poison herself, then?" Pol said. He tweaked the binding cords, and they fell to the ground as he stood in front of his brother.

Bythia began to blink. She swayed on her feet and collapsed to the floor. "That wine was meant for you, Landon!" Those were her last words before her eyes rolled up into her head, and she collapsed to the floor.

Landon put his hands to his head. "No!" he cried out.

"There's the proof." Pol picked up Landon's sword and pointed it at his brother.

His stepbrother sat back down and cringed. Pol let Landon stew for a bit.

"What do I do now? You're the smart one. What do I do?" Landon begged, looking up at Pol with pleading in his eyes.

A figure stood at the door. Regent Tamio entered the room.

"Kill him," he said to Pol, without emotion.

Pol threw down the sword. "No."

"I order you to kill him."

Pol shook his head. "Landon is the King, and you are the King's subject. You ask me to kill him? That would make me a traitor, wouldn't it?"

Tamio looked disgusted. "You are making it difficult for me, boy.

I had other plans for you, but this will be better, much better for me." Tamio flicked his wrist, and Pol found himself frozen in place. He tried to figure out what kind of tweak Tamio had performed, but he remained in place.

Landon rose and ran behind his desk, holding the chair as if it were a shield. Tamio stepped to Pol and picked up Landon's sword. "You'll be caught with this in your hand, My Prince, getting revenge on the King and Queen. What a crime!"

Landon obviously caught on that his life was in danger from the Chief Guard. Tamio advanced on Landon.

Pol couldn't move, but could he use his magic. He levitated one of his boot knives up to his shoulder with the point facing the Chief Guard. All Pol saw was Tamio's back.

"I'll be taking your place, Fairfield," Tamio said. "The Emperor will agree to it with the trouble your father has stirred up, allying himself with South Salvan. But these things are evidently above you." Tamio raised the King's sword over the King of Listya.

Landon closed his eyes and cringed, covering his head with his arms.

The knife disappeared from Pol's view as he 'moved' it into Tamio's heart.

Tamio's stricken face turned to Pol. "What have you done?" his voice came out as a croak.

"I have saved my brother's life," Pol said as he watched Tamio collapse. Landon's sword clattered to the floor as Tamio died.

Pol wondered if the tweak was a stiffening of his joints. He spelled a counter and fell to the floor, but he quickly got up.

"Are you going to kill me?" Landon pressed himself against a bookcase. He held his hands close to his chest. Pol had never seen his stepbrother show such fear.

"Why would I do that? I said I saved your life. Didn't you hear me?"

"You've changed," Landon said, looking up at Pol, and not relaxing one bit.

Pol shrugged off his comments. He helped Landon to his feet. His brother let Pol help sit him in his desk chair.

"I'll write down a few suggestions to get your new rule going." Pol wrote down Greenhill's name and the other interviewers from the past two days. "These people may not be your friends, but you need to find Listyans who will help you. If you marry again, marry a Listyan girl. Immediaately stop the stupid taxes and the other measures that Bythia put into place. You'll only succeed if the people see you as a benefit. Do you understand?"

Landon nodded, but Pol doubted if he was listening.

"I'm taking Anna Lassler," Pol said.

"Who?"

"Bythia's healer. The Queen doesn't need one anymore." Pol glanced at her body. "I'm also taking Demeron with me." He showed the certificate of title to Landon. "Signed by the Emperor, see?"

Landon nodded again, still bewildered.

"I'm leaving Listya in your hands. Rule the country well, or there will be another Tamio ready to take your head, but I won't be here to save you, then. Do you understand?"

"I understand. Why are you doing this for me? I've never treated you well," Landon said.

"As I told Tamio," Pol shook Landon's shoulder, and shuddered. He voiced his unexpected revelation. "You are my brother, no matter if I want you to be, or not."

~ ~ ~

Chapter Thirty-Seven

~

P OL MET DEMERON CLOSE TO THE GUARD HEADQUARTERS. Pol wore
his guard uniform, and stood with his saddlebags. He put them on
Demeron, always a struggle with the tall horse. Anna stood by him,
wearing street clothes with a big bag hanging from her shoulder.

He pulled out the empty message portfolio and trotted to the
castle gate with Anna sitting behind. "I have a message that needs to
go out tonight. It's an emergency. Let me through with the healer." Pol
waved the message case. "Quickly!"

The guards muttered, but they recognized Pol and let him through.
He rode through mostly empty streets. Men and women were leaving
the taverns for home as the pair threaded their way through town.

"Get Mansen to the boarding stables before noon. I've got to
extract Searl." He let Anna off where she directed and proceeded to
the stables where Pol had placed the cart and Searl's horse and then lay
down to sleep on musty hay.

~

Pol woke up and changed clothes. Queen Bythia's demise hadn't
yet been announced, and there had been no alarm about Pol's actions
the night before. He stopped by an inn and purchased a pot of stew for
the jail and a bag of bowls and spoons. As usual, the guards seized the
stew and began to wolf down the food. Pol watched as they ate before
he walked down the aisle to Searl.

"You're back," he said.

"I am. Now it's time to go."

"Here? The guards."

Pol laughed. "Don't worry about them. We just have to wait a few more minutes." Pol used his power to unlock the cell door.

"I could have done that," Searl said.

"Hey!" Pol said. "I'm going to take all the credit." He gave Searl a smile and led him out of the dungeon. All along the corridor, the guards lay on the ground with grins on their faces.

"You drugged them?"

"Minweed from your garden. Somehow the last twenty-four hours has been filled with irony." Pol said.

Searl's eyes goggled.

Pol pulled on his guard coat and escorted Searl out of the city jail. They walked to the stable.

"Anna!" Searl said. "I'm sorry I'm a mess." He put his arms around his daughter, and then around Mansen.

Pol stood apart watching for any intruders. While they talked, he pulled out the cart and hitched it to Searl's horse. Then he dug up the two bags of money and put them in his saddlebag.

"Time to go," Pol said, taking off his uniform coat and tossing it back into the stall. He hoped that would be the last he'd have to wear it.

There was a line to get out of the city. By now, stories of the Queen's death at the hand of Regent Tomio and King Landon's heroic attempt to save his wife were on every tongue.

"Aron Morfess?" Carlon Winters pulled up alongside Pol. "Where is your grandfather?"

Pol looked at Mansen, and realized that he had to make up some kind of story.

"He's back in Alsador, in the city jail," Pol said.

"I don't think so," Winters said, looking at the cart. "This must be the son-in-law. Where is the daughter?" His gaze didn't leave the cart.

They approached the guard who eyed the three of them.

"What's the matter?" Pol said.

"Some trouble in the city. An old man escaped from the city jail with his grandson."

From the guard's comment, Pol and Searl were sought by the

city guard, not Landon. His brother wouldn't hesitate to include a description of Demeron.

"If we see them on the road, we'll send them back to Alsador," Winters said.

He looked at Pol and Mansen. "Let's go, men." Winters looked back at the guards. "I vouch for these two. They are my servants."

The guard waved them on, and they were soon on their way out of Alsador.

Pol's eyes bored into Winters' back. Why had the man inserted himself into their affairs? It didn't matter since the man's action allowed them to easily slide past the guards.

Pol looked in the mirror and changed his dark hair back to his normal silvery blond. Searl still slept on the bed behind them. It had taken all four of them threatening Searl to leave him, without funds at the inn, before he agreed to take a bath. Pol made sure the clothes Searl had worn to jail had been burned.

He walked down to the common room for a meal with Anna, Mansen, and Winters. As he stepped into the room, he noticed Valiso Gasibli sitting with Searl's daughter and her husband.

"What are you doing here?" Pol fought off the confusion that he felt.

"I have business with the Abbot, so I'm accompanying you all to Deftnis," Val said. He grinned in his cold way. "You're probably wondering where Carlon Winters is, aren't you?"

Pol heard Winters's voice coming from Val's lips. "Seekers are also masters of disguise," Pol said, amazed that Val's transformation had fooled him so thoroughly. He remembered Searl's comment about Winters' disguise.

"You get to learn that in advanced classes," Val said. "I owe you an explanation. The youth, who was Regent Tamio's last project before you showed up, suspected a coup. Ranno sent me to investigate. You wouldn't believe how surprised I was to run into Searl and you."

"Valiso Gasibli, surprised?" Pol said.

"It does happen," he said, drily.

"I kept my eyes on you two, and went about my investigation.

I was surprised again," he bowed to Pol, "when I found you working for Regent. I had no doubt he would figure out who you were and accelerate his timetable."

"So you knew he was going to kill Landon?"

Val nodded. "You knew the pattern that developed as well as I did," Val said. "I was right behind you in the castle and heard your conversation with Anna, here." Val gave her a little bow. "At that point, I just kept out of the way, unless I was needed. You did very well, for a beginner."

Pol snorted. "I am a beginner, aren't I?"

"A very good one," Anna said, patting Pol's hand.

Pol folded his arms. "Was this another test?" He hoped he didn't sound too petulant.

Val laughed, a real laugh this time, and ruffled Pol's hair. "A very good one!" he echoed Anna's comment. "I didn't have to do anything but monitor the situation."

"Landon might have killed me," Pol said.

"You know better than to say that. Once I knew Searl cured your heart, few men with a sword could defeat you. You've noticed that no one at Deftnis likes knives, but how many times have my lessons saved your life?"

Pol just nodded and ground his teeth. He knew he hadn't been used, but he felt like he'd been left flailing in a windstorm.

"Wilf Yarrow is the Emperor's man," Val continued, "and will take care of rooting out the South Salvans. I let a few of the more trustworthy nobles know that Landon will need some help. I don't think you'll have to worry about your brother, not your step-brother."

Pol felt his neck flush. "You heard me?"

"Hazett will be proud of you when he hears of this," Val said. He seemed to be enjoying the conversation too much in Pol's view. "My report to him had left Alsador before I met up with you at the city gate."

Pol squirmed in his seat. He hadn't intended anyone to know about his conversation with Landon. He didn't know what to do, now that he had finally avenged his mother's death and was startled by the fact that he no longer desired to destroy his siblings. He'd have to do some work on re-adjusting his own pattern.

~~~

Epilogue

~

Eight days later, the five of them looked across the choppy ocean at Deftnis Isle. Summer was in full force, and the monastery would soon empty out for Harvest Break. Pol groaned at the prospect of riding across that rough water, along with Searl and Val.

"I'm not going to live on that island, Father," Anna said. "I had enough of that place when I was growing up."

"Then stay in Mancus."

"There is nothing for us here. We left Alsador without money and—"

"Don't worry," Searl said. He tossed the fat purse of weeder money to Mansen. "Set up an ironmongery in Mancus. You can even get contracts for weapons from the monastery. Anyway, I want to be able to bounce my grandchild on my knee."

"But my healing?" Anna said.

"I'll be coming over often enough," Searl said. "It's time you learned how to properly use magic, and there is no one better to teach you." He grinned and rubbed his chin. "Maybe it's time to start a nunnery."

They rode down to the town and left their horses at the stable where Pol had first separated from Demeron nearly a year ago.

"We'll get you back over to the isle as soon as the ocean calms." Pol said to his horse.

I can wait as long as they feed me grain.

Pol grinned and patted his horse's jaw.

Searl, Val, and Pol boarded the boat that would take them back to the Isle. Anna and Mansen stood on the pier, waving.

Pol looked at the seven monks and Val sitting around the table where he usually took lessons from Vactor. Searl and Pol had already given their tale, and Val had backed them up.

"So what are we going to do with you?" Abbot Pleagor said to Pol.

"I'm cured," Pol said.

"You are, but I don't know if I can have a fifteen-year-old Gray roaming around the monastery."

"Gray? I'm just a Level Four."

The Abbot waved Pol's ten tests from Searl's cabin in his face. "This is the standard set of Seventh Level attributes."

Pol looked a Vactor. "Tell them it isn't so," Pol pleaded.

Vactor shrugged. "It is. You can color your hair, create your own spells."

"Val made disguises," Pol said.

"I would hope he could. Val is Eighth Level."

"A Black?" Pol glared at Val. He already knew Val was a much higher level than he had ever let on. "You lied to me."

Val looked back with emotionless eyes. "So?"

Searl raised his hands to calm things down. "Steady, boy. Listen to Val."

"Yes, listen to him," the Abbott said.

"Actually I've ridden all the way to Deftnis with a mission, Pol," Val said. "The Emperor is concerned about South Salvan, and King Astor's ambitions will not end with the death of his daughter…"

If you liked The Monk's Habit, please leave a review where you purchased the book. An excerpt of Book Three, *A Sip of Magic* follows.

An Excerpt From

A SIP OF MAGIC
The Disinherited Prince — Book Three

Chapter One

POL CISSERT LOOKED AT SEVEN MONKS AND VALISO GASIBLI, who Pol called Val, sitting around the table where he usually took magic lessons from Vactor. Searl Hogton, the Master Healer, and Pol had already given their account of what happened in the foothills of the Wild Spines, and Val had backed up their adventures in the Listyan capital of Alsador, where Pol had eventually saved the life of King Landon, his estranged brother.

"So what are we going to do with you?" Abbot Pleagor, the head of Deftnis Monastery, said to Pol.

"Searl cured me," Pol said. He didn't know if it was an appropriate answer, but the vast improvement of his health had been about all he could think about since he had returned to Deftnis Isle from his quest to find Searl.

"You are, but I can't have a fifteen-year-old Seventh Level magician roaming around the monastery."

"Gray? I'm just a Fourth Level."

The Abbot waved the list of Pol's ten tests that Searl had insisted he pass before they could leave the Spines. "This is a set of Seventh Level attributes."

Pol looked at Vactor. "Tell them it isn't so," Pol pleaded.

Vactor shrugged. "It is. In addition, you can color your hair and create your own spells."

"Val made disguises," Pol said.

"I would hope he could. Val is Eighth Level."

"A Black?" Pol glared at Val. "You lied to me."

Val looked back with emotionless eyes. "So?"

Searl raised his hands to calm things down. "Steady boy. Listen to Val."

"Yes, listen to him," the Abbott said.

"Actually I told you that I didn't ride all the way to Deftnis just to accompany Searl back to the monastery," Val said. "The Emperor is concerned about South Salvan and King Astor's ambitions will not end with the death of his daughter. I had intended to find a suitable Second Level magician, but with your improved health, you are the ideal candidate to help me fill a vital mission for the Empire."

"I just returned." Pol said. "I spent the last three months finding a way to stay here, and now you want me to leave? King Astor wants me dead, and you want me to go to Covial, the South Salvan capital, to spy on my worst enemy?"

"Yes. Except you won't be going to Covial, but Tesna," Val said.

"After Coram, the Tesnan spy tried to kill me three times!"

"You won't be going as Pol Cissert, or Poldon Fairfield, but under the guise of a young noble's son, already accepted to Tesna. He is sixteen, but now that you are growing, you'll be able to take his place."

Pol frowned. He didn't want to leave the monastery when he had fought so hard to return. "I still want to stay here."

"As much as I enjoy seeing you learn, Pol, you present problems at your age," the Abbot said. "Your education is still somewhat of a patchwork. The next youngest gray is twenty-two years of age, and he is considered a brilliant prodigy. You are adept at many spells and have no idea of what else you can accomplish. Your previous ill health prevented you from even attempting some basic Third Level spells—"

"Like magic lights?" Pol never could muster the energy to tweak the pattern of air that would generate a cold white light. He agreed with the Abbot. "So, that means I need to spend more time learning. That's what Vactor and I were doing before I had to leave last Spring."

"Val can help with that as you travel," Vactor said.

"But I don't want to go," Pol said. He felt like a child that had been given a new toy, only to have it confiscated by his parents. "I looked forward to coming back."

Silence met his comment. Pol looked at the faces, all of them reflecting back some level of disappointment at his reluctance.

"I'll be doing more Seeking?" Pol said, looking at his former Seeker teacher nod. He knew he couldn't back out of this task, so he reluctantly said, "I'll do it. I suppose I have plenty of time to return, now that I won't be dying anytime soon."

"At least not from your formerly bad heart," Searl said, with a sly grin.

Pol felt uncomfortable walking around Deftnis Monastery wearing the gray cord of a Seventh Level magician around his waist. He still slept in the dormitory, but the Abbot told him that would end when he returned from Tesna, no matter what happened. He withdrew from his classes, since he was months behind.

Paki, his companion from Borstall Castle and Kell, who accompanied them to retrieve Searl, took his elevation in stride as Pol sat down with them for dinner. They had already gotten together with Darrol Netherfield and Searl Hogton to talk about what went on after they had left Pol with the Searl, the addicted Master Healer.

"There is talk about you leaving us at Harvest Break," Kell said.

Pol could only nod. "It's a secret mission, but I'm heading east."

Paki squinted as he worked his brain, probably thinking of what Pol's mission could be. "Is it dangerous?"

Even now, Val had been closed-mouth about the details other than the fact that he would be headed for the monastery at Tesna, and that it would, indeed, definitely put him in peril. "I don't know much more than that," Pol said.

"Can we go with you?" Kell said.

Pol shook his head. "I don't know yet. I do know that I won't be going to Borstall. I'm learning a few of things that I'll probably never use."

Paki made a face. "More political stuff, huh? At least you don't have to finish all of your classes like Kell and me. I feel like I'm in jail."

"Life always changes," Pol said. He didn't tell them that politics wasn't what Val was drilling him on. "Anyway, when Harvest Break starts, you can go down to Deftnis Port any time you want."

Paki grinned. "That's right. I can hardly wait, but that might not happen."

"Oh?" Pol said.

"I'm going home to see my mother."

"Borstall Castle might not be a welcoming place." Pol worried about Paki returning to where they both had grown up. Even though Pol wouldn't be with them, he worried about vindictive siblings.

"Not to worry. I'm taking Kell with me," Paki said. "He has an uncle who has a family trading office in Borstall. They have ships that go back and forth from Volia."

"Yeah," Kell said. "My father won't mind me visiting Uncle Wester. He's always wanted me to know more about the family business. We can stay with him."

Pol smiled. They would be all be headed east, but to different destinations. "I'd be a little uncomfortable in Borstall."

"So you're mission works out for everybody," Paki said. "We'll miss you, but then you'll probably miss us." He laughed.

"Probably," Pol said, knowing that he envied them their freedom.

When Pol walked into the little classroom off the Monastery library, Darrol stood and greeted him.

"How are you, Pol?" Darrol said. "We haven't gotten together very much since you returned."

"What are you doing here?" Pol said. "Are you going to join my classes?"

The former Borstall Castle guard nodded. "I am. Val asked me to come by and listen in. It looks like we are going to do some more traveling together."

Pol raised his eyebrows. Val didn't say they would be accompanied on their trip, but Pol was glad of it so he broke into a smile. Val continued to intimidate him, since the Seeker was full of information that he seemed reticent to divulge, so Darrol would leaven awkwardness that Pol was sure to feel traveling alone with Val.

Val walked in and told them to sit. He looked at Darrol, and then at Pol. "Now that Darrol is coming along, let's summarize the mission. You are already accepted into the Tesna monastery as an acolyte from a noble family in Boxall. Your mission is to find out how King Astor intends to use the monastery to rebel against the Empire."

"But Darrol—"

"Darrol's coming along to keep me company. I'll be camped close by, and you'll be sending me messages on your progress."

Darrol narrowed his eyes. "I'm going to be your nursemaid?" he said.

Val turned up a corner of his mouth. His smile always looked like more of a sneer to Pol. "I need someone to fetch and carry, Darrol."

"I'm happy to do that, if it will help Pol," Darrol said. A year ago, he had become Pol's sworn man, no matter if Pol wanted him or not.

After nodding, Val said, "It will. I'll need you to fetch messages. We haven't yet determined how that will happen, since I've only been to the Tesna monastery once, and that was years ago." He looked at Pol.

"I'm ready," Pol said. He said it, but Pol was still a reluctant participant.

"No you're not. Now that you know all about your new family in Boxall, we concentrate on Tesna. I've got the latest plans of the place. I want you both to listen carefully…"

~

Searl looked down on Pol as he lay on the familiar examination table in the Deftnis infirmary. "Everything looks stable to me," Searl said. "I do good work. You've already started to catch up on your growth and you'll be seeing more changes in your body, so don't be too alarmed that you begin to grow as tall as other fifteen year olds."

Pol took a deep breath and jumped off the table. "No chance that your changes will reverse themselves?"

Searl mirrored Pol's sigh. "We can all die tomorrow. I can't be certain, but there isn't any deterioration, and it's been weeks since I did my work. You are feeling better, aren't you?"

Pol nodded. "I feel stronger every day."

"You're smart enough to look out for yourself."

"Just like I looked out for you?"

Searl smiled and nodded. "Same thing." He put his arm around Pol. "I owe you more than I can say. I knew I was wasting away in the cabin, and you arrived to save me." He kept nodding his head. "Now I have better things to look forward to than to lay back on my bed and welcome minweed oblivion."

"I'm happy about it too," Pol said.

"Come back safe and sound, Pol. You have lots of friends who are looking for you to succeed."

Pol smiled. Indeed he did have friends, even the Emperor had helped him, and now he went on this mission to pay back Hazett III, the Emperor of Baccusol for saving him from certain death in his former home, Castle Borstall. Now he would have to go into the heart of the enemy, Tesna Monastery.

At least he wouldn't have to worry about running out of strength in a critical situation.

~ ~ ~

~ A BIT ABOUT GUY

With a lifelong passion for speculative fiction, Guy Antibes found that he rather enjoyed writing fantasy as well as reading it. So a career was born and Guy anxiously engaged in adding his own flavor of writing to the world. Guy lives in the western part of the United States and is happily married with enough children to meet or exceed the human replacement rate.

You can contact Guy at his website: www.guyantibes.com.

†

BOOKS BY GUY ANTIBES

THE DISINHERITED PRINCE

Book One: The Disinherited Prince

Poldon Fairfield, a fourteen-year-old prince, has no desire to rule since his poor health has convinced him that he will not live long enough to sit on any throne. Matters take a turn for the worse when his father, the King of North Salvan, decides his oldest will rule the country where Pol's mother is first in the line of succession followed by Pol, her only child. Pol learns he has developed a talent for magic, and that may do him more harm than good, as he must struggle to survive among his siblings, now turned lethally hostile.

FANTASY - EPIC / SWORD & SORCERY / YOUNG ADULT

POWER OF POSES

Book One: Magician in Training

Trak Bluntwithe, an illiterate stableboy, is bequeathed an education by an estranged uncle. In the process of learning his letters, Trak finds out that he is a magician. So his adventures begin that will take him to foreign countries, fleeing from his home country, who seeks to execute him for the crime of being able to perform magic. The problem is that no country is safe for the boy while he undergoes training. Can he stay ahead of those who want to control him or keep his enemies from killing him?

Book Two: Magician in Exile

Trak Bluntwithe is a young man possessing so much magical power that he is a target for governments. Some want to control him and others want to eliminate the threat of his potential. He finds himself embroiled in the middle of a civil war. He must fight in order to save his imprisoned father, yet he finds that he has little taste for warfare. Trak carries this conflict onto the battlefield and finds he must use his abilities to stop the war in order to protect the ones he loves.

Book Three: Magician in Captivity

After a disastrous reunion with Valanna, Trak heads to the mysterious land of Bennin to rescue a Toryan princess sold into slavery. The Warish King sends Valanna back to Pestle to verify that the King of Pestle is no longer under Warish control. The Vashtan menace continues to infect the countries of the world and embroil both Trak and Valanna in civil conflict, while neither of them can shake off the attraction both of them feel towards each other.

Book Four: Magician in Battle

Trak saves Warish, but must leave to return the Toryan princess. He reunites with his father, but is separated again. Circumstances turn ugly in Torya, and Trak returns to Pestle to fight a new, unexpected army. Valanna's story continues as she struggles with her new circumstances, and is sent on a final mission to Pestle. The Power of Poses series ends with a massive battle pitting soldier against soldier and magic against magic.

FANTASY - EPIC / SWORD & SORCERY / NEW ADULT

THE WARSTONE QUARTET

An ancient emperor creates four magical gems to take over and rule the entire world. The ancient empire crumbles and over millennia. Three stones are lost and one remains as an inert symbol for a single kingdom among many. The force that created the Warstones, now awakened, seeks to unite them all, bringing in a new reign of world domination—a rule of terror.

Four Warstones, four stories. The Warstone Quartet tells of heroism, magic, romance and war as the world must rise to fight the dark force that would enslave them all.

FANTASY - SWORD & SORCERY/EPIC

Book One: Moonstone | Magic That Binds

A jewel, found in the muck of a small village pond, transforms Lotto, the village fool, into an eager young man who is now linked to a princess through the Moonstone. The princess fights against the link while Lotto seeks to learn more about what happened to him. He finds a legacy and she finds the home in her father's army that she has so desperately sought. As Lotto finds aptitude in magical and physical power, a dark force has risen from another land to sow the seeds of rebellion. It's up to Lotto to save the princess and the kingdom amidst stunning betrayal fomented by the foreign enemy.

Book Two: Sunstone | Dishonor's Bane

Shiro, a simple farmer, is discovered to possess stunning magical power and is involuntarily drafted into the Ropponi Sorcerer's Guild. He attracts more enemies than friends and escapes with his life only to end up on a remote prison island. He flees with an enchanted sword containing the lost Sunstone. Trying to create a simple refuge for an outlawed band of women sorcerers, he is betrayed by the very women he has worked to save and exiled to a foreign land. There, he must battle for his freedom as he and his band become embroiled in a continent-wide conflict.

Book Three: Bloodstone | Power of Youth

When usurpers invade Foxhome Castle, Unca, the aging Court Wizard of the Red Kingdom, flees with the murdered king's only daughter, taking the Bloodstone, an ancient amulet that is the symbol of Red Kingdom rule. Unca uses the Bloodstone to escape capture by an enemy and is transformed into a young man, but loses all of his wizardly powers. Unca must reinvent himself in order to return the princess to her throne. Along the way he falls in love with the young woman and must deal with the conflict between his duty and his heart, while keeping a terrible secret.

Book Four: Darkstone | An Evil Reborn

As the 22nd son of the Emperor of Dakkor, Vishan Daryaku grows from boy to man, learning that he must use his unique powers and prodigious knowledge to survive. He succeeds until his body is taken over by an evil power locked inside of the Darkstone. Now Emperor of Dakkor, Vishan is trapped inside, as the ancient force that rules his body devastates his homeland while attempting to recover all of the Warstones.

As the amulets are all exposed, the holders of the Moonstone, Sunstone, and Bloodstone combine to fight the Emperor's relentless drive to reunite the Warstones and gain power over the entire world. The armies of Dakkor and the forces of those allied with the three other stones collide on a dead continent in the stunning conclusion of the Warstone Quartet.

~

Quest of the Wizardess

Quest of the Wizardess chronicles the travels and travails of young Bellia. After her wizard family is assassinated when she is fourteen, Bellia seeks anonymity as a blacksmith's helper. When that doesn't work out as expected, she flees to the army.

Her extraordinary physical and magical skills bring unwanted attention and she must escape again. After finding a too-placid refuge, she takes the opportunity to seek out her family's killers. Revenge becomes her quest that takes her to a lost temple, unexpected alliances and a harrowing confrontation with her enemies.

FANTASY - EPIC/NEW ADULT-COLLEGE/COMING OF AGE

The Power Bearer

How Norra obtained the power and the extraordinary lengths she went through to rid herself of it.

What's a girl to do when all of the wizards in her world are after her? She runs. But this girl runs towards the source of her power, not away from it. Along the way she picks up, among others, a wizard, a ghost, a highwaywoman and a sentient cloud. Through thick and thin, they help Norra towards her goal of finding a solution in a far off land that no one in her world has even heard of.

YOUNG ADULT EPIC FANTASY

Panix: Magician Spy

Panix has life by the tail. A new wife, a new job in a new land that has few magicians and none of his caliber. His ideal life takes some unexpected downturns and Panix finds himself employed as a spy. He has no training, but must make things up as he goes if he is to survive the politics, betrayal, war and, at the end, his own behavior.

FANTASY - ADVENTURE

THE WORLD OF THE SWORD OF SPELLS

Warrior Mage

The gods gave Brull a Sword of Spells and proclaimed him as the world's only Warrior Mage. One big problem, there aren't any wars. What's a guy to do? Brull becomes a magician bounty hunter until the big day when he learns he not only has to fight a war with the magicians of his world, but fight the god that the magicians are all working to bring into being. He finds out if he has what it takes in Warrior Mage.
EPIC FANTASY

Sword of Spells

Read about Brull's beginnings and earlier adventures as a bounty hunter of magicians in the Sword of Spells anthology.
EPIC FANTASY

THE SARA FEATHERWOOD ADVENTURES

Set in Shattuk Downs, a reclusive land in the kingdom of Parthy. Sara Featherwood could be a Jane Austen heroine with a sword in her hand. There are no magicians, wizards, dragons, elves or dwarves in Shattuk Downs, but there is intrigue, nobility, hidden secrets, plenty of adventure and romance with a bit of magic.
FANTASY ~ YOUNG ADULT/COLLEGE
FICTION ~ WOMEN'S ADVENTURE

Knife & Flame

When Sara Featherwood's mother dies, her sixteen-year-old life is thrown into turmoil at Brightlings Manor in a remote district of Shattuk Downs. Life becomes worse when her father, the Squire, sets his roving eye on her best friend. Dreading her new life, Sara escapes to the Obridge Women's School. Seeking solace in education doesn't work as her world becomes embroiled with spies, revolution, and to top it all off, her best friend becomes her worst enemy.

Sword & Flame

If you were a young woman who had just saved the family's estate from ruin, you'd think your father would be proud, wouldn't you? Sara Featherwood is thrown out of her childhood home and now faces life on her own terms at age seventeen. She returns to the Tarrey Abbey Women's School and is drafted to help with the establishment of the first Women's College in the kingdom of Parthy. Now in the King's capital of Parth, life confronts Sara as she learns about family secrets, which threaten to disrupt her life and about resurgent political turmoil back home that turns her scholarly pursuits upside down as she must take action and use her magic to save her family and her beloved Shattuk Downs.

Guns & Flame

At nineteen, Sara Featherwood has done all she can to help establish the first Women's College in the kingdom of Parthy. That includes a pact with the kingdom's Interior Minister, to go on a student exchange program as payment for eliminating opposition to the college. Little does Sara know that her trip to a rival country is not what it seems and as the secrets of the true purpose of her trip unravel, she utilizes her magic to escape through hostile territory with vital secrets, but as she does, she finds herself drawn back to Shattuk Downs and must confront awful truths about those close to her.

THE GUY ANTIBES ANTHOLOGIES

The Alien Hand

An ancient artifact changes a young woman's life forever. A glutton gladiator is marooned in a hostile desert. An investigator searches for magic on a ravaged world and finds something quite unexpected. A boy yearns for a special toy. A recent graduate has invented a unique tool for espionage. A member of a survey team must work with his ex-girlfriend in extremely dangerous circumstances. A doctor is exiled among the worst creatures he can imagine.
SCIENCE FICTION

The Purple Flames

A reject from a Magical Academy finds purpose. A detective works on a reservation in New Mexico, except the reservation is for ghouls, demons, ghosts, zombies, and the paranormal. A succubus hunts out the last known nest of vampires on earth. The grisly story about the origins of Tonsil Tommy.

In a post-apocalyptic world, two mutants find out about themselves when their lives are in imminent peril.
STEAMPUNK & PARANORMAL FANTASY with a tinge of HORROR

Angel in Bronze

A statue comes to life and must come to terms with her sudden humanity. A wizard attempts to destroy a seven-hundred-year-old curse. A boy is appalled by the truth of his parents' midnight disappearances. A captain's coat is much more than it seems. A healer must decide if the maxim that he has held to his entire career is still valid. A fisherman must deal with the aftermath of the destruction of his village.
FANTASY

~ ~ ~

Guy Antibes books are available at book retailers in print and e-book formats.